About the Authors

Kelli Ireland spent a decade as a name on a door in corporate America. Unexpectedly liberated by Fate's sense of humour, she chose to carpe the diem and pursue her passion for writing. A fan of happily-ever-afters, she found she loved being the puppet master for the most unlikely couples. Seeing them through the best and worst of each other while helping them survive the joys and disasters of falling in love? Best. Thing. Ever.

USA Today bestselling author **Jules Bennett** has penned more than fifty novels during her short career. She's married to her high school sweetheart, has two active girls, and is a former salon owner. Jules can be found on X and Facebook (Fan Page). She holds competitions via these outlets with each release and loves to hear from readers!

Sara Orwig lives in Oklahoma and has a deep love of Texas. With a master's degree in English, Sara taught high school English, was Writer-in-Residence at the University of Central Oklahoma and was one of the first inductees into the Oklahoma Professional Writers Hall of Fame. Sara has written mainstream fiction, historical and contemporary romance. Books are beloved treasures that take Sara to magical worlds. She loves both reading and writing them.

Sunrise on the Ranch

February 2026
**City Lights,
Cowboy Nights**

May 2026
**Long Roads,
Last Chances**

March 2026
**Once Burned,
Twice Loved**

June 2026
**Gold Spurs,
Wild Horizons**

April 2026
**Bold Boots,
Fierce Hearts**

July 2026
**Her Boss,
Her Rancher**

BOLD BOOTS, FIERCE HEARTS:
Sunrise on the Ranch

KELLI IRELAND

JULES BENNETT

SARA ORWIG

MILLS & BOON

All rights reserved including the right of reproduction in whole or in part in any form. This edition is published by arrangement with Harlequin Enterprises ULC.

This is a work of fiction. Names, characters, places, locations and incidents are purely fictional and bear no relationship to any real life individuals, living or dead, or to any actual places, business establishments, locations, events or incidents. Any resemblance is entirely coincidental.

Without limiting the exclusive rights of any author, contributor or the publisher of this publication, any unauthorised use of this publication to train generative artificial intelligence (AI) technologies is expressly prohibited. HarperCollins also exercise their rights under Article 4(3) of the Digital Single Market Directive 2019/790 and expressly reserve this publication from the text and data mining exception.

® and ™ are trademarks owned and used by the trademark owner and/or its licensee. Trademarks marked with ® are registered with the United Kingdom Patent Office and/or the Office for Harmonisation in the Internal Market and in other countries.

First Published in Great Britain 2026
by Mills & Boon, an imprint of HarperCollins*Publishers* Ltd
1 London Bridge Street, London, SE1 9GF

www.harpercollins.co.uk

HarperCollins*Publishers*
Macken House, 39/40 Mayor Street Upper,
Dublin 1, D01 C9W8, Ireland

Bold Boots, Fierce Hearts: Sunrise on the Ranch © 2026 Harlequin Enterprises ULC.

Cowboy Strong © 2016 Denise Tompkins
Single Man Meets Single Mum © 2014 by Jules Bennett
That Night with the Rich Rancher © 2016 Sara Orwig

ISBN: 978-0-263-42161-3

Printed and Bound in the UK using 100% Renewable Electricity
at CPI Group (UK) Ltd, Croydon, CR0 4YY

COWBOY STRONG

KELLI IRELAND

To my father-in-law,
a large-animal veterinarian who looks and
sounds enough like Sam Elliott to terrify folks.
I think it's the moustache. I've got your number,
though. Ranger cookies.
Love you.

1

TYSON COVINGTON LEANED against the end of the trailer and waited on the person he considered his personal dealer in ecstasy to deliver. It wasn't as though he was addicted. He could stop any time he wanted to. He just didn't want to. The level of feel-good that was about to change hands was insane. And *cheap*. It could be worse. *Much* worse.

"Number seventy-two," the matronly woman in the portable kitchen called as she slid his order through the trailer's narrow delivery window and across the short counter. "Funnel cake, extra powdered sugar, and a large lemonade."

Ty stepped around the corner of the trailer. "Thank you, ma'am." He tipped his hat to her before tucking the plastic cup between his arm and body, juggling the grease-stained paper plate in his hands.

If he ever met a woman who could whip these up for him? His single days would be over. For regular funnel cake access, even *he* would consider marriage.

A large barn fan kicked on and swept away the extra

powered sugar. Ty clutched his plate tighter as the dense cloud of sugary goodness dissipated in the air.

Ty tore off a wedge of the hot treat and shoved it in his mouth. Sucking in a breath at the burn, he inhaled a lungful of powdered sugar. All the willpower in the world couldn't stop him from choking. He coughed hard and blew out what looked like a face full of illegal substance all over the back of a nearby cowboy's dark denim shirt.

Oops.

Still, he wasn't about to let something as ridiculous as a second-degree burn to the mouth or a personal confrontation destroy the pleasure of the first bite. There was something about rodeos that just made funnel cakes taste better.

He glanced around and let the sights, sounds and smells momentarily take him over. Man, he loved rodeos. Listening to the scratchy amplification of the announcer's voice boom over the subtle, hive-like hum of the crowded stable area, Ty thought that was probably how God sounded as He called out the scores for those entering heaven horseback. And if, for some reason, Ty couldn't enter heaven horseback? He wasn't sure he wanted to go.

Shod hooves hit the dirt pack with sharp clips as owners unloaded horses nearby. Others were arranging stalls, wiping down hides until they shone under the lights and generally working with their animals. Some—both animals and owners alike—were high-strung. Others were old pros, comfortable with the routine common to every competition. Even one with stakes as high as this. The banter between the cowboys, half bragging and half bullshit, resulted in sharp laughs now and again.

Ty relaxed a bit.

He wandered into the community barn and stopped in front of the stall he'd been assigned. Shifting to lean against the bottom half of the Dutch door, he chewed rapidly and tried to breathe with more care—in through the nose, out through the mouth. His eyes still watered enough his vision blurred. Yeah, he could've taken a big swallow of lemonade, but he wasn't a wuss. Besides, some things were simply sacrosanct. Funnel cakes were up there on that list, so he'd eat his cake like a grown man or not at all.

Gingerly shifting the paper plate around, he took a second bite. The first burn was bad enough that the second and then third hardly registered. Glancing around, he took a healthy swallow of lemonade, his shoulders sagging as the cold assuaged the scalding heat.

Still not a wuss, since no one witnessed the momentary weakness.

A dark velvet nose slipped over his shoulder and huffed, sending the plate—and the treat—flipping end over end out of his hand. The plate rolled away and came to a stop next to a bale of hay. The delicacy hit the hard-packed dirt with a *thwap*—facedown.

Tyson glanced over his shoulder at the big, wide eyes—one brown, one blue—doing their best to appear innocent and full of curiosity. He scowled. "Don't look at me as if you were being deprived, you big mule. You *know* I would've shared a bite when it cooled off."

The horse flapped his lips at his owner in a not-so-subtle demand.

Fighting a grin, Ty picked up the cake and retrieved the plate, gently slapping the two together to knock away most of the dirt before tearing off dusty chunks and feeding them to his horse, Doc Bar's Dippy Zippy Gizmo. But as far as the ladies were concerned, he went by Gizmo. The stud horse had the disposition of a labradoodle crossed with a bullmastiff—gentle, playful, loving and strong as an ox with a heart that just wouldn't quit. He was also developing quite the reputation with breeders in the area for passing on both his disposition and superior skills to his get. Demand had become so intense eighteen months ago that Ty had put the horse on a breeding hiatus. He hadn't wanted to, but he couldn't keep up the breeding demand and the competitive circuit. One or the other had to give.

The stud horse was only six years old. On the fringes of entering his prime, as far as competition went, and the idea of pulling him off the rodeo circuit when he'd really begun to shine seemed incredibly unfair to both of them. They'd worked hard to earn the points, and money, necessary to make it onto the pro roster. That had been followed by hard work and a lot of long hours in the truck and trailer as they traversed the country, attending every event they could. The end goal had always been the same—earning a spot on the National Cutting Horse Association national finals roster and a chance at the more than four million dollars in prize money.

It still didn't feel real.

Winning would entitle Ty to demand premiums for Gizmo's stud services, to be even more selective in breeding and creating the Covington line of Quarter horses, a line he'd named Bar None. Like Doc Bar before him, Gizmo was the seat of what Ty was determined would go down in the Quarter Horse Hall of Fame as one of the finest lines ever.

He didn't want to create a mass-market Quarter horse.

He wanted exclusivity, a name for his horse and himself, a legacy that would make him his own man, no longer overshadowed by his brothers.

Ty was pulled from his thoughts as a crowd of spectators walked by the stables discussing the horses and their odds. It didn't matter that it was December in Fort Worth, Texas. People from around the world had flown in for this. They'd hang out, see the city's sights and spend a little money. But come tomorrow, these same people would be in the stands, cheering on the stars of the rodeo circuit.

On the streets, limousines ferried international horse breeders and buyers—men and women who Ty hoped would come out to watch Gizmo in action and see what Ty had worked so hard to cultivate in the genetics program he'd started in his teens. They would watch with the open intent of either investing capital in Ty's program or passing on him.

No. Pressure.

Ty shook his head. Thinking that way gained him nothing. What he *needed* to do was focus on Gizmo, keep him healthy and happy and energized. The horse was nearly psychic. If he sensed Ty was off, the two would end up out of sync, and that wouldn't serve either of them well. That meant Ty had to find that inner place where he could simply exist, the place he'd spent so much time as a child, the place no one could reach him.

But his mind threw one more curveball before he could shut himself down. What if he actually took the top title? The little bit of funnel cake he'd eaten wadded up into a thick lump and sank deep in his gut, settling like a ship's anchor. If he won, the recognition would take him places he'd dreamed of going all his life.

Ty studied his horse with a critical eye. Known as a grullo, Gizmo was a rare dun color—deep blue-gray body; black mane, tail and leg markings; a black dorsal stripe; and a pale face mask. Gizmo often sired colts with dun coloring thanks to a rare genetic marker, and as his predictability in colt color went up, so did the stud fees Ty could charge. Grullos were rare. Every dime of that money helped fund Ty's breeding program as well as his ability to travel the rodeo circuit and pay the exorbitant entry fees, not to mention helping cover the costs of hiring extra cowboys to cover him at his family's dude ranch. But what mattered most was Gizmo. Ty had loved the lunk since the colt had taken to following him around only a few days after birth.

"Doesn't seem to matter where we are. I always find you making moon eyes at that damn horse," said a highly familiar, decidedly feminine voice, coming from a dozen or so feet to his left.

Ty's lips twitched as his body came to life, fueled by raw awareness. "Not true."

"How do you figure?"

He ran his fingers into Gizmo's forelock and scratched. The horse's eyes drifted half closed. Ty glanced toward his stable neighbor, lifting a single brow as he offered a lazy smile. "Sometimes he makes moon eyes at *me*."

Mackenzie Malone, heiress to the Malone Quarter horse breeding empire and the most challenging competitor in the arena, considered him openly. Then she slipped into her horse's stall, disappearing from view. "Disturbingly true," she called, her voice muffled by the thick wooden wall that separated them. "True enough, in fact, that I'm not exactly sure how to reply."

"I would say that depends on whether or not you're

still seeing that suit. What was his name? It was a city... Kincaid? Watson? Portland? Nashville?"

"His name was Dallas." Thick walls or not, her amused response came through loud and clear.

"Still seeing him?" he pressed. It took a few minutes for her to stick her head around the corner and answer with a grin. Every second he waited deepened his vague but persistent unease.

"Nope. Turns out he had a very weird penchant for... Never mind. The answer is no. I'm not dating the city boy anymore." One eye narrowed. "Why?"

Desire for the fiery redhead quickened his pulse, prompting Ty to move away from Gizmo and peer into Mackenzie's—Kenzie's—stall as she moved back inside. "Just want to make sure you know there's no need to be jealous of Gizmo, darlin'. Since you're city-free, I'll let you make moon eyes at me anytime."

"'Let me,' huh?" Her laugh was rich yet delicate, the sound enticingly deceptive. She might look like a fragile waif and sound like an angel, but she was a powerful threat in the arena and hell's own temptress between the sheets. "Keep dreaming, Covington. I don't make moon eyes for anyone, but particularly for bed partners who park their boots by the door instead of under the bed with the intent to stay awhile."

He hadn't heard her complain before. Their longstanding history in the arena had always been fun. Before a rodeo, they'd establish the ground rules, the winner gaining something he, or she, wanted to experience together, though it had always been in bed. These postcompetition hookups allowed him to blow off a little steam and manage any residual adrenaline and ramped-up aggression after the long days on the rodeo circuit.

He and Kenzie had skipped a few opportunities to knock boots in the past, but only when one or the other was temporarily involved with someone else. And it was *always* temporary. Neither of them was programmed for long-term relationships, and that was what he adored about her. No expectations, no threat to either's independence and no hard feelings when he and Gizmo took home the top prize instead of her and her mare, Search for Independence, or Indie, which they did more often than not.

Still...here they were, chasing each other for spots in the finals, knowing they'd likely end up in a face-off at some point in the competition.

Ty absently pulled a piece of a gum out of his shirt pocket, his mind shifting to the first elimination early tomorrow morning.

Gizmo tossed his head and bugled, knocking one front hoof against the stall door, his eyes never leaving the sweet treat Ty held between two fingers.

"Fine. Take it. Your breath is horrible anyway." He handed the horse a piece of bubble gum and fought not to laugh as Gizmo seemed to grin, delicately plucking the treat from Ty's fingertips.

"Sometimes I wonder if Gizmo realizes you're more than a walking, talking soda jerk of sugary goodness."

Gizmo shoved him hard with his nose. Ty stepped away, just out of reach of the horse's flapping lips. "Enough," he mumbled, gently pushing Gizmo's face from his shirt pocket. "You're embarrassing me."

The horse tossed his head and continued to chew his gum with exaggerated enthusiasm.

Unfurling the in-stall water hose, Kenzie filled Indie's water buckets, watching to ensure the mare didn't step on the hose as she moved around, inspecting the new space.

"So," Kenzie called out to Ty, "how's the dude ranch endeavor going?"

Ty leaned against Indie's stall door. "It's been far more successful than we thought it would be, actually." They'd have to have another two years before they were in the black regularly. No way was he revealing that to a Malone, though. Wouldn't surprise him if her family lit winter fires with random dollar bills they had lying around their ranch. Kenzie had never known the hand-to-mouth existence he'd lived for a large part of his life. She couldn't understand.

Shaking off the discomfort of the chasm of differences in their socioeconomic positions, Ty continued, "Cade's fiancée has been amazing at getting us prime advertising and exposure. Thanks to her efforts, we were rated a five-star resort. She's pretty great."

"I heard Cade had popped the question." She twisted the spigot off before coiling the hose. "You like her?"

"I do. Quite a bit, actually. She's just what he needed." From any other woman, Ty would have weighed the comment for its jealousy component. Not with Kenzie. She was far too practical, and for that he was grateful. But it wasn't gratitude that resulted in the small twinge of emotion that pricked his heart. Truth? He had no idea what it was. And he had no intention of putting it under his internal microscope for evaluations. Some things were better off left alone, and this was one of those things. Besides, there was a bigger elephant standing between them.

He intended to take the title at this rodeo, and probably from this very woman.

Kenzie Malone moved through Indie's stall with the ease born of thousands of hours doing the same repetitive tasks for a variety of horses, some of them hers but most her father's. Indie was all hers, though, and the mare was special. She was one of the first fillies out of a line Kenzie had started the moment she'd received the first half of her trust six years ago. She'd been eighteen.

The animal was an anomaly at five years old. Indie possessed more intuition, more instinctive responses than could be cataloged. Riding her was a dream. All Kenzie had to do was keep one leg on each side of the saddle and park her mind in the middle. The horse did the rest. Indie knew where to step, when and why, and that left Kenzie with less to do than fans might believe. Yet riding Indie always provided a thrill—almost as much as the man currently lingering in the doorway.

Every inch of Ty Covington's six-three frame was delectable. She wanted to run her tongue through the hollow at the base of his throat…again. She wanted to taste the salt and sunshine on his skin…again. She wanted to nibble her way to the waistline of his jeans and dip her fingers below the band of his boxer briefs, tease the root of his arousal before taking him…again.

It dawned on Kenzie that she should probably spare them both the public humiliation and turn the hose on herself before she mentally stripped Ty naked. Face flushed, she pulled her hat off and ran Indie's polishing rag over her head, wiping away the excess sweat. Not much she could do about the shortness of breath or the way her nipples pearled beneath her T-shirt. That was simply the way she responded to Ty. Each time. Every time.

Aware it wouldn't take the man long to pick up on her

interest, she focused on tasks that would keep the horse between them. But Ty, being Ty, managed to charm the female in Indie, moving her away from her hay net to accept the small pieces of apple Ty offered. The horse's move left Kenzie with a head-to-toe view of the cowboy.

She was torn between thanking the gods for his perfection and cursing the same deities for the distraction the man created by simply *being*. Broad shoulders, a muscular build, dirty-blond hair that was a good four weeks past the point of trimming, brown eyes richer than the most expensive chocolate, large hands, strong jaw and lips made for kissing—all things that drew her. But what really flipped her switch was his confidence. True confidence, though, not arrogance.

For a man who looked the way he did and had so many notches in his bedpost it resembled a totem pole, that was saying something. And as if that weren't attractive enough, she had to include his sense of humor, compassion, friendliness and easy compatibility—in public, but particularly in private. It was the recipe for the perfect man. Or would have been, save one thing.

Tyson Covington couldn't stand postsex *anything*. No cuddling. No pillow talk. She'd never had the chance to wake up to his sleep-rumpled face the next morning because he'd *never* spent the night. He made a mad dash for the door before she could ask him to stay. It had started out as a relief. Now? Kenzie wasn't as comfortable about his urgency to get out of her room once they were both satisfied. And it was *always* her room.

She turned away from him, worrying her bottom lip with such ferocity it hurt.

"It's not like you to turn your back on me, Malone." From her peripheral vision, she watched the man step closer and tip the brim of his hat up to better reveal those dark brown eyes. "What's bothering you?"

The simple question, so softly worded, totally caught her off guard. He'd always been playful. This quiet concern was new, and it threw her off her game. It was the only reason she had for answering, "Just thinking."

"About?"

"You." Heat rushed across her cheeks. This wasn't how they worked, and she doubted he'd take the change well.

She didn't see him move, but suddenly he'd spun her around and pressed the front of her body against the darkest corner of the stall wall. Running his hands up her arms, he stretched her out, her wrists captured in one hand.

Kenzie yanked on her wrists and arched her back.

Ty kicked her feet wide and, bending at the knees, rubbed the ridge of his impressive erection up and down the seam of her ass. Bending forward to cover her, his lips brushed the edge of her ear as he spoke. "Ground rules stay the same as those we set at regionals. Winner gets his—or her—fantasy night. Or do you want to modify the game for the big show?"

His hot breath tickled her ear and made her shiver.

Her body responded of its own accord, her back arching again to better present her ass, her arms pulling against his hands, her head canting farther to the side so he might have better access to her neck. His actions fed a primal need in her to be taken, claimed, while her mind screamed that they were in public, could be caught. And wasn't that the crux of being with Ty? There was always a risk, always that touch of spontaneity that was his calling card, that thing that always made sex as fun as it was pleasurable.

Ty let her neck go without warning. Then he stretched her arms higher, forcing her to move to follow them up the wall. "When did little Kenzie Malone decide she liked a little exhibitionism?" he whispered, moist lips barely brushing the top of her ear.

"When did the cowboy who established *love 'em and leave 'em* decide to stick around long enough to do it right?" she countered.

Ty grabbed her hip and spun her to face him. Wedging a thigh between her legs, he rubbed against her sex with firm strokes. Not once did he tear his gaze from hers. "Where's this coming from, Kenzie?"

"If you'd park your boots beside the bed instead of being so damn afraid to take them off at all, I would imagine there would be a lot you'd learn about the women you call 'lover,' Covington. Including me." The brazen statement held within it a poorly disguised challenge, one he clearly heard.

He hauled his body back, eyes wide, and let go of her arms before spinning for the door and stalking out.

She never had the chance to ask him to stay.

2

THE NIGHT WAS passing slower than any Ty could remember. The second hand on the clock ticked and paused, ticked and paused, seemingly searching for the energy to tick again. He tossed and turned, went down to check on Gizmo, then went back up to his hotel room to toss and turn again. He needed to blow off a little steam, and sex was his preferred method.

And his mind was locked on one particular redhead, a woman he'd had numerous times but never could get out of his system.

It wasn't as though Ty was actually into exhibitionism. He'd just wanted to push the fringes of experience and try something new, and she'd always been safe—as well as seriously fun—to play with. And bless the powers that be, darling Kenzie hadn't balked. His pulse quickened. Hell, if anything, she'd asked him for more. But he hadn't been certain how much "more" was wise in the barn.

He'd also had a fleeting moment of insecurity, wondering if she'd want more of what he'd offered just then or more of him in general. The former he could provide, and gladly. He'd always liked women, had always been insistent that everyone left satisfied. But him offering more than what the moment afforded all parties? No. That type of "more" had never been on the table. Ever.

His rolled over and punched his pillow.

Earlier, the competitors had drawn for their bracket positions, and he'd drawn third out of fifty riders. It was a crappy pick. He'd have much preferred to ride somewhere between thirtieth and thirty-fifth so he knew how hard to push Gizmo and how much showmanship was required to keep his horse in the top ten while still preserving enough energy to really clean up if he was called to a tiebreaker.

Flopping onto his back, he stared at the shadowed ceiling. Insomnia sucked. Bad. Insomnia alone sucked worse. He really needed some feminine company to get his mind off all the people who'd be watching him and Gizmo, both live and on TV. The pressure of those anticipated stares grew heavy in the silence, then heavier still, until he thought he might not be able to draw a breath due to the weight on his chest.

The bedcovers tangled around his feet as he lurched upward. He got his feet underneath him, shoved his room key in the pocket of the complimentary robe before tugging it on and then grabbed his cell as he headed for the door.

He hit 6 on speed dial and waited as the call connected. When she answered, he let out a breath he hadn't realized he'd been holding.

"Why are you calling me—" covers rustled and her jaw cracked as she yawned "—at one thirty in the morning?"

Thoughts of her in bed, her lithe body clad in little—or nothing—made him adjust his robe for better coverage. "What room are you in?"

"You're looking for a booty call from the wrong woman. I'm sleeping."

"You lost the wager." He spoke so fast his words ran together.

Silence.

"I beat you at regionals, so I entered nationals with a points lead. Means I get my fantasy fulfilled first," he pressed.

"We aren't on the boards yet."

Her cautious tone worried him, made his response sharper than he'd intended. "Actually, we are. I went to check on Gizmo and Indie earlier tonight, make sure they were settled, and end-of-season scores have been posted."

"Well," she mused, "I suppose that puts you on top of me."

His cock kicked hard enough there was no hiding it. Thankfully, the hallway was empty. "On top's not where I want to be."

She chuckled, the sound sleep heavy, sultry. "You realize that if I beat you here, I'll top you in points and earnings for the year."

His brow creased. "No. Just until the next rodeo season starts."

"Not by your logic. You're saying you get to have your fantasy tonight because you're ahead in points in a competition that hasn't started. Well, this exact same competition won't start again until December next year, so I could feasibly be ahead of you in points until they post next year's regional totals on the nationals boards. Same thing you're doing, just building out the timeline."

His mouth went dry and he stopped, resting his shoulder against the wall. "You're making me think this was a bad idea."

"Good or bad, it was *your* idea, Tyson," she said softly. "Room 1134. Show up and own it, or hang up and don't. But make up your mind in the next five minutes or I'm going back to sleep and I won't answer after that. Not the phone, and definitely not the door."

The line went dead. If he showed up now, he'd be accepting the fact that she was right—his terms had been pretty broad and rather unclear. If she beat him, could she, *would* she, want to see him for the next year? That would take this thing between them outside their established bounds of competition romps. Make it more than an occasional tryst. As in…dating.

The idea didn't repel him, and that alone should have been enough to turn him right around and have him back in his room before he lost what was left of his mind.

He decided not to give the thought too much attention, though, so he pushed off the wall and resumed his trek toward the elevator bank.

He reached the elevators just as one opened and dumped off a group of highly intoxicated bridesmaids supporting one barely conscious bride. To a woman, they looked him over as if he were the best thing they'd seen all night. While he wasn't entirely comfortable with it, he still smiled and flirted a little before stepping into the elevator car and winking at them as the doors closed. It was, after all, what anyone who knew him would have expected of him.

He punched the button for the eleventh floor and ignored the way his belly dipped as the car started its upward climb.

Because he knew with the kind of certainty that discomfited a man that the belly drop had nothing to do with the elevator and everything to do with the woman in room 1134.

KENZIE HAD BEEN fast asleep when her cell phone rang. Part of her had known before squinting at the bright caller ID who it would be. The other part of her had grumbled and threatened to go back to sleep, right up to the point she swiped the answer button on the screen and heard Ty's voice. His seductive teasing? Pretty much expected. Lust swamping her like a johnboat with a cannonball hole in its center? Not so much.

After disconnecting the call, she lay there considering her parting shot. *He's not going to show up after I challenged him like that.*

She had no idea where the idea to challenge him had come from. She'd only known she wasn't about to simply roll over and let him have his way with her because he was coiled tighter than a self-winding watch on an MMA fighter's wrist. It didn't matter that she wanted him just as bad and was wound just as tight. The principle of the thing mattered—the principle and their agreement.

Well, that added to the fact that he wasn't one to fish the same pond over and over if the catch was too easy. He needed the challenge, and it had to come across as near defiance if a woman thought to reel him in for even a single passionate night.

And she posed a more authentic challenge than most.

What she needed was to have a quality man chasing her, not someone simply after the Malone name or associated fortune. As the sole Malone heir, she'd learned this lesson by age fourteen.

At fifteen, Jack Malone, her father and her idol, had pulled her aside to administer some of the best advice Kenzie had ever received. "When we lost your brother, others assumed I'd want another son to pass the Malone legacy on to, but you know—" he'd gripped her arms "—you *know* I wouldn't trade you for all the Spanish gold hidden in the ocean's depths. And when it comes to taking a man as husband, I won't make that choice for you. I don't care if the man you fall in love with is an artist, a pilot, a musician, a doctor or a garbageman. I set your trust up for you to be well-off, so your man doesn't have to be rolling in money to make you happy." He'd taken her by the shoulders then, his grip just this side of painful. "I have loved your mother through both lean years and flush times. Money can't make a marriage, let alone a *happy* marriage," he'd said softly before clearing his throat, voice gruff when he'd refocused on Kenzie. "You find the man you want to wake up to for the rest of your life, the man you can't help but give your heart to, and you marry *him*. Just promise me you won't elope, baby girl. You're my one shot to publicly blubber as father of the bride."

Now here she was, waiting on a man she desired and equally admired to come to her room at her invitation. "Sheer irony. Nothing more," she whispered, stretching her clasped hands above her head. She should probably brush her hair before—

The rap at her door, soft but firm, had her throwing the covers back at the same time her heart lodged itself in her throat. *He showed up*. She wouldn't overanalyze it, wouldn't overthink it. She'd just enjoy it.

Padding across the room in her cami and thong, she peered through the peephole and bit her bottom lip. Ty stood there, hands in his pockets, and grinned at her. That man wore a borrowed robe better than anyone she'd ever seen. "Hopeless," she muttered, unsure whether it was him she spoke about or herself.

She opened the door.

Ty slipped inside, bare feet silent on the carpet. He swiftly shut the door and, grabbing her around the waist, spun and pressed her against the wall. Lips, full but soft, teased along her jaw, and he whispered, "Missed you."

Don't believe him, her mind volunteered. *You're no one special to him. After all, he's known as the Rodeo Romeo.*

She stiffened.

Lifting his head to stare down at her, Ty's gaze roamed her face. "Something wrong?"

"No." She smiled absently. "I'm good."

He curled a finger under her chin and lifted until met his stare. "Surely you can do better than that."

"It's the middle of the night, Ty. 'Good' is pretty damn spectacular."

He laughed quietly, pulling her into his arms and backing her to the bed. "I'll do my best to make sure you don't regret answering your phone."

"Your first task is keeping me awake."

He nipped her ear. "This is my fantasy, Malone. That starts with you being awake and receptive to my cunning seduction."

"And it ends with?"

Again he lifted his head, but all signs of teasing

had disappeared. Dark brown eyes bored into hers, the weight of their intent scattering goose bumps along her skin. "It ends with you screaming my name."

Her mouth formed a small O, but no sound emerged. She was too surprised at his directness to utter anything more than the most fundamental thought. "When did you get so serious about sex?"

Ty leaned forward, his lips brushing hers as soft as a butterfly's caress. "When you answered your phone. I need you as much as I want you tonight, Mackenzie."

The way her name rolled so richly off his tongue made her whimper.

She should answer. She really should. But the words were stuck in her throat behind her thundering heart.

He wants me, needs *me.*

Never had he admitted to anything more than "craving" her. The hunger to hear him confess it again almost had her asking for him to repeat his words, but pride intervened. Then he slid a hand between them, deft fingers manipulating her sex with skill born of experience, and all thoughts of admissions evaporated. Heat built between them faster than sheer winds from a prairie storm's dry line. He'd never been this way with her, never been anything more than a fun bed partner she enjoyed when their paths crossed and she was in the mood. This man? He was different, in control, almost predatory. Closing her eyes, she gripped the looped cotton weave of his robe and let her head fall back, gasping slightly when he laid his lips to the hollow of her throat.

His huffed out a small laugh against her skin. The smell of mint hit her—*toothpaste*—as his breath wafted up, strong and clean.

"Kiss me," she murmured, tossing his hat aside in order to run her fingers through his hair.

"Demanding little thing," he answered, weaving a hand of his own through her mass of curls and fisting it in her hair just tight enough her eyes widened. He stared at her for several seconds before placing his cheek next to hers, so close that his lips caressed her ear as he spoke. "Tonight's my fantasy. You agreed to the terms when I called. Clear?"

"You going to bite me again?" she asked, exhaling slowly.

"Absolutely."

"Then, hell yes, we're clear, but only if you quit stalling."

Ty chuckled as he shrugged out of his robe and stood before her, gloriously nude and unashamed of his body. His abs tightened as she touched the muscled ridges and valleys, tracing the chiseled six-pack of his torso, the ropy lengths of muscle in his arms and the corded strength in his legs. The way his lats cut down his abs and framed his long, thick arousal. She let her gaze linger there, and that seemed to be his undoing.

Scooping her up, he sank onto the bed and rolled to his back, placing her on top of him. He ran a hand around the back of her neck and pulled her down as he rose toward her. Stopping millimeters from their mouths colliding, his hot breath washed over her.

She licked her bottom lip. They were so close her tongue brushed over the soft skin of his full lower lip. The faint taste of mint lingered there as the scent did on his breath.

Ty's eyes flared, pupils dilated as he closed the last of the distance between them, claiming her mouth without hesitation. Tongues dueled, lips sucked and harsh breaths wound together in something akin to demands, not requests, made by desperate lovers.

It was a war she wanted to fight forever, one she might never want to win.

Lying back, he encouraged her to straddle his hips. He bent his knees, pushing her forward. Her dark red curls fell in a curtain around them to create the sensation they were cocooned, the world forever far away. He broke this kiss, the rapid rise and fall of his chest mirroring hers. "Hell's fires, woman. Give a man a chance."

Kenzie traced his bottom lip with her thumb, clenching her thighs around his hips when he nipped her finger. "Chance to what?"

"Seduce you." In a swift move, he rolled her over. "It was supposed to be a drawn-out seduction, with me doing the seducing."

"And..." Kenzie prompted.

"I'm the one being seduced. Your mouth should come with a warning label."

"It does," she said, lowering her face to his and kissing him slowly this time, in a leisurely exploration, tasting him, sipping from his mouth, running her hands over his pecs and wrapping her legs around his waist.

He broke away only to bury his face in the crook of her neck. "You wreck me."

"And that's a bad thing?" she teased, tracing her fingers lightly down his rib cage.

Ty sucked in a breath and shivered. Without looking, he reached over the edge of the bed and dug through his robe, retrieving a condom. "I can't wait, Kenzie. I wanted to, but this first time is going to be rough, fast. I need…" He shrugged, fumbling with the wrapper until, cursing, he sat back on his knees and sheathed his length. "I really want…" he began again.

Those words again—*need*, *want*—used in relation to her. "We're dancing to the same tune, Ty."

Eyes narrowing and mouth tightening to a thin line, he took her arm and gently pulled. "Roll over." She followed his direction only to have him grasp her hips and lift. "On your knees, Mackenzie."

She'd barely assumed the position when he pulled her down his entire length with enough strength to make her cry out with a surprised thrill. "Tyson!"

He pushed her shoulders to the mattress. "Arms wide."

She complied, but slowly, earning a quick slap to the ass that set more than her skin on fire. He rubbed his hand over the stinging skin and whispered words of encouragement to her. Then he began to thrust and retreat. All she could do was feel, experience and indulge in Tyson.

His fingers dug into her hips as he pumped faster. "Hold on to the sheets and don't let go."

Arching her back and lifting her rear higher earned his praise as well as a heartfelt curse. "Can't…baby… I can't…" He reached around her and found her clitoris, manipulating it almost frantically as the arm that held him up shook and his rhythm faltered.

Orgasm crashed into her and she offered his name to the heavens in a soulful cry, his voice joining hers. Their fingers wove together, tightening, as they grounded each other through the emotional onslaught.

When it passed, Kenzie relaxed her hand and made to turn over, but Ty gently lowered himself onto her back. "You know better than to think we're done, darlin'."

"It's late, Ty," she contentedly murmured into the pillow.

He rained kisses all over her shoulders. "It's never too late for round two, Mackenzie."

Hiding her face in her pillow, she smiled.

That was exactly what she'd hoped he'd say.

3

TY LET KENZIE drift off to sleep around 4:30 a.m. before quietly gathering his things to leave. Door open, the light from the hallway cutting through the room's darkness, he glanced back. She looked like a fallen angel with her nude body spread across the bed, lips kiss swollen and hair in disarray. Long lashes fluttered against her cheeks and opened enough to reveal the brilliant blue of her eyes. Her soft sigh revealed her immediate understanding that he was leaving.

Normally that would be Ty's cue to go. But there was something about Kenzie, something about the way she'd given herself to him tonight, that rode his conscience. For the first time, Ty wanted to stay, to see the night through and wake up to her face in the morning. It was the strangest sensation, this foreign need to wake up with a woman in his arms. Not just any woman, but *this* woman.

He strode back to the bed. Ignoring her unguarded surprise, he bent over her and kissed her, all tongue and teeth and heat. She responded, arching into the hand he placed on her breast and wrapping a hand around the arm parked next to her head.

The ever-simmering ember of desire that lay between them fanned to life, the flame licking at the base of his spine as his shaft thickened.

"Stay," she whispered against his mouth, tracing his bottom lip with the tip of her tongue.

He tried to imagine waking up to her beautiful face, tried to imagine her hair spread over his pillow. Sure, he could see it, but he could also imagine it being the beginning of something much larger, something he hadn't ever believed he would want. The longer he thought of the possible consequences, the more actively hesitation shoved at his willingness to try. It took only seconds for hesitation to win the battle, if not the war.

Ty stood. "I can't, darlin'. You know I've got to be up early." Without a word, she watched as he retied his robe with fumbling fingers. "I'll see you in the morning?"

Still, she said nothing.

He left as quickly as he'd arrived, anxiety driving him into the hall and all the way to his room. Whatever she'd wanted from him sexually, she'd definitely gotten. Beyond that? He refused to examine their exchange too closely.

Sleep dogged his heels when, several minutes later, he slipped into his room and quietly shut the door. He'd preset the alarm on his smartphone before knocking on Kenzie's door, ensuring he'd be up early enough he wouldn't have to rush to the barn. Shuffling through the dark room, he paused to set the desktop radio alarm as a backup, shed his robe and then collapsed onto his bed. The air conditioner's sharp *click* preceded the smell of refrigerated air, slightly canned and stale, as it swept across the room. For all that he preferred the outdoors, the artificially cooled air was bliss on his overheated skin. Air-conditioning always helped him sleep.

The robe tangled around his legs and he kicked at it even as he tried to retrieve the covers. No luck. The cooler he grew, the more determined he was to simply stop fighting and give in to sleep. Without at least a few z's, it would be pointless for him to show up in the arena in—he cracked one eye and peered at the clock—less than four hours. Gizmo deserved more than that from him. His eyes drifted shut.

Sometime later, he woke with a start and the absolute, sickening certainty he was late. A quick check of his watch proved his instincts right. Very. He glanced at the desktop clock and realized it was an hour slow. If he'd depended on that alarm alone, he'd have missed the competition altogether.

My phone. Where the hell's my phone and why didn't that alarm go off?

He'd last had his phone in his robe. He dug through the pockets. *Not there.*

Didn't matter. There wasn't time to hunt it down. The rules required him to be ready and warming up thirty minutes prior to his call time. He had less than an hour before he and Gizmo were due in the competition arena, less than twenty-five minutes before he had to be in the warm-up ring.

Yanking on jeans with one hand while he tried to pull on his shirt with the other proved fruitless and forced him to slow down. Man, he had *not* wanted to start nationals this way. He got himself together and sprinted from the room, rode the elevator to the lobby and raced through the crowds. He uttered apologies as he clipped folks left and right.

Another glance at his watch as he waited to cross the street to the temporary stalls said he had thirteen minutes to prep Gizmo and get him to the ring.

Damn it. Not enough time.

The light changed and he kicked into an all-out sprint through even heavier crowds. His stomach plummeted when—from twenty yards away—he saw the top of the Dutch door was already open. He slid to a stop in front of the stall...and gaped.

Kenzie stood there casually brushing the horse's tail. Gizmo had been saddled up, his reins looped over the wall-mounted hitching ring. His splint boots rested in the tack bucket she'd hauled out with her.

"What are you doing?" The question whipped across the distance, sharp enough to cause Gizmo to bob his head and paw the ground in protest.

"Why, I'm putting pretty polka-dot bows in your manly horse's tail before I paint his hooves 'I'm Not Really a Waitress' red by OPI, of course," Kenzie answered, just as brittle. "That way you might fool the steers, mesmerizing them with his handsome appearance. Just a hint? Right here, a 'thank you, Kenzie' wouldn't be inappropriate."

Ty stared at her, his eyebrows climbing into his hairline. "You're such a smart-ass." Grabbing the splints, he knelt in front of his horse and, moving quickly, yanked the Velcro straps in place.

"And you're behaving like a real jackass." She tossed the steel comb at him. "I came down to feed Indie and saw you hadn't taken care of Gizmo. The longer you went without showing up, the more I began to think it might be helpful if I lent a hand. I actually just called your cell to make sure you were up. My bad, seeing as you clearly have this under complete control. I suppose I should tell you to ignore the voice mail where I yell at you to get your butt in gear."

She moved past him and he instinctively stood and grabbed her arm. "I'm sorry."

"Yeah, you are," she bit out. "Now let go."

He tightened his hold. "No. Look, Kenzie. I'm truly sorry. You have to understand, I *need* this…"

Her brow furrowed when he trailed off. "Need what?"

He stopped himself just short of explaining the prize money was necessary for him to expand his breeding operation, and he was glad. As a Malone, she wouldn't understand his desperation to claim the prize money. It fueled his drive every day. Instead of answering, he shifted his approach. "I appreciate that you stepped in and helped." He shrugged, the skin across his shoulders tightening until it was too small to comfortably cover his large frame. "Thank you."

She eyed him with open disbelief, as if she knew it hadn't been what he'd started to say. In the end, though, she let it go with a "Sure. Whatever."

Ty moved around her to tighten Gizmo's cinch before he led the stud into the barn alley. "I hate to run, but I have to check in at the warm-up ring."

"Go. I'll be in the stands."

"Taking notes on how it's done?" he teased, mounting his horse.

"Nope. Watching arena conditions, checking out how worked up the steers get and gauging what the judges seem to be scoring on most heavily." She tapped her chin and then met his eyes, grinning. "Oh, yeah. And just how hard I have to bother to beat you."

Ty laughed. "One of the things I admire most about you, Malone, is your warped sense of entitlement." The minute the words left his mouth, he knew he'd stepped in it. Her face went stony and her spine ramrod straight. He opened his mouth to say something lighthearted, but she cut him off.

"I had no idea you thought so little of my skill, Covington." She crossed her arms under her chest and took a step away from Gizmo. "Normally I wouldn't address such nonsense, but this is one thing I'm compelled to settle. You may consider me 'entitled,' but I work every bit as hard as you do, if not harder. I put in just as many hours in the saddle, in the barn and on the computer to perfect my breeding program. No one can claim that's done with any sense of entitlement since I do it all myself. I'll pit my work ethic against yours *any* day."

She spun on her heel and stalked off, weaving through the crowd with a kind of fluid grace no one else had ever mimicked, let alone matched. For such a petite woman, she seemed taller, more sure of herself than ever. That she hadn't apologized for her legacy but rather had bitch-slapped him with it raised his opinion of her mightily. And that she'd walked away without sparing him a glance? He shouldn't find it sexy, but he did. Not many women were built of sterner stuff than that.

Ty wheeled Gizmo toward the warm-up ring and urged the horse into a trot. Once again, he called out apologies for his speed, but he was down to the wire.

The ring loomed closer.

One of the registrars moved to shut the gate for the next round of competitors—*his* round. He had to make it through before that gate closed or he was considered a no-show. That was *not* happening.

He spurred Gizmo forward. They sprinted for the gate, the horse's hooves pounding across the packed dirt and into the softer substrate of the ring before the registrar could respond.

"Sorry," Ty called, waving a hand in acknowledgment to the officials. He trotted over. "I had a small snafu this morning, but I made it."

"Barely," one of the men groused.

"He's here on time, William," said a woman next to him, eyeing Ty with open interest. "Leave him be. Name?"

"Tyson Covington and Doc Bar's Dippy Zippy Gizmo."

She made a note before pulling out Ty's competitor number. "Need help pinning this to your shirt?"

William snorted and pushed away from the table. "Keep your jeans on, Kathy. I'll help him."

She blushed, handing over the number.

Ty dismounted, and the man pinned the competitor's number across the shoulders of his shirt. "This'll be your number for every event you compete in. Keep it pinned to your shirt when you're on your horse for any reason." He gave Ty a friendly punch to the shoulder and stepped away. "A word of warning, though. You come through that gate at anything other than a slow trot next time, and I'll see that you're marked absent on the roster."

"That's hardly fair," Ty said as amiably as possible as he remounted Gizmo.

"I'm not so worried about fair as I am about competitors following the rules. The rules say you're here before that gate closes." He held up a hand when Ty started to protest. "Yes, you were here, but only because you ran the last hundred yards. That's not the spirit of the rule, son."

"Sir." Ty tipped his hat and spun Gizmo away, silently fuming at having been called out. What made him the angriest, though, was that the man was right.

He warmed Gizmo up with a small herd of steers. The horse seemed anxious, and Ty worked to first settle Gizmo and then himself. He tried to shake the nagging irritation of having been taken to task twice, first by his friend with benefits and second by a registrar and complete stranger. Neither sat well with him.

The announcer's voice came over the loudspeaker to announce the first competitors. Ty listened to the crowd's reaction as the first horse and rider hit their marks. The pair left the arena and their score was called shortly thereafter. Not bad, but definitely not strong enough to put the other cowboy on the boards or in the money at the end.

Ty absently listened as the next cowboy put his mount and the selected steers through their paces. He scored far better than the first rider. *A contender.*

Then it was Ty's run.

A deep breath, a swift pat to Gizmo's shoulder, then Ty reined his horse toward the arena entrance.

Showtime.

KENZIE FOUGHT THE urge to skip Ty's showing altogether. He'd pissed her off. More than that, he'd hurt her. It wouldn't have been such a shock if she'd expected it, but she hadn't. Not from him.

"'Entitled,' my ass," she spat, weaving her way through the crowds that were collectively pushing their way into the bleachers around the arena. She'd never been entitled. In fact, she had never been meant to be the Malone heir, and had no qualms with that particular fact. But the abrupt death of her older brother, Michael, had set her on the undesirable path that forced her to be both daughter and surrogate son to The Malone. Her father. The man who could do no wrong in the Quarter horse community.

Oh, she loved him. Wildly, in fact. He was an amazing father and friend, and most kids never experienced that rare combination. But the reality was that once she'd lost her brother, Kenzie had become the de facto heir to the Malone legacy. It wasn't something she'd ever wanted, and never, ever at that cost.

It left her trying to fill some big shoes, to live in the darkness of two shadows—Michael's, the up-and-coming rodeo star who had been the perfect older brother and ideal son, and her dad's, an infamous horseman who'd always been successful at everything he did. Kenzie wasn't perfect, and she failed as often as she succeeded. It was obvious to those around her she'd never be as good as they were.

So even insinuating she was either spoiled or entitled was the highest insult anyone could throw her way and was guaranteed a reaction. *I've earned every step forward I've taken. No one has handed me anything.*

Okay, yes. There was her trust fund. But no amount of money was worth the price she'd paid. Besides, there was certainly no dollar figure that automatically gave Ty, or anyone, the right to use words that hurt her.

If Michael were here, none of this would have happened. She wouldn't have inherited so much money, so no one would dare comment. The crushing sense of obligation to be both perfect daughter and replacement son wouldn't exist.

Three short beeps sounded. *The competition clock.* She slowed. Stopped. The crush of people worked their way around her. The first competitor was in the arena and working his, or her, group of calves. Applause followed the spectators' collective gasp.

What had happened? Curiosity ate at Kenzie. She moved with purpose toward the arena and then into the stands.

She slipped into the Malone arena-side box, bought with Malone money, respected because of the Malone name. Not hers—not yet—but her father's. He'd been a national champion in cutting, reining and roping, and his high score still stood. She'd grown up proud of him. Now? She wanted to beat him.

A small smile pulled at the corners of her lips at the same time someone opened the box and walked in, folding down the stadium seat beside her. Years in the man's presence told her who it was before she even looked into his sun-lined face. "Hey, Dad."

He slid down in his seat before draping an arm around the back of her seat. "You here to figure out a way to win or for the eye candy?"

"Dad!" The word escaped her on a rush of laughter. "You don't say things like that to your daughter."

"Hey," he exclaimed. "I'm hop. I know what's what."

"That would be 'hip,' and no, no, you don't."

He gently cuffed the back of her head. "Smart-ass."

He shifted his attention to the ring. "So who's our biggest competition this year? Still that Covington man from New Mexico? Didn't they get into some financial trouble, have to set their place up as a dude ranch to salvage it or something?"

Kenzie fought to keep her face straight. It wasn't that her dad didn't respect the hard work the Covingtons had put into saving their ranch. What bothered him was that, when he'd heard Gizmo's owner was in financial straits, Jack Malone had made a fair offer for Gizmo in an effort to help a fellow cowboy out. Even more, though, he'd wanted to get his hands on the stud horse. He hadn't taken Ty's rejection well. Of course, Ty hadn't taken the gesture as it was—at least mostly—intended, either. She'd never talked to either man about it directly, but she'd heard about it from both of them and more than once.

Her father didn't press for an answer right then, so she settled into her seat, watching the first competitor struggle to keep his calf separated from the herd. Horse and rider were out of sync. It took less time for him to lose the calf than it did for the rest of the herd to scatter. A mild round of clapping ceased when, in a fit of irritation, the rider viciously yanked the horse's head to the side and spurred him out of the arena.

Kenzie flagged down a server and asked for a program. Finding the horse and rider, she made a note regarding the horse's stall number. One benefit of having money? She could scare the man into responsible behavior with threats she could definitely follow up on. Oh… and she could buy his horse. She'd be doing both before she returned to Colorado.

Her attention shifted to the event again.

The second rider pulled a slightly above-average score, and he was clearly pleased with his performance.

That put Ty and Gizmo up next.

Kenzie took several deep breaths and blew them out with absolute control. Her dad rolled his program and slapped it against his palm repeatedly as he leaned forward to get the best view. With breakfast over, the noise level rose sharply due to the sheer volume of humanity moving in. Footfalls rumbled on the upper-level bleachers as more and more spectators filled the last vacant seats. What had been a low-level hum had grown to a near cacophony of sound. Even an experienced horse and rider could suffer from the distraction, and neither Ty nor Gizmo were accustomed to performing in indoor arenas this large. Sound seemed to echo back at both horse and rider and could fracture the focus of either. Or both.

The herd holders positioned a new group of yearlings for the incoming pair and then backed off, waiting.

At the opposite end of the arena, the gate swung open in a sweeping arc. Ty and Gizmo emerged from the dark tunnel at a lazy trot. Gizmo's head was low, the reins hanging loose. The horse seemed indifferent, almost half asleep, and Ty, with his chin to his chest, could have been napping. Their leisurely approach quieted the crowds even as it ratcheted spectator tension to a new high.

Kenzie moved to the edge of her seat. *What the hell is he thinking? The judges are going to score him down for looking so—* The buzzer sounded and she gasped.

With no visible cues from Ty, Gizmo's ears flipped forward, alert, and he started for the herd, the intent in his movements balling the cattle up. Horse and rider eased into the mass of cows and separated the first steer, peeling him away from the others with brutal efficiency. Ty and Gizmo moved in parallel harmony. The cowboy kept his hands down, his reins slack in order to give Gizmo his head. The stud horse never faltered. A whirling dervish, he spun, wheeled and darted left and right with both athleticism and showmanship that stunned not only Kenzie but the crowd, as well. She'd never seen the pair like this, had never known Ty to ride *this* professionally yet make it seem absolutely effortless.

Someone broke the silence with a whistle. Another voice shouted encouragement.

Anxiety created a solid mass between her shoulder blades. An invisible band tightened around her chest and made every breath she drew as painful as it was necessary. She wanted to scream at everyone to keep quiet, to let the pair work. If it wouldn't have generated an even larger distraction, she'd have done just that.

But Ty and Gizmo ignored every potential distraction. The horse worked the yearling and prevented his return until Ty deemed it time. Then, together, they put the animal back in the shuffling herd.

Next they sorted a much bigger steer out of the group. Obviously irritated, the steer charged the horse. Gizmo didn't give ground, instead rapidly placing himself, cross bodied, in between the steer and the herd. Confused, the steer stumbled and stopped. Gizmo took advantage of the other animal's hesitation to push him farther from the herd.

The big steer sprinted one direction, then spun and sprinted the other, trying his best to get by Gizmo. The horse wasn't having it. He met the steer's every move with a countermove that kept the animal separated from the herd.

Then on a particularly hard turn, one of Gizmo's leg splints came loose.

Kenzie's stomach dropped.

The horse ignored the support failure, charging forward to stop the steer. He slid to a stop and whirled to meet the other animal's next move.

Gizmo pushed off with his front feet, forced to make a rapid change in direction to head the steer off. The unsupported fetlock flexed and twisted in a totally unnatural manner. The cannon bone bent and the horse screamed, the sound sheer agony. The horse's momentum was unstoppable, and both Ty and Gizmo went down, the horse's right front hoof flopping sickeningly as he rolled over Ty.

Kenzie didn't think, didn't listen to her father's protests as she rose, refused to heed his restraining hand on her arm. She shrugged him off and vaulted the pipe fence, heading across the arena as fast as she could. Soft, ankle-deep dirt pulled at her feet like quicksand. The sound of her breath swamped her awareness as she pushed forward. She had to get to Ty *now*.

On some level, she was aware of onlookers shouting and the announcer's voice booming and the herd holders trying to keep the yearlings back so they didn't create more chaos. None of it mattered. What mattered was the horse groaning and unable to get up, his shredded fetlock already swelling. Even more? His rider. The man. Lord have mercy, the man...

Tyson.

His hat had been crushed in the fall and then flung several feet from the spot where he'd hit the dirt and gone completely still. She fixated on the hat as she ran. She knew Ty was within feet of the hat but couldn't bear to look at him too closely. One glance, one *single* glance, had dragged up memories that darkened the periphery of her consciousness, reminding her of Michael and the way he'd lain, preternaturally still in the dirt after his fall. She'd silently urged her brother to get up as he always did, to dust himself off and curse his horse and start again. But he hadn't risen. Not ever again.

No. No, no, no! her mind shrieked as her lungs worked harder than industrial bellows to provide her with air, to keep her moving, to keep her focused on that damned hat.

She couldn't lose someone else, couldn't watch another man she cared about die doing what he loved. She'd wouldn't recover from that a second time.

Move, Ty. Just once. Move.

Her heart hammered out a frantic rhythm in her chest. She stumbled, fear making her clumsy. Landing on her hands and knees, Kenzie crawled the last half-dozen yards to the unmoving man.

No! Her singular denial translated to a silent wail.

The closer she got, the easier it was to see he wasn't quite right. His eyes were closed, and his head... His head was canted at a strange angle. Dirt packed one ear and caked the near side of his face. And his chest failed to rise and fall.

Ty wasn't breathing.

"Please, God, no." Her broken plea was lost to the sounds of the announcer, official personnel and the crowd's frantic buzz. She ignored it all, kneeling next to him and grabbing his hand.

Ty's chest shuddered as he gasped, seizing a short breath. For ages, nothing followed. Then another short, gasped breath.

She squeezed his unresponsive fingers. "Ty? Tyson? Tyson!" she yelled, scared to touch him anywhere else even as she longed to shake him hard enough to rattle his teeth. "You answer me, damn you!"

Nothing.

"Don't you dare do this to me," she whispered. The harsh words brimmed with anger, demand and fear.

Sirens chirped and forced her to look up. The ambulance and EMTs were headed their way. The vet's emergency truck and flatbed trailer followed.

Gizmo...

Still gripping his hand, she leaned forward. "You fight, Covington. *You. Fight.*"

His fingers spasmed against her hand. One booted foot flopped to the side only to lie perfectly still again. Then his eyelids fluttered. The deep mink of his irises showed for a split second before his eyes slipped closed.

"You stubborn man! Gizmo needs you. Wake up and deal with this catastrophe. I'm not cleaning up after you. Do you hear me?" she demanded. Hysteria's sharp claws scrabbled their way up her spine as the seconds passed and he didn't answer. "Tyson!" She squeezed his hand hard enough to grind the bones together.

His fingertips pressed into her hand, the movement faint but undeniable.

A man and woman raced up to her, and she recognized Cade Covington before he skidded to a stop. Eyes wide, he fixated on Ty, and when he spoke, his deep voice trembled. "Tyson." He grabbed his female companion's hand, uttered a pained sound and then pulled her against his body.

She wordlessly folded into him, her eyes fixed on Ty and brimming with tears.

The ambulance stopped a few feet away, and two EMTs hopped out. One grabbed a body board as the other, already gloved up, approached. He crowded her out, the act far from gentle. "I need you to leave the ring, ma'am."

"Like hell," she snarled. She had to stay, couldn't leave him, not like this. *Wouldn't* leave him. "He's mine." The lie emerged without conscious thought.

The man shot her a sharp look even as he pulled on blue nitrile gloves. "Your husband?"

She didn't even hesitate. "He's. Mine."

He scrutinized her before lifting one shoulder and getting to work. "Fine, but stay out of my way."

Cade stared at her, skepticism filtering through his initial shock at her declaration.

She ignored him, ignored everyone but Ty and the EMT. Terror wove its way around her heart and up her throat, stopping just shy of spilling out her mouth on a keening wail. Focusing on the EMT, she managed to rasp out a desperate "Help him."

She heard raised voices behind her. Eli Covington and a woman she assumed was his new wife stood with rodeo vet. The three of them were arguing as Gizmo lay there, his sides heaving, hide slicked with sweat.

"The animal is in pain," the vet said. "Putting him down would be the humane thing."

"I'm about to hit you so hard your dentist won't need to worry about which teeth to keep. I guarantee that'll result in pain. Yours." The woman, tall enough to look at the man eye to eye, stepped close enough to invade his personal space. "You suggesting I put you down then, too? As a matter of 'humane' treatment?"

"That's different," the man objected. "I'm human."

She pointed at Ty's still form. "You euthanize this horse, you might as well put him down, too, because you'll destroy him and everything he's worked for."

Eli said something low to his wife.

She rounded on him. "Don't you dare tell me not to get worked up! I don't care if I'm six weeks' or six months' pregnant. Neither my hormones nor the baby responsible for them changes right and wrong."

Ty squeezed Kenzie's hand again, stronger this time but still far weaker than he should have been capable of. His eyelids fluttered before he ground his teeth and opened unfocused eyes. "Save..."

"We're working on saving you, Mr. Covington." The EMT scowled. "You've got to be still, though. We have to establish how much damage the accident caused your cervical spine."

"Screw spine," he whispered brokenly. His pain-filled gaze roamed wildly, skipping over her face and coming back. He fought to focus. "Giz... Save..." Tears rolled down his temples, and he squeezed her hand harder. "Please, Kenzie."

"I'll do what I can," she answered, voice husky.

"No." His tears flowed faster. "Promise."

"You have to calm down, Mr. Covington." The EMT pulled a syringe and loaded it. "I'm going to give you something for the pain before we transport you."

"Promise!" he rasped, grasping Kenzie's hand hard.

"I promise," she choked out, but his eyes had already drifted closed, and she had no idea if he'd heard her before the drug hit.

His hand relaxed. She clung to him, unwilling to let him go.

"Where are you taking him?" she asked, standing as they lifted the body board.

"Medevacing him to Baylor's trauma center."

Kenzie looked at Cade. "Go with him. I'll check in later after I take care of Gizmo."

"Take care of him how?" Cade demanded.

"Don't worry, I have a vested interest in ensuring the horse survives."

Cade's fiancée narrowed her eyes. "Ty didn't mention anyone else having a vested interest in Gizmo."

"Have you talked to Ty about his business dealings since he's been here?" Kenzie asked with feigned arrogance.

Cade arched a single brow. "No."

"Then, I don't expect you to know that I bought into the horse here or that I'm funding part of your brother's breeding program." Any other time it would have bothered her how easily she lied. Not right now, though. Too much was at stake. "I won't let my investment fall apart."

"Gotta go, folks," the EMT called.

"Do what you can," the short-haired woman said, grabbing Cade's hand and hauling him toward the ambulance. They hopped inside, the ambulance driver slamming the door closed behind them before racing for the driver's seat. The ambulanced chirped and, with lights flashing, took off.

Kenzie turned to the rodeo vet. "What's the prognosis?"

"Unless you own the horse—"

"I have a vested interest, yes." *How many lies would a cowgirl issue if a cowgirl could issue lies?* The answer was simple: as many as it took. "Let's consider the broken parts mine, so tell me what I'm facing here."

"He's torn ligaments and tendons in his fetlock, and I'm going to wager he's also fractured his cannon. We've got a Kimzey leg saver on its way, but the damage…"

He shrugged. "He'll require serious surgical intervention. If he's worth anything at all, get him to Ohio State University."

Eli's wife paled. "You're talking thousands just in transport."

"Make it happen," Kenzie said, crossing her arms and widening her stance.

The vet arched a brow. "You realize that between emergency transport and initial treatment you're looking at fifty to eighty thousand dollars?"

"You signing the checks?" she asked quietly.

"No."

"Then, don't worry about the costs."

"We have to, though," Eli murmured.

Kenzie shook her head. "No, you don't." Facing the vet again, she tucked her hands into her jeans pockets and did the one thing she hated doing. She threw her name at the doctor with the force of a major league pitcher's fastball. "I'm Mackenzie Malone, Jack Malone's daughter." The vet's eyes widened and he opened his mouth to say something, but Kenzie shook her head. "There are only two things I want to hear from you. First, I want this horse's flight number to the airport nearest Ohio State University. Charter a plane if necessary. Second, I want the in-flight pain management plans for him so I can clear that plan with my own vet."

The rodeo vet stiffened. "I assure you—"

"I listed the two things I need, Doc, and your assurances weren't on the short list." Dismissing him to do his job as she'd seen her father do a thousand times, she faced the Covingtons. "Ty's being lifted to Baylor. You two go there. I'll stay with Gizmo."

"Don't let them put him down. Please, Ms. Malone."

Eli choked on the words and looked away, but not fast enough to hide the sheen of tears in his eyes.

"Just Kenzie, and I give you my word I'll do my best to avoid that very thing, Mr. Covington."

The woman pulled out her admission ticket and grabbed a pen from a vet tech. She scribbled on the back, then handed the card to Kenzie. "I'm Reagan Covington, large-animal vet and Eli's wife. Call me with the drug names and I can explain what they're giving him."

"Will do. Now you two go on. Ty needs you, and frankly, I can make things happen faster if I have a little room to play the bitchy heiress."

Both Covington and his wife issued their thanks before jogging toward the nearest arena exit.

Kenzie went to her knees by Gizmo's head. She stroked his jaw and murmured soft words of encouragement. It took her several moments to summon the courage to meet his gaze. When she did, her heart broke for him. His nostrils blew hard, froth decorated his lips and neck, and the whites of his eyes showed clearly. He hurt. Worse than the pain, though, was his obvious fear. It was as if he had some inkling of just how bad off he was, and he was terrified.

That made two of them.

4

Kenzie knew the exact moment her dad entered the fray. Things started to happen at twice their normal speed. The vet became respectful versus argumentative, and that—*that*—pissed Kenzie off more than anything. As a petite woman dominating the leaderboards in a man's sport, she had to earn every iota of respect she received. Carrying the Malone name only made it more difficult. There were always the behind-the-back allegations that she'd never have made it this far if it hadn't been for her father. For all that it was bull, the quiet whispers stung. The song "Should've Been a Cowboy" by Toby Keith rang true. Neither the title nor the lyrics said it was a blessing to be a cow*girl*. She wouldn't allow them to push her aside because she was female.

Shoving her way through to the vet, she stepped up beside her father and shot him a hard glance through dark lashes. "I'll manage this, Dad."

"Seemed to me you could use a little help."

"Nope. He—" she jabbed a finger in the vet's direction "—will do better when he learns a little respect for women and a hell of a lot *more* respect for animals."

"There're better ways to get what you want, Mackenzie."

"Well, right now Gizmo's down, so tossing the last name around will have to do." Rounding on the very man under discussion, she ignored the people milling about, the weight of the crowd's collective stare and, above all, she fought to keep her attention off the pain poor Gizmo was suffering. He had to come first. She focused on the one man who could truly help him. "Dose him with dermorphin so we can get him in a hoist and moved."

"I need proof you have authority over the animal, ma'am, because he's registered under Tyson Covington's name."

"I already explained this. I bought into him prior to the accident." She didn't think twice about uttering the lie again. Not until she realized her father had overheard.

"Excuse us for a second." He took her by the arm and led her a few steps away. Jack Malone's eyes were bright, glittering with a type of predatory anticipation she'd never seen outside competition. "I've been trying to get Covington to sell me half rights to Gizmo for over three years. How did you manage it?"

"Feminine wiles?" A question and not a declarative statement. Guilt tightened her throat, the sensation spreading to her chest. She'd always been honest with her dad. She'd been his shadow as long as she could remember. How could she lie to him, particularly about something he wanted so badly? Easy. She couldn't. Opening her mouth to admit her deception, he plowed forward in excitement.

"I'll have Alyssa make arrangements to get this horse to Ohio State and the Galbreath Equine Center's emergency medicine team." He pulled his cell and called his barn manager. "Alyssa, I need you to charter a flight for an injured horse—Fort Worth to the nearest airport to the Galbreath Center." He paused then shook his head. "No, not Indie. Kenzie managed to buy into Covington's Dippy Zippy Gizmo just before the stud was injured." Another pause. "I have no idea how she managed to do it. We'll get details later. Right now, that horse has to get on his way. I'll have Kenzie book the next flight to Columbus since she should be on the ground before the horse in order to receive him. Tell the Center to do whatever is necessary to save this animal. Cost isn't an issue. I'll call you back shortly. Thanks, Alyssa."

Kenzie wanted to puke. The lie had taken on a life of its own and was about to cost her father a hell of a lot of money. She couldn't live with this, couldn't let him foot the bill and then find out the truth. "Dad, maybe you shouldn't do this. I don't actually—"

"Honey, it's all right. I trust you implicitly. You'll be my eyes and ears, acting in my stead to make sure this horse gets the best of everything." He pulled her into a bear hug. "I'm so glad we're finally partnering with the Covingtons and have the means to help save this magnificent animal."

Guilt hung in her throat, both bitter and sour. "I haven't been—"

"I know you haven't ridden yet, Kenzie, but don't worry, honey. You're amazing on horseback and you're young still. There'll be more opportunities for you to chase my record. I'm proud as hell that you're putting others' well-being in front of your own success." He stepped away and grasped her shoulders before meeting her gaze. "Call me with your flight details." His attention drifted to the horse, who lay in the soft arena dirt, sides heaving, one front fetlock terribly swollen and distorted in a macabre, stomach-churning manner. "You remind me so much of Michael, thinking on your feet like this."

She'd lived to ease her parents' pain after Michael's death, worked her ass off to be good enough at everything she did to make them proud, and here she was, hearing the words for the first time.

The irony wasn't lost on her. Jack Malone, known for his honesty and straightforward talk, wasn't *proud* of her based on her own merit. It had taken things beyond her control and one whopping lie to hear the words she'd longed for from him.

Sure in the knowledge she was dooming herself by letting the truth stay buried, she hugged him hard before starting for the end of the arena where the golf carts were kept. She got a driver to return her to her hotel, stuffed all her belongings into her suitcase and less than forty minutes later was in a hired car bound for the airport.

She dug out her cell phone, pulled up the internet and paused. If she called her dad now, she could come clean, tell him she'd pay for the horse's care from her trust fund. She wouldn't have to live with the immense burden so many lies created.

She closed the web browser and pulled up her dad's cell number.

Her thumb hovered over the call button.

I trust you implicitly.
I'm proud as hell that you're doing the right thing.
You remind me so much of Michael.

Confessing now would destroy his pride in her, would make him regret losing Michael all the more because her brother never would have backed himself into a corner like this.

"Way to go, Mackenzie," she muttered, closing the phone function on her smartphone and returning to the web browser.

It only took a few taps of the screen on the airline's booking page to have her seated in 3A on the next flight to Columbus, Ohio.

Kenzie dropped her phone in her messenger bag, then settled back into the seat. The image of Ty's broken body flashed through her mind. She shivered.

There was more to this than just her father's pride in her. At least part of the reason she was going through with this was the sheer terror she'd witnessed in Ty's eyes. She'd felt an emotional connection with him, a shared purpose that bound them together in this. She could save him, save his horse, where she'd failed Michael that day. Now she might set the past to rights by saving Gizmo, and in turn, giving Ty a reason to fight harder to recover, to live.

And she needed him to live. In the privacy of the backseat of the car, she could admit she cared about him. Cared far more than was wise, no doubt.

But for a split second when she'd first approached Tyson after the accident...

His chest hadn't moved.

Hers had stopped in kind.

He'd had no pulse.

Hers had stalled without even an indignant sputter.

His eyes hadn't fluttered.

She'd been unable to blink.

He'd been as still as death.

And a part of her had died.

The thought alone was enough to make her throw herself into Gizmo's well-being. Being near the horse would put her near Ty, and it would give her time to work out how to handle her dad. And she could avoid looking too closely, or even at all, at the complicated emotional chaos she'd faced when, for that split second, she'd thought she'd lost Ty forever.

T%%Y KNEW THINGS WERE%%, at best, pretty damn bad. If someone would've taken the time to explain just *how* bad, he'd have appreciated it. Chances were good they assumed he couldn't hear them, though. Seeing as he couldn't currently force his eyes open, it was a fair assumption. But it was still wrong. During the many moments of dark lucidity, he heard every word.

As it was, the best he could do was focus on squeezing his hands or flexing his feet when instructed. No matter how miserably he knew he'd failed, strangers' voices praised him. Now and again he'd hear a voice he recognized. That was when he'd fight hardest to open his eyes. The effort always proved too much, but it wasn't enough to take the fight out of him. He needed to know what had happened, needed to see the truth in the faces around him. Those faces wouldn't lie to him.

Yet no matter how hard he fought against the pain that enveloped his brief battles to remain conscious, he continued to surface to darkness and descend into darkness.

So he listened.

And heard the same phrases over and over.

"Cervical involvement at C2 and C3."

"Neurological impairment unknown."

"Long-term prognosis undetermined."

"Lucky to be alive."

He was aware he lost blocks of time, but was sure that time had passed because the voices of his caregivers changed. Day and night ceased to exist. The hum of machines and the squeeze and flex commands from those voices became his only constant.

That was why it surprised him when he finally rose from the darkness and found the room blindingly bright. He opened his mouth and a very feminine sob escaped. More confused than ever, he closed his mouth, but the sobbing continued.

Not him, then.

He blinked slowly. When he forced his eyes open again, a woman with a penlight hovered over him. She lifted first one eyelid and then the other, flashing the light in his eyes. The beam pierced his skull as wave after wave of nausea rolled through him.

"Uh," Ty managed to grunt in protest.

"Glad to hear you're finally protesting all the poking and prodding," she said on a smile. "Can you manage to squeeze my fingers, Tyson?"

Concentrating, he squeezed as hard as he could.

"That's good. Better than yesterday."

Her comment, couched in cheerful enthusiasm, didn't fool him one bit. He was weak as an abandoned calf in mid-January. Hopefully his chances of survival were better.

He blanked out again. When he opened his eyes, the sobbing was softer, removed from him somehow, and two male faces loomed over him. Ty tried to raise his hand, but it seemed heavier than a concrete footer. Licking his lips, he tried to nod his chin. No go.

Will nothing move?

Machines beeped with mechanical urgency, reflecting his rising panic. The hushed *whoosh*-pause, *whoosh*-pause of a ventilator made him want to choke on the tube down his throat. Eyes wide, he was ashamed at the tears that trailed down his temples as his panicked gaze sought those of his brothers'. He managed to raise the first finger on his right hand. A nurse rushed into the room.

She went to a monitor just outside his field of vision and murmured, "Tyson, honey, you have to calm down," as she manipulated the machine and made the incessant *beep-beep-beep*ing stop. Fishing around in her pocket, she pulled something free.

Ty strained to see what she'd come up with. It wasn't by sight that recognition hit but instead by the lethargic weight that stole over him and began to pull heavily on his consciousness.

Damn if she didn't sedate me when I just woke up.

He was frantic to stay awake, but it took only seconds for his vision to blur and his brothers to become optical twins—two of Cade, two of Eli.

The soft sound of feminine tears stopped.

"Rest, Ty." Cade's voice was rough, as if it hadn't been used in ages.

"We'll be here when you wake up," Eli added, reaching down to grip Ty's hand.

He'd have felt a whole lot better if he'd been able to grip that hand back. Then the pharmaceutical cocktail hit and took him down before he even registered the count.

TKO.

5

It had been almost seven weeks since Mackenzie arrived in Ohio with Gizmo, and there were two things she knew with relative certainty. First, the horse couldn't have had better care. Second, January was the worst possible month to visit Ohio.

She tugged the neckline of her jacket higher and blinked rapidly, the wind freezing her eyes and burning her chapped lips as she rounded the corner of the building and sped up in her effort to reach the heated barn.

Inside, Kenzie went straight to Gizmo, pulled her hands out of her pockets and slipped the big guy a couple of sugar cubes. She slowly rubbed his face, jaw to muzzle and back, and murmured to him as the vet, Dr. Trey Harris, removed the vet wrap and nonstick pads that covered the surgical sites. The pins had come out and the horse was bearing weight regularly, yet for all that, his foot still looked like something from a horror flick. The incisions were healing fine, but there were still angry welts where the surgical pins had been inserted in both his fetlock and pastern, and all around the last of the sutures the skin was raw and red. The swelling had abated, though. Enough so she could see Gizmo's improvement. Still, the idea of the pain he'd endured—still endured—made her throat tight.

"When—" The one word came out scratchy, so she forced herself to slow down and breathe before facing the vet. "When can the big guy go home?"

Dr. Harris glanced up at her and one corner of his mouth curled up in a slow, lazy smile. "You getting tired of staring at my pretty face?"

Laughing, Kenzie shook her head. "You're easy on the eyes but you're not a cheap date, Dr. Harris." She sighed dramatically. "I just don't see a long-term future for us."

The vet, easily her father's age or older, chuckled, never ceasing his ministrations to the leg and ankle he'd essentially rebuilt the day Gizmo, and she, had arrived. He didn't answer her, though.

So she pressed. "I was hoping to move his care to the ranch before the end of the month. Is that reasonable?"

"What kind of care do you have in place for him at home?"

"The barn is clean and dry but certainly not a sterile environment. However, I can have a cement pad laid for him and rubber nonslip floor tiles installed. And once I have a return date, I'll arrange a sling and will incorporate whatever physical therapies you recommend. I can have my vet fly in to check on him, and Ty's sister-in-law is a large-animal vet, too. Then there's you." She batted her eyes at him. "I don't suppose you'd make a couple, maybe three…or four, house calls, would you?"

"I'm available." He fluttered his lashes at her and

made fish lips. "But like you said earlier, I'm an expensive prospect."

"Only the best for this guy." She patted Gizmo's neck.

Dr. Harris sobered. "I'm serious. It would be pretty costly to buy my time in such large chunks because I'd have to bill you for the hours away from the clinic."

"Sure, but leaving him here long-term can't be much, if any, cheaper. Along with vet bills, I have to consider feed, board, grooming and his handler's fees, as well as my own room, board and rental car. It all adds up fast. Flying you in to visit him would, by all accounts, be more reasonable."

"True. I just want you to understand there will be additional costs to having me examine him on site, and those visits will occur subject to my availability."

"If the horse needs it, trust that I'll do it."

"Fair enough." He paused when he hit a sensitive spot and the horse twitched and then pawed the air as passively as a 1,200-pound animal could. "So whose barn should we make arrangements to deliver him to?

Kenzie jerked upright, stiff as a board. "The Covington barn. Why?"

"Just wondered whose home he was going to since your dad and Covington are equal partners now."

Her brow furrowed. "Who said my dad was an equal partner?"

"That would be—" he gestured toward her "—*your dad*."

"If there's a partner in this, it isn't Jack Malone." Her shoulders sagged a fraction. "It's me."

"You don't seem happy about that."

"It's complicated." She didn't offer any more because there wasn't more to say. That and she didn't want to start any rumors. When Dr. Harris opened his mouth, she cut him off with a sharp shake of her head. "Let's leave it at 'complicated.' How soon can I get him home?"

The vet worked his fingers down Gizmo's leg, along the cannon bone that had been fractured in the accident. "I'm admittedly pleased with how clean he's healed." Standing, he brushed off his hands and then shoved them into his coat pockets, considering her. "Let me finish up here, get a new set of X-rays and we'll talk dates. I'm guessing you'll hang around until I'm through?"

Don't I always? "Sure." The metal cribbing rail on the stall delivered a shock of cold when her jacket sleeves slipped up as she leaned forward to rest her arms on the door. Sure, Colorado was cold, but it wasn't as cold as this. There was snow in Colorado, but that meant ski season opened, not that the snowbirds fled south.

South.

She was far more snow bunny than bird, but she'd be heading south with Gizmo. That meant she'd be facing off with Ty sooner rather than later. Her stomach did this weird gymnastics routine. If the vet up here had heard about the "partnership" she'd asserted where Gizmo was concerned, it was safe to assume Ty had heard the same. Though that was pure speculation, seeing as she hadn't talked to him. Not yet. Kenzie had limited all correspondence to email exchanges with Reagan. Her logic had been simple: by limiting her emails to Reagan, and *only* Reagan, Kenzie didn't have to worry about what she'd said to whom and when she'd said it. There were fewer chances she'd have to stretch the truth in different directions to better support the tales she'd already told.

Except with her dad. She'd tried to clear that up.

Man, she'd tried. But every time she brought up the horse's progress, her dad always launched into some grand speech about how proud of her he was and how she was doing the right thing by both families, helping the Covingtons pay medical bills they'd never have been able to afford all while praising her for "this great new partnership that's getting the Covington boy's superior genetics program integrated into our herd." How was she supposed to tell him the whole thing was a sham she'd cooked up in a split second because she hadn't wanted to be separated from her prime competitor who was, by the way, her lover? That was bound to go over well.

And how was she supposed to tell him she was spending Malone money on a horse their family had no rights to? Most of all, how was she supposed to tell her dad she'd lied to him, to everyone, and that she was nothing at all like Michael? She was never meant for this, to be son and daughter, sole heir and youngest child.

"I can't," she whispered, the two-word admission carried away by the howling winds outside.

"I'll make arrangements to have the horse cleared for travel in roughly two weeks, provided you agree to follow my instructions for his recovery and therapy."

Shoving her hands into her pockets, she forced her spiraling thoughts to step aside, giving her whole attention to the doctor. "Two weeks?"

"At the outside, yes." The vet glanced at Gizmo's front foot. "Swim therapy would really help him strengthen that joint and encourage faster strengthening of the muscles and tendons that support his front end." Dr. Harris pulled his toque off and scrubbed one hand through his short hair. The effect left him looking like he'd uncovered an irritated hedgehog.

Kenzie grinned. "I'll have a pool installed."

"Of course you will," the vet said with an answering smile. "And stop laughing at my hair."

"Can't," she admitted, her grin widening. "You've been hiding a hedgehog under your hat the entire time. It's as if suddenly you're not the man I thought you were."

He gave her a mock dirty look. "My wife says the same thing."

Kenzie couldn't control her laughter. "Smart woman," she said between peals.

"Get out of my barn, kid," the older man groused good-naturedly. "I've got to get this guy ready to go."

She sobered enough to add, "I'll make sure your aftercare plan is followed to a T."

He nodded. "Go ahead and book his flight for the first of February. I'll have him ready by then. You ready to take this on?"

Her thoughts scattered like dandelion fuzz in the face of a hopeful child's breath. She could get the horse home, arrange to have his therapy taken care of and see Gizmo emerge as strong as he would ever be. But the horse wasn't the only factor. The Covingtons would expect answers. Her dad would expect results from a partnership that didn't exist.

And Ty? She shouldn't have anything to worry about. She'd done what she had to do in order to ensure his wishes were carried out. Facing him would be hard, admitting she'd lied to save Gizmo even harder. But she'd do it without apologizing.

She shifted her gaze to the horse, reaching out to

straighten his forelock. "I guess there isn't any other option, is there?"

And that was the hell of it.

There wasn't.

6

SOMEONE HAD ARRANGED the furniture to create what Ty called his "parking space" in front of the big picture window in the main house's living room. He sat there far too often, looking out over the little bit of ranch the view afforded. To the east, he watched as one of the hired hands crested the hill on horseback, bringing in the newest group of guests from their first trail ride. The horses all looked good. Ty would have to thank Cade for making that a priority despite all his other responsibilities. Not that his brother wouldn't have done it on his own, but Ty knew the horses were being paraded for his approval. Probably to make him feel like he was part of things. But he wasn't. Not anymore. The cowboy never would have brought them so close to the house otherwise.

A sigh escaped him, sounding far too close to self-pity for his comfort. Provided he was careful, didn't reinjure his neck and did all his physical therapy, his disabilities were temporary. Knowing that wasn't enough to curb his frustrations, though. Or his fears. Never in a million years had he thought his life would end up like this. He'd been arrogant. Vain. Assumed himself invincible. Now he rode an electric wheelchair instead of his horse.

Gizmo.

The stud horse would be home today, arriving three days after Ty had. He was anxious, scared to see the horse who was more than just "an animal" to him, afraid Gizmo had suffered more than Ty had imagined. And imagine he had. He'd thought of Gizmo a thousand times every day. He'd created the worst-case scenarios over and over as he tried to spur his memory to recall the details of the fall. Sure, his family had discussed the accident with him, but he'd chosen not to watch the replay on the DVR. There was no doubt in anyone's mind, least of all his own, that he'd take it hard. Still, if things had been as horrible as he imagined, the horse wouldn't have come through with the positive reports from the vet. And *only* the vet.

Not once had Kenzie called him. Not once had she reached out to let him know how Gizmo was recovering or talk about this mysterious agreement that had been forged between them. Pride kept him from admitting to his family that he had no recollection of the agreement. He hadn't wanted Gizmo's care interrupted. Selfish? Yes. That didn't change the truth behind his choice, though.

He wasn't stupid. There was no way he, or the ranch, could have afforded to cover the costs of the Galbreath center. So he'd kept quiet, fighting to remember what he'd agreed to. The one thing he knew? Whatever agreement they'd struck had been after the accident, because he recalled with great clarity everything that had happened before he'd gone into the arena. Ty resented her for preying on his weakness and her choice not to communicate with him. Sure, she'd been emailing Reagan as the veterinarian who'd take over Gizmo's rehab when he came home. Reagan had relayed the messages.

But Kenzie hadn't called anyone, hadn't reached out to *him* at all. She had to know how bad he wanted the information. She understood what this horse meant to him, probably better than anyone. She understood what losing Gizmo would do to his breeding program, to *him*. Why? Because she understood him. Or so he'd thought. Seemed he'd misjudged her character. Badly.

A dust cloud rose from the road that led into the ranch from the south. A horse hauler rounded the slight bend in the drive. The sun gleamed off its bright white-and-chrome exterior. Ty squinted. Behind the hauler came a fancy truck-and-trailer combo he didn't recognize.

"Someone's here," he called through the house, doing his best to ignore the faint bitterness in his words. Before, he'd have slapped his hat on and headed out to meet the truck. Now? He'd been reduced to reporting the goings-on. Nothing more.

Heavy footsteps were followed by lighter, decidedly feminine ones. "Who is it?" his sister-in-law Reagan asked as she peered over his shoulder.

"Fancy setup," his eldest brother and Reagan's husband, Eli, commented. "Has to be Gizmo. I can't imagine him arriving in anything less with a Malone arranging his travel."

Reagan laid a hand on Ty's shoulder and glanced back at Eli. "Says the man who lived alone in a six-thousand-square-foot house."

Ty forced a smile. "Make sure they put him in the first stall past the tack room, would you?"

"Sure." Reagan slipped her sunglasses on and headed

for the door. "Might be handy to have the attorney around if there are forms to sign."

Eli's voice drifted back to Ty as he followed his wife. "Is that all I am—your legal monkey?"

"Just be grateful I haven't sold you to a traveling circus."

Ty listened as the front door closed and muffled their voices. He wheeled his chair from the window so he faced away from the scene outside. He envied them the sunshine on their shoulders, the breeze in their faces and open air around them. The ability to walk without limitations or fear of falling. To ride out across the pasture. To see the new foals that had arrived in his absence. Those little ones wouldn't know him, would consider him an unidentified threat, and that sickened him. He'd never missed the birth of a foal, never missed the chance to rub them down and be there every day thereafter. Now? It would be ages before he could get to the barn, get involved, get to know the babies.

"Hello, Ty."

The feminine voice startled him. He'd been so lost in thought he hadn't heard anyone enter. He spun the chair toward the intruder. Recognition was as effective as a punch to the gut. "Mackenzie Malone. Couldn't spare a call, huh? So why are you here now? Come to check out the crippled cowboy? Or did you come in to write a check in the hopes you'd buy some goodwill? I expected better of you."

Her cheeks paled and she reacted as if shoved, taking a step back before recovering. "Feeling's mutual." She lifted her chin a notch, her eyes narrowing. "And I didn't come into the house to buy anything. I was there, in Texas, when you were hurt. Unfortunately, no one bothered to tell me your attitude was maimed along with everything else." Kenzie stepped closer and propped a hip on the sofa arm, one leg slowly kicking back and forth as the other one held her in place. "I didn't immediately announce myself because you were brooding. I thought I'd let you get it out of your system. Looks as if that isn't happening, so brood away."

"You didn't spend two weeks in a coma. You didn't nearly lose your life on national television. Both your legs work just fine. Riding is a joy you indulge in and take for granted every damn day. So don't you come in here and judge me, Mackenzie." There was a world of accusation in his words, a world he hadn't intended to tap into. "Go back to your gilded castle and play at breeding quality horses. You have no right to be part of this, no right to be here."

She stiffened, her eyes widening before she schooled the emotions chasing one after another across her face. "Don't have the right?" Her lips thinned. "I beg to differ."

"Begging's a good place to start, sweetheart." Ty leaned against the wheelchair's armrest to catch every single word, every expression, anxious to have it out with the woman who'd run off with his horse the first chance she had. The same woman who had forgotten him as soon as she'd taken what she wanted, and it hadn't been him. It surprised him how much that stung, but damn if he'd admit it. He curled one lip up in a half smile, half snarl. "Go on, then. I'm waiting."

Her eyes narrowed to finite slits, blue irises sparking wildly. "I'm sorry?"

"That's the way. Is this the first time you've ever groveled? Keep it up. You'll get the hang of it."

She opened her mouth only to snap it shut and stare at him. Seconds passed before she spoke again. "What's your damage, Covington?"

"Are you *blind*?" he half shouted. "My problem is I'm *sitting*, Malone, and it's not because I'm lazy. I'm here, stuck in this damn house, watching as some stranger delivers my horse—*my horse*—and parks him in a stall in heaven only knows *what* condition!" Yep. Full-on shouting now. He wasn't proud, but he wasn't going to apologize. She had it coming, keeping information on Gizmo sequestered the way she had. He'd understood the horse was getting the best care possible, but nothing in life was free. At some point, she'd want something in return.

Crossing her arms, she stood.

"Lording it over me, huh?" he continued. "That you can stand and I can't? Feel good to finally be able to beat me at something?"

Her lips all but disappeared in that beautiful face. "Of all the people outside your immediate circle, I'm most aware you were as injured as Gizmo. But don't you dare, *dare*, throw down the verbal gauntlet unless you're prepared to take the gloves off, too."

"I had a right to know about my horse, to see him settled today!"

"Like hell you did!" she shouted in return. "You're in no condition to handle that horse right now. You'd despair, and he'd know. He's a sensitive animal. He has to focus on getting through physical therapy, very much like you do. He deserves every chance to make as full a recovery as is physically possible, or everything that's gone into saving him was wasted. Same goes for you. There's a pattern here, in case you're not seeing it. Fifty bucks says you're yelling at me because you're making asinine assumptions about how I pity you, sitting in the house in the wheelchair." She sucked in a breath and blew it out on a harsh exhale before pushing forward. "Do the responsible thing for once in your life and put someone else's needs in front of your own. Don't go see Gizmo until you can keep from treating him as if he's crippled. And do yourself a favor. Stop forcing everyone else to regard you, and treat you, the same way."

Every bit of heat drained from his face as Ty listened to her accusations. He nodded, fighting to swallow the emotion clogging his throat.

She stepped forward and loomed over him.

The move forced him to roll his eyes up to see her. "Step away, would you?" he bit out.

"Move your chair."

"You coldhearted—"

"Don't you dare finish that sentence." One degree further and the ice in her voice would have rimed the windows. "I know you've been handed a raw deal, but don't let yourself be reduced by circumstance to calling a woman foul names. You're a better man than that. Or you were." He started to defend himself, but she waved a hand between them and spoke over him, drowning out any defense he might have delivered. "I'm exhausted, I haven't been home in two months and I missed my chance at nationals because I was playing nursemaid. You owe me courtesy—no, you owe me bone-deep *gratitude*." Blue eyes sparked wildly as heat climbed her cheeks. "I'm not willing to negotiate on that. Like it or not, you owe me."

He closed his eyes and blindly steered his chair away from her. They both knew she'd taken the gloves off with that last comment.

Tyson Covington rarely owed anyone, and when he did? He always paid up.

Always.

KENZIE STORMED OUT of the house, a sticky miasma of dark emotion roiling through her. Fear. Heartache. Frustration. Compassion. Fury. There were more—so many more—but none she'd ever thought she'd have to deal with in relation to Ty Covington.

Liar.

"Damn it, Mackenzie Malone, you knew what you were getting into with this." The impact of her cowboy boots on hard earth punctuated each step. Yanking her ball cap off her head, she slapped it against one leg in time with her stride as she headed to the barn with new purpose.

She wouldn't walk away from Gizmo. She'd known him since he'd started traveling with Ty as a yearling to get used to shows. She'd watched him from his first performance. From day one, he'd been magnificent. One of the worst moments of her life had been looking into his pain-filled eyes that seemed to plead with her for salvation. Any salvation.

She usually harbored incredible guilt about using her trust fund—guilt that half that money used to belong to a brother she'd cherished. Guilt that all the money in the world couldn't bring him back.

Not this time. This time the money had managed to save someone.

But for all she'd operated on the belief she'd done right by Gizmo and Ty, the man had proved in a matter of minutes that this thing between them—this debt incurred, this debt owed—would stand between them.

The thing that made her angriest was that he had jumped all over her for doing the very things he'd asked her to do. How could she ever win against someone who asked for an immense favor and then punished her for giving him what he'd asked for?

No, she hadn't called him. There was a reason, though—a reason she wasn't ready to face, let alone own.

Pausing, she leaned against the shiny trailer, shocked by the cold when she touched her forehead to the metal. "Take your own advice and suck it up." Wide-open space swallowed her quiet words, protecting her from being overheard.

Okay, fine. I'll deal with the truth. She'd known Ty would have trouble talking around the neck brace. That he wouldn't be able to cope with verbal updates on Gizmo's condition, particularly when it had been iffy whether the horse would ever walk again.

She thumped her head against the trailer. "Chickenshit." Louder than her last admission, but the harsh accusation was still for her ears alone.

Truth, then, she thought. *Real, hard truth.* She'd known she'd be returning Gizmo to the Covington ranch. She'd see her commitment through to the end. She didn't shirk her duties or shy away from the hard stuff when it came down to brass tacks. But she hadn't been sure she could face Ty's condition. He would walk again, but no one knew how well. And ride? That was up in the air at the moment. And ride Gizmo? That was so far in the future that the calendar hadn't even been printed yet.

"Truth," she said again, the self-command a rough one. It was all these things and more that scared her, but seeing Ty broken had been enough to nearly drop her to her knees.

The vibrancy of the man had been diminished by both circumstance and the reality he now faced. She could see it in his face, that knowledge. That moment when she'd stepped into the house, that moment when she simply observed the near hopeless desperation on his face, had ripped her heart out. When he'd rounded on her, she hadn't blamed him. Not one bit. But pride wouldn't let her take poor treatment from him, either. She was in over her head where that man was concerned.

She'd spent the past two months lost in a world of probabilities and survival statistics. She hadn't applied those to the man who meant so much to her. At least, not until she saw him. Now? The idea that he might not ever be 100 percent again made her want to scream at the heavens over the injustice.

"You look as though you could use this."

Kenzie spun around so abruptly she knocked the ceramic mug out of the redhead's hand. Rich, dark coffee splashed out in flash-frame movement, the cup tumbling to the ground and shattering.

"Sorry." The redhead rushed forward. "I'm so sorry. I didn't mean to crowd you at all. I was only trying to get out of this blasted wind—"

"It's all good," Kenzie said, interrupting. "I promise. I was just—"

A dark-haired woman stepped up to join them. "I hope you're going to finish that sentence with 'going to see if Gizmo was settled.' I swear, the big guy's moping without Ty."

On cue, a horse's bugle cut across the wind that whipped across the plains. The sound would undoubtedly carry to the house, and Ty would cringe. It would hurt him to hear the horse calling for him when he was unable to get down to the barn.

What if I was wrong earlier? What if the best thing for Gizmo is to see Ty? And if Ty witnesses the proof of Gizmo's improvement, maybe he'll want to be part of that. Maybe...

She straightened. "Do you guys have a golf cart here, or one of those all-terrain Mules people use around the barn?"

The dark-haired woman held out a hand. "I'm Reagan, Dr. Matthews—or Dr. Covington, I guess—Eli's wife. We sort of met at the rodeo and we've been exchanging emails over the past couple of weeks. Yes, we have half a dozen golf carts for guest use and four Mules for the cowboys to haul feed, tack and such. Why?"

Before Kenzie could answer, the other woman stepped in and took one of Kenzie's rough hands in both of her smooth, slender ones. "I'm Emmaline, Emma for short, and the last name's about to be Covington."

Kenzie squeezed Emma's hand in recognition. "You were the woman with Cade in Fort Worth."

"Yes." Emma blushed prettily.

Reagan shifted her attention to Kenzie. "The 2014 Kawasaki Mule with the four-inch lift kit and all-terrain tires has the best ride. Will that work?" she asked as she dug a key ring out of her pocket and began sifting through them. Finding the right one, she pulled it off and handed it over.

"Just like that?" Kenzie asked, surprised.

"I assume it has to do with getting Ty out of the house."

Kenzie nodded at the doctor. "It does."

Emma glanced at the house before meeting Kenzie's

curious stare. "He's changed, and we don't have a clue what to do for him. If you have a plan, I'm all for it."

"Can he walk at all?" Kenzie asked as she slipped the key into her jeans pocket and cracked her knuckles.

"A little. He's anxious, but he can do it. Just doesn't like us to watch him practice." Reagan considered Kenzie, seeming to weigh her next words. "He doesn't ever leave the house."

"I'm sure he's worried about how he'll be treated by the ranch hands. He's worked with them a long time?" Kenzie asked.

"Yeah." Reagan watched as one of those very hands rode a horse in close to the barn at a lazy trot, calling out a welcome to someone mending fence. "He's known them for years. Why?"

"He won't want them to think less of him." She shrugged under the weight of the women's curious stares. "It's pretty normal, really." Kenzie flushed when Reagan shot a quick glance at Emma, the look on her face asking how a rodeo-circuit cowgirl would know what was "normal" for a person recovering from an injury. She fought not to hunch her shoulders. "I majored in psychology. Graduated magna cum laude."

Reagan's entire assessment changed, her stance relaxing and her shoulders dropping some. "Very good to know. And everything you said is true. We've been coddling him a little too much."

Kenzie watched the goings-on around them for a minute before pulling the key out of her pocket and returning it to Reagan. "He'll feel safest with his brothers. Have them bring him down tomorrow after breakfast. If he protests, pick up his damn chair and carry him to the barn. Just make sure the area's clear." She closed her eyes for a brief moment and listened to Gizmo's second bugle. "I'm going to do what I can to ensure the horse is up for the visit."

She dug her truck keys out of her pocket.

"Where are you going?" Reagan asked, clearly confused.

"I need to get my own mare home and make plans to be back tomorrow for Gizmo's first physical therapy session."

Reagan shook her head, reaching behind her to begin braiding her hair into a French braid as she spoke. "It'll be easier if you just stay."

No. Oh, no. I'm not *getting roped into being the one to deal with the injured cowboy because these folks aren't willing to. No, no, no.*

But when Kenzie started into the—first—hundred reasons that came to mind as to why she couldn't… shouldn't…*wouldn't* stay, Emma stepped in. "Truly. There's a one-bedroom cabin vacant. It's nearest the barn and set up as a honeymoon suite. No one's renting it at the moment, so you're free to use the space. And your mare can stay here. I'm sure the barn will be okay for her." At Reagan's wheezed laughter, Emma's gaze snapped between them. "What? What did I say?"

The slightly shorter woman shook her head, swinging the tail of her braid. "The Malone barn is nicer than our house, Emma. Nicer, even, than the house you and Cade are building."

"I don't know about that," Kenzie objected, but once again, her input was overrun with the doctor's practical assessment.

"Look, Ms. Malone—"

She held up a hand. "Kenzie, please."

"Kenzie, then. It's no secret you're the sole heir to the Malone fortune. That's all well and good. That money has undoubtedly afforded you a different life than most have led, particularly here. 'Different' doesn't equal better or worse. Just...well, *different*."

"You're The Malone's daughter?" Emma's clear capitalization of her father's name made Kenzie want to smile, but she refrained. Barely.

Instead, she gave a single nod. "I'm sure you and I have our differences, but I know the value of hard work. My dad has money, yes. That didn't excuse me as a kid from chores any more than it exempted me from having to make my way through the dips, dives, turns and resentments of the male-dominated sport of cutting." She sighed and scrubbed her hands over her face. She was so tired, and at this point just wanted to lie down.

Emma fidgeted, twisting her fingers together until she formed a fist. She paused and seemed to struggle with whether or not to speak her mind. Finally she blurted out, "Are you the one who paid Ty's hospital bills?"

Kenzie didn't answer. She refused to admit she'd helped the man who'd been so wretched to her only moments ago. And she was sure that she, and her motives, had been the topic of many a Covington discussion.

She wound her hair up and then absently tucked it under her ball cap, trying to buy time.

The two women opposite her shared a look, and then Emma stepped forward and hugged her. "For all you've done for us, for all you've done without any reason other than it was the compassionate thing to do, stay. Please. Give us a chance to at least repay your kindness with some of our own."

Guilt wrapped around Kenzie's spine like a ribbon around a maypole.

Multilayered.

Fast.

Bright.

Tight.

Yet what these women shared, this tight family bond, was everything Kenzie had missed in her own family since Michael died, everything she craved. They were offering her a place inside that inner circle. It was too good to turn down. Impossible to refuse. Under the guise of the partnership, she could rediscover what it meant to have whole family unit, not a broken interpretation of what might have been. She could have this place, this space, this sense of belonging, even for the short time left until she handed Gizmo's recovery wholly to Reagan. It was selfish, but she wanted to experience what it felt like to be part of something outside the Malone name, something that had been built on hard work, sweat, tears and genuine talent versus parental expectation, unavoidable responsibility to grieving parents and the burden of obligation based on nothing more than her last name and bank balance.

This could blow up in her face on an epic scale. Ty could accuse her of lying and she'd have nothing with which to refute his allegations other than her own assertion she'd only done what he asked her to. Except the whole partnership thing. That was a big ol' lie. Nothing more, and nothing less. She should say no. She should get out of there before the brothers became involved and a similar obligation led them to open their homes, and their lives, to her.

Gizmo bugled again. The horse's third call echoed

across the open air, forlorn and lonely, a spirit lost between what had been and what now was.
That did it.
"Okay. I'll stay."

7

CADE AND ELI had insisted Ty get some sunshine this morning. Unfortunately, his brother's driving skills in the Mule had gone from pretty damn bad to downright crappy. Eli didn't seem *capable* of missing the rocks and staying out of the ruts as they traveled through the heart of the ranch. They were all fighting to keep from grunting and groaning as they crept along, every movement exaggerated thanks to the pace Eli insisted they keep. Ty would be lucky if he didn't refracture his neck or end up knocking a kidney free and having it land in the heel of his boot.

"Almost there," Cade called to him.

"Forced cheerfulness doesn't suit you," Ty snarked.

"No?" Cade asked with even more false enthusiasm. "Then, you know how I feel after living with your cranky ass the past couple of weeks. Being a total jerk hasn't suited you…or those of us who have to put *up* with you."

"Cut it out, both of you." Eli's reprimand was as effective as dry tinder tossed into a burgeoning wildfire.

"I don't understand why you insisted I come out this

morning." Ty, facing backward and with Cade at his side to help stabilize him, was beginning to sweat with the effort to stay upright. "This is stupid. I should be resting."

"All you do is 'rest,'" Cade answered with air quotes. "You're not putting much effort into your physical therapy, you're not doing the exercises in between sessions, and frankly, you're approaching the point where I'm going to take you for a walk one of us doesn't come back from. Hint? I'll make it home just fine."

Ty's temper shot north. "I broke my damn neck, Cade. What would you have me do? Jump right into the middle of the life I led? Maybe take a local girl out for a night of dancing and a little fun? Or better yet, why don't I get in the saddle and see how *that* goes?"

"Chickenshit," said Eli from the front seat.

Ty's jaw fell open as far as the brace would allow it.

Cade caught the look on his face and laid a hand on his shoulder before speaking to their eldest brother. "That might be taking it a little far."

"No, it isn't. If he's going to treat his body as if it's this fragile palm frond, getting up each day and refusing to push himself to grow and get stronger, then I'll call it like I see it. *Chickenshit*." The Mule coasted to a stop, and the putter of the engine died when Eli pulled the key. "The truth sucks, particularly when you—*either* of you—don't want to hear it."

"Did you hear a word I said?" Ty demanded, forcing himself to slip from the rear-facing seat and, with the aid of his walker, get his feet under him before slowly rounding on Eli. His next words died on his lips, though, when he realized where they'd brought him.

The barn.

And that meant...

Gizmo.

"No." Voice hoarse, eyes gritty, Ty stumbled, but Eli and Cade each grabbed an arm to steady him. "I can't do this. Take me to the house. Now."

"You want to go back?" Eli let him go and slipped into the driver's seat, cranked the engine over and took off at breakneck speed. "Walk," he shouted as he sped away.

"I can't..." He shuffled his feet around until he faced Cade. "I can't do this."

"Huge difference between *can't* and *won't*." His older brother settled the walker in front of Ty and moved out of reach. He pulled out an apple from his pocket and tossed it to Ty. "Time to stop lying to yourself. You may not *want* to do this, but you can. Suck it up and get it over with. Tell Gizmo I said hello. I'll be within shouting range if you run into trouble." Then Cade spun on his heel and walked away, rounding the corner of the barn and disappearing from sight.

Movement in the barn told Ty he wasn't alone. That he couldn't see who it was irritated him. He didn't want this. Didn't want to be stared at as if he was some crash-test dummy. Didn't want to be the topic of conversation in the bunkhouse. Didn't want to be the subject of discussion. Didn't want anyone's pity. He could withstand—had withstood—a lot, but not that. Never that.

Cade's accusation that Ty had thrown in the towel stung. He'd tried so hard to retain some sense of himself, that same sense of humor, the same wit and flirty banter with the opposite sex. It didn't come easy. Not when his life had been reduced to a series of moments, a few breaths that refused to come and a heart that stopped beating. And yeah, it had happened that way. It was the one thing he remembered in an otherwise void of blackness.

He remembered he'd been looking at Kenzie when his heart stopped. She'd watched him fight for every breath he could steal, witnessed his heart stall out, and she'd stood there and cried as darkness took him under. She'd wept for him, but not once had she reached out to him.

Sure as hell kept her hands all over my horse, he silently muttered.

Shifting his walker to face the gaping maw of the barn door, he took his first step toward the dim interior. Paused. A second step. Another pause. His breath came hard and shallow. His head felt extremely heavy on his fragile neck. Walking took more concentration, more sheer effort, than it ever had. Sweat dotted his nape. He wanted to return to the comfort of his wheelchair. His heart, that defiant organ, thundered in his chest, and he waited, sure in the knowledge that it could quit again without warning. Every sensation was horrible in its own right. Combined? He was overwhelmed with the urge to tear the barn down with his bare hands, one board at a time, in lieu of being emotionally deconstructed in the same fashion.

"I can't." Wiping his brow, he glanced around. "I can't do this."

He struggled to keep his balance as he attempted to maneuver the walker toward the house. Lord help him, he was as weak as a newborn foal. His legs refused to stabilize. He had to get out of here, though, and he'd do it on his own. Pride would keep him upright far longer than stamina ever would. And when he ran out of pride? When he couldn't go any farther without help? He'd call his brothers. They could pick him up and drive him to the house. This was, after all, their fault. He never would have come down to the barn of his own free will. This was a mistake—an *epic* mistake.

Then Gizmo called out, the sound heart wrenching.

Chest tightening impossibly, he took finite steps until he was pointed toward the barn again. Moving slowly, fear bore down on him with every step. By the time he crossed the threshold into the barn, his defenses had been thoroughly stripped away, his emotions raw and exposed.

For better or worse, he stood where it had all started—where he'd found a way to live, to be more than the youngest Covington, more than a playboy screwup, more than he'd ever thought he'd be with more than he'd ever thought he might have.

He'd had everything he'd wanted.

Then that bitch Life had found a way to take it all away from him.

KENZIE HAD HEARD the Mule stop, then charge away. Voices had risen in confrontation before Cade had announced he was leaving Ty to fend for himself. She was confident the middle Covington brother hovered nearby, though. He wouldn't leave his younger brother alone to fend for himself. She knew Cade well enough to be sure he was far too loyal for that.

Then she heard the shuffle-step, shuffle-step of Ty's progress. She wanted to go to him, to help, but he had to do this for himself. Her job was to stay out of the way. She'd only observe. If an issue arose that put either Ty or Gizmo at risk, she'd text one of the brothers. Or, heaven forbid, both.

She was glad she'd changed her mind about Ty visiting Gizmo. Both animal and man would heal faster if they had each other to lean on. A bond like these two had was as rare as it was beautiful.

When Ty neared the barn, Kenzie slipped into the deep shadows between the haystack and the tack room to best watch the man move. The determination on his face had been tempered by a bevy of other emotions, all of which were horrible to witness. His stop-and-start gait left his footing unsure, and he leaned on his walker so heavily the wheels sank first into the soft dirt and then, when he reached the barn, the mulched alleyway bisecting the stalls.

He stopped inside the giant doorway and closed his eyes, and she thought he might have given up. Half of her wanted to rail at him for quitting while the other half wanted to go to him, wrap him in her arms and offer to help carry the burden. In an abstract way, they'd been that person to each other over the past few years. This, however, was different. *Decidedly* different. This wasn't about mutual gratification or losing a couple of hours to pleasure to get one's mind off something. Rather, it was about choosing to embrace life instead of letting circumstance steal it from a loosened grasp.

She stayed where she was.

Ty finally opened his eyes and focused his gaze on Gizmo's stall.

Kenzie originally wanted to put the horse in the stall at the far end of the barn, where it would be easier to access the swimming pool she was having installed. It dawned on her she hadn't mentioned the pool to anyone here. Oops. She'd get on that as soon as this moment with Ty and Gizmo passed. Right now, though, the man and his horse were the priority. The family had entrusted her to see to Gizmo's well-being while they were focused on Ty.

They trust me.

The knowledge stole her breath. Fist pressed to her abdomen, she forced herself to breathe slowly. That was when it happened.

A gelding in stall five, halfway down the stable alleyway on the north side, stuck his head over his stall door and spotted Ty. The horse went nuts. Pawing the door, he tossed his head and snorted, rolled his eyes and stretched his lips out, flapping them like sheets in the wind.

Ty saw the animal and froze. "Gilligan," he croaked, the sound raw, the painful reality undiluted. "I'll get to you in a minute, my man."

More horses appeared, peering out of their stalls to see what the hullabaloo was about. Recognizing Ty, they neighed and stomped their feet and gave every sound of joy one might expect from an excited herd of horses.

Kenzie grinned and then glanced at Ty to gauge his reaction. What she found wiped the smile off her face.

Ty stood staring at Gizmo's stall, eyes wide as tea saucers and face as pale as cream. He shook. Not mild shaking, but the kind that was closer to a seizure. He stared straight ahead, his gaze narrowed on the stall door in front of him where no head had emerged.

Then, Gizmo was there. He moved with a faltering gait, his head bobbing in counterbalance to his limp, but it didn't change the fact that his head appeared over the stall door.

Ty physically sagged so much he nearly fell. Shoulders shaking, she watched as the man she'd always known as strong, indefatigable and hardheaded fell apart. He moved forward through sheer force of will.

Tears spilled down the cheek he unknowingly presented in profile to her. His lips moved in what she would guess could only be an invocation, and Gizmo's ears strained toward the man as if he listened to every word.

Ty finally made it to the horse and stopped.

With incredible tenderness, Gizmo lowered his head and pressed his broad face into Ty's chest. The animal loosed an audible sigh that said more than the most powerful words ever would.

Moving with infinite care, Ty rested one hand on the side of Gizmo's cheek and bowed his head. Tears fell faster. "What the hell were you thinking, you giant lunk? Nothing—no prize, no winnings, no title—*nothing* is worth what you put us through. If you thought different, you're an idiot." The last was offered with such soft condemnation that it was impossible to know whether Ty was referring to himself or his horse.

Gizmo didn't move, just leaned into Ty and held perfectly still as Ty ran his hands over every inch of hide he could reach. The horse's long-lashed eyes slowly closed as he relaxed further. His bottom lip wobbled, and Ty smiled, the reaction softening the grief that had etched itself onto his face.

Never had Kenzie witnessed such a private reunion, and she hated herself more than a little for hiding in the shadows and watching such an intimate moment.

The other horses calmed down as Ty continued to talk, their faces turned toward him, ears perked and eyes alert.

It was only their silence that allowed Kenzie to hear his next statement.

"You and I both know that if it wasn't for Kenzie, you wouldn't be here right now. It changes things between us, me and her. Before? It was fun. I think it might have even been headed somewhere. I don't know. But now? I owe her a debt I can never repay. I *owe* her. And we can't ever go back to what we had before. Hell, *none* of us can go back to what we had before. At least you lived—" Ty's voice broke, and he fought to regain control. "She saved you when I couldn't." He let go of the walker and placed his other hand on Gizmo's chin, lifting his head so they were face to face. "Her money did for you what I couldn't—got you the best of everything. I wouldn't ever have been able to afford the Galbreath Center. She's done right by us, so I have to set my pride aside and find a way to thank her." He closed his eyes. "I wish I could reset the clock on this whole thing, but there's no such thing as a do-over. Not for you. Not for me. Not for her. And definitely not for me *and* her."

The floor fell out from under Kenzie. He thought there could have been more between them? That maybe, just maybe, they could have been something?

The words changed everything. And nothing. He resented the financial debt that he'd incurred, and she resented that money could create issues where none need exist. But she understood why he saw it as something he could never set right between them. It was debt she'd accrued based on a single promise—a promise she'd made when she'd thought she might lose Ty. The raw feelings she had for him meant she'd given her word without thinking, and she'd followed through on her promise because that was just who she was.

It would have been so much simpler if she hadn't fallen for him, if she'd remained detached instead of letting the walls between them crumble, the same walls she'd worked so hard to create when they'd first met. But she hadn't. She'd opened the door to him and begun to fall for the one man from whom she'd sworn she'd never expect more than fun and respect.

Hidden in the shadows, she watched Ty with Gizmo. Her heart ached as if it had been pierced. She swallowed the sound of distress that choked her. There had to be a way out, a way that everyone could get what they wanted, what they *needed*, and no one had to get hurt.

There just had to be.

8

TY FOUGHT TO control his emotions. If he got stressed out, Gizmo would pick up on it. But seeing his horse like this, stiff and hurting, divided him. One half wanted to rage against the injustices heaped upon each of them, him and Gizmo. The other half wanted to fold into himself and crumple to the floor until someone came along and picked up the pieces. He'd never been a man to give up when hardship reared its head. But this was more than your average hardship. This particular experience was better described as having been TKO'ed by Hardship and beaten up by his posse members, Pain, Misery and Hopelessness.

A small sound caught his attention, a noise a horse wouldn't make. He grabbed his walker and, legs trembling with exhaustion, faced the direction of the sound. Narrowing his eyes, he stared into the sliver of dense shadow between the end of the tack room and the tall base of the haystack. At first he saw nothing, but, as his eyes adjusted to the limited light, he realized someone was standing there.

"I know you're hiding back there. Come on out." His

tone was intentionally gentle but left no room for either discussion or dissention.

The shadowy figure shifted, stopped and then stepped into the light.

He'd expected a guest, someone who'd been caught in the barn when Eli and Cade had kicked him out of the Mule. What he got was his worst nightmare and deepest desire all rolled into one.

Mackenzie Malone.

"What the hell are you doing here?" he demanded, the soothing cadence of his earlier words lost to immediate temper.

"I was out here checking on Gizmo when you showed up. I tried to leave, but I couldn't get the door at the end of the alleyway to open. The latch stuck. It left me either confronting you or trying to wait you out. I chose the latter." She shoved her hair off her face on a huff. "How did you figure out I was here anyway?"

"You need to learn to keep quiet if you don't want to be discovered skulking about."

"I wasn't skulking."

"Fine. Let's call it what it is—sticking your nose where it doesn't belong." He snatched his walker up and did his best to make tracks for the barn door, hollering for Cade and Eli as he went. When his brothers failed to appear, Ty quietly cursed them. *Freaking brothers. They know she's out here.*

Working to keep his breathing level, he forced one foot in front of the other in as fast a retreat as he could muster. Even his best efforts couldn't stop his temper from spilling out of his mouth. "'Fess up. How are they getting you to do their dirty work, watching over me? You obviously don't need the money, and we clearly don't have it to spare, so that's not it. What did they promise you?"

"Can't I simply do something because it's right?"

He hated the way her voice seemed smaller, swallowed by the empty space above them. "You and I don't have that kind of relationship."

"We've never had anything that remotely *resembles* a relationship, Ty." Kenzie moved toward him, her hips swinging as they always did when she was walking off a good mad...or building up to one. "You always made it perfectly clear we were friends with benefits. Never anything more. I accepted that without comment and without fussing. So don't you go throwing attitude at me, acting as if I've somehow wronged you by doing *exactly* what you asked me to do. I used my own discretion in saving Gizmo's life. And my judgment calls kept him from being put down and guaranteed he'd recover. I gave him a chance at life. The least you could do is offer up, oh, I don't know, a thank-you. But you won't, will you? Or is it that you can't, Ty? Which one is true?" She closed in on him. "Both, I'd wager. Why? Because it's so clear that you're pissed at the world, angry about the hand that's been dealt you. It's inhibited your ability to do anything more than feel sorry for yourself."

She'd closed the distance between them and was leaning into his face as she threw out that last word. Fury raced through his veins, chased by guilt at the way he'd lashed out at her and the knowledge she was right. The hell he'd admit it, though.

She smirked, her eyes never leaving his as she goaded him further. "Surely the ever-argumentative Tyson Covington has *something* to say."

Ty didn't think, didn't consider the consequences.

He just gripped the back of her neck and pulled her into him. Their mouths came together without apology, without compromise, without softness. This, this primal thing that always hung between them, proved bigger than words and defied any tenderness his wounded heart might crave. He needed passion, needed to know he had survived, needed to feel something—*anything*—other than the ever-present pain.

He owned the kiss, sure of himself in this one thing. She responded to his wordless directions, sighed into his mouth and gave herself over to the driving force of his desire. Still, she didn't let him dominate her but made him work for it, made him chase the particular tilt of her chin, the touch and retreat of her tongue, the nibble of her teeth on his lips.

Her chest brushed against his.

Ty didn't think too much about keeping his balance. He simply held on and let her come to him, encouraging her to take what she wanted and give him what he needed in exchange. Somehow, though, his need seemed larger, more visceral, than simple desire. Of course, given the way his body responded, his cock hardening in a painful rush and his heart thundering so loudly in his ears that he struggled to hear anything else, he wasn't going to dismiss the power of desire.

Kenzie moved again in an effort to better accommodate the limited motion his neck brace allowed. Despite the clothing between them, he could feel her nipples harden against his chest. Then she sighed his name. It was her response that grounded Ty in the moment, gave him his footing and offered him the kind of reassurance he'd been searching for since he'd woken from the coma. Here, with her, he found safety, a surety of self, a sense of purpose. He could give her what she desired. And what she desired was him.

Yet the experience of holding her in his arms wasn't all that simple. True, he wanted nothing more than to lose himself in her, to take the warmth she offered and let her spend the morning convincing him that he was, indeed, alive. He also wanted to rail against her for things that weren't her fault—the fact that she had two good legs, strong arms, a steady gait and, above all, the freedom to do as she pleased.

Conflicted, he pulled away, ending the kiss.

Her eyelids fluttered open and she blinked, her pupils wide enough they almost consumed the cornflower blue of her irises. "It's hard to fight with you when you kiss me senseless."

One corner of his mouth kicked up despite the fact that he tried his best to not smile. "That's the point."

"Yeah, well, it's cheating." She smiled, contentment radiating from her in waves.

The realization she was happy nearly knocked the wind out of him. *How can she stand here and be happy?*

Fighting to regain control of the moment, he glanced over her shoulder at Gizmo, who stood with his head up, ears forward and eyes bright. Ty shook his head and then forced himself to meet Kenzie's gaze. "It's not cheating. I've just never been one to depend on words when actions get the job done without complicating things."

And with her, it always worked that way. Words hadn't ever been necessary between them. In fact, words tended only to muddle things. Without words, what existed between them was, and had always been, a simple case of mutual want that ruled the moment and drove their actions.

She closed her eyes and breathed deeply. "No sense complicating anything."

"You know I don't do complicated, darlin'."

She stiffened, her fingers digging into his arms. The smile that had pulled at the corners of her mouth disappeared, her expressive face closing down.

Ty wanted to retrieve the words, take them back. He wanted to figure out how to say what had to be said—that he wasn't available for more than the moment, never again, not even for her—without stealing that blissful look from her face. But his old man had taught him early on that words, once offered up, could never be taken back.

KENZIE TRIED NOT to react. Honest.

She failed.

And she didn't fail on a minor level. This failure proved epic. And the longer Ty's words looped through her mind, the more her reaction gained first traction, then speed and finally purpose.

She'd heard him admit to Gizmo that there might have been something between them. Then to her face he'd crushed that hope.

She knew her eyes had shuttered, knew her face wore a neutral expression. It was a tactic her father had mastered for negotiating, as well as in difficult social situations. Her dad used the opportunity to craft a strategic response. Kenzie had spent a lifetime emulating the very same affect but had never expected it to come in so handy. She was surprised to realize that, for her, strategy wasn't a factor. She needed the time to figure out how she was going to hide the body, because killing Tyson Covington had taken on spectacular appeal.

Stepping away from the man lest she strangle him, she gave a curt nod. "Sure thing, *darlin'*. Why complicate somethin' so simple as a friends-with-bennies arrangement, right?" Her tone was so caustic it should have burned the barn down around them.

"Kenzie, I—"

"No need to finish that sentence," she volunteered. "Mixing up something as straightforward as this is foolish. I get it. You made sure of that."

He tried to smile at her, but whatever he saw in her face made that smile falter. "I should go."

"Typical." The single word cracked across the air like a rifle's report. "Things get uncomfortable and you find the nearest exit." She crossed her arms under her breasts. "Go on, then. Call one of your brothers. They'll be the fastest way out of here for you. Eli!" she shouted. "Cade! Bring the Mule, would you? This cowboy wants to ride into the sunset." She rounded on Ty, chest heaving. "I'm sure they'll be here in no time, rushing in to save their little brother from assuming responsibility. And since you won't—assume responsibility, that is—I will. I'll manage Gizmo and his recovery."

Ty's eyes blazed with undisguised anger. "Excuse me?"

"I said—"

"I heard what you said," he snapped. "It isn't a matter of me *choosing* not to manage Gizmo's recovery, and you know it."

"No, Ty. What I 'know' is that you're supposed to be recovering from an injury. Instead, you're acting as if you're sitting around waiting to die. What I 'know' is that if you don't get your ass down here and invest in your animals, someone's going to do it for you. I can't speak to your other horses, but as far as Gizmo is concerned, that someone will be me." Realization almost blinded her. This was her chance to solidify the lies and make them truths. "If I have to take over, I'll do it based on the extreme investments—both financial and personal—that *you* requested I make to ensure Gizmo's well-being. That was the foundation of this partnership after all."

"Like hell!" His shout reverberated through the barn. "I want the partnership dissolved."

"Yeah? How, *exactly*, do you suggest we accomplish that? Are you going to repay me for doing exactly what you asked me to do, Ty? For being financially responsible for all of the medical bills and seeing the horse through recovery? Or maybe you think if you walk away, it will just *go* away. Is that it? Do you honestly believe I should have done it—*any* of it—without expecting fair recompense? After all, you said it yourself just moments ago. We don't have the kind of relationship that would warrant me doing something out of the sheer goodness of my heart."

"What heart?" he spat.

"Obviously the one Daddy bought me as my sweet-sixteen present. It was black, to match my truck." Her stomach pitched and rolled like a dinghy on a violent sea. She'd never lorded money over anyone. Ever. But she couldn't turn back now without losing the ground she'd gained. This had become as much an issue of defending her pride as covering her lies.

When she'd been in college and struggled with a senior-level business class, her dad had sat her down and explained that negotiations were much like poker. There was a little shuffling, a lot of bluffing and even more posturing. If you sat at a table where you were unsure about the other players, the most important thing to do was salvage the hand you were dealt. That meant playing it smart, hard and close to the chest. It made your opponent wonder what you held, and it bought you time to convince him that, even with a total crap hand, you were bound to win. The point, he'd said, was to hold until you were forced to fold.

Kenzie stared up at Ty and narrowed her eyes as he did the same.

She. Wasn't. Folding. Not on this. Not ever.

She took a large step backward and crossed her arms. "You don't get to choose in this, Ty. Not when you left me with both personal and financial responsibility for Gizmo's care. You left me alone!" she shouted. "You left me to decide whether to euthanize that magnificent animal and put him out of his misery, or walk the road to recovery with him *because you wouldn't*." She looked at Gizmo's stunning gray-and-black coloring, those ice-blue eyes watching her with a shrewd awareness that always unnerved her a bit. "You want to settle this?" she asked so quietly Ty instinctively leaned toward her.

"You know I do," he said through gritted teeth.

She faced Ty then and let the hammer fall. "I'll accept short-term breeding rights to Gizmo as full satisfaction of all monies owed."

"Like. Hell," he said again. He pulled his cowboy hat off and tunneled his fingers through his hair. "He's off-limits, Malone."

"I've invested more than twenty thousand dollars in your medical bills. I've also sunk more than eighty thousand dollars in your horse's bills. Where he's concerned, I'll see another twenty-three thousand dollars in the pool installation and ten thousand dollars in miscellaneous physical therapy costs."

All color drained from Ty's face. "I didn't realize..." His Adam's apple bobbed. "I'll repay you. With interest. We'll set something up. Just leave Gizmo alone." He swallowed hard enough for her to hear it, and then he dropped his own hammer. "Please."

She ground her teeth together, ashamed of herself and furious with him for pushing her into this. *Save Gizmo*, he'd pleaded with her after she'd thought she'd lost him, the man she'd begun to care for despite her best efforts to remain detached. She'd gone further than he'd likely ever expected her to go, and despite it all, he wouldn't give her an inch in return. He still considered her genetics so inferior to his that he refused to allow Gizmo to be part of her breeding program.

She sucked in a sharp breath, the dry, icy air burning her lungs even as it froze them. No. He couldn't use her like this. She wouldn't be some bottomless ATM that spewed cash on demand and never had a single deposit in return. If she didn't set this boundary, she'd never be more than this to him. She opened her mouth to say just that, but Eli pulled up in the Mule.

Ty began his shuffling turn toward the barn door and his best—only—means of escape.

"Everything okay?" Eli called, all good cheer and hopefulness.

"As okay as it can be when you have a rabid fox in the henhouse and find your shotgun's out of ammo," Ty answered.

Eli shot Kenzie a glance. When she didn't respond, his eyes narrowed. "What happened?"

"Nothing." She managed to issue the single word

without her voice wavering. Chest tight, she forced herself to continue. "Your brother wasn't aware I'd expect repayment for both his and his horse's medical bills."

Eli's eyes tightened at the corners before he offered a shallow nod. "We'll manage as a family."

"No, we won't." Ty stumbled, but he righted himself before either she or Eli could grab him. "I'll work it out. I have a few horses I can sell."

Kenzie's heart constricted as Eli erupted in a veritable tirade. She knew it would kill Ty to sell part of his breeding stock. Yes, he'd retain the heart—Gizmo—but the body would be weakened. Could she be responsible for that?

That wasn't the part that ate at her, though. She'd never acted the part of a spoiled diva, not like this, and she was beyond mortified.

Eli helped Ty into the backseat of the Mule and Cade appeared as if summoned, sat next to his younger brother and shot Kenzie a glare that, in theory, should have turned her to stone. He'd obviously heard enough of the exchange with Ty to draw his own conclusions.

Freaking fabulous.

The brothers pulled away, Ty's entire focus on Gizmo. The man she'd given up her dream of nationals for never once looked at her as the Mule rounded the bend and headed for the main house.

Kenzie retrieved her cell and called home.

9

JACK MALONE ANSWERED on the third ring. "Hey, baby. What's new? Everything going okay at the Covington place?"

"I need to talk to you about that, Dad," she replied softly as she moved toward Gizmo's stall. The stud horse watched her, anxious for the treats she carried. He nosed her pockets, lipping loose fabric eagerly and huffing at her. Determined not to add his disappointment in her to everyone else's running tally, she pulled out a couple worse-for-wear sugar cubes and, pinning the cell phone between her ear and shoulder, offered the sweets to the horse one at a time.

"You're there, aren't you?" The elder Malone's voice had a faint echo thanks to crappy cell service. That connection didn't disguise his concern, though.

She sighed. "Does it make a difference?"

"Of course it matters, honey. I want to know where you are. That way, if you need me, I can ride in on my white horse. A man can't just charge blindly, you understand." When she didn't respond to his teasing, he sobered. "You came by, loaded Indie up and then left without speaking to me. I haven't seen you in two months." He paused, his breath rasping across the microphone. When he finally broke the silence, his tone came across far softer than before. "Are you okay? Has something happened? You can talk to me, Mackenzie. Always. About anything."

Her shoulders hunched. The implied censure, delivered with parental effectiveness despite the fact that she was twenty-four years old, worked. "You weren't home when I picked Indie up. That's all it was."

"You could have waited," he countered. "Any one of the hands would have told you I'd be home before sundown."

"Sorry." She hated having apologies wrung out of her, particularly because she never could do the same in reverse. Moving away from the apology altogether seemed prudent. "I had to be at the Covington place to arrive with Ty's stud." She reached out and tickled the lips of the horse under discussion.

"I understand." Her father took a deep breath. "How is Gizmo?"

"Fair." She heard a tractor fire up on his end. Kenzie imagined the way the belch of diesel exhaust would sully the cool Colorado air of the Malone place, could see the way the fields sloped away from the mountains, could almost feel the rumble of the big engine through her torso. "You feeding this early in the season? I thought the grass looked pretty good."

"I want to increase the protein intake of the yearlings in pasture one, so I'm pulling a few round bales to run down to them. Have some good blood on the ground, thanks to you."

His pride in her, so evident in both word and tone,

made her squirm. That she'd lied to him and, worse, let that lie run on, gain a life of its own and encourage him to develop expectations of her she'd never be able to live up to? She had to shut it down. "Dad, I..." She stalled out.

"What's wrong, honey? Talk to me."

He loves me more than I deserve. This was the man she'd loved all her life. This was the man she related to with such ease. This was the man she'd always sought advice from over the years, particularly after losing Michael. And in return, he'd begun to talk to her about the ranch the way he once had talked to Michael. He'd learned to trust her instincts and valued her input because she never pulled her punches, never simply said what he wanted to hear because he was Jack Malone. Not until now anyway. That particular realization doubled the weight of her guilt. She had to admit she'd lied. He wouldn't stop loving her, wouldn't turn her away, wouldn't shut her out. Not as Ty had.

But when she opened her mouth, it wasn't the truth that came out. Instead, she found herself recounting everything that had just happened, from the family's insistence that she stay on the ranch to listening to Ty's private monologue with his horse to the harsh words more recently exchanged. The only thing she omitted was the kiss. When the last of her troubles passed her lips, the only response she got was one of absolute silence. Nausea rushed up her throat so rapidly she fought not to choke on it. "Dad?"

"He's reneging on the partnership?" The hostility in the question was hardly banked.

"What? No! Not exactly," she said. "He doesn't remember—" *Because there's nothing to remember*, her subconscious interjected. *Go on. Tell him. Tell him that you not only lied, you kept the dishonesty running for months between the two of you. You've had ample opportunities to come clean. Tell him you didn't because... Why? Why haven't you?* She couldn't explain it to him because she didn't have a remotely plausible answer for herself.

"What is it, then?" Jack Malone pressed. "Because I know what you've spent."

"Are you checking up on me?" The idea appalled her.

"Not checking up so much as ensuring you had everything you needed while you were in Ohio."

"Sell it to someone else, Dad. You know my initial trust fund deposit was enough to live off for the rest of my life. You don't have to watch over me."

Jack Malone hardly paused, let alone yielded his position. "I've seen the checks you've written, Mackenzie. That man has sure as hell taken your money without batting an eye. I will *not* have him take advantage of your kindheartedness."

She stepped away from Gizmo, her hands trembling so hard she feared she'd drop the phone. Pinning it between her ear and shoulder, she shoved her hands into her pockets and fought for calm. If her dad believed Ty had taken advantage of her, there would be hell to pay. She had to stop the momentum she could feel him gaining as his parental instincts kicked in. "Dad, it's not what you think."

"Then, what is it, Mackenzie? Spell it out for me, because from where I sit? It looks very much as if he's abused your generosity. You can't let people spin some bullshit story just to get what they want from you, particularly when you're dealing with this kind of money and no return."

"I thought you were fine with it." The words were strained, the air in her lungs slowly pushing out as an invisible band of panic six inches wide torqued down on her ribs, increasing in pressure until black dots danced through her vision.

She had to slow down, regain control of the moment, her emotions, her situation. Now. Before it got worse. Panic attacks had been daily events after her brother died until intensive counseling and medication had taught her how to control them. Then they'd stopped. She hadn't had an attack in years. This one had struck so fast she hadn't been able to talk herself down.

"Dad," she whispered, panic winding its way through that single word.

"Mackenzie?" Jack's tone changed in an instant. "Talk to me, baby girl. I can hear you breathing hard. What happened? What upset you? Was it me? I'm so sorry, Kenzie. Just slow down, we don't have to deal with this right now." The sound of ice clinking against glass preceded the *glug* of liquid splashing into the same. He swallowed hard, then his voice was back, smoother, calmer. "Slow down, Mackenzie. Just slow down." He took another sip, smaller this time. "This isn't easy for either of us."

"What?" she wheezed. *Awfully early for him to hit the bottle.* "What do you mean?"

"The panic. It's chock-full of the worst moments of our lives. You relive it, I relive it." He sighed, the sound weighted. "You were too young to lose your brother, let alone see it happen." The sound of another sip. "It tore us all up."

"I know." Forcing herself to draw slow, deep breaths, Kenzie refocused on Gizmo. "It won't hurt me to practice a random act of kindness, Dad."

"Financially? No, it won't, though I'm a bit irritated you're wasting Malone money on a man trying to back out on his promise. A person's only as good as his word, and you know I'm right. But that isn't the only position to consider. There are the emotional costs you're incurring." He waited. When she didn't respond, he continued, his voice rougher, harder, less compassionate that she'd ever heard it. "I won't have your heart broken by some two-bit country kid who thinks he can bat his eyes at you, promise you a partnership and get you to fork over the cash to see him through a hard spot."

"You did *not* just imply I'm too…too…*female* to be able to hold my own with a 'two-bit country kid,'" she said on a raw whisper.

"If Michael were here, I'd have him over there right now to see that the Covington kid kept his word. Your brother would have done it, too."

"Dad—" she started, paused, then started again. "Dad, I'd like to think Michael would have trusted me to handle this on my own. And I'd like to think you would do the same." The irony wasn't lost on her. She was asking for his trust when she was giving nothing trustworthy in return. She'd never hated herself quite so much as she did right then.

"Your mother and I are concerned about you, honey. You're living a very lonely life right now, chasing that national title like it's the be-all and end-all. Now you've created this partnership that could make your line into something, and you're less interested in it than you are in the man who's trying to screw you out of your fair share."

"If you only knew," she muttered.

After an interminable silence, a silence in which Kenzie felt the pressures of his expectations building in her chest, he spoke. "Losing Michael wrecked this family." The words were offered like a reverent eulogy, not a decade-old memory, and it stung.

"I'm well aware of that. I lived through it," she said in a tight voice. *It* and *the aftermath*.

"Don't get smart with me." Jack Malone paused, seemingly searching for the right words. "Michael's loss left a hole in our lives, a hole we'll never fill again. Not because we don't want to, mind you, but because we can't. If that makes us a little overprotective of you as our only child, you'll just have to come to terms with it. You're all we've got left."

Her father continued, but Kenzie hardly heard the last of her dad's words before disconnecting the call. The conversation had stopped for her when he'd said she couldn't fill the hole that had been left by Michael. She'd spent a decade trying so hard to be both son and daughter to her parents, to be a strong enough personality to fill that emotional vacancy her brother had left. She'd failed on an epic level. Now, knowing her efforts to be both daughter and lost son to her parents had failed? Hearing him say it out loud? Fully aware she'd only be disappointing him further when she admitted her deception? Well, she hadn't thought she'd be able to hate herself any more. How miserably wrong she'd been.

TY COULDN'T GET the taste of Kenzie off his lips. He brushed his teeth. He drank a Coke. He considered smoking a cigar. That only reminded him of their last game of strip poker, the one where he'd been down to one sock and his boxers. She'd been tossing out cards while wearing nothing but a green dealer's visor, her bra and a black thong. A cigar had dangled from the corner of her mouth. Light had danced through her hair, and every time she'd moved, her smooth skin had pulled taut over that flat belly. Sure, it had been sexy. But it was nothing compared to the way her lips had wrapped around the butt of the cigar and kicked up at one corner when he'd lost the next hand in spectacular fashion. Oh, and his boxers. He'd lost those, too. She had immediately declared herself the winner and claimed him as her prize.

They hadn't slept that night.

"Damn it!" He slammed his closet door shut and collapsed into his wheelchair so hard he had to put a foot out to keep from tipping over. Settling, he wheeled over to the window in his temporary bedroom and looked up. "I'm seriously getting sick of this."

He shoved the window open a crack. A rush of crisp, snow-laden air washed over him and made the hair on his arms stand up at the chill. He needed the opportunity to cool off. Kenzie had left his blood so close to the boiling point that he couldn't think. Even now, all he wanted was to get his hands on her again and to have her put her hands on him. He just had to get her out of his system, then he'd see her off the ranch and out of his life. For good.

He heard the sound of a single horse's hooves pounding the earth. He stretched to peer out the window.

Who is it? Windows are too tall. So either stand and see or sit and wonder, Covington.

Curiosity won the internal debate as the sound grew

nearer, the tempo increasing as the horse picked up speed in order to charge up the hill.

The rider's sticking to the road. Is something wrong? Has something happened? Could be one of the ranch hands on his way to fetch either Eli or Cade.

He wanted the cowboy to be coming after *him*, coming to ask *him* for advice, ask *him* for help. It used to be that way. Not anymore. No one asked him for anything anymore.

Everyone from Kenzie to Eli had told him that was his own fault. Their theory? If he'd make an effort to re-engage not only with others but with life in general, folks wouldn't feel so awkward about approaching him. They'd start to seek him out again. He just had to make sure they knew they were welcome. But that was the problem. He wasn't at all sure they *were* welcome. He didn't want to be gawked at, didn't want to be—

Those pounding hooves drew closer still.

Screw it. He wasn't standing up. He was too tired and he hurt, no matter how little Kenzie thought of his excuse. *Excuse...*

"Damn if she's going to get me questioning myself," he groused. "Incoming!" he called into the house. Then he waited.

No answer.

"Hey!" he hollered. "I said there's a rider incoming!"

More silence.

Temper brewing, Ty grabbed the windowsill and pulled, hoisting himself up to peer out the wide but narrow bank of windows that ran nearly the full length of the wall. The breeze carried the smells of dust and crushed grass and animal through the window. Fresh and pungent, they tickled his nose and wordlessly encouraged him to draw in a deep breath. Then he choked when he recognized the rider, hunched over the animal's neck, riding hell-bent for leather up the main road as she headed deeper into the ranch.

Kenzie.

She didn't take in nearby scenery but kept her gaze focused far ahead. She didn't stop when a cowboy called out to her. Strangest of all, she didn't acknowledge a group of young kids, their trustworthy little ponies plodding along in single file as they carried their charges home from a trail ride.

Kenzie morphed into the Pied Piper around children. Little cowboys and cowgirls alike flocked to her at exhibitions and rodeos, clamoring to gain, and keep, her attention. She loved the littlest ones most, though she never admitted it.

So to see her fly by kids, her mare's jets set on wide open, without offering a greeting? No. That rang all kinds of bells, each of them chiming "wrong" in a different tone.

Ty watched her go, her shape growing ever smaller as the wind carried her dust trail off at a brisk clip. Never easing up, she and her mare crested the hill behind the house and disappeared. He sank into his chair, lost in thought. What kind of skeleton did a woman have in her closet that held that much sway over her? To chase her out into the elements in such a blind panic?

Wasn't me, that's for sure. She had no problem holding her own with me out there. Frustrating woman, calling it as she sees it. To hell with everybody else's opinion. And changing her mind is as ridiculous as trying to take that goat from the T. rex in Jurassic Park. *You know you'll never walk away with more than the blood-*

ied scraps of your pride, and that's after *you scrape the pieces together.*

"She's not right about me," he said to the empty room. Sitting deeper in his chair, he rubbed his aching belly. He should fix a sandwich or something to ease the mild nausea that had settled deep in his gut as he watched her thunder past the house. "She's not right," he repeated with more force.

That was when he stopped, stunned at the realization of what he'd just done.

He'd controlled his descent from the window to the wheelchair. And he'd done it without help or a single conscious thought. For the first time since the accident, he'd moved without stiff reserve and fearful awareness of every ache, pain... Hell, every threatening twinge.

With his mind tangled up with what had just happened, Ty absently moved toward the doorway, intent on wheeling himself to the kitchen...and came face-to-face with Reagan. Heat flamed across his cheeks at her stunned appearance. His chin came up a notch. "What?"

His sister-in-law looked at him, then his chair and then him again. She raised a hand and held it halfway to her mouth before letting it fall. Her eyes were wide. "You stood. On your own. With so little effort. How? When? And why didn't you tell anyone you could do this, Ty?" Skepticism vied with amazement in that green-eyed gaze. It unnerved him. Yet no amount of curiosity could dim the inherent compassion shining from her, a beacon of hope in the muted afternoon light.

Tugging at his collar, he slumped a little. He couldn't explain it, seeing as he couldn't make sense of it himself. All he knew was that he'd stood when he'd needed to and it hadn't hurt the way he'd both anticipated and grown accustomed to. He had expected excruciating pain. The kind that stole a man's breath and rendered him unable to speak, to breathe, to utter a cry for help. But it hadn't truly hurt.

"Ty?" she pressed.

"I don't know, okay? I wanted to stand up, so I did." He could add that he'd been desperate to identify the rider, that he'd needed to know why the cowboy had been riding so hard while Ty sat in his chair, worthless. Standing had been spontaneous, the results both exhilarating and terrifying. "You've seen me walk. What's the big deal?"

"The 'big deal' is that none of us thought it was so easy for you. We all believed you had excruciating pain and that's why you were clinging to the chair so hard." She sighed and, pulling her ponytail free, rewrapped the hair higher on her head. "What's going on, Tyson?"

He gripped the chair's armrests so hard the skin over his knuckles appeared bleached. "It's not that simple."

His barked response didn't faze Reagan. "It should be. If you're capable of doing more, then do more. Period. You need to get back to physical therapy. You need to stop sitting around doing nothing, letting your muscles atrophy. What you've been doing? It's giving up, Ty."

He jerked back and hissed at the sharp movement.

The reaction was instinctive but not necessary, because it didn't hurt. It wasn't comfortable, sure. But there was a world of difference between discomfort and *hurt*.

"Well, I'll be damned." Ignoring her, he wiggled out of his brace. Then, with a tentative touch, he traced the line of his surgical scar down his cervical spine. No acute pain.

"Ty?" Reagan pressed.

He glanced at her, jaw clenched. "I don't want to stand up." She started to say something, likely to protest, but he gripped the wheels of his chair and shoved them forward. "Don't confuse my not wanting to do something with me giving up. Two totally different things. Make sure you get that part straight when you tell Eli."

With that parting shot, nasty as it was, he rolled through the door and down the hall, forcing himself to consider sandwich condiments in lieu of soul-rattling comments. He'd take mustard over manhandling any day. And wasn't this embarrassing, his life reduced to sandwich analogies and defending himself to the ghosts of conversations present and past.

Still doesn't mean either of 'em is right.

He rolled on.

10

KENZIE HAD NO idea how far she'd gone before Indie slowed of her own accord. Lathered sweat lay in foamy patches along the mare's neck. Chest heaving, the animal slowed to a brisk walk, her head bobbing with pleasure at the hard run.

Knotting the reins, Kenzie rested them and then laid them over the horse's withers before lying down, her spine parallel to the horse's. A little hissing noise—air between her teeth—instructed the mare to drop to a far more casual pace. The *clop-clop-clop* of the horse's hooves on dry, winter-hardened ground sounded out a rhythm roughly one-fourth as fast as Kenzie's heart rate.

Somewhere nearby, cows called their calves to their sides, disturbed by the sudden appearance of horse and rider.

Let them chatter. It's what parents do.

And just like that, everything her dad had said to her raked across Kenzie's raw nerves again. Her shoulders twitched.

Indie shied away from the movement, the skin along Kenzie's back shifting hard in protest.

"Easy," Kenzie said, calm and firm, as she resituated herself in order to keep from ending up in the dirt. The walk to the barn would be a long one.

The horse snorted and tossed her head.

"You and everyone else, always with your opinions." She rubbed her wind-burned cheeks and stared up the darkening sky. The bone-chillingly cold air was infused with the crisp scent of snow. The sky would let loose before sundown. The cloud cover hung around like the wind's hired muscle, conveying to everyone that things were going to get ugly. It was only a matter of time.

As if in agreement, Indie kept her stalwart pace but made a wide circle that pointed them toward the barn.

Kenzie wasn't ready to return, but she didn't fight the horse's instinct when it came to the weather. Or anything else, really. She just hated the idea of facing the Covingtons right now, having to load Indie and all their gear and start the arduous journey home. And through miserable weather, no less. Just…ugh. But staying here wouldn't be an option. Not after today's confrontation with Ty.

She hadn't meant for it to get out of hand, but the opportunity to save face, to make the alleged partnership legitimate instead of a lie, had been too tempting. That whole "resistance is futile" thing proved true. Hurting Ty hadn't been anywhere on her impromptu agenda, but despite her good intentions, it had happened. The trust between them now fractured, she had no idea how to move forward. There would be no sidestepping the truth—that she'd tried to force his hand where it came to securing Gizmo's stud rights for the Malones' Quarter horse breeding program.

But he'd hurt her, too, when he'd said he'd sell off some of his stock. He would do it, violate that almost sacrosanct rule of keeping your best blood at all costs, simply to ensure he would be done with her. And that was what this was mostly about. The undisguised anger in his gaze had said he wanted her and her horse gone yesterday. After all, Indie was a mare. If he wasn't diligent in protecting Gizmo's honor, Indie may seduce him, get pregnant and demand child support.

"Such an idiot." Kenzie huffed out a breath, watching it condense on the air into a thick, white cloud. "We're not seducing his horse."

Really, though, did he hate her so much, think so little of her and her breeding program, that he'd go so far as to cull his own herd to satisfy the debt between them? She thought she'd been clear that simply allowing her to introduce Gizmo's genetics into her line would render the debt paid in full.

Ty's selling off a handful of horses he'd worked so hard to develop simply wouldn't do. There had to be another solution, one where they could both get what they wanted.

Drumming her fingers against one thigh, she didn't realize the wind had shifted directions and now blew straight out of the north. Since she was headed south, that put the thirty-mile-per-hour "breeze" at her back… and carried away any sound coming at her with an into-the-wind approach. Including that of the oncoming horse and rider. Kenzie had no forewarning other than Indie's sudden halt.

The mare raised her head, ears trained toward the stranger and unknown horse.

Scrambling to sit up with as much grace as she could muster, Kenzie reached out to grab the reins. She curled her fingers around the thin leather strips but couldn't stop herself from sucking in a sharp breath.

Her lungs promptly froze.

She'd been preoccupied, but not so much she hadn't realized the cold had been leaching into her and stealing what mediocre warmth she had left as the wind hammered her. The problem? She hadn't realized just *how* cold she'd become. And cold killed.

Eli reined in beside her, his mount a good deal taller than Indie. The man's furious stare pierced Kenzie with unabashed animosity. "What the blue blazes were you thinking, charging off into an unknown ranch like that with weather threatening to thrash us within the hour?"

That he thought to ride out here to make sure she was okay? She could almost call the action chivalrous. Almost. That he was railing at her the way a concerned parent would a small child? She couldn't, in good conscience, call that anything but overbearing. How typical.

Ignoring Eli, she nudged Indie into a swift walk.

Eli wordlessly wheeled his mount in beside her and kept the same pace.

"If there's something in particular you want, spill it," she called out over the now-howling wind. "Silent lawyers make me nervous."

"They should." He glanced at her before settling his Stetson lower over his brow to block the wind. "What's going on between you and Ty?"

There it was—the question she didn't want to answer, mostly because she didn't know how. She could offer a thousand speculative responses, but there was only one answer she had that would be accurate, though not terribly revealing. "Nothing." *Not at the moment anyway.*

"You claimed him as yours in the arena," Eli countered. "That doesn't say 'nothing' to me."

Damn. He had to have an elephant's memory, didn't he? She was so tired of dancing around the truth, trying to make sure she kept her stories straight, that she gave up and blurted out the truth. "We were friends and, until the accident, occasional lovers. Nothing more, nothing less."

Eli nodded, not sparing her a glance but rather seeming to file her answer away for future retrieval. They rode in silence. The first snowflakes began to fall as he spoke again. "Where does the partnership regarding Gizmo come into play, then?"

She swallowed so hard she nearly choked. There was no answer she could offer that wouldn't expose her as a liar, nothing she could say that would absolve her of the fact that she'd manipulated everyone in order to do what Ty had asked of her, even if he didn't remember asking. Painted into an uncomfortable corner, Kenzie chose to say nothing. It was her best—*only*—defense.

Eli kept shooting short glares her way, waiting on her answer. He finally snapped. "Look. I know you and Ty are at odds. I get that. I'm not asking you to spell out specifics, but I have to understand what you mean—or meant—to him."

She twisted to face the man at her side. "What are you talking about?"

"You raced by the house earlier."

"So?"

"That action got him out of his chair." Eli reined his horse in front of Indie and stopped Kenzie and her mare. "On his own. He got up and stepped to the window on his own."

Torn between cheering at Ty's initiative and wanting to rage at the fact that he wouldn't do more for himself, she again defaulted to remaining silent. It was safer that way.

Eli glared at her.

She returned his stare without apology.

His curse was hot enough it should have melted the snow gathering on his hat brim.

Kenzie only arched a brow.

"You're baiting me, so I won't apologize for my language." He dragged a hand down his face, over his mouth, and then wrapped it around the back of his neck. Tension sang off his body. Sensing his anxiety, his horse fidgeted. Eli ordered the animal to settle. The command proved as effective as telling an alligator to go vegan. The big gelding wanted none of it.

"If you don't calm down, you're going to end up in the dirt," Kenzie offered with casual indifference.

"Probably." Eli relaxed his grip on the reins, settling his butt into the cantle before visibly forcing his shoulders to relax. "I'm just going to lay it out there, then. Cade and I are both sure you're lying about this whole partnership thing."

She sucked in a breath and the pervasive cold burned her lungs. Before she regained the ability to speak, and therefore respond, Eli pressed on.

"Problem is, we can't prove it. Ty doesn't remember anything from the point he entered the ring to the actual moment he woke in the hospital. You could make any number of absurd claims and there'd be nothing we could do to refute it." He shot her a shrewd glance. "That doesn't mean the absurdity of the claim will hold in court, mind you."

"Get to it already."

One corner of his mouth twitched upward before he forced it into neutral submission. "Cade and I talked about it, and I drew the short straw of discussing our plan with you."

"So far, you haven't discussed a dang thing," she ground out, her nerves so frayed she wondered they weren't sparking.

"We want you to stay and get Ty on his feet—"

"No." Her response was immediate.

"Not negotiable. In return, we won't challenge your claim to Gizmo's stud services. You'll get him, on your property, for ninety days." He rubbed his red nose. "We'll also repay you everything you've spent on my brother and his horse. It'll take us a while to figure out where the money's going to come from, but we'll make it work. With interest as well, though it'll have to be reasonable or the dude ranch will suffer." He did grin when he met her gaze this time. "Unless you're willing to take Monopoly money."

She huffed out a laugh, her breath condensing on the air. The snowflakes had become little beads of ice, pelting her exposed cheeks as the wind whipped around her. "I'm afraid I tried the Monopoly-money approach at age five after I broke one of my Dad's trophies."

"Yeah?"

"I tried to pay him off in pink bills and hotels. Ironically, he took it. I still ended up grounded for breaking the trophy when I'd been warned to leave it be." The memory was a fond one now that she could look at it through the lens of time and with the benefit of age. Her dad had been so serious, accepting her payment and then sending her to her room. He'd come up later and revoked riding privileges for a week after lecturing her on responsibility. Michael had sneaked her out twice in the following seven days to ride with him. Man, she'd loved him so much.

"Sounds as if you had a good father."

Kenzie's throat tightened. "I had… My family's amazing."

"Why the past tense?" Eli asked, openly curious.

"I lost my brother when I was a kid."

"I'm sorry." Eli reached out and fleetingly touched her arm, then withdrew. "I can't know the reality of losing a brother, but I do know the horror of thinking I lost one."

"Yeah." The word was little more than a breath lost to the wind's next gust.

"Stay, Kenzie. No matter the fight earlier, whatever you were to him hasn't died. That much is obvious."

"What do you expect me to be able to do that the doctors and therapists can't?" she demanded. "I'm the one person he's hell-bent on despising at the moment."

"Don't be so sure he despises you." He shot her an amused glance, his smile revealing dimples no woman should have to combat. "And you're a woman with resources. I doubt there's much you can't accomplish when you set your mind to it. Particularly where this man is concerned." He snorted and moved his horse a few strides away from her and Indie. "Let's just say the doctors and therapists don't hold the same type of influence over him that I'm willing to wager you do."

"You want me to—"

"Help him find himself again, Ms. Malone. You're the only one he's responded to, the only one he seems willing to engage with. Bring him back, not only to himself but to us. Please." When she didn't immediately respond, he pressed on. "Do this and…we won't contest your *right* to Gizmo's stud services." He glanced up at the sky. "Looks as if it's about to get ugly." With that, Eli spurred his horse forward.

"The weather or this thing with Ty?" she shouted to the eldest Covington's retreating form. He didn't answer, so she shouted a second, more relevant question. "What does Tyson think about this arrangement?"

If he answered, she didn't hear him. The snowstorm had intensified to near whiteout conditions, Eli's silhouette fading fast.

She urged Indie forward. The mare didn't need more than a free bit, and she took off after the man and horse, who were getting harder to see by the second.

Almost two hours later, Kenzie stepped into the one-bedroom cabin she'd been given and shut the door. She struggled out of her wet boots, her feet so cold they were tinged blue. Next came the soaked jacket, and then she started peeling off the jeans. That was when she remembered her last question to Eli: "What does Tyson think about this arrangement?"

He never answered.

"Sneaky freaking lawyer," she muttered.

Tossing her jeans into the stacked washer-dryer combo, she padded toward the bathroom on near-frozen feet. She needed a hot shower to thaw out. Then she'd reassess. The hardest part of the whole thing was that it was a half blessing as well as a half curse. She'd have to get Tyson to be vulnerable by doing the very same.

How far can you take it without crossing the line marked This Point is Too Far?

She'd had a hard time living with the lies she'd told so far. What would it do to her to manipulate Ty into recovery? How deep an emotional marshland would she have to traverse to secure his buy-in? And finally, how many more lies could she—*would* she—have to tell to get out of this mess?

That was all disturbing enough. But a single question she hadn't been brave enough to ask hung around, nagging at her conscience, demanding its due.

At what point, if any, did she confront the feelings she and Ty had been so actively avoiding? The ones that had been coming to a head prior to the accident?

Fear choked her.

What if he doesn't remember that, either?

If she had to, she'd make him. Lord only knew how, but she'd find a way, because his reaction to what they'd had then said everything about how he felt about what they might have now.

How do I make a man closely examine something he doesn't even want to glance at?

The answer was so easy that she grinned. You teased a little. You made it desirable. And then you made it irresistible.

Outside, the worst storm northern New Mexico had seen in thirty years raged on.

It was nothing compared to the storm brewing in her heart.

ONLY HALF-AWAKE, TY opened his eyes to find that the sunrise had set the world on fire, reflecting off the dazzling snow packed outside. He must have dozed off and left his curtains open last night. And he must have left the door unlocked, too. Because there was someone in his room.

Light created a brilliant nimbus around the individual. He blinked his eyes, trying to bring her into focus. Her? Yes, her. The swell of hips, the narrow shoulders and the outline of long hair pulled up in a sloppy topknot said she was female. She turned a bit. High breasts and a tight ass presented a tempting profile.

No, she wasn't "female." She was 100 percent authentic *woman*.

Below the covers, his cock stirred. He jolted, tipping his chin down as far as he could with his neck brace on but loose. How long had it been since he'd woken with his typical morning arousal?

"You awake?"

In the haze of half-sleep, he wondered for a moment if she was talking to him or his groin. "Has to be you," he mumbled, blinking faster.

"Who else?"

Grumpy tone or not, her voice glazed his skin and wound around his senses. Allure and sensual promise. That was what she was. He recognized it. Recognized *her*.

His cock shifted. Arousal crowded out everything but the memory of his hands on her body. Her response and his overwhelming desire to fill her senses and her mind.

Her. It was her. She'd been responsible. Mackenzie Malone.

"What are you doing here?" he rasped, throat dry from another night of sleeping on his back and breathing through his mouth.

"Came to check in on you."

His stomach did a lazy, nauseating roll. "I thought we left things pretty clear yesterday."

"They may have been clear for you, but I still have some things to work out. Besides, I can't leave now anyway." She gestured absently toward the window. "Snowed in."

Ty cleared his throat and half rolled, half flopped to a sitting position. Straining against his neck brace as much as he dared, he lifted his flat stare to hers. "I told you I'd pay you back."

"You really should know me better than that. I'm not worried about the money." With cautious steps, she moved to the edge of the bed.

"Then, what is it that has you so worried you're in my room at—" he looked at the clock "—barely six thirty in the morning?"

"May I sit?"

Before he could deny her request, his erection punched at the single-button fly of his flannel sleep pants. The damn thing would leap into her hands if Ty didn't keep it quarantined.

She noticed his physical reaction. Her answering smile revealed a single dimple. Years of knowing each other as intimately as they had created another private joke they would laugh over in the future.

There is no future.

Ty struggled to keep from shifting toward Kenzie as the mattress dipped with her slight weight. Their hips brushed. His erection strained toward her.

Eyes crinkling in unabashed amusement, she tipped her chin toward his lap. "I assume New Mexico has strict laws about keeping crotch creatures like that chained for the public's well-being."

He barked out a laugh. "Crotch creatures?"

She shrugged. "You have a better name for it?"

"As a matter of fact…" he started.

Kenzie waved him off. "Of course you do. Pretend I didn't ask." Twisting her fingers together, she settled her hands in her lap and trained her gaze on them.

The longer she sat like that, Ty wondered if he should prod her to say or do something. After all, she'd come to him. Then she spoke.

"I have a proposition for you."

Used to be conversations that started like that would have been full of promise. Now? Not so much. Anger burned through him, its heat far more brilliant than the sun on the pristine snow. "There's no point propositioning a broken man, Mackenzie. And in case you somehow failed to notice, *I am broken*." The words lashed out with enough force they could have—should have—drawn blood.

Her chin snapped up, those fiery eyes blazing. "You aren't broken."

He chuffed out a bitter laugh and closed his eyes. *Instant anger—just add a dose of disabled cowboy*. "Right. Just go, Mackenzie."

"Don't know what I was thinking." She pushed off the bed, nearly toppling him over.

"Go easy there, Sasquatch," he muttered as he regained his balance.

Halfway to the door, she froze. Her steps were slow, precise and measured as she rounded on him. "Go. Easy." She arched a shaped brow with more sarcasm than had likely ever been conveyed by a single facial gesture. "You'd like that, wouldn't you? If I—hell, if *everyone*—went 'easy' on you." A wicked smile curled her lips up. "How long are we supposed to dance around you and your fragile psyche, Covington? What's the timeline here, because it's already getting old."

"What, you need to know how long you should pretend compassion?" The second he said it, he realized he'd pushed her too far.

Kenzie's eyes narrowed to furious slits. "Pretend compassion, is that what this is? When have I *ever* pretended? When have I *ever* been anything other than sincere with you?" She flinched, a shadow flitting through her gaze. He started to call her on it, demand an explanation, but she was already moving toward him with a hip-swinging grace any blues singer would have been proud to work. Closing the distance, she gently pushed him backward on the bed before crawling up his body like the lithe lover she'd once been to him. She braced one hand on either side of his head and leaned forward until their eyes met.

Heart in his throat, Ty reached up and pulled her hair loose so it cascaded around them. The thick curtain of waves hid them from the world. He tucked a rogue curl behind her ear. "What are you doing, Malone?"

"Making a point." With extreme gentleness, she slid her jean-clad core up and then down the length of his erection.

He hissed. "Which is?"

Leaning into him, she stopped with less than a breath between them. When she spoke, her lips moved over his. "This doesn't feel like the body of a broken man."

He began to breathe heavily, his eyes widening. "I can't do this."

She brushed a featherlight kiss over his lips. "At some point you've got to get back in the saddle, cowboy. Now's as good a time as any."

"Kenzie," he started, her name little more than a growl. "If this is about Gizmo—"

"Ty, your horse is in the stable. Leave him there." Slipping forward that last fraction, she claimed his mouth in a soul-stealing kiss.

She lit him up from the inside out. He was the sun to her solar system.

Alive. Feel so alive.

He ran his hands through her hair, reveling at its silky weight. Fisting his hand in her hair, he canted her head to one side and encouraged her to take the kiss even deeper, to give up some of the control she clearly struggled to maintain. The need to own the moment swept through him like a Chinook wind, melting the remnants of his heart's long winter solstice. For the first time in ages, he was warm. More than warm. Heat burned through him, chasing away the cold.

In her arms, Tyson Covington was reborn.

11

KENZIE BROKE THE kiss so she could simply look at the man beneath her. She touched his face, tracing a fingertip over his lips, up one cheekbone and then down. The hair along his stubbled jawline had grown out enough that it was on the verge of losing the prickly feel and becoming soft. She loved the way his hair was both light and dark. It was reflective of the man himself—the part people saw and the shadows he carried inside. She understood him. Probably more than he realized and definitely far better than he wanted her to.

He nipped the pad of her finger as she traced it over his lips again.

She instinctively pulled away and then pressed two fingers to his lips. When he kissed the sting, part of her relaxed. This was Ty. Simply Ty. He wasn't a stranger but a familiar lover. A man her heart recognized, craved, dreamed of more often than not. Looking at him now, it was as if she was seeing him for the first time all over again—the rush of attraction, the need to glimpse his smile, the desire to hear his laughter and, even more, to be responsible for it. Above all, though, was the yearning to touch him.

So she did.

Hands trembling so slightly she didn't think he'd notice, she reached out and undid the first Velcro strap on his neck brace.

Ty jerked away, eyes wide. "I can't take the brace off."

"Shh." The rip of the next strap seemed louder than the first.

"Seriously." His hand rested atop her wrist to stop her from removing the next strap. "Please, Kenzie. I can't do this."

She paused, taking in the undisguised fear on his face. "Can't or won't?"

He slid his hand to encompass hers and squeezed. "I don't..."

Cupping his face with her free hand, she pulled gently against his grip, giving him every opportunity to really resist, to stop her, to hold on to his fear and put it in front of his desire.

His gaze locked on hers and, eyes wide, he let his hand fall away.

She knew it was the ultimate gesture of trust. He'd handed over the keys to his fear, stepped aside and allowed her to rule the moment. No way would she abuse that. Moving with ultimate care, she pulled the third and fourth straps. Then she lifted the top of the brace away.

Fine tremors ran through Ty, transmitting his concern to her through every point where they touched.

Movements precise, care for the man tempering her hunger for him, Kenzie set the brace on the floor.

"I can't reach it," he said, voice strained to the point of breaking.

"You won't need it," she countered quietly.

"But what if I—"

"Enjoy yourself," she finished for him.

His brows drew together. "Huh?"

"What if you let your inner playboy loose and take a chance?"

He shook his head and froze.

Her heart stuttered. "Did you hurt yourself?"

"No," he answered slowly. "But what if I do?"

She closed the distance between them, feathering her lips over his in tiny kisses. "What if you *don't*?"

"It could happen, Kenzie. If I'm not seriously careful—"

"We'll take it slow." She pulled back a fraction. "Isn't the potential pleasure worth fighting through the fear? If we have to stop, we will. I swear to you I'll stop before I let anything hurt you, Tyson."

With slow deliberation, he threaded his fingers through her hair. "This is like losing my virginity all over again."

She grinned. "Why do I love the idea that I'm the one divesting you of your pseudo-innocence?"

"Because you have a very wicked side, Miss Malone." His smile grew and reflected in his eyes. "Coolest part? I've always wanted my very own Mrs. Robinson, and now I've got her."

Kenzie's laugh bubbled out, sultry and full of every unspoken promise she longed to make, from the generally innocent to the decidedly *not*.

Mrs. Robinson indeed.

Closing the distance again, she took the kiss deeper, angling her mouth over his so all he had to do was receive her. After a tense moment of consideration, he responded in kind. Hands searched, touched and learned; mouths tasted; tongues stroked and breaths came shorter and then shorter still. Here, in Ty's arms, no matter that she set the pace, she knew a sense of peace she'd been missing. She had longed for this, for him, ever since he'd walked out her hotel room door in the early morning on the day of the accident.

There had been moments, lonely and terrifying, when she'd wanted to leave Ohio, leave Gizmo in the vet's capable hands and go to Ty. But she hadn't. Hard as it had been, she'd honored his request that *she* see his horse well. Now that she had Ty, though, she wasn't about to let go. Not until someone forced her hand.

Those were thoughts for another time, though. This? This man tentatively coming to life beneath her? He was all that mattered.

His hot lips skated over hers, more demanding now than they'd been moments before. It thrilled her that he'd grown more brazen. She wanted both his capitulation and the masterful demands he typically made of her body. She wanted it all, to rule and be ruled, touch and be touched.

Her name was an invocation on his lips, a plea to her for something her conscious didn't quite understand but that her subconscious grabbed at greedily.

Kenzie ran her hands down Ty's sides, smiling against his mouth when he sucked in a breath. "Ticklish?"

"No," he replied, wiggling to get his shirttail out from under him and over his head. "Not even a little."

She dragged a blunt fingernail down his side, and he squirmed, trying to get away.

"Fine! Quit," he said, laughing. "I am ticklish. Now stop distracting me."

"What am I distracting you from?" she teased.

He looked up at her, face suddenly solemn. "I don't want to miss a single moment."

Pain blossomed in her chest, and for a second, she wondered what it was that could ache like that and yet make her crave more of the same. Then he cupped her breasts, gently rolling her pearled nipples between his thumb and forefinger. All thought turned to ash at the wave of desire that burned through her. Core aching, she moved to straddle his waist, to position herself to take what she needed.

His hands stilled. "Go easy, Kenzie."

"I promise. Just don't stop." She pressed her hands over his, encouraging him to manipulate the tender swells of her breasts with tiny squeezes of her fingers. "Please."

"I'll never deny you, baby." His hips surged when she pressed her sex against him, his groan the only thing soft about the moment. Or him.

She arched her back, one hand holding his to her breast while the other was parked on his thigh to help give her leverage as she rode him with a slow, hip-rolling motion. Drawn into the ageless rhythm, he gripped her thigh, pushing and pulling to help set the pace.

It had been so long, too long, since she'd been here with him. She didn't want to let the moment go, wanted it to last forever, but her body's needs were more immediate than her emotional ones. What her body wanted was achievable *now*. No reason to deny either of them the pleasure of connection and release.

Ignoring his wordless protest when she moved off his lap, she stood and stripped with perfunctory movements, more anxious to return to him than she was to make the action a seduction. The avaricious look on his face as his eyes roamed over her body said she achieved the latter regardless.

Kenzie crawled up Ty's body, stopping midway to untie his pants. She worked them down his hips and over his feet, tossing them clear of the bed.

With him lying before her without a stitch of clothing, she'd never been so grateful for the fit and finish the good Lord had bestowed on this man. He was beautiful, head to toe.

She could have looked at him for ages, explored his body and learned every peak and valley. Instead, she straddled his lap again, reveling in the heat of him against her sensitive skin. "No underwear. If you'd been in a car wreck, Tyson, you'd have scandalized the nurses."

He arched a brow at the same time he grinned, the look one of guileful amusement. "You know me, Kenzie—always ready and willing to play patient."

"You're incorrigible."

"Every man has aspirations. That one word sums mine up quite nicely."

Shaking her head, she leaned forward and nipped his earlobe. "Stop talking, Tyson." She didn't give him a chance to respond. With deft hands, she reached between them and positioned his arousal, then worked her way down his thick length. He stretched her. She reveled in the near discomfort his size caused. She hadn't been with anyone else who'd made her feel so much, made her long to embrace her sexuality and experience everything a skilled lover could offer. Particularly a skilled lover who knew her body so well.

In the past, he'd always seen to her needs first. Today,

though, she reciprocated his every touch, returned his every encouragement tenfold through words, sounds and intimate touches. He fought her at first, trying to make her reach the pinnacle alone. She was having none of it. Where she went, she ensured he followed. This was an exercise in mutual gratification.

She rode him with long, slow strokes, losing herself to the feel of him beneath her, the way his hips thrust up as she sank down, the way his deft fingers pulled her release to the surface, drawing it closer and closer with every careful manipulation. Her chest rose and fell, faster and then faster still.

Beneath her, Ty whispered her name. He dug his fingers into her hips and pulled her down his length as she sank low. His thrusts grew deeper, harder. The sounds of their lovemaking—the touch of skin on skin, the tender words and soft encouragements—filled the small room.

The fluttering of her release began to build, that intangible feeling that something huge was bearing down on her, something bigger than she could control, too large to define, too much for her skin to contain. The pleasure rushed at her suddenly and then over her, shattering her with brutal efficiency. She couldn't stop herself from bearing down on Ty and crying out, the magnitude of what he drew out of her too large for words.

Losing the graceful rhythm he'd kept, he gripped both her hips fiercely. Driving into her with thrusts so powerful he nearly unseated her, he followed her over the edge with a shout.

Kenzie closed her eyes and simply lived in the moment. No past. No future. Just the present existed. It was the only thing that mattered. She'd come too close to losing the chance to experience him even one more time, to losing *him*, and she didn't want to go through that ever again.

There had to be a way out of the mess she'd made, a way to ensure everyone got what they most wanted—Ty could keep Gizmo, the brothers could keep Ty whole, and she...she could simply keep Ty.

TY LISTENED TO his heart. The act had become habitual, the first thing he did every morning and the last thing he did at night. He had to count out one hundred consecutive beats before he could do anything else. The organ—muscle? Or would it be a morgscle?—tattooed a repeating design against his rib cage. He forced his breathing to slow as he discreetly checked his pulse.

One sixty-four.

Not a bad postexertion rate.

Postexertion. He grinned. *Postcoital, buddy. That would be post*coital.

His bedroom rodeo queen shifted beside him. She rested her head on his shoulder, her moist breath skating across his sweat-slicked skin.

Chilled, Ty fumbled for the edge of the quilt.

Kenzie sat up and pushed the thick fall of hair over her shoulder. "Any reason you're manhandling the bedding like that?" She grabbed the edge of the quilt and then paused. "Ty?"

He closed his eyes. "Leave it alone, Kenzie."

"Can't." She traced his stubbled jaw with the pads of her fingers.

"I mean it."

"Still can't," she murmured. "It's okay to be angry. It's also okay to admit you're scared. You suffered a horrific injury. Makes sense you'd want to use caution as you ease back into things." Her thumb drifted over the fullness of his lower lip. "What doesn't make sense is why you're so willing to accept suffering and settle for survival instead of fighting to live."

She doesn't understand.

His heart rate picked up speed, and Ty wondered that the morgscle didn't bruise as it threw itself against his sternum harder and harder. That would be bad in its own right, having a bruised morgscle. Fixated on the repeating thump of his heart, he started counting out the beats.

One, two, three, four, five—

"Ty?" She cupped his jaw.

Shit. Have to start over.

He pulled free of her touch.

One, two, three—

"Seriously, Ty." Completely unself-conscious, Kenzie moved to straddle his hips before putting a hand on either side of his face. "You have to slow down. You're going to have a full-blown panic attack if you don't."

"You don't get it," he said through clenched teeth, his nose flaring on each exhale and nearly sucking closed on every harsh inhale. "You don't know what it's like, Mackenzie."

"What *what's* like?" she asked with undisguised concern.

"You can't understand how it feels." He dropped his fist to his chest, daring that damn morgscle to defy him again, to fail to carry out its responsibility. "You haven't ever…" An invisible band around his chest began to crank down, cutting off his air supply and making his heart pound so loudly in his head he struggled to hear anything else. "I think I'm having a heart attack."

Her grip on his face tightened. "Look at me, Tyson."

He shook his head, two short, fast jerks of the chin. "Get off me. Go get help. Please."

"If I call your brothers, they're going to bring in paramedics. Given the remoteness of the ranch, you're going to end up with a Life Flight helicopter in your front yard and guests ogling the cowboy they've only heard about but haven't ever seen. They're going to airlift you to Amarillo where they're going to give you something from the benzodiazepine family of meds to get you to calm down."

"Move!" he wheezed. He pulled her biceps and twisted his hips, trying to move her.

No luck.

"First you have to look at me." The unforgiving authority in her voice demanded he comply.

Fear gripped him with all the fury of a pit bull after a fresh bone. All his life he'd been written off as someone who needed micromanagement, a dreamy-eyed kid with his head in the clouds and a quick smile that lacked substance. That stopped now. He was a grown man, and it was about time people started treating him like one. He'd survived more in the past two months than most people encountered in a lifetime, from the injury to the loss of memory to the pain of recovery. Resentment burned in him as he met her stolid stare.

"Tell me where you are."

"Under you."

One corner of her mouth kicked up. "Do you remember the last time you were there? It was in Fort Worth."

"I can't—"

She continued, talking over him. "You said it wasn't where you wanted to be then, either."

"Clearly, I was an idiot. Now move."

"Clearly." She stroked his hair off his forehead. "I didn't hurt you then, and I won't hurt you now." Continuing with the soothing motion, she talked. And talked. And talked some more. She told him about her favorite nice restaurant—San Francisco Steak House—and how she'd once driven seventy miles just to get to her favorite drive-through burger joint—Whataburger.

She told him how she'd had to argue with the salesman when she'd bought her last pickup truck because the man believed "a lady should never need four-wheel drive." That particular story had been delivered with several eye rolls.

She told him how she'd ended up getting drunk in college one night when she and some friends had gone bowling. She'd allegedly bowled the best game of her life—274—chomping on an unlit cigar and sporting a Hawaiian shirt she'd won off an elderly man on the neighboring lane. It was all alleged because she couldn't remember anything after the third game. And then she'd grimaced as she recounted the raging hangover the following morning.

She told him how she'd missed her senior prom because, even at seventeen, horses had mattered more than boys, and she insisted she'd never been as boy crazy as her friends had.

"Not until you met me anyway."

Kenzie smiled down at him, the look in her eyes no longer challenging but rather filled with humor and the warmth of good memories. "Sweetheart," she said as she waggled her eyebrows à la Groucho Marx, "you were never a boy." She leaned forward and gently nipped his chin. "You still drive me crazy, though."

His hands moved of their own volition, coming to rest on her bare hips. "Feeling's entirely mutual."

"What are we going to do about that?" The question, while delivered in a light tone, had a thread of seriousness woven through it.

He considered her, tracing his thumbs over the slight swells of her hips, letting them dip into the shallow depressions in front of her hip bones. "Hard to say. You going to keep talking me down from panic attacks?"

She lifted one shoulder in a casual shrug. "Why not? I can't do anything with the horses. Not until the snow melts anyway. How long does it usually stay on the ground?"

"Could be days, could be weeks. Never can tell around here." He shifted under her, settling his burgeoning erection against her core. "About the panic attacks—I suppose we'll have to work something out. You're a hell of a lot cheaper than my prescription."

He had the sinking feeling she would prove herself to be far more addictive, though.

12

KENZIE COULD HAVE lolled around in bed all day without complaint, but there were chores to be done. With snow on the ground, it was all the more important that the animals were taken care of. She'd see to Indie and Gizmo, but she had no intention of doing it alone. Nope. If she had to hog-tie and drag him, Ty would come along.

Standing at the foot of the bed, jeans in hand, she considered the man lounging amid the rumpled sheets and wadded-up pillows. "You look thoroughly pleased with yourself."

"Darlin', what I just did is the equivalent of tagging a twelve-point buck with a single shot from a rickety bow sporting a crooked arrow less than ninety seconds into the first day of hunting season." Clearly proud, he hooked an arm behind his head. Propped up like that, he was the perfect picture of sanguine masculinity. His flinch wouldn't have been noticeable if she hadn't been looking for it.

"You okay?" she asked with intentional indifference, making it a point to focus on getting into her jeans and then searching for her socks and boots.

"Couldn't be better."

"Sore at all?" she pressed.

"In the best possible way."

Gotcha. She rounded on him, unable to tamp down her smile. "Awesome. Then, get up."

He stared at her as if she'd just gifted him with a wheelbarrow full of horse apples and expected gratitude for the fresh load of crap. "Get...up?"

"You can get down if you want to, but you'll still have to get up to do it."

"Funny girl." The teasing in his tone was still there, but beneath it ran an undercurrent of unease. "You're joking."

"Not in the least." She sank onto the bed and wiggled her cold toes into thick socks before reaching for first one boot and then the other. "I've got a ton to do today, and I need your help."

She could do everything on her task list by herself, and in fact she'd planned her day that way, not expecting company. But this little lie was one she could—*would*—live with, and gladly. She could even ignore the way her skin seemed to shrink a bit at the ease with which she prevaricated.

Let it go, Malone. No harm, no foul.

Standing, she grabbed a ball cap off the hook by the door and set about feeding her hair through the opening above the strap and then tightening it. "Didn't know you were a Denver Broncos fan," she said, pointing at the logo on the cap. Maybe she could get her dad to give up his fifty-yard-line seats. She and Ty could grab a Sunday-afternoon game, maybe spend the night in Denver and—

"Did you hear me?" he demanded, interrupting her mental weekend planning.

She glanced over her shoulder. "No. Sorry. What was that?"

"I said I'm not leaving the house."

She fisted her jacket in her hands. She didn't want to do this. Didn't want to fight with him, or to shame him or bully him into finding the motivation he needed to get off his ass and live again. She wanted him to want it on his own. The way he'd wanted her.

Setting her jacket on the corner of the bed, she crossed her arms under her breasts and faced him. "I don't understand."

"There's not much that needs explaining," he countered. "I'm still recovering, Kenzie. If I go out there, I could slip and fall, refracture my neck, damage my spinal cord worse than I did originally." He shook his head minutely even as he reached for his brace. "I could be hurt worse this time, maybe even paralyzed."

"'This time'?" Kenzie parroted, confused. "What do you mean, 'this time'? You planning on taking another header? Or maybe you intend to roll around in the snow with Gizmo and try to set a new world record for making snow angels while horseback. Wait. I've got it. You're planning a wrestling match with the colt in stall seven, aren't you?" She dug deep and retrieved a shallow smile. "He's not huge, but he's stout as hell. I wouldn't recommend it."

Color drained from his face and left his appearance pastier than Elmer's Glue save for two small bright spots that rode high on his cheeks. "You're just like everyone else. You're not *hearing* me on this."

"Oh, I hear you just fine. The difference between me

and 'everyone else' is that I refuse to kowtow to your temper tantrums or tiptoe around your irrational fears. I'm sick of this, and I haven't been around you even a fraction of what your family has. I'm not going to stand around and let you come up with any more excuses about why you can't do more than feed yourself pureed peas someone else fixed for you. This stops now, Tyson." She fought to keep from grinding her teeth as she decided just how hard to push him. At his mulish look, she pulled the emotional rip cord and let herself free-fall. "Put on your big-boy Pull-Ups and get out of bed already. You're freaking twenty-five years old."

"Twenty-six."

"What?"

"I turned twenty-six while I was in the hospital."

"And you think that fact—that you're older—works in your *favor*?" she exclaimed. "Did you fracture the logic center of your brain, too?"

He scowled at her, jaw set in a mutinous, hard line.

She pressed on, unwilling to give up the ground she'd made. "You proved you're man enough to get the job done—and more than once—this morning. Time to get that flannel-clad ass out of bed and back in a pair of Wranglers,cowboy."

"No." He pushed himself up, hands shaking as he tightened the neck brace's Velcro tabs. "You don't get to come in here like some…some…"

"The phrase you're searching for is 'knight in shining armor,' but that doesn't fit with your image of yourself, does it?" She spoke so low she knew he had to strain to hear her. Damn if she'd speak any louder. "Because then you'd be the damsel in distress. Truth is, you *are* the damsel on the railroad tracks in this little vignette.

But no one tied you down. There is no mustache-twirling villain to blame. There's only you. And now your private audience is throwing popcorn at you as the train bears down, yet you're just lying there shouting about the injustices you've been dealt. Get over it, Tyson. Cut the invisible ropes you've bound yourself with and get up already."

"Don't you stand there and pretend to understand what this is like for me."

"Oh, I don't have to pretend. I *know*. I've lived this before, Tyson. Always on the outside, but this is a familiar glass house." She grabbed her jacket and stormed toward the door, her throat burning with words she hungered to say but knew she'd regret, words she'd never be able to take back. She didn't want his pity, but she wanted him to understand that he wasn't the only one hurting. Not even close.

Spinning to face him, she clutched her jacket in one hand and yanked the borrowed ball cap off with the other. "I was thirteen when I saw my only brother killed in an accident eerily similar to yours. But it wasn't during a show. It was in the middle of an open-range branding. An exceptionally large bull calf got squirrelly. Michael roped him." She swiped at the single bead of sweat rolling down her temple. "But the calf fought, got wadded up in the rope. Michael's horse didn't have the experience to get out of the mess, and the three of them went down. Two of them got up. My brother wasn't one of them."

Wide-eyed, Ty opened his mouth and then closed it when she made a stop gesture with her hand. "Don't."

She'd achieved her goal—shocking him—with incredible efficiency. But the undisguised pity he didn't even try to hide proved more than she could bear. She felt the first emotional fissures open, the sensations not unlike someone dragging the tip of sharp needles along her skin. Superficial scratches that would provide weaknesses, places that would split with the right amount of pressure.

But the next words out of his mouth created a kind of emotional epoxy that bound everything together. "I'm so sorry. I didn't know. If I had…" He trailed off, his eyes closing as he fought to find the words.

She would spare him that much, at least. "How could you have known? You were fifteen. I wasn't even on your radar at that point, so it wouldn't have meant anything to you. Not on a personal level anyway. But my life was forever changed. Mom totally withdrew, first from her charitable and volunteer works and then from society altogether. It was as if she lost her will to live."

Ty's brows drew together in apparent anger. "I realize she lost her son, but she still had you."

He hit so close to the heart of her decade of hurt, becoming invisible in the shadow of a good man's death, that she took a physical step back. She couldn't go there. Not with anyone, but particularly not with him. How could he understand the consequences of Michael's death? How could he possibly grasp the fact that his love-'em-and-leave-'em approach felt very much the same to her? She couldn't. Not without turning those fissures into gaping wounds.

Instead, she pressed on. "While I pretty much lost Mom, Dad began wrapping up his rodeo career. He gave it all up so he could be there for Mom. So while I lost my mom's awareness, I gained my dad's time and attention. He turned that focus on me, on helping me become national champion." What she didn't say was that she'd followed that path for her father, stepping directly into Michael's boots. She'd never been able to fill them, though. Not for either parent.

"What about you?"

She whipped her gaze up to meet his. "What do you mean?"

"Just that. Your mom basically withdrew from life to grieve. Your dad gave up his career to come home and take care of your mom, but he also fought to keep Michael's memory alive by encouraging you to chase championship titles on the rodeo circuit. What did you do to grieve?"

Kenzie reached out and grabbed the edge of the dresser as black spots danced through her vision. "I managed."

"That's not what I asked."

Swiping at tears she was fighting not to shed, she cursed her own vulnerability. She hadn't want to show it to anyone, but particularly this man, who was notorious for running at the first sign of anything complicated.

You wanted him up and moving under his own power? You're going to get your wish. This ought to have him hotfooting it out of the county by noon.

That thought cut the last tethers of her emotional control. Fear and anger, thoroughly aged and seasoned by time, welled up and exploded out of her in a rush of almost unintelligible sound. "You want answers? Get your ass out of that bed. Better yet, make it to the barn and I'll give you all the intimate details."

"I don't think I can make it—"

"Then, ask for help. But bottom line? If you want answers badly enough, you'll find a way to get to the barn. Come find me there, Ty." *Want me enough to try.* "I'll answer your questions." *Need me enough to push past the obstacles.*

Michael's death had left her with an aching loneliness no one had ever been able to fill, partly because she hadn't opened herself up to anyone enough to expose the hurt she wore like a mantle every day. And she'd never allowed anyone to get close enough that they might catch even a glimpse of her most broken parts. She'd never found anyone she trusted enough to understand her, to understand the pain and the yearning.

Until now.

Ty understood. She just needed to get him up and moving, to reinvest himself in his life and be active again. He would emerge stronger. He just didn't know it yet.

But she'd used her brother's memory paired with bribery to get him to do it.

Information.

The thing it turned out he wanted most was information, and it was there, within his reach. He had only to move, to walk, to make an effort and lay claim to it. She'd set a beginning point—the bedroom—and an end point—the barn. If he made it from one to the other, she'd answer the questions he wanted to know.

But in the process, she risked her own emotional devastation. Those fissures of grief would split, exposing a dark abyss. When that happened, she'd survive only if he was there for her.

She *needed* him to need her.

TY LAY IN BED, his mind a roiling mass of thoughts and ideas and realizations he'd failed to work out over the years he and Kenzie had been first friends and then lovers. Just now, she'd thrown out what amounted to more than a double-dog dare—get out of bed to get the answers he craved. Then she'd fled the room as if all the regret in the world nipped at her heels. Seeing her inherent bravery stripped of fight, reduced to flight, wrecked him. That he couldn't give chase pissed him off.

"And just what do you think you'd do if you caught her?" he asked himself aloud. He'd like to think he'd rescue her from the heartache of her past, but in reality, there was no way to take the hurt away or undo what she'd experienced.

And how do you think you're any different? Who do you expect to compensate you for what life's put you through? his subconscious demanded.

Understanding drove the air from his lungs like a sucker punch. He was no different, and there was no compensation that would give him back what he'd lost. Not any more than he could return her brother to her or compensate her for his loss.

Which meant she was ultimately right. He'd been behaving like the proverbial damsel in distress, waiting on the hero to show up and rescue him.

Shifting to his side, Ty swung his feet off the edge of the bed, the momentum helping him lever himself up to a sitting position. Dark spots marred his vision and he blinked repeatedly. He'd been in bed too long, had spent too much time lounging. His muscles were almost useless, and his bones were so heavy they felt as if they'd been cast out of concrete. He wanted to lie back down and pull the covers over his head. How had he let himself go so badly?

Easy. Whereas he'd once lived large, life now scared him because it had scarred him.

His fingertips traced the four-inch knotty line of scar tissue that disappeared into his nape. The hair had finally grown back where the surgeons had shaved it in December. Strobe-like memories of the day of the accident drifted through his mind, mental Polaroid images he'd carry with him forever. Some were blurry, some were clear and there were others that were nothing more than black slides with no value. The brightest memories, though, were when he woke from the coma…and the night before it had all gone down.

He remembered everything about his and Kenzie's last night together. The smell of her perfume, the slip of the sheet that revealed one luscious bare hip, the passion, how she'd silently watched him leave the room—all of it was fresher, more easily retrievable than memories of his last phone call home. He lingered over the image of her lying in the tumbled bed, skin flushed and appearing well loved. He'd recalled that last image more times than he would cop to, no matter who was doing the asking.

The accident had messed him up, left him reeling as he'd fought to recover not only physically but, as she'd pointed out, emotionally. What he needed was to jump-start his life, to reengage on a more meaningful level. Raking one hand through his hair, he considered what it would mean to him to take over this alleged partnership. He'd have to get her to tell him…

I'll answer your questions.

There it was. His out. It was almost too easy.

He tightened his fingers and gripped his hair. She'd said it herself. If he made it down to the barn, she'd tell him what he wanted to know. What she'd failed to do was qualify the topics he could question her on. She'd left herself wide-open.

All he had to do was set aside the fears that were welded to his soul and then haul his broken backside to the barn.

13

ENTERING THE BARN after fighting knee-deep snowdrifts, Kenzie huffed out a sharp breath, watching as it condensed on the bitter cold air. This morning hadn't gone the way she'd expected. It was supposed to have been fun, full of her and Ty's signature teasing and laughter. The passion had proved too intense for that, though. And then her past had risen up and taken over the emotional bus, turning what had been a *Hope Floats* moment into a *Speed* film snippet complete with the bus going airborne, the crash landing imminent.

Grabbing a rake, shovel and cart from the equipment room, she set about cleaning the stalls she was responsible for. She started with Indie, hoping Ty would come in time to help with Gizmo. Her mare was quiet, absorbed with her grain ration, allowing Kenzie to work mindlessly as she replayed the conversation with Ty this morning, shying away from the hard parts.

She was nearly finished when she heard the sound that froze her where she stood. Booted feet. Steps slow and measured, the person entered the barn.

He showed up.

Adrenaline trilling through her veins, she set the pitchfork aside and stepped into the alleyway to find a cowboy she hadn't met emerging from the tack room.

He glanced up, seemed to recognize her, and his face shut down. All he said was "Sleigh ride for the guests," as he passed by, silently harnessing up a pair of draft horses before leading them out the opposite end of the barn.

Clearly, word about her "designs" on Gizmo had made it down the campfire gossip chain and made her persona non grata on the ranch.

"I swear," she muttered, scooping up another forkful of straw that needed replacing. "Men are far more active gossips than women." She glanced at Gizmo. "Present company excluded, but probably only because English isn't your first language." He nodded his head dramatically, and she laughed. "You're such a smart-ass."

She continued cleaning, the morning's conversation stuck on Repeat in her mind. She couldn't get it to stop, only to pause at highly relevant places or comments. Sweat trickled down her back, a ticklish, itchy line of irritation. Stepping over to the edge of the open stall door, she backed up to the corner and rocked side to side to scratch the itch. Her bra had dampened from the exertion, too. Glancing around, she shed her jacket and reached under her shirt to unhook her bra and wiggle out of it. Shoving it down the arm of her jacket, she tossed the garment on the nearest clean straw bale in the barn's alleyway.

"Better," she breathed.

Resuming her duties, she tried to ignore the building guilt that held down the trigger on her nerves. Movements jerky, she finally stabbed the shovel tip into the ground and leaned on the handle, closing her eyes. As pervasive as the cold was, it couldn't compare to the frost that rimed her emotional center.

Can't believe I used Michael's memory that way.

Exploiting her brother's death was wrong in a variety of ways, but she was far from the first to use it as a tool. Her mother had used it to get her father to quit the rodeo circuit. Her father had, in turn, used it as a manipulative tool to get Kenzie to take the professional rodeo circuit seriously, encouraging her to take over where Michael left off—"in Michael's memory," of course. Her maternal grandparents had used Michael's death to prod Kenzie into going to college because "Michael would have wanted it." Her paternal grandparents had suggested she could keep Michael's memory alive by riding with his bridle and reins in each event. At age fourteen, she'd balked, even cried, at the heartache caused by holding reins stained by her lost brother's sweat. They'd grown stern and told her how much it would have meant to Michael, as well as how much it *would* mean to her father, *their* son, to see that bridle worn in their grandson's memory.

The list went on; everyone from family members to friends to neighbors had exercised their right to gain what they wanted either for Michael or because Michael would have wanted it. She had despised them all for sullying her brother's loss that way, and yet here she was, finally succumbing to this warped expression of grief.

Only Ty had ever given her relief from the memories. He'd never asked because he'd never known, and that had suited her just fine. She could be normal with him, not the daughter/granddaughter/sister/cousin/friend who linked people to Michael's memory. She'd been Mackenzie Malone. Period. Sure, he'd known she was an heiress. But until the accident when he'd pleaded with her to save Gizmo, until she'd invested over one hundred thousand dollars of her trust fund money into saving Ty's horse and covering his medical bills, her money hadn't mattered. And for a few hours last night and this morning, she'd totally forgotten about the whole mess money and obligation and memories created. She'd just been Kenzie Malone in the arms of the man she loved.

She gasped. The man she loved...

No. Not possible. She'd be a fool to fall in love with a man like Ty.

Yet the longer she looked at what she felt for the man and what she'd done for him, the more she realized what a fool she really was.

She staggered across the wood chip–covered floor and crashed into the stall wall. Chest heaving, she shook her head and watched the fall of her hair move in slow, measured sweeps. And still, her internal argument carried on.

Love? This isn't love. This is...something else. But not love. It couldn't be.

How did she know, though? She'd never been in love. Not romantic love. Not spend-your-life-together-forever love. No. This couldn't be *that*. Not with Ty. She might have strong feelings for him, feelings so vibrant they marked her a neon idiot, but love?

"No," she whispered, thumping the edge of her fist against the thick wooden wall.

Her mind drifted back to the conversation she'd had with her father when she was only a teen. His words, so profound even then, had stuck with her.

I don't care if the man you fall in love with is an artist, a pilot, a musician, a doctor or a garbageman, he'd said.

He'd made absolutely sure she understood that the amount of money her potential spouse had—or didn't have—meant little to nothing, that her inheritance afforded her the means to choose a life partner based on love alone. How would her dad feel about Ty? Would he hold true to his word? He'd been proud that she'd managed to secure a partnership with Gizmo's owner, but also protective when he'd believed Ty was taking advantage of her. What would he think of her falling in love with that man?

"This isn't going to end well," she whispered.

Twisting, she leaned her shoulders against the stall and thumped her head against the wooden wall. How had she ended up here, of all places? She'd been struggling with her developing feelings for Ty even before the accident, but not once had she suspected they ran this deep. What would he do if she told him?

Probably grab his passport and disappear into a Brazilian jungle, she thought with an involuntary smile. But then he'd probably charm a young woman in some undiscovered native tribe and have to move on to Siberia when the respective father took offense to Ty's practice of short-shelf-life relationships. A small laugh escaped Kenzie at the thought of Ty being the only person with a tan in Siberia.

She'd be willing to bet he didn't sport tan lines, either.

That image led her mind straight back to a montage of memories, all of them centered around the myriad ways he'd pushed her body to new heights, had encouraged her to embrace the pleasure he could offer and then seen her to her own end before achieving his.

Her nipples pearled.

The response had nothing to do with the cold and everything to do with her cowboy. She couldn't let her need for him supersede his want of her. Not without consequence. But she hadn't been able to help it, hadn't been able to reject the psychological convenience of using Eli's promises as her excuse to see Ty.

In the quiet aftermath of lovemaking, when heart rates thundered and minds weren't quite clear, she'd been able to tell herself she was doing it to help Ty. It had also been a way to hoist her butt out of the sling she'd so efficiently parked it in with the very first lie. She could let Eli assume the responsibility of Ty's wrath over breeding Gizmo, get out of the partnership claiming that the ninety-day rights to the stud horse satisfied the debt owed, and she wouldn't have to tell her dad she'd made the whole thing up. If Ty was up and mobile before she left, even better for the Covingtons and her conscience.

A cold gust of wind curled around the door and stirred up straw motes. The pungent scent of animal grew sharper on the crisp, dry air. Outside, the merry jingle of sleigh bells and the hiss of wide steel runners over snow advertised the passage of the sleigh on its way to the chow hall to pick up guests. She envied them the view of the ranch, pristine as it would be. Nothing could beat the views from solitary vistas and the otherworldly quiet of snow-packed plains in either New Mexico or Colorado.

She longed to share a moment like that with Ty. They'd cover up with blankets and share a carafe of hot cocoa… Leaning her head back against the wall, she sighed and let her eyes drift closed. It would be idyllic. Except for the fact that Ty would know their driver. No fooling around for them, then. Maybe they could go out together, just the two of them. She'd driven a team before, and the smooth pull over snow wouldn't jar Ty's neck. He'd probably appreciate getting some fresh air and a firsthand look at the ranch. Heck, he might even enjoy taking the reins. If she could figure out who to ask... Maybe Eli? She'd get on that this after—

"You're fired."

The deep voice shocked her out of her romantic reverie. She shoved off the wall and spun toward the voice, knocking the shovel over in her haste. The handle snagged on the side of the stall trolley with a wood-to-plastic *thwack* that made her wince. But it failed to dislodge her heart where the stupid organ had welded itself to her larynx and wasn't giving up ground.

"We Covingtons run a tight ship, Ms. Malone. Daydreaming isn't allowed."

A slow, sensual smile on familiar lips made her knees weak.

Ty tipped the brim of his hat up, those mirth-filled dark eyes ringed with even darker lashes peering down at her. "Unless, of course, you were thinking of me. Then, I'll not only keep you, I'll see that you're promoted for exercising stellar judgment and exceptional taste."

She should have issued a witty reply, should have told him she didn't work for layabouts, should have said... something. Anything. But all she could focus on was the last sentence.

He'd keep me.

Throat inexplicably tight, she knew with the certainty that darkness always yielded to light that her grief had yielded to hope. Somewhere in the recent past, at a time she hadn't been wise enough to recognize, her heart had tipped the scales from "like" to "love" where this man was concerned. It changed nothing because he didn't know. Not yet. But for Kenzie?

It changed everything.

Ty watched Kenzie struggle through a string of emotions, her eyes darkening even as the color leached from her face only to come back in a rush, her cheeks flushed and rosy. Her eyes didn't lighten, though, and he wondered what had gone through her mind. Half of him wanted to ask while the other half shied away from anything powerful enough to steal the voice of such a straightforward woman.

"Why are you looking at me like that?"

"You came," she said. How she packed two simple words with so much weight he'd never understand.

"I did."

"I didn't think you would." She rubbed her nose and glanced away. "Not really."

"I wanted the answers you promised me."

Her shoulders sagged a bit. "Fair enough."

"You okay?"

"Fine," she said, the lie evident. She met his hard stare, but her gaze lacked the emotion that had filled it only moments before. "Great."

"Liar."

"Prove it."

"You promised to answer any question I asked if I hauled my bedbound backside down here. I did, so hold up your end of the bargain."

Her short bark of laughter could have shattered glass. "Sure. Let's get right to that."

"I'll ask again, Kenzie, and don't feed me some line of bull. Are you okay?"

"I've been better and I've been worse." She shifted her gaze to the stark white landscape, squinting as the sun reflected off the smooth surface of the snow. "This morning was full of surprises."

Michael.

He should have realized discussing her brother's loss would leave her a little raw. "Look, about that. I'm truly sorry."

She offered him a shallow smile. "Sure. Thanks."

Setting that aside because he wasn't sure what to do with it, he couldn't help but poke at her a little. "So which is it? Are you fired, or you moving up the food chain here at the Covington family dude ranch?"

She started to answer only to stop, clear her throat and start again. "Did you actually say, 'I'll not only keep you'?" she deadpanned. "With lines like that, it's a wonder you Covington men aren't single forever. 'I'll not only keep you…' Idiot."

He laughed, the sound stirring the horses and bringing large heads over stall doors. Except for Gizmo. Kenzie had left his stall open as she worked. Now the grullo stud nudged her aside as gently as a twelve-hundred-pound animal could and made straight for Ty.

He had dreaded this moment for months now, truly facing Gizmo again with nothing between them. Heart pounding brutishly and with no finesse whatsoever, Ty fought to ignore it all—the heart that beat too hard, the sweat itching between his temple and hat band, the giant animal he'd loved from birth, the way his neck ached a bit without his brace, the woman watching it all.

The horse stopped in front of him, those pale, long-lashed eyes considering Ty with wisdom far too vast for a horse. He nodded his head in short, slow movements, a silent demand of sorts.

Ty raised a trembling hand toward Gizmo.

The horse stepped into the touch. Dropping his head, Gizmo pressed his broad forehead into Ty's chest and let loose a sigh of heartrending contentment.

Ty swallowed repeatedly, trying to force down the emotion that flooded his throat, alternately squeezing it tight and filling it so full he couldn't breathe. His eyes burned. Damn if he'd cry, though. The only tears he'd shed over this whole thing had been shed in private, and he wasn't going public at this point. No way.

Instead, he gritted his teeth and raised both hands, resting one on each side of Gizmo's face. "Brought you something."

The horse didn't move.

He leaned in closer. "Candy."

Gizmo raised his head and then, without warning, reached out and pulled Ty's hat off his head. With a toss worthy of a California beach bum spinning a Frisbee out over the sand, the horse launched Ty's hat to the side before beginning to mouth the pocket on his shirt.

Ty felt it happen before he could control it. He burst out laughing. Digging out the Blow Pop, he unwrapped it, used his pocketknife to snip the stem and offered the confection to the horse.

Gizmo snatched it up, bit down and grunted, nostrils flaring. Flicking his tail, he chewed and chewed, the crunching unnaturally loud. Then the treat was gone and he was nosing at Ty with more intent.

"One more, you giant addict, but then I'm cutting you off." Ty pulled out a jumbo-size Tootsie Roll, unwrapped it and broke it into three pieces. He fed them to Gizmo one at a time.

As if he understood this was it, the horse savored these more, actually drooling as he chewed.

"I take it no one fed his sweet tooth," he said quietly, running his hands all over Gizmo's face and neck.

"That is…" Kenzie gestured to the horse and then to Ty. "He's addicted and you're his dealer. I mean, you realize that, right? And I *did* give him sweets, just not quite as many. I mean, sugar cubes and apples and—"

"Sugar cubes are child's play and apples don't count."

"I did the best I could." Her voice was stiffer than her spine, which was poised to shatter.

He realized then that she'd taken his teasing as criticism. That hit him harder than having stirred up her old grief. He needed to keep things light between them, needed to ease the pall that seemed to hover over her like a dark cloud. "Darlin', you know I'm yanking your chain." He glanced around. "So what was it you wanted my help with?"

She watched him closely, her gaze guarded. "You up for it?"

He wasn't about to admit he was wearing down, and fast. He needed to get the answers he'd come for. "Bring it on."

"I'll put these tools away. You get Gizmo back in his stall." She retrieved the pitchfork and tossed it into the little trolley.

"And then?"

"Then you're going to drop your drawers. The rest should be pretty self-explanatory."

Tyson stood stock still for a split second. "You going to inoculate me?"

She grinned, but the gesture was off. Her words, however, weren't. "Not exactly. But if you want to be patient to my nurse, that's fine with me."

Mouth dry, he struggled to issue the command that would direct Gizmo to return to his stall. Took two tries, but he managed.

"Hurry up, you giant slug," he whispered harshly. "Your buddy here has a date with a cowgirl-cum-nurse he hopes will be even half as naughty as she just sounded."

He shut the door behind the horse and latched it before slowly facing the interior of the room...and Kenzie heading toward him. The look on her face was impossible to interpret, divided as it was between forecasting personal injury and powerful pleasure. But when she caught him staring, she smoothed her features and blinked slowly as she licked her lips.

Something was clearly wrong. He wasn't sure what it was, wasn't sure she'd own it even if he pressed. The one thing he knew, could relate to, was the mind's desire to cede control of the issue to the body's ability to find a simpler solution. Whatever hurt she bore or anger she harbored would be soothed by this, this thing between them. And her reaction in this, her need for him, was the part of her he understood with startling clarity because her needs mirrored his—for touch, taste, companionship, comfort, home. *Each other.*

He reached for his belt buckle long before she was within arm's reach.

14

Kenzie grabbed the front of Ty's jacket and pulled him into her.

One more time, she silently pleaded. *Just give me one more time with him, and then I can live with the consequences.*

She would do her level best to control the moment, to give only enough of herself that Ty wouldn't realize what she felt for him. She would take as much as she could so she would have the memories to dole out to herself a bit at a time for the rest of her life. It would have to be enough because she had no alternatives. Not until Ty made his move anyway.

He pulled her into his arms on a self-satisfied sigh. "You're like an addiction, Mackenzie. One I can't seem to get enough of. I come down from the high you create to find I'm already craving my next hit." He pulled her even closer to his body so they were pressed thigh to thigh, belly to belly, chest to chest. "And I want you to hit me again."

Her laughter wasn't as light as she intended. "Never

ask a woman you've recently irritated to hit you, Tyson. Not without at least qualifying the request."

He pulled away and looked down at her. "I'll take whatever you dish out, woman. No complaints."

A hard shock coursed through her, head to toe, and she jerked in his embrace. *He doesn't mean that, has no idea what he's saying.*

Brow furrowing, he stared at her with undisguised confusion. "Problem?"

No answer would have sufficed. Instead, she tightened her grip on his jacket and ran her other hand into his hair before pulling him back to her. "You talk too much."

"Yeah?"

"Yeah."

"Then, shut me up," he whispered, the heat of his breath scalding her chilled skin.

A slight pull against his head and their lips met and their mouths fused, welded by the power of their passion.

Kenzie took what he offered and demanded more, taking his mouth with a proprietary sense for which she refused to apologize. She wanted as much of him as she could garner, as much as she could claim without scaring him. Was she selfish? Yes. But was the behavior necessary? Even more so.

Passion flared between them, the sound of his quickening breath and her hammering pulse drowning out all but the sharpest sounds. She experienced him without reservation, memorizing the smoky flavor of coffee on his tongue and the pinewood smell of soap saturating his skin. The well-worn flannel shirt beneath his jacket had pilled after so many washings and created a rough texture underneath her fingers. Almost panting, the sound of his desire escalated in her ears until she matched him breath for breath. Then his arousal punched at the zipper of his jeans, its heat juxtaposed with the cold shock of his large belt buckle.

Slipping her fingers under his waistband, her nails gently scraped the head of his erection.

His hips thrust forward, pushing more of him into her hand.

Smiling, she ended the kiss—for now—and backed across the barn. "Awfully anxious for a man who had sex less than two hours ago, aren't you?"

"You're responsible for this, Malone." The growled words were almost pained.

"Then, step it up, cowboy." She slid her fingers deeper into his boxer briefs. "Stop dragging your feet."

"Where are we going?"

She tilted her chin toward the tack room. "I'm about to show you a new way to ride."

His eyes nearly bugged out of his head and he lurched forward, all but knocking her over in his urgency to get them both through the doorway.

The door crashed open on the dimly lit room. Smells of leather and saddle soap, both familiar and comforting, saturated the room. Everything here was well organized. Saddles for the guests perched on numbered wall pegs while the larger saddles used by the Covingtons and the ranch's cowboys were all stored over oak barrels that had been mounted length-wise on short legs. Each saddle's stirrups and cinch were flipped over the seat. Bridles and reins were hung on shorter pegs, the name of the horse printed above the headstall. There were bits and pieces of leather as well as spare equipment parts in different bins. Buckets filled with currycombs, sweat scrapers, hoof picks, hoof oil and more lined the bare wood shelves. It looked like so many other tack rooms but still had the feel of the Covington place to it—organized but exuberant, profitable but still fun.

Kenzie intended to stick to the fun part, if nothing else.

Leaving Ty standing with his back pressed to the closed door, she located his saddle and wordlessly moved toward it.

"I can't ride." The croaked admission came from Ty with such little force the words almost didn't make it to her.

She spared him a quick glance before setting to work cinching the saddle to the barrel as tight as she could get it and adjusting the stirrups so his feet would clear the ground. "Everyone has to get back in the saddle sometime, baby."

"Kenzie, I…" He cocked his head and considered her actions. "I'm mounting a *barrel*?"

"Only so I can mount *you*," she said as casually as if she'd offered him the day's weather forecast.

Crossing to her, Ty paused at the saddle and considered it. When he didn't move any farther, she patted the tooled leather seat. "Nothing's changed about this in hundreds, even thousands of years. One leg up and over."

"Right. Because people ride barrels all the time." Though the words were liberally seasoned with humor, his eyes were solemn.

"Fine. We'll go about this backward, then." She turned the little space heater up and then locked the door. With a mocking sigh of despair, she shucked her boots and then shed her layered tops. The heater wasn't keeping up, and goose bumps broke out over her skin.

That didn't stop her, though. She stripped out of her jeans before stepping back into her boots. Rounding on Ty, she realized she'd never felt more cherished, more wanted than she did right then. And it was all due to the look of unadulterated hunger on his face. Hunger *she* had put there.

"Lose the boots and jeans, cowboy, and then park that fine ass of yours in the saddle, feet on the floor," she said, voice husky. "I'm not telling you again."

"You don't have to." He kicked his boots to the side, pulled his jeans and briefs off and crawled into the saddle. A little yip of shock escaped him when his bare butt hit the cold saddle leather. "I trust you're going to do something about this cold?" he said through clenched teeth.

It took her a moment to form an answer. All she could think was that he looked like every cowgirl's dream, sitting there with his cowboy hat tipped up, his flannel shirt pushed back over his hips and framing his arousal, that firm rear propped against the saddle's cantle, muscular legs flexing as he pressed the balls of his feet against the wood floor. He was the epitome of male beauty and the manifestation of feminine desire.

Moving through a haze of want, she let her feet carry her to him. She planted her hands on his chest and gently pushed.

It was a testament to his trust in her that he leaned back, never checking how far he'd have to go before he met security.

When his shoulders touched the wall, she drew a deep breath. "Hands on the skirt, grip the edges."

He followed her commands, gripping the leather skirt

on the saddle and curling his fingers into the fleecy underside.

"Lock your elbows." She waited for his compliance before issuing her last directive. "Don't let go until I tell you to."

"Bossy little thing," he murmured. Then he went silent, watching with wide eyes as she stuck one booted foot into the shortened stirrup and swung her opposite leg over the saddle—and his lap—to park that foot in the other stirrup.

She ended up in the saddle backward, facing him and straddling his lap. Bracing her hands on the wall, one on either side of his head, she leaned in to kiss him—small, teasing nips that drew groans of frustration and approval from Ty. Rolling her hips back and forth resulted in a delicious sexual tension as her sex rubbed over the underside of his shaft and drew even deeper sounds from him.

Kenzie deepened the kiss at the same time she managed to slide the tip of Ty's arousal home, slowing sinking down his length until she took him all the way to the hilt.

Ty let his head fall back with a shout. He reached for her, but she slapped his hands away.

"Hands on the skirt or this stops. Now."

He glared at her, dark eyes wild. "Don't drag this out."

"Impatient much?" she teased.

"Kenzie..."

She rose as high as she could without losing him, and leaving one hand on the wall and gripping his shoulder with the other, she took him in again. Moving with controlled grace, she rode him hard, leaning forward to whisper in his ear all the things she'd dreamed of doing with him, to him and for him since they'd been apart. She was graphic.

He obviously didn't mind.

She rode him harder as the wave of pleasure grew within her, taller and wider and so dense it blocked out all thought, all reason, all sensibility.

"Let me hear you, baby," he ground out, clearly fighting to hold out as long as he could.

That wave of pleasure crested, hung suspended for the briefest second before crashing down and dragging her under. He was her point of reference, her anchor, her true north in all matters of the heart. She hated him for it as much as she loved him.

And love him she did.

He followed her into the abyss, seemingly willing to drown with her.

She buried her face in his neck and mouthed the one thing she most needed him to know and most needed to hear in return. *I love you.*

That she couldn't say it aloud infuriated her. She was better than that.

Sitting up, she knew she had to tell him, even if for no other reason than he should hear it before they talked about where they'd gone wrong. He deserved the truth. She took a deep breath at the same time he reached out and ran two fingers down her throat and paused between her breasts.

He looked up, a sea of emotion churning in his gaze. "Kenzie, I… You need to know that I…"

She held her breath. If the Fates were fair in any way, he'd tell her first, would admit his heart was hers.

He glanced down, coughing to clear his throat. "I never thought this would be so hard."

"Go on," she encouraged.

He gave a short nod. "Sure." When he looked at her, the depth of his emotions hadn't changed, but the flavor had. "There are things I have to understand, questions only you can answer."

She all but fell out of the saddle, fighting not to run for her clothes.

Her heart sang him a love song; his couldn't even manage to hum the chorus in tune because he wasn't interested. Answers meant far more to him than anything else.

That was when she knew she'd never get what she needed most from him.

Love.

TY LEANED AGAINST the tack room wall, the rough wood of the planks snagging loose strands of hair as he sagged. It was cold in the little tack room, but it wasn't totally miserable thanks to the small portable heater they ran in the heart of winter to keep things from shrinking. He tilted his head back and grinned into the darkness of the high ceiling. The heater had done its job for him, too.

No shrinkage here.

He loosed a soft chuff of laughter. Even though the words were issued internally, he found the testosterone-fueled pride in them funny.

Glancing at Kenzie, he watched her gather her clothes, her back to him. No need to keep up appearances if she wasn't paying attention, so he leaned more heavily against the wall. Gravy, but he was worn out. He hadn't had this much sex *before* the injury. Not that he was complaining. No way. The reality that he wore down so quickly was just discouraging. For what seemed like the hundredth time this morning, he mentally slapped himself for letting his physical conditioning get so far away from him.

I totally pulled the tied-to-the-tracks damsel in distress routine. Crap. I hate it when she's right.

"What are you scowling at?"

Kenzie's rich, sexy-as-sin voice coiled around him. If voices were ranked for seductive powers, she'd be in the ninety-ninth percentile. It just didn't get better than her voice in the dark. He pulled a fleece saddle pad off the wall and settled it over his lap in an attempt to hide her effect on him. Miserable failure as far as the effort went.

She raised her brows in mock disbelief. "Eli's not old enough to be hunting down little blue pills, so where'd you get one?"

"I don't need one any more than he does." Indignation, thy name is wounded male pride.

"You certainly don't, but that?" She gestured to his reviving erection. "That's not normal. Not even for you."

He huffed out a short laugh. "What do you mean, not even for me?"

"Easy. You're a total hound. You've been without sex for more than two months and you obviously needed to burn off the excess drive. But seriously? Three times in as many hours?" She grabbed her jacket and stuck her hand first down one sleeve and then the other before emerging with her bra. "That's damned impressive for a twenty-six-year-old."

"You're not suggesting I'm too old to hold my own? And did you just pull your bra from your jacket sleeve?" He scrubbed a hand over his face. "I don't remember putting it there."

She chuckled, her hair hiding her expression as she

bent forward at the waist and hooked the band behind her with deft movements. "Long story, but I took it off before you got here."

"Why?"

"Like I said, long story." She slipped into her body shirt and then retrieved her flannel.

Then what she said hit him. Not the little bits and pieces. No, it was the core of her original statement. *You're a total hound. You've been without sex for more than two months and you obviously needed to burn off the excess drive.*

Did she really think so little of him? Worse, did she think what had happened between them was nothing more than a quick romp to burn off excess sexual energy? Something suspiciously akin to shame burned through him, and he didn't like it. At all. Tugging at his collar, he let his gaze roam the room. He tried to focus on the condition of the other cowboys' gear. He stared at the shelf with the hoof picks and short cans of hoof oil. He made a mental note to get more of the heavier oil on hand for the remainder of the winter. He considered the state of the room and the fact that it likely hadn't been cleaned out since before his accident. But his mind, for all he tried to avoid it, kept winging back to her statement.

Parking his feet in the stirrups, he grabbed the saddle horn and pulled himself upright. His back and neck ached. The muscles along his spinal cord objected to his repositioning, screaming and shaking in exhausted protest.

Whatever.

What she'd said, the assumption she'd made about them, reignited the fear he'd been harboring since she showed up in his room early this morning. Part of him knew he was being irrational. Things had always been casual before, so why wouldn't they be so now? But the other part of him, the part he rarely allowed to come out and play, was reeling at her dismissive attitude. Before he considered the consequences, before he weighed the pros and cons, he simply asked the thing he suddenly most wanted to know. "What's this about, this whole sexcapade, this morning and again now?"

She twitched as if she'd been bitten by a horsefly.

His stomach plummeted. "Mackenzie?"

Focusing her gaze anywhere but on him, she worked to hastily button her shirt.

"You missed the first one." That his proffered observation was so calm startled him. No, he'd never been one to lose his temper, to strike out when hurt. But this was a familiar hurt under unfamiliar circumstances. His mind swung open the doors of his past and suddenly he was four again and remembering his earliest experience with rejection. His father had refused to teach Ty to ride because he was too "flaky." The old man had insisted Ty keep his feet on the ground until his head was out of the clouds and he learned to be more practical where the animals were concerned. He'd deemed Ty's affection a weakness. He'd rejected Ty's love.

So Eli had taught him to ride. His old man had instead taught him not to overinvest in emotion that could be used against him.

He'd done just that, though, by letting Kenzie know how much Gizmo meant to him. He'd created and exposed his own Achilles' heel when he'd begun to wonder if there could be something more between him and the woman across from him.

And she'd used that weakness to her advantage. She'd exploited him when he was down and out. She'd positioned herself perfectly to get her hands on the only thing he'd guarded more carefully than his heart.

His horse.

It was a stupid thought to fixate on, but his mind dogged it like a border collie on a belligerent steer, herding it closer and closer until Ty remembered his dad's exact pitch and tone, his articulated disappointment in the dreamer Ty had been and the voiced expectation of Ty that really boiled down to his dad having no expectation at all. It had been the first time Ty had realized that who he was might not be good enough.

While his dad was long gone, he experienced the same realization now, that he wasn't good enough for this woman. His value came from what he possessed, not who he was.

Floorboards creaked as Kenzie shifted foot to foot, anxiety bleeding from her like a grievous wound.

"Answer me," he said quietly, all traces of the dreamer in him gone.

"Ty," she all but pleaded, her voice soft, wrecked even.

A world of hurt was delivered with that one word, one syllable. "You told me you'd answer my questions if I came down to the barn. I'm here. Hold up your end of the bargain, Malone."

Chewing on her lower lip, she silently wrapped her arms around her middle. Hands restless, she finally fisted her shirt's loose flannel, clutching it so tightly her knuckles bleached out. Still, she stared at the floor and refused to look at him.

The longer she stalled, the more frantic his imagination became in filling the silence until he couldn't take it anymore. His worst fear manifested itself in a burst of terror-driven accusation. "You don't want me. You're not here for *me* or my recovery and well-being. You're only here to protect whatever bullshit arrangement you crafted that would let you get your hands on Gizmo."

Her chin snapped up. Eyes wide, she spoke in a whispered rush. "I didn't talk you into anything."

"I might not remember the accident, Kenzie, but I *know* I didn't offer to partner with you." Chest heaving, muscles weak, he still forced himself to kick his feet free of the stirrups, swing a leg over the saddle and stand. He wouldn't square off with her sitting down like some invalid.

"You don't remember! There's no way you can be sure."

His stomach plummeted at her desperate attempt to turn this back on him. He wasn't having it. "I may not be sure, but you have no proof."

"I have my word."

"If you did what I think you did, your word's not worth anything anymore, Mackenzie."

"What are you getting at, Ty?" she choked out.

"Did you lie?" he demanded. When she didn't immediately answer, didn't offer a vehement denial, he thought he might be sick. Swallowing convulsively, he asked again. "Did. You. Lie?"

"Yes," she whispered.

"What?" The question exploded from him on a broken gasp. His heart plummeted. Unreliable thing that it was, the muscle-organ didn't bounce when it hit the inner heel of his left boot.

The damn thing shattered.

15

INSTINCT URGED KENZIE to salvage the situation, to explain why she'd done what she'd done, then make it right between them. One look at Ty's face, though, and she knew with absolute certainty that that was no longer an option.

Fury slowly bled over his countenance, replacing the raw, unadulterated shock of her initial admission.

She'd always intended to tell him the truth. Every day that passed had made it harder, though. Her realization only an hour before that she loved this man had totally thrown her and scattered her good intentions to the four corners. Understanding and despair collided in her and left her reeling, exposed and terrifyingly vulnerable. Worse, she'd been a fool, had never expected him to call her out like this, to use her promise to talk about Michael to garner an admission of guilt from her. "Ty, I—"

He sliced his hand through the air, cutting off her explanation. "Don't." Breathing so hard he was nearly panting, he gripped his shirt and yanked it away from his chest. "Just...don't."

She stepped closer, hand outstretched. "Are you having a panic attack?"

His movements were almost spastic, uncoordinated even, as he pushed off the wall and shuffled toward the barred tack room door. Shoving things out of the way with total disregard, he wrenched the door open and gasped, breath condensing on the rush of cold air. "You don't need to pretend anymore."

Her mind slowed, comprehension warped by the tendrils of panic spreading through her. "Pretend?"

"I get it, Kenzie. Your dad's been after me for more than two years, trying to get me to stud Gizmo out to the Malone Quarter horse empire." He barked out a bitter laugh, and she recoiled. "You know, I just realized that's about the same time you showed up in my life." He shot her a hard look. "Was that what this was all along? An attempt to get me to fall for you so I would sell Gizmo's baby batter to you? Because you realized you couldn't beat me in genetics otherwise?"

Kenzie stood still as death while inside she figured she more closely resembled a crash-test dummy—arms akimbo, head at an odd angle, one foot twisted the wrong way. She should answer him. She knew that. Yet words eluded her, refusing to coalesce into any semblance of coherent thought. Her mind was a landfill of expired good intentions and discarded hope. So she stood there, silent, and bore the wrath of the man she would have done anything for—had done *everything* for—cringing when his smile grew brittle, hard but breakable.

"I think the worst part of this is that you used my memory loss to your advantage to gain the thing you wanted most from me. *Gizmo*." He spat the horse's name like a vile curse. "He's all that mattered to you. And the second you saw an opening, you took him under the guise of a false partnership."

"I saved him," she objected.

"You saved him so you could use him," Ty countered.

"I did what—"

"What you wanted, Mackenzie," he shouted.

"What you asked me to do!"

His grin was colder than the wind chill at the peak of the Sangre de Cristo Mountains. "See? I can't dispute that because *I don't remember*." His voice had been cold, but his eyes suddenly became glacial. "And that's why you brought Indie, isn't it? You intended to breed her to Gizmo while proximity wasn't an issue. Nice, Kenzie. Real nice."

She met that desolate gaze head-on. "No." After months away with Gizmo, she'd simply wanted her horse's company. She'd needed to be able to ride when she wanted to and without asking for the equine equivalent of a Hertz rental car. But her response didn't matter. All Ty was willing to see was the worst possible interpretation of what she'd done and why.

Jaw knotted, skin pale and lips almost nonexistent in his face, Ty stared at her, unblinking. "I want you to pack whatever's in that cabin, get your gear and your horse out of my barn and get off my land before I call the sheriff."

Kenzie straightened at the threat. "And just what are you going to report, Ty? That the woman you've been sleeping with off and on for years spent over one hundred thousand dollars on you and your horse, and she screwed you senseless this morning?"

One corner of his mouth curled up, the expression uncharacteristically cruel. "No. I'm just going to report she screwed me."

She'd expected heartbreak to sound like a gunshot. It

didn't. There was a very quiet internal fracture, a tiny gasp. Then came the onslaught of pain, an emotional riptide that pulled her under. It stole her breath. It darkened her vision. It wrapped tentacles around her chest and bore down. It hurt more than anything ever had.

"Get off my ranch, Mackenzie, and don't come back." No steadier than the town's resident drunk on a weekend binge, Ty stumbled out of the tack room and out of the barn.

By the time Ty made it to the house, the fear of falling had surpassed "probability" and moved straight to "inevitability." That was why he didn't shout when he collapsed in the foyer. He couldn't *sit* up, couldn't *get* up, so he simply lay there and fought to catch his breath.

The door opened, exposing his clammy skin to a blast of outside air. He shivered, silently fighting through the additional discomfort it caused. Screw that. It hurt. *He* hurt. All over. He rested his forehead against the hardwood floor and groaned.

"What the…" Cade's large hands ran over his back and arms, searching for injury. "Talk to me, Tyson," he ordered, voice gruff. "Tell me what happened."

"Life. And don't go soft on me. Not now." Using arms and legs weaker than a newborn foal's, he fought to roll himself over. Cade tried to help, but Ty uttered a sound suspiciously growl-like, and the larger man backed off. "I'm not a freaking damsel," Ty said through gritted teeth.

"Damsel?" Cade said, confused. "I'm at a loss here, man. What does a damsel, or being one, have to do with you being sprawled out on the floor?"

Irony, you're a real bitch. "Everything. And nothing." If it wasn't so painfully true, he'd have laughed. If only…

Using the last of his reserve, Ty managed to roll over.

Cade tried to help him sit up, but Eli chose that moment to open the door. Caught unprepared, Cade was shoved forward. Ty had to give credit where credit was due, though. His older brother managed to throw himself clear of Ty's semiprone form, presumably in an attempt to keep from crushing him.

"What are you two pony jockeys doing crouched in front of the door?" Eli demanded absently as he dumped his wet boots into the boot tray.

Ty cradled his face in his palms and batted his eyes at his eldest brother. "Oh, you know. Hanging out. Discussing fashion trends and the latest *E! News* gossip. We were going to use the living room, but furniture is so passé. It's all about casual living now."

"Smart-ass." Eli looked Ty over. "You fall?" he asked quietly.

"Flat on my face."

"Break anything?"

My heart. "No."

Eli offered Cade a hand and then the pair turned to him. "Let's get you up, then."

As a unit, they worked to help him to his feet and continued to support him until they made it to his room and perched him on the side of the bed.

Cade pulled Ty's boots off and Eli helped him get laid down on the bed. Ty ignored the soft scent of perfume on the sheets.

Kenzie.

Ty struggled to sit up. "I need to change my bed before I lie down."

"You're worn out, Ty. Leave it for now," Eli answered. "We'll handle the sheets later, when you're up to it."

He couldn't stand it. "I want the sheets changed. Now."

Eli faced him with slow deliberation and arched one brow. "Do I look like Cinderella?"

Anxiety rose within him. Fighting to draw a slow breath, to calm himself down, Ty considered his options. He didn't want to admit that the smell of her would make him crazy, didn't want to own the fallout, the fact that he'd been had. Lying here with her scent surrounding him, though? Totally worse.

Chucking pride aside, he looked first at Cade and then Eli. "Mackenzie Malone lied." That was, apparently, all it took to free the words he'd held in check. He dumped the whole story at his brothers' feet, starting with how he'd first met Kenzie and ending with him walking away from her less than an hour ago. Nothing was left out. Nothing was off-limits.

When he finally finished, Cade and Eli were quiet. He didn't understand. He hadn't expected them to grab their ropes and scout the tallest tree for a hanging, but neither had he expected them to hold their opinions to themselves. They were all opinionated. Always had been. Rule of thumb said they were also brutally honest with one another under every circumstance. Nope, he didn't get their silence at all.

"She lied. She admitted it." He rubbed at the crease between his eyebrows. "So why do I suddenly feel like a total dick?" Shifting around in bed, he adjusted his pillows and looked first at one brother and then the other. The way they both avoided eye contact sent up his internal "shark in the water" flag. "What did you guys do?" No answer. He pushed himself higher up his headboard. "One of you will tell me or I'm calling the women in."

"No need for that," Cade said, sinking to a crouch beside the bed.

Ty rustled up a teasing smile. "Chickenshit. Emma's a total softy."

His older brother quirked a brow, the gesture speaking volumes even though all the man himself said was "Keep telling yourself that, little brother."

Eli pulled up the room's only chair, dropping into it as though he bore the weight of the world on his shoulders. He still wouldn't look at Ty.

The action, or inaction, seasoned his brothers' hesitation with discomfort and flavored it further with guilt. He was about to call them both on it and demand answers when Cade finally broke the silence.

"You have to understand, Ty, that we thought we were going to lose you, first physically—" he reached up and pinched his upper lip hard enough to turn it red "—and then emotionally." Blue eyes met Ty's brown ones. "You checked out on us after you came home. None of us in this house were willing to risk losing you, either physically or mentally."

Ty stared at the other man. "When you did you go all Dr. Phil on me?"

Cade didn't bat an eye when he answered, "When it seemed to all of us that you'd stopped caring whether you lived or died."

He flinched. "Well, that was about as subtle as a kick in the nuts."

Cade exploded off the floor, at eye level one minute and in Ty's face the next. "You want subtle, discuss the nuances of fine wine with Emma. From me you get the hard truth, little brother." He grabbed Ty by the front of the shirt. "There's not one of us who wouldn't have done worse than we've done if it meant saving your sorry ass when you were too broken to do it yourself."

Blood rushed through Ty's head at a frenzied rate, the swooshing white noise so powerful it almost drowned out the sound of his voice in his head. "What have you done?"

Cade looked over at their eldest brother.

"Answer me," Ty shouted, startling the two men and bringing Emma racing into the room.

"What happened?" she demanded, breathless. Her gaze traveled the room and came to rest on Cade's ruddy complexion. "You told him."

Ty zeroed in on his future sister-in-law. "They haven't told me anything."

She joined the rank and file, fixing her gaze anywhere but on him.

"Emma. Please." He didn't remotely regret the pleading in his voice. Every second that passed left him feeling sicker, more certain he'd somehow committed the worst mistake of his life.

Emma moved to stand by the side of the bed, edging Cade out of the way and, at the same time, placing herself between Ty and Eli. "Get out."

"This is between us, Emma." Eli's admonishment was soft yet firm.

"I would have respected your position if you'd admitted everything when you and Cade first concocted the idiotic plan. But you didn't. Now you're refusing to tell him what you've done because you don't have the guts to own your mistake."

"I would've thought you'd have learned from that," Reagan said from the doorway.

"I did." Eli stood and faced his wife. "He's my baby brother, Reagan."

"He's a *grown man*, Eli. You and Cade have to stop trying to keep life from happening to him." The brunette closed the distance to her husband. "I'm with Emma on this. Get out."

Cade crossed his arms over his chest. "What are you going to do?"

"What you two should have done from the beginning," Emma answered. "Give him the truth." Cade opened his mouth, no doubt to argue, and Ty watched Emma shut the big man down with a single look. "If you'd owned this before, I'd have kept out of it. You didn't, which means Reagan and I are going to clean up the mess you two have made. We don't need your help—"

"Or your blessing," Reagan added.

"To do it," Emma finished with a nod to the other woman. "Respect me on this, Cade. I told you that you and Eli were wrong to try to manipulate Kenzie."

Ty forced himself to sit up. "Come again?"

"Out. Now," Reagan said, her tone brooking no argument, and yet it was compassionate for all that.

His older brothers left the room. Eli was pulling the door closed behind him when he paused. Staring at the floor for a moment, he seemed to need to work up the courage to face Ty. When their eyes met, Ty's breath seized in his chest at the sheer remorse on Eli's face. "I'll ask you to remember one thing. We did this because we weren't willing to lose you. Nothing, *nothing*, is worth that."

Then he closed the door.

Side by side, the women Ty loved like family faced

him. And what they told him upended everything he thought he knew.

But he'd been right about one thing.

He was a total dick.

16

BETWEEN WHITE-KNUCKLED driving conditions, pulling a trailer over snow-packed roads, changing a flat tire halfway home and trying to figure out how to break the truth to her dad, Kenzie was ready to drop long before she saw the sign announcing that Cheyenne Wells, Colorado, was seventeen miles ahead. She took the next exit, crossed under the Malone gate and began the last leg of her journey home. Winding her way across the ranch, she let herself take in the sweeping grassland and strong five-wire fences that ran to the moonlit horizon. It was a good thirty minutes of dirt roads, muddy potholes and creative curse words before the mare barn came into view.

Parking out front, she rested her forehead on the steering wheel, the only sound that of the engine ticking as it cooled. Eyelids heavy, she may have passed out for a minute before jerking upright at the rap of knuckles on the driver's-side window.

She powered the glass down with a touch before shutting the engine off. "Hey, Andy. You're up late."

"Could say the same for you."

She couldn't stifle the jaw-cracking yawn, only nodding in response.

The weathered cowboy leaned back and made a show of examining her truck and trailer. "Looks as if you drove through every snowdrift and salt spill you could find."

"They treated the roads pretty heavily for ice so it wasn't too... You know, I was going to say it wasn't too bad, but that's a bald-faced lie." And she was done with those. For good. Even if it hurt, it was the truth or nothing from now on.

Opening the door, she hopped down from the cab. "The salt needs rinsed off, but it'll have to wait until tomorrow."

"That's a first."

"What's that?" she absently asked.

"You puttin' off caring for your precious truck." He shook his head and grinned. "You two ought to write your love story down for future truck owners, Mackenzie. I'm stuck in a mediocre relationship with mine, and you give me hope I might just find 'the one' if I keep searchin'."

She felt the color leave her cheeks. Such a profound statement given what she'd left behind earlier today.

Roll with it, Malone.

Dredging up the last of her emotional reserves, she managed a small smile. "Funny guy."

"Suppose only a fool gives up hope, though, huh?" Andy slapped the halter lead he held against his leg. "Came out to check on Bean's labor."

Impossible as it seemed, Kenzie perked up. "Bean's foaling?"

"Said so, didn't I?" Andy glanced over his shoulder. "The Malone's in there with her now."

Her knees simply folded and she went to the ground.

Andy dropped the lead and went to one knee beside her. "Malone," he called, low but strong.

"No," she croaked. "Don't call him."

"Too late." The cowboy stood and slipped into the darkness at the same time Jack Malone appeared.

Her dad sank to a crouch beside her, running his hands down her arms. "What's hurt, baby?"

My heart. "Nothing." *I'm bleeding out.* "I'm fine, Dad."

"You're sitting on the ground, your skin's the color of chalk dust and corral slop is soaking into your jeans. And from the sounds of it, your horse is protesting being left in the trailer." He reached out and gently removed her hat. "Talk to me, Mac."

The use of her nickname made her throat tighten. It was the name Michael had bestowed on her when he'd found out their mom had dared deliver him a sister instead of the brother he'd requested. Michael had refused to call her "a girl name," and Mac had stuck.

"I'll get your mother." Her father made to stand.

"No," she all but shouted as she reached out and grabbed his arm. A single tug pulled him off balance and down he went, landing with a squelching sound on the ground beside her. "Please."

The look of surprise on the infamous Malone's face eased the tension in her, but not as much as his comment did. "You're going to be the one to tell your mother later why I had to go—what's it called when you don't wear underwear beneath your britches? Commandeering? Soldiering?" His face brightened. "Going mercenary!"

She laughed as heat infused her cheeks. "You have to stop with the modern slang, Dad. It's called going commando, and no, I don't want to tell her why you're going to shuck your underwear in the barn."

He reached over and yanked on a piece of her hair. "You just landed me on my ass in the muck, kiddo. It's soaked through my Wranglers and my unmentionables are now soggy. I'm ditching 'em as soon as I can. I think there's a pair of clean coveralls in the barn I can pull on."

She plugged her fingers into her ears and began to chant, "La, la, la, la." Then she met his amused gaze. "I'm not pulling my fingers out of my ears until your lips stop moving."

He grinned.

She dropped her hands. "I'm ruined. You realize that, right? No daughter needs to know these things. As far as I'm concerned, you and Mom are Ken and Barbie."

"I don't get it."

"You have no defining—" she blushed furiously and waved her hands about "—*parts*, Dad. *Parts*."

His booming laughter was answered with coyote chatter, their yips and barks carrying across the night breeze from who knew how far away. Wiping away tears, her dad grinned down at her. "Ken and Barbie. Does that make you… What was that teenage kid's name?"

"Don't," she said, smiling. "Don't even try to remember Skipper's name, Dad. You'll ruin childhood memories by renaming her something like Petunia."

"Fair." He reached out and tucked a loose strand of hair behind Kenzie's ear. "You never were much for dolls."

"They weren't—"

"Horses. I know." His smile was wistful.

She suddenly felt as if she were five again and the world, *her* world, was centered right here on Malone land. Leaning over, she rested her head on her father's shoulder. "I needed that, Dad. Thanks."

"What's going on, baby girl? Talk to me."

"What makes you so sure anything's going on?" She was stalling, but she couldn't help it.

"Don't bullshit a bullshitter, honey."

She nodded, fighting the wave of nausea that rose up her throat. "I want to..." Resting a hand on her chest, she forced herself to meet her dad's open gaze. "I should to talk to you before I see Mom."

"Sure." He whistled and Andy reappeared. "Do me a favor and walk Kenzie's mare out and then put her up."

"Sure, boss." Andy moved with bowlegged agility, unloading the horse and moving away with her before Kenzie could summon an effective protest.

Jack Malone turned to her. "So spill."

She sucked in a breath and held it to a slow count of ten before letting it rush out on a harsh exhale. Every cell in her body was screaming at her to flee, seeming to understand this was a fight she'd never be able to win. Fighting down the urge, she rose, moved to the wooden corral fence and scrambled up to the top rail, where she perched, waiting for him to join her.

Her dad followed, standing in front of her with a suspicious look on his face. Crossing his arms over his chest and widening his stance, he took two deep breaths and schooled his features. "Go on, then."

If she was going to deal in hard truths, she might as well start with him. She'd spent her whole life trying to please this man, but never more so than over the past decade. Not once had she felt she'd succeeded. What she had to tell him now would irrevocably cement her sense of failure. She'd survived a lot of crap over the years, but she wasn't sure she could survive this.

Her dad considered her, then closed the distance between them. Reaching out, he gently took her hand and cradled it in his own. "You know there's nothing you can say or do that will make me stop loving you, Mac, so out with it. What's been eating at you?"

"I lied to you." *Nice finesse, Malone. Nothing like hurling it at him via fast-pitch.* The truth hung there, suspended in flight. It had been offered and, apparently, received, and neither sender nor recipient was sure what to do with it.

He finally offered a short nod. "Okay. About what?"

She'd known from the moment she got into her truck and headed home twelve hours ago that she would have to tell him everything or nothing. There would be no CliffsNotes version.

"You won't stop loving me." A declarative question if ever there was one.

"There's nothing in the world that could make me stop loving you, Mac."

Then, everything it is.

Decision made and reassurances offered, there was no point in stalling. So she didn't. Starting with the admission that she and Ty had been lovers, she ran through the entire course of events, wrapping up with the details involved in her long trip home.

There was only one topic she didn't address: the fact that she'd fallen in love. That in the midst of the continual heartache involved in healing physical wounds and the terror of learning to recognize her true self, she'd fallen in love with Tyson Covington.

There would be fallout from her actions and the choice to keep this one fact to herself. It was one of life's simple truths—cause and effect. A Japanese man had even created a kind of chart—an Ishikawa diagram—to make results traceable and repeatable and to identify weak points. Whoever Ishikawa had been, he'd no doubt have a heyday with her psyche. She was so messed up she probably would have broken the initial diagram. Hell, she'd probably have broken the theory *behind* the diagram. Whatever. All she wanted right then was her dad's reassurance that it was all going to be okay.

The longer she waited, the longer she stared at Jack Malone's neutral countenance, the more her internal panic levels escalated. They were fast approaching DEFCON Total Emotional Annihilation when he finally spoke.

"Why lie, Mac? I was proud of you for doing the right thing for the right reasons—helping someone in need, helping someone who couldn't take control of a horrifying event." He parked his fists on his hips before exhaling through his teeth. Staring at a point on the ground somewhere between them, he quietly asked, "Why lie about any of this?"

Mackenzie nearly came out of her skin when the answer came from behind her.

"Love makes a woman do crazy things." Stella Malone, Kenzie's mother, stepped out of the shadows, climbing the fence to sit next to her daughter. A look of contrition decorated the older woman's face, emphasizing the fine lines that good makeup and bright smiles usually hid.

Kenzie glanced between her mom and dad, confused. "When did you come down from the house?"

Stella's shoulders rose and fell with feminine grace. "When I heard your father laughing. He rarely laughs like that. I wanted to know what was happening and be part of it." She reached out and took Kenzie's grimy hand. "Appears I got here a little late."

"I'm glad you came," Kenzie managed before the first fat tear broke over her lower lashes. She rubbed at it with undiluted aggression. "I'm so sick of crying over this. It seems as if that's all I've done all day." She drew a shaky breath and, clutching her mom's hand, forced herself to lift her face to her father's. "I'm so incredibly sorry, Dad. I didn't mean to do anything more than secure the right to save Gizmo like Ty asked me to do. I know what it's like to lose your hope." Her voice broke, and she had to clear her throat before continuing, "I didn't want that for Ty. Beyond that, I don't have any excuse for my behavior."

Her dad simply stood there, his chin tucked to his chest, refusing to meet her eyes. When he spoke, his voice had dropped two solid octaves and gone gravelly. "Do you love him, Mackenzie?"

"Does it matter?" The question could have been rhetorical. It wasn't. And her parents knew it.

"Get on up to the house and get cleaned up. I want you to stay with us for a few days." Spinning on his heel, he started for the barn.

Her mother's hand tightened around hers.

"Does it matter?" Kenzie asked again, louder this time.

Jack Malone answered without slowing, without turning around. "It changes everything."

THE SUN WAS going to melt Ty's brain. That or it would cause the useless gray matter to spontaneously combust given the level of alcohol he had consumed last night. He rarely drank and never to excess, but last night had been his major exception. There was no doubt he'd come close to pickling his organs.

A pitiful groan sounded from somewhere near the foot of the bed.

Ty stretched one leg and was met with a flexible but solid object.

The toe punt resulted in a muffled, "Ow. Quit it." Bedding rustled. "Man, you have the bluntest toes. They're like little battering rams."

Ty blinked slowly, forcing his eyes to adjust until he managed to squint in the face of certain death. His mouth was so full of cotton he expected he could have spun yarn straight out of it.

At least then I'd do something useful with my piehole.

"What happened?" a different, deeper voice asked.

Cade.

Ty lifted his head, shocked at the volume the drumming between his ears immediately escalated to. *Wow*, he mouthed, gripping his temples. "Shh." At the hissed command, the invisible musicians banged harder on their drums.

If they were within reach, he'd pinch their little heads off.

Bastards.

As if it were their fault.

Why am I thinking of them as sentient beings?

Refocusing, he realized Eli had crashed along the foot of the bed while Ty had ended up crossways. He rolled over, and the entire room pitched. He slammed his eyelids closed, gripped the edge of the mattress and swallowed repeatedly. Bravery didn't return to him for several minutes. He hated throwing up.

When the worst of the spinning nausea passed, he chanced a peek through half-slit lids to find Cade curled up on the floor. The larger man had fallen asleep again, but he wouldn't stay that way. Sunlight crept across the floor with every progressive tick of the clock's hand. In less than half an hour, Cade would be hit full in the face with the morning sun.

Ty squinted harder. "At least I won't suffer alone."

The aroma of fresh-brewed coffee crept through the room.

He groaned his appreciation.

His brothers responded in kind.

He tried to grin but his face almost broke, and the drummers in his head went wild.

"Rise and shi— Hell's bells, boys." Reagan sounded choked. "It smells like a bar down here."

A booted foot crunched over what he assumed were peanut hulls, adding a thundering bass line to the chorus in his head.

"What did you three do last night?" she demanded.

Ty threw an arm over his face and mumbled, "Tried to figure out women. Apparently the answer does *not* lie at the bottom of a bourbon bottle. Who knew?"

Eli must have moved because the mattress shifted. "No shouting. Have a little respect for the dead."

A soft feminine cough preceded a second woman's voice. *Emma.* "Cade?"

"What Eli said. Dead. No shouting."

Emma laughed softly. "You know, I figured you'd cut yourself off before it got this bad."

"Would have, but there's apparently a man code. I got my card last night," he answered, a little pride woven through the evident misery.

Ty blindly held out a hand. "I'm not married to you or getting married to you, so I get coffee first."

"Why?" Eli groused, sitting up and cradling his head with a pained look.

"Because you, my brothers, are going to get feminine sympathy. I'm going to get—"

"Your ass kicked," said a stern male voice he didn't recognize.

His brothers staggered to their feet and put themselves between him and the door.

Always with the saving me. Kenzie was right. I'm the freaking damsel of the Covington clan.

The thought of her ripped the painful wound of the truth open all over again. He'd drunk to forget. Apparently, "amnesia in a bottle" was temporary and not only caused physical hangovers but provided a sustainable fuel source for emotional ones.

Gripping the iron headboard for support, he rose to his feet. One look at the man in the doorway was all he needed to realize the shit storm that was about to rain down on him. "Good morning, Mr. Malone."

17

THERE HAD BEEN heated words, shouted accusations and one very creative threat involving an electric cattle prod that left Ty fighting the urge to look behind him with every step away from the house he took. Total chaos had ruled for several minutes until Reagan had loosed a sharp whistle that had nearly rendered Ty and his brothers deaf, mute and blind as their skulls shattered.

Jack Malone had scoffed at the three of them. "For your sake, I hope you don't always expect to find the solution to your problems in the bottom of a bottle." With that, he'd spun on his heel and started down the hall, heading for the front door. He'd paused there, gripping the doorknob. "Get yourself cleaned up and meet me in the barn, Covington."

"You ask for one, you're going to get all three of us," Cade had responded, the low, slow words as clear a threat as if he'd handed the older man a formal challenge.

"I don't do threats, young man. You should remember that." He'd stepped into the brilliantly clear, brutally cold day. "I'll deal with Tyson alone or not at all." It would have made sense for him to slam the door. That he'd shut it with controlled care expressed his anger far more effectively.

"Crap." Ty sank to the edge of the bed. "I'm not up for this."

"It's my fault." Eli sat next to him and leaned forward, resting his elbows on his knees and his forehead in his hands. "I'll deal with him."

"No."

They all peered up at Emma.

"This is Ty's mess." She'd glanced at each of them in turn, her gaze coming to rest on him as compassion paired with the hidden hard-ass in her. "I love you, but it's time you started cleaning up after yourself."

"Told you," Cade muttered, the corners of his mouth twitching.

Ty rose again, forcing himself to stand without hanging on to anything...or anyone. "You're right." He glanced around the room. "Anyone interested in checking out my junk when I get dressed should stay. Everyone else? Out. I'll deal with this."

And that was where he was now—headed to the barn to find out what particular pound of flesh Jack Malone had come for.

The snow had been cleared between the house and the barn, but the downhill trip still proved exhausting. Getting home was going to suck. Picking his way into the big building with careful steps, Ty was forced to remove his sunglasses to peer through the barn's dim interior. "Mr. Malone?"

The man stepped out of Gizmo's stall. "Wanted to see what my daughter's money paid for. Appears it was to save a fine horse and an irresponsible man. Seems that would give her fifty-fifty odds of making sound financial decisions with her inheritance in the future, wouldn't you say?" He didn't wait for an answer, instead turning his back on Ty dismissively as he shut Gizmo's stall door and continued to look over the horse. "He's a beautiful specimen."

"He's not a 'specimen.'" Ty knew Malone was provoking him, knew better than to let the man get to him. But that he'd basically reduced Gizmo to nothing more than a sperm factory really pissed Ty off. "'Specimens' are found in petri dishes, Mr. Malone. Gizmo is both my companion and business partner. He's also going to provide the next big genetics push for the breed." Ty tilted his Stetson back and crossed his arms over his chest. "You're well aware of that or you wouldn't have been working so hard to breed three of your mares to him."

"That's fair." Malone shifted and propped an elbow on the stall door. "But let's be honest, Mr. Covington. You'd have to sign over exclusive breeding rights to the Malone ranch if you ever thought to reimburse my daughter for the financial investment she made in you and your 'business partner.'"

Ty's stomach hit the dirt and started digging, because apparently ground level wasn't sufficient for how far his stomach intended to fall. "I want to be clear here, Mr. Malone. I always intended to pay her back, with interest, for the investment she made in me and my horse."

The infamous rodeo cowboy pushed off the door and strode across the hitching area toward Ty, his steps sure, his temper brewing. "Damn skippy, you will."

"The dude ranch is mortgaged, but we're realizing a healthy profit. While I can't repay her in a lump sum, I'm willing to—"

"Shut up." Malone stopped inches from him, but they

were still effectively toe-to-toe. "You want to know what this cost her? I mean *truly* cost her?"

"She gave me the figures, Mr. Malone."

The older man snorted and shook his head, yanking his hat off. Malone tilted his chin back and stared at the ceiling for so long that Ty looked up, too, just to see what he was staring at.

Turned out it was nothing and everything—nothing visible, everything intangible.

"She told you about her brother." Jack Malone's words were half statement, half accusation.

"She did."

"Did she tell you she was the first one to reach him after he and his horse went down?"

A whole new level of understanding hit Ty like a sucker punch to the solar plexus. Clearly, she'd withheld a few critical details from her description of that day.

"I didn't think so," Malone said quietly. "She was thirteen, Mr. Covington. She was thirteen and worshipped her older brother with every cell in her little body." He ran a hand around the back of his neck, the ropy muscles in his forearm tightening as he lowered his chin and glanced at Gizmo again. "I'm going to assume she also left out the part where she tried to perform CPR on Michael and how we had to pry her off him to let the medic get to my son."

"No, sir. She didn't share any of that."

"She wouldn't have."

"May I ask why?"

Malone spared him a short look before shifting so he faced the open barn door. His face had drawn tight, his lips thinning into an almost invisible line. "She witnessed Michael's accident, just like she did yours. She watched Michael draw his last breath, Mr. Covington." He faced Ty then. "Just like she did with you."

The world fell out from under Ty. There one moment, and simply gone the next. He'd known—*known*—that his heart had failed, that he'd stopped breathing. He hadn't told anyone for fear they wouldn't believe him.

But she'd witnessed the whole thing.

His vision blurred like a snowy TV screen, and Ty found himself sitting on the ground and being supported by the very man who'd put him there. Granted, it had been with words—*truth*—but he was there all the same.

"She thought she'd lost you, Tyson." Malone spoke so softly that his words were almost swallowed by the open space in the cavernous barn.

Almost. But not quite.

"She told me she screamed for you. They tried to get her to leave your side, and the only way they'd let her stay was if you were tied together somehow. She knew how much you avoided relationships. She chose the lesser of what she considered the two evils as you'd see them—a business partnership. Then you were breathing again, and you pleaded with her to do whatever was necessary to save your horse. She took you at your word, spun a few yarns and did exactly as you asked. And what did you do?" he asked, voice rising. "You emotionally brutalized her, you jackass! You cast her out!"

Ty choked on the wad of emotions trying to make their way out of his mouth. There were a hundred, a thousand things to say. None of them were for this man, though. He needed to speak to Kenzie. No. Not just speak to her. He needed to see her. There were things he had to say. Some of them he didn't understand completely, but he'd figure it out on the way.

Feet on the ground, he leaned forward and propped his forearms on his bent knees. His chin dipped forward. To hell with worrying about pulling on his neck. Her reality was bigger than his fear.

He'd never thanked her. Not really.

Malone must have felt he'd given Ty long enough to process his words because the man pressed on. "She lied, Tyson, but it was for good reason."

"My brothers explained a lot of this. Apparently Eli and Cade decided to offer her breeding rights to Gizmo if she helped me." He looked up then, an unhappy smile pulling at his mouth. "I wasn't the best patient."

"So I heard."

Ty chuffed out a sardonic laugh. "I'm willing to bet she downplayed just how horrible I was." His smile softened. "That's how she is."

"True." Malone sank to the ground beside Ty. The other man's face relaxed a fraction. "You understand she turned them down, your brothers and their offer."

Shame burned his cheeks. "I do."

"Fair enough." The older man looked out over the corrals outside the barn, where several guests were getting ready for a trail ride. He watched them without speaking, seeming to use their activity to distract him as he gathered his thoughts.

Ty was willing to wait. He had enough to think about himself.

He'd accused Kenzie of some horrible things, had taken her money with unintentional disregard to her perpetual worry that it was her money people valued over her.

If he could turn back time, he'd assure her that it was *her* he wanted access to, not her checkbook.

Access.

That was really what he'd wanted, what he'd taken for granted. She'd always been there when he wanted her, and it had been more often than not. He'd chafed when she was involved with someone else, blaming it on his temper. But he'd missed that cue, too.

"I'm an idiot," he whispered, shock bleeding through him in a cold rush.

He hadn't been angry.

He'd been *jealous*.

Just as he opened his mouth to explain to The Malone that he needed to call Kenzie, now and not later, the man spoke. Tone quiet and firm, he kept his focus on the ranch guests clambering into borrowed saddles on borrowed horses and having the best time doing it. "Do you understand *why* she couldn't leave your side, why she would have lied, cheated, stolen or worse to ensure she had a place there?"

Ty started to answer, but Malone shook his head. "Think before you answer. Really think, Tyson."

He rubbed his belly in an attempt to soothe his roiling gut. "She felt as if she could make it up to her brother for not being able to save him."

Malone sighed. "You're as big an idiot as I feared." Shifting around to face Ty, he met and held his gaze. "There's no do-over where Michael is concerned. There's no 'making it up to her brother.' Her choices, all of them, were for you."

Kenzie has his eyes.

It was all he could think. Well, that and the fact that he missed the hell out of her. She'd been gone twenty-four hours and he wanted her back. Here. With him. If it meant dealing with her overprotective old man in order to get to her, he'd do it. He was going to find a way to pay her back every penny she'd spent plus interest. He wanted, *needed* her to know this had never been about money, that his wanting her here wasn't to secure his financial future. Sure, he was and would always be grateful she'd saved Gizmo's life, but he hadn't asked her to because of the balance in her bank account. He had asked her because he trusted her to do what was necessary, to protect the one thing that meant something to him. *Gizmo.* But that equation was no longer accurate. Over the years, that one thing had become two.

He had his horse.

But now he wanted her.

Shock made him drop his arms. His jaw followed of its own accord.

He'd never wanted a woman in his space. He'd never wanted a woman in his home. He'd never…taken a woman in his own bed. No. Not *a* woman. *The* woman.

It had taken him years, a near tragic event and a painful recovery to realize what this woman meant to him.

He loved Mackenzie Malone.

The Malone was right. He was an idiot.

Seeing recognition set in, Kenzie's dad nodded. "Took you long enough." A small, somewhat sad smile emerged as he stood and offered Ty a hand. They faced each other, nothing but one woman in common. Malone nodded. "See you in Colorado," he said softly. Then he started for his car.

"Thank you, Mr. Malone," Ty called, running out of the barn, already thinking of what he needed to pack, how he'd handle the logistics and how fast he could get on the road.

Malone didn't stop, just raised his hand in acknowledgment. "If I'm going to lose her to you, son, you might as well call me Jack."

Kenzie had no idea where her dad had gone, and her mom was a freaking vault on the subject, offering nothing more than "He had some business to take care of."

So the first day Kenzie was home, she slept. All day. It had been months since she'd had a full night's sleep, and she overindulged. Let the world call her a princess. She didn't care. She'd earned the right to twenty-four hours of solid z's.

She probably could have slept through the second day as well, but she forced herself out of bed. She wanted to see Bean's new foal and get the name recorded so the baby's registration could be filed without delay. She and her father had high hopes for this breeding between one of her program's top mares and a new stud horse from Montana.

Grabbing a small bottle of orange juice as she passed through the kitchen, she also snagged her jacket off the hall tree and then headed outside.

The wind whipped across the plains, biting through her jeans as if they were made of tissue paper and chilling her straight to the bone. Her hand shook as she sipped her juice.

Should've grabbed coffee.

A door slammed somewhere ahead, the sound ferried by the wind. She picked up her pace when she saw her dad's pickup parked near the barn's office. With him in residence, the barn should have been a busy place. It was vacant. Someone had left the door at the end of the stable alley open, though. That had turned the alleyway into a wind tunnel, chilling the barn's normally snug interior.

All four of the ranch's border collies were curled up outside the office door, a sure sign her dad was inside. Those dogs followed The Malone everywhere. It was a standing joke around the place that while he was good with horses, he was magic with dogs. Truth was, he was magic with both of them.

She reached for the door, intent on letting herself in, then paused when she realized her father was talking to someone. The wind made it impossible for her to make out the conversation, but one thing was very evident. There were at least two men inside. Someone said something and then there was a third, distinctive voice.

Three men. One's Dad.

Had to be horse business. Normally she'd be involved, but after her impromptu return home, he was probably giving her some recovery time. She stepped back over the sleeping dogs and made her way to Bean's stall, stopping several times along the way to scratch a neck or rub an offered nose.

Bean moved to greet her with a soft whuffling noise and a gentle nudge to the shoulder. Deeper in the maternity stall, movement caught Kenzie's eye. A tiny dark foal with a single white sock and a crooked facial blaze lurched to her feet. Unsteady on spindly legs, the little blue roan made her way to her mother's side, nosing the mare as she looked to nurse as a clear reward for her efforts. She suckled for a moment and then turned her attention to the stranger who had captured her mother's attention. Without hesitation and sporting a jaunty step, the foal came forward as confident as could be and sniffed Kenzie's proffered fingertips.

Her heart swelled. "You made a beautiful baby girl, Bean."

The foal nibbled at her fingers, milk teeth blunt but definitely present.

"None of that," Kenzie admonished. Reaching out, she stroked the silky blue-black coat, already dreaming of what the future might hold for such a self-assured little girl. The possibilities seemed endless. It lifted Kenzie's spirits when she'd privately despaired that Ty had broken something in her—something that would take a lifetime or more to repair.

Ty.

She missed him. Bad. But the potential between them had been destroyed, erased so efficiently it might have never existed after he kicked her out of his life. The hurt swelled up, pressing against her heart. Her vision blurred with unshed tears. She resented the fact that he could cast her aside as he had, that she was the one who bore all the hurt, all the blame, all of his anger in this. Not for the first time, she wondered what Eli had *told* Ty, if anything, about the brothers' proposition. Had he confessed his own attempt to manipulate the situation? Had he admitted to Ty that she'd shot him down? Or had he taken the easy road and let her be the fall guy? She'd never know, and that bothered her.

How long would she hurt; how long would it be before she stopped loving the man who'd broken her heart?

Bean nudged her again, demanding her attention.

"Sorry, baby." Rubbing the mare's head, she contemplated the foal. She'd need a strong name, something that would resonate on the rodeo circuit. Kenzie grinned. "Baby, you just got named. Lyssa Bean's Domino Effect."

"I like it."

Kenzie physically jumped even as her heart stalled.

Startled, Bean moved between the stranger and her baby, laying her ears back and flicking her tail in agitation.

"Kenzie, please. At least face me."

That voice. Heaven save me, that voice.

She shook her head.

Strong but gentle hands rested on her shoulders and encouraged her toward him anyway.

Her shoulders twitched.

His grip tightened.

She drew as deep a breath as her leaden lungs would hold and forced herself to meet the gaze of the man who'd broken her heart.

Tyson Covington.

He ran a hand down her arm and wrapped his fingers around hers. "I need to talk to you."

"I, uh…" She cleared her throat, furious at herself for being so soft. "No." She pulled her hand free and sidestepped him, heading for the safety of the office—and her father. "You were pretty clear, Tyson. I got it—*get it*. There's nothing left to say."

He caught up and stepped in front of her. "Yeah, actually there is."

She tried to step around him again but he kept darting in front of her until she finally stopped, glaring at him. "Get out of my way. Or better yet, why don't you try this on for size. It should be familiar enough. Get off my ranch."

He winced.

The urge to comfort him made her want to scream. Shoving past him, she focused on her dad's office door and picked up the pace, certain Ty wouldn't dare move fast enough to catch her. He'd be too worried about reinjury.

That was the only excuse she had for squealing when his hot hand gripped her biceps and pulled her around to face him.

"Stop running." The command was harsh and low.

"Oh, that's rich coming from you," she snapped, pulling free of his grasp. "You, who holds the record for the fastest bed-to-door sprint in the history of lovers worldwide. Go on, Tyson. Show me how it's done."

"In case you missed it, Malone, I ran *to* you, not away."

Her retort stalled, tripping off the end of her tongue in something that sounded suspiciously like "Whumah-ah-ah."

"I have no idea what that means, but I'm going to interpret it as, 'Go ahead, Ty. You have my undivided attention.'" He pulled an envelope from his back pocket and used it to gesture to a short stack of straw bales. "Have a seat. There are a few things I need to say to you."

She sat, not because he ordered her to but because her legs simply gave out.

He dragged a hand down his face. "Thanks."

If she hadn't been so hyperfocused on the surreal moment, she wouldn't have seen the way his hands shook. But she did. Part of her softened toward him at the sight, and she hated herself a little more.

He suddenly broke away from her, then surprised her by walking back and thrusting the envelope at her. "My stamina sucks so I'm on a bit of a timetable here. I had this whole speech worked out, knew exactly what I was going to say, but it never comes out that way, does it? I think it would be easiest to let the paperwork speak for itself."

Kenzie accepted the papers and sat there, staring at the sealed envelope that bore the logo from the legal offices the Malone ranch used for just about everything. "What..." She glanced between the envelope and Ty several times. Swamped with equal parts anxiety and confusion, her mind shut down and her mouth ran off without a map. "You're suing me?"

"What?" Ty shouted, eyes wide. "No! Lord, no. Just... open the damn envelope, Mackenzie. Then I'll explain."

Her hands shook so badly she dropped the envelope. Twice. But she finally got the flap open and pulled out three sheets of paper. The first was a short, handwritten statement.

I, Tyson Hollister Covington, hereby acknowledge the debt owed and the amount established by one Mackenzie Anne Malone in the amount of $112,742.88. I hereby accept responsibility for that debt with the intent to repay it, in full, via a lump-sum settlement. Said settlement shall satisfy all monies and related interest owed.

Ty's signature had been notarized by one Elijah Covington, Esquire.

Her father's hand had added the following:

In recognition of the loan made by the Malone family to one Tyson Covington, the settlement agreement is accepted as proposed.

Below her father's signature, the notary public from the ranch's law firm had affixed his seal.

That had been the third male voice coming from the office.

Fingers numb, she let that sheet drift to the floor. "I didn't lend you the money, Ty. I gave it to you."

"I asked you for it, and we need to be clear before we can move forward. Keep reading."

Kenzie moved on to the next page. It took a second to realize what she was looking at and another to process it. Gasping, she shot to her feet. "No. No, no, no."

He took her by the arms and settled her back on the straw bale. "Yes, Kenzie. Read it."

The registration and ownership for Doc Bar's Dippy Zippy Gizmo had been transferred to her name. She was listed as the horse's sole owner.

She knew her eyes were wild when she met his solemn gaze. "No, Tyson. I can't take Gizmo. I won't. I never wanted this."

"Which is exactly why I'm doing it." He ran a finger along her jaw. "Keep reading."

Hands shaking wildly, her voice vibrated with emotion. "No."

"Please. For me."

"You have no right to ask me to do anything for you. Not anymore."

"I hope to change your mind." He bumped her knee with his. "Now read."

She fought to focus on the third sheet, a letter composed in a surprisingly legible hand—one she recognized from the first page.

Mackenzie,
Sometimes people screw up. Other times they royally screw up. And rarely someone will screw

up so bad that the magnitude of their mistake actually registers on the Richter scale. I've been told that the United States Geological Survey recorded and reported a seismic disturbance day before yesterday. The disturbance was recorded at roughly 10:44 a.m. and was located at 35.9439° N, 104.1931° W. (In case you're curious, that happens to be just outside Roy, New Mexico.) The USGS has said that, based on the available information, their experts believe the event occurred when a total asshole shed every ounce of common sense he allegedly possessed and made a snap judgment. It was the snap judgment and the resulting fallout that caused the disturbance. Apparently, it was the largest event caused by a single individual in recorded history.

You see, I'm the one who set off the Richter scale. I'm the jackass.

I tried to rationalize the event. Apparently the English language hasn't come up with words that convey that particular level of moronic behavior just yet. I'm on it, though, and will let you know when they're available.

Next, I looked for an excuse in a bottle of bourbon. It wasn't there.

I tried to argue with a very wise man who drove over eight hours in crappy weather to come to his daughter's defense. I argued with that man, that father, and told him he'd neglected his daughter by treating her like a poor replacement for the son he'd lost. I have the bruise on my shoulder from the one punch he threw to prove that this man, this father, loves his daughter for all her own strengths and weaknesses. Nothing more. Nothing less. That collective experience revealed just how far a good man will go to ensure his child is protected.

I looked in the mirror then and realized I'm not a good man. But I want to be.

More important, good or bad, right or wrong, I want—need to be your man.

Movement made her look up in time to see Ty dig something out of his pocket and drop to one knee.

"I've talked to your dad. He's a very smart man who loves you very much. He insisted I call your mom, too, because apparently she would make my balls into earmuffs if I didn't let her get her own threats in before I set foot on Malone land." He grinned at her. "You might think you spent the past decade living in your brother's shadow, but they made it clear to me that they never felt that way. They love you because you're you, Mac."

The sound that escaped her was far closer to a sob than she cared to admit, but it was all too much.

Reaching out, he took the letter from her limp fingers and dropped it at her feet. "I think I remember what the rest of it says."

"Okay," she whispered, terrified to hope. Despite the fear, despite the negative voices that told her she was a fool to lay her heart in this man's hands, she set her hurt aside, silenced her pride and listened with her heart.

Ty took both her hands in his and stared at her. "This is harder than I expected it to be."

"The easy road is for cowards and barrel racers."

He grinned. "That's my girl."

Her eyes widened even as her heart tripped and her breath caught. The way he looked at her, the way his eyes softened at the sight of her panic, overrode her urge to run.

"That's my girl," he repeated, softer this time. "And that phrase says it all. It sums up all my hopes, my dreams, my desires, wants and needs. It's more than I ever thought to find in this life. If only I'd been smart enough, brave enough, to open my eyes sooner, we could have had all this time together, and I never would have had to listen to you talk about city boy. What was his name? Nashville...Seattle...Buffalo..." He gently pulled her into his embrace.

And she went. Her heart, so broken less than an hour before, had never been so full of love for this man. "Dallas. His name was Dallas."

"Give me a chance to make you forget him, Mac. Give me a chance to wipe out every man who came before and to wipe the floor with any man who believes he has a chance after."

"How long do you think it'll take?" she asked. "My memory's pretty good."

"God willing, darlin', it'll take a lifetime. Just say the word." He lowered his lips to hers, and then waited.

"Yes," she said. "My answer to you will always be yes."

* * * * *

SINGLE MAN MEETS SINGLE MUM

JULES BENNETT

To Jill, Amy and Inez. I love you three more than the frozen yoghurt we devour. Thanks for the road trip and all the laughs. May we have many, many more!

One

*O*omph!

Out of nowhere, Ian Shaffer had his arms full of woman. Curvy, petite woman. A mass of silky red hair half covered her face, and as she shoved the wayward strands back to look up, Ian was met with the most intriguing set of blue eyes he'd ever seen.

"You okay?" he asked, in no hurry to let her down.

He'd taken one step into the stables at Stony Ridge Acres and this beauty had literally fallen into his arms. Talk about perfect timing.

The delicate hand against his shoulder pushed gently, but he didn't budge. How could he, when all those curves felt perfect against his body and she was still trembling?

He may not know much about the horse industry, but women... Yeah, he knew women really well.

"Thank you for catching me."

Her low, husky voice washed over him, making him

even more thankful he'd come to this movie set to see to his client's needs in person...and to hopefully sign another actress to his growing roster of A-listers.

Most agents didn't visit movie sets as regularly as he did, but he sure as hell wasn't missing the opportunity to keep Max Ford happy and allow prospective client Lily Beaumont to witness just what a kick-ass, hands-on agent he was. Given his young age, the fact that he was known as a shark in the industry happened to be good for business.

Ian glanced to the ladder that stretched up into the loft of the spacious stables. His eyes narrowed in on the rung that hung vertically, the culprit of the lady's fall.

"Looks like your ladder needs repairing," he told her, looking back to those big, expressive blue eyes.

"I've been meaning to fix it," she told him, studying his face, his mouth. "You know, you can let me down now."

Yeah, he was probably freaking her out by keeping her in his clutches. But that didn't stop him from easing her down slowly, allowing her body to glide against his.

Hey, he may be there to concentrate on work, but that didn't mean he couldn't enjoy the samplings of a tempting woman when an opportunity presented itself.

Keeping his hand on her arm, Ian allowed his gaze to sweep down her body. He justified the touch by telling himself he was looking for signs of injury, but in all honesty, he simply wanted to get a better look. If this was what they called taking in the local scenery, then sign him up.

"Are you hurt anywhere?" he asked.

"Just my pride." Stepping back, forcing his hand to fall away, she brushed her fingers down her button-up plaid shirt. "I'm Cassie Barrington. And you are?"

He held out his hand. "Ian Shaffer. I'm Max Ford's agent."

And if all went well, he'd be signing Max's costar Lily,

too. There was no way he'd let her go to his rival agency without one hell of a fight first. And then maybe his very unimpressed father would see that Ian had become a success. He was a top agent in L.A. and not just hanging out at parties with women for a living. He'd become a powerful man in the industry.

Though the parties and women were a nice added bonus, Ian enjoyed stepping away from the glamour to be on set with his clients. And it was that extra touch that made him so successful. Between forging connections with producers and getting to know the writers and actors better, he could place his clients in the roles best suited to them.

The role Max was playing was perfect for him. The top actor was portraying the dynamic Damon Barrington, famous horse owner and former jockey. And for Ian, escaping L.A.'s hustle and bustle to spend time on a prestigious Virginia horse farm was a nice change of pace.

"Oh, Max mentioned you'd be coming. Sorry for falling on you." Her brows drew together as she gave him a quick assessment. "I didn't hurt you, did I?"

Ian shoved his hands into his pockets, offering her a smile. She could assess him anytime she wanted. "Not at all," he assured her. "I rather enjoyed the greeting."

Her chin tilted just enough to show defiance. "I don't make a habit of being clumsy…or throwing myself at men."

"That a fact?" he asked, trying not to laugh. "Such a shame."

"Do you make a habit of hitting on women?" she asked.

Unable to resist the gauntlet she'd thrown before him, Ian took a step forward, pleased when her eyes widened and she had to tip her head up to hold his gaze.

"Actually, no. But I'm making an exception in your case."

"Aren't I lucky?" Her tone told him she felt anything

but. "Max should be in his trailer. His name is on the outside, and I believe another trailer was recently brought in for you."

Apparently she was in a hurry for him to be on his way—which only made him want to stay longer. Finding someone who didn't care about his Hollywood status, someone who wasn't impressed with his power and money, was a refreshing change. The fact that someone was curvy, wore jeans as though they were made to mold those curves and had expressive baby blues was the icing on the proverbial cake.

"So you're the trainer and your sister is the famous jockey?" he asked, crossing his arms over his chest.

The warm late-spring sun beat against his back as it came through the wide doors of the stable. Summer blockbuster season was just around the corner and, hopefully, once the film wrapped and he'd signed Lily, his agency would still be on top. His ex-partner-turned-rival would no longer be an issue.

He'd started working for an agency right out of college, thanks to a referral from a professor he'd impressed, but some lucky breaks and smart business sense had had him quickly moving to open his own. Unfortunately, he'd taken on a partner who had stabbed him in the back and secretly wooed most of their clients in the hopes they'd work exclusively with him in a new venture.

For the sake of his pride, he had to win Lily over and get her under contract. But how could his mind be on business with this voluptuous distraction before him?

"You've done your homework," she commented. "I'm impressed you know about me and my sister and our different roles."

"I do my research. You could say I'm pretty hands-on as an agent."

"Apparently you're hands-on with everything."

Oh, that was such a loaded statement—one he wouldn't mind exploring if he had the time. His eyes held hers as he closed the gap between them. The pulse at the base of her throat quickened and her breath caught as she stared, unblinking, at him.

Damn work responsibilities. But surely a little flirting, hell, even a fling, would make this an even more riveting trip.

"Everything," he whispered. "Let me know if you ever want an experience."

When her gaze dropped to his mouth again, Ian resisted the urge to grab her, to taste her. There would be plenty of time for…anything she was willing to give. Besides, wasn't the chase half the fun?

"I think you know where my trailer is."

And because he'd probably crossed some sort of moral, ethical boundary, Ian turned and walked from the barn, leaving her with her mouth open.

Well, this was already the most exciting movie set he'd ever visited and he hadn't even seen his client yet.

Cassie tightened her grip on MacDuff's lead line. He was still new, still skittish, but she was working with him every single day and he was showing improvement. Every now and then he'd let her father, Damon Barrington, ride him, but he had a touch that every horse seemed to love.

At least MacDuff had quit trying to run from her. Now, if she could just get him to understand her silent commands that he had to mimic her pace and direction when they walked.

Her work with MacDuff and the other horses was just one of the many issues that had ended her marriage. Derek had wanted her to stop spending so much time with the "strays" she brought in. He'd insisted she stop trying to save every animal, especially when she'd become pregnant.

Cassie would never stop trying to save animals...especially since she hadn't been able to save her marriage. Her husband had obviously loved women and liquor more than her and their baby. His loss, but the pain still cut deep.

She focused on the line, holding it tight and trying to keep up with the routine because she was running a tad behind now.

Of course, she'd been thrown off her game already this morning after falling into the arms of that handsome, bedroom-eyed stranger. For a split second she'd wanted to revel in the strength with which he held her, but then reality had slapped her in the face, reminding her that she'd fallen for a smooth talker once. Married him, had his child and hadn't seen him since.

Well, except when he'd shown up for the divorce proceedings, mistress in tow. As if that busty bleach blonde would ever play stepmom to Cassie's precious baby. Hell. No.

Cassie swore she'd never let another man play her for a fool again, and she sure as hell wouldn't get swept away by another pretty smile and sultry touch.

Unfortunately, when she'd fallen into Ian's arms, she'd forgotten all about that speech she'd given herself when her husband had left. How could she have a coherent thought when such strong arms were holding her flush against a taut body? No woman would blame her for the lapse in judgment.

But no more. Cassie had her daughter to consider now.

With sweet Emily just turning one, Cassie knew she'd definitely gotten the best part of her marriage, and if Derek didn't want to see their baby, he was the one missing out.

So, no more sexy men who thought they were God's

magnificent gift to this world. Although Cassie had to admit, even if just to herself, that her insides had tingled at Ian's touch. He'd been so strong, had smelled so...manly and had looked in her eyes as if she truly was a beautiful, desirable woman.

She hadn't felt anything but frumpy and still a bit pudgy since having Emily. The extra weight that refused to go away coupled with her husband leaving her for another woman were damaging blows to her self-esteem. Yet, Ian had held her with ease, which wasn't helping her ignore the potency of the mesmerizing man.

Getting swept away by another handsome man with sultry eyes and a powerful presence wouldn't do her any good. She had to concentrate on helping her sister, Tessa, win her way to the Triple Crown. They'd worked side by side nearly their entire lives, always with the dream of being Triple Crown winners like their father. And here they were, about to make history, and Cassie couldn't be more excited.

When Cassie had been too far along with her pregnancy, her father had stepped up to train Tessa. This racing dynasty truly was a family affair.

One race down, two to go.

The fact that the Barrington estate had been turned into a film set was icing on the cake. A script surrounding her father's legacy, legendary racing and past winning streak had piqued the interest of Hollywood A-listers, and, suddenly, the horse farm was all abuzz with lighting, sound guys, extras and security.

Cassie actually loved seeing her father's life played out by Max Ford, the handsome, newly married actor. And playing the role of her late mother was beautiful Southern belle and it-girl Lily Beaumont. So far the two were doing an amazing job, and Cassie couldn't wait to see the final product.

To cap off the racing season, Cassie was moving full throttle toward opening her own riding school for handicapped children. Since having her own child, Cassie wanted to slow down, and she'd always had a soft spot for kids anyway...something she'd thought she and her ex had in common.

Launching the school would be one more step in the healing process. So now she just needed to keep saving up—she wouldn't dream of asking her father or anyone else for money—to get it off the ground.

"Daydreaming?"

Keeping a firm grip on the lead line, Cassie glanced over her shoulder to see Tessa moving toward her in slow, cautious steps. MacDuff really did get treated with kid gloves by everyone until he learned they were his friends.

"Maybe just a little," Cassie admitted, gently pulling MacDuff into a soft trot. "Give me just a few minutes and we'll get to work."

Tessa shoved her hands into the pockets of her jeans. "I'd rather hear what has my big sister so distracted this morning."

Cassie rolled her eyes at Tessa's smirk and quirked brow. She led MacDuff forward a few steps, stopped and moved back a few steps, pleased when the stallion kept up with her exact number and didn't try to fight her.

He was learning. Finally.

"I'm always amazed at how broken they seem to be," Tessa said softly. "You have this patience and gentleness. It's almost as if they know you're determined to help them."

"That's because I am." Cassie reached up to MacDuff's neck, offering him praise. "He's just misunderstood and nobody wanted to work properly with him."

"He was abused."

Cassie swallowed as she led MacDuff back to the stables. The thought of someone beating him because he hadn't had the right training sickened her. She'd known he'd been abused on some level, simply because of how he'd arrived all wide-eyed and nervous and then threw Tessa the first time she'd mounted him. But the second any horse, rescued or not, stepped onto Stony Ridge Acres, they were treated like royalty. No matter their heritage. Yes, they bred prizewinning horses and bought from a long lineage of winners, but it wasn't always about the win.... It was about the love and care of the animal. And since Stony Ridge was a massive farm, they could take in those strays Cassie had a soft spot for.

She'd always loved watching the trainers her father had for his horses. Years ago, female trainers had been frowned upon, but her father had insisted women were more gentle and less competitive by nature than men, thus producing better-tempered horses—and winners.

"You didn't happen to see a certain new hunk on the set this morning, did you?" Tessa asked as she pulled out the tack box and helped to brush MacDuff.

Cassie eyed her sister over the horse's back. "Aren't you engaged?"

"I'm not dead, Cass." Tessa brushed in large circular strokes. "I'll take your lack of answering to mean you did see him."

Saw him, fell into his arms, got lost in those sexy eyes that could make a woman forget she'd been burned...and maybe reveled in that powerful hold a tad too long.

"Even you have to admit he's one attractive man," Tessa went on.

"I can admit that, yes." Cassie switched from the currycomb to the dandy brush. "I may have had an incident this morning involving that loose rung on the ladder to the loft and Mr. Shaffer."

Tessa stepped around MacDuff's head, dropped the brush into the tack box and crossed her arms over her chest. "Okay, spill it. You know his name and you said 'incident.' I want all the details."

Cassie laughed. "It's no big deal, Tess. I fell off the ladder. Ian happened to be there, and he caught me."

"Oh, so we've gone from Mr. Shaffer to Ian."

"He's Max's agent and apparently visits his clients' film sets. We exchanged names," Cassie defended herself. "Seemed like the thing to do since he was holding me."

"I love where this story is going." Tessa all but beamed as she clasped her hands together.

Laughing, Cassie tossed her brush aside, as well. "No story. That was pretty much it."

"Honey, you haven't even mentioned a man's name since *you know who* left and—" Tessa held up a hand when Cassie tried to intervene "—your face seemed to brighten up a bit when you said his name."

"It did not," Cassie protested.

Tessa's smile softened. "If you want to argue, that's fine. But he's hot, you finally showed a spark of life about a man and I'm clinging to hope that you haven't given up on finding love. Or, for heaven's sake, at least allowing yourself a fling."

Cassie rolled her eyes and patted MacDuff's side. "Just because this romance business is working for you doesn't mean it will for me. I tried that once—it didn't last. Besides, I have no time for love or even a date between training with you and Emily."

"There's always time. And, romance aside, have a good time. A little romp with a sexy stranger might be just what you need," Tessa said with a naughty smile. "Aren't you the one who forced me to take a few days off last month? You have to make time for yourself."

Cassie had conspired with Tessa's now fiancé, producer Grant Carter, to whisk Tessa away during her training and the filming of the movie. Grant had wanted to get Tessa far from the limelight, the stress and the demands of their busy schedules, and Cassie had been all too happy to help because her sister needed a break.

Tess had found the right man, but Cassie seriously doubted there was a "right man" for her. All she required was someone who loved her and didn't mind her smelling like horses more often than not, someone who would offer stability in her life, make her feel desirable and love her daughter. Was that too tall of an order?

"I'm not looking for a fling," Cassie insisted, even though she'd pretty much already envisioned a steamy affair with Ian.

Tessa raised a brow. "Maybe a fling is looking for you."

"I just met the man. I'm sure he's not going to be around me that much anyway, so there's very little chance of seduction. Sorry to burst your bubble."

"Maybe you should show Ian around the estate," Tessa suggested as she went to grab a blanket and saddle for her racing horse, Don Pedro.

Cassie sighed, closing the gate to MacDuff's stall. "I don't want to show him around. Max is his client—he can do it."

"Max is going to be busy filming the scene with Lily down by the pond. I want to make sure we're there to see that taping."

Cassie smiled and nodded in agreement. She loved watching the two actors get into character, loved watching her father's reaction to reliving his life through the eyes of a director, and there was no way she'd miss such a monumental scene. This was the scene where Max would propose to Lily. The replay of such a special moment in her parents' lives was something she had to witness.

"I'll make sure we're done here about the time shooting starts," Cassie assured her sister. "All the more reason I don't have time to show Ian around."

"Now, that's a shame."

Cassie and Tessa both turned to see the man in question. And just like with their earlier encounter, the mere sight of him caused a flutter to fill her belly. Of course, now she couldn't blame the sensation on the scare from the fall... only the scare from the enticing man.

"I'd like to have a look around the grounds if you have time," he said, looking directly into her eyes, seeming to not even notice Tessa.

Cassie settled her hands on her hips, cursing herself when his gaze followed her movements. Great, now she'd drawn his attention to her hips...not an area a woman wanted a man looking.

"I thought you went to see Max," Cassie said, refusing to acknowledge his request.

"I saw him for a brief moment to let him know I was here. He actually was talking with Grant and Lily."

Cassie cast a glance at her sister, whose face had split into a very wide grin. *Darn her.*

With a gracefulness that would've pleased their late mother, Tessa turned, extended her hand and smiled. "I'm Tessa Barrington, Cassie's sister. We're so glad to have you here at the farm."

Ian shook Tessa's hand as the two exchanged pleasantries. He finally settled his gaze back on Cassie. Did those eyes have some magical power? Seriously, why did she have to feel a jolt every single time he looked at her?

"Go ahead and show Ian around, Cassie. I'm fine here."

If Cassie could've reached out and strangled her sister

with the lead line she so would have, but then Ian would be a witness.

"It will have to be tomorrow or later this evening." No, she wasn't too busy right now, but she wouldn't allow Mr. Hollywood Hotshot to hold any control over her. "I'll come find you when I'm ready."

"Well, I'm going to walk Don Pedro out," Tessa said. "It was a pleasure to meet you, Ian. Cass, I'll see you later."

Great, now they were alone. Cassie would definitely kill her sister for that little stunt.

Ian stepped closer, and Cassie held her ground. This was her property and no matter how charming, how sexy and how…

Damn, he smelled good. She lost all train of thought; Ian's masculine scent was enough to render her mind blank. How long had it been since she'd been with a man, felt his touch?

Too long. So why did this man with an inflated ego turn her on? Could she not attract the right kind of guy just once?

"I can wait till tomorrow," he told her. His eyes searched her face as a hint of a smile played around his lips. "I'm a pretty patient man."

Placing a hand on his chest to stop him may have been a mistake. A jolt of awareness tingled up her arm. The strength, the chiseled pecs beneath her palm… Yeah, she was very aware of the sexiness that encompassed Ian Shaffer.

"I appreciate the fact you're taking the time to use your charm on me, but I'm too busy for games. Besides, I'm pretty sure I'm a lot older than you."

Ian shrugged. "Age hadn't entered my mind."

Cassie laughed. "I'm pretty sure I know what entered your mind."

He stepped forward again, giving her no choice but to

back up until the gate to a stall stopped her. Ian put one hand on either side of her head, blocking her.

"Then I'm sure you're aware I find you attractive." His eyes dropped to her mouth, then traveled back up. "I can't wait for that tour, Cassie."

He pushed off the stall and walked out of the stable. When was the last time a man had caught her attention, inspired her sexual desire so fast? The danger of falling into lust scared her to death.

But she had to be realistic. There was nothing special about her. And if she did allow herself to act on these very new, very powerful emotions, she highly doubted he'd remember her name in a few months.

No way could she succumb to his charms.

Two

Cassie's parents had been married nearly twenty years when her mother was killed suddenly in a car accident. She'd always admired the love her parents had for each other, always wanted a marriage like that for herself.

Unfortunately, a happy, loving marriage wasn't in the cards for her. And hindsight was a harsh slap in the face because Cassie realized she'd probably married Derek too quickly.

She'd craved the love her parents had had and thought for sure Derek—the Barringtons' onetime groom—had the same outlook on marriage.... As in, it was long-term and between only two people.

How could she trust her feelings for a man again? Cassie swiped the tear from her cheek as she headed back toward the stable. The sun was slowly sinking behind the hills surrounding the estate. Spring was gradually turning into summer, giving the evenings just a bit more light.

The day's filming was complete and the scene she'd just witnessed had left her raw and hopeful all at the same time.

Max Ford and Lily Beaumont had beautifully reenacted Cassie's parents' proposal. Cassie had heard stories, had seen pictures of her parents' early love. But to witness that moment in person… Cassie had no words for how precious the experience had been.

She'd stood with Tessa off to the side, and even with the directors and producers stopping and starting and rearranging in the middle of the scene, the moment had captured her heart.

Added to that, each time she'd glanced at Ian, his gaze had been on hers. He hadn't even bothered trying to hide the heat that lurked in those dark, heavy-lidded eyes. Thankfully, at one point he'd slid on his aviator shades, but his dominating presence still captured her attention…and her hormones.

There went those lustful emotions again. She couldn't afford to get swept away by a sexy body and killer smile. Lust was the evil that had overtaken her once before and look where that had gotten her. Oh, she didn't regret her marriage because she had Emily, but the pain from the rejection and having her love blatantly thrown back in her face was humiliating. Who wanted to be rejected?

Cassie reached the stable, intending to work with MacDuff again, but her eyes moved up to the rung of the ladder that still hung vertically.

She'd meant to mention the problem to Nash, the new groom, but between the emotional shoot and a certain hot agent plaguing her mind, she'd simply forgotten. Besides, he'd been so busy today cleaning out all the stalls, she really hated to add to his list.

Her father took pride in his stables, always making sure everything looked pristine and perfect. Cassie would bite the bullet and fix the ladder herself. At least working on something would keep her mind off Ian…hopefully. Her tendency to fix things and have everything in her life make sense would have to be satisfied with just this piece of wood for now. The Ian issue—and she feared he was fast becoming an issue—would have to wait.

She grabbed the hammer and several long nails from the toolbox in the equipment room. She shoved the nails in her back pocket and held on to the hammer as she climbed the ladder that stretched to the loft of the stable.

The setting sun cast a soft glow into the structure. Horses neighed, stomped hooves and rustled in their stalls. The sounds, the smells—none of it ever got old. Cassie loved her life here and she looked forward to bringing her daughter up in such a beautiful, serene environment.

During her four years of marriage, she'd been away from the estate. Even though she and Derek had lived only ten minutes away, it just wasn't the same as being on the grounds. Cassie loved living in the cottage, being with the horses and knowing her family was all right here helping with her emotional recovery.

With her tears mostly dry, Cassie sniffed. Crying had never been her thing. Anger fit more into her life, especially since she'd been abandoned only two months after giving birth. Tears hadn't brought her cheating husband back, not that she'd wanted him after the fact, and tears certainly weren't helping her raise her daughter or move on like the strong mother she needed to be.

Halfway up the ladder, she eyed the broken rung, then carefully slid it back into place. Widening her stance as far as she could to balance her body while holding the hammer, she reached around into her back pocket for a nail.

"I can help you with that."

Cassie glanced over her shoulder to see Ian at the base

of the ladder, his watchful gaze raking over her body. *Great.* She had red-rimmed eyes and a red-tipped nose, she was sure. She was not a pretty crier. She always got the snot-running, red-splotchy-face and puffy-eyes look.

Cassie slid a nail out and turned back around to place it against the wood. "I've got it, but thanks."

She knew he hadn't left, but Cassie didn't say anything else as she worked quickly and repaired the rung. With a hefty tug on the wood, she made sure it was securely in place before she started her descent. Just as she'd gotten to the last rung, Ian moved his hard body against hers, trapping her between the ladder and a most impressive chest. Her body was perfectly aligned with his, causing ripples of heat to slide through her. They were both fully dressed, but the sensations spiraling through her had never occurred before, even when she'd been completely naked with her ex.

Yeah, she was doomed where this sexy stranger was concerned.

Cassie swallowed, closed her eyes. Ian made her aware of just how feminine she was. When was the last time she'd felt desirable? Was it so wrong to want a man to find her attractive? After being married to someone who kept looking elsewhere for his desires to be fulfilled, Cassie knew she was probably grasping at any attention at this point.

She also knew she didn't care—not when his body was so hard, so perfectly perfect against hers. Not when his soft, warm breath tickled the side of her neck, and not when his masculine aroma enveloped her.

"What are you doing here?" she whispered.

Ian slid his arms up to align with hers, his hands covering hers on the wood. "I saw you walking this way. You looked upset."

No. He didn't care. He couldn't. Not this soon and not about her. Sexual desires were clouding his mind…and hers, too, apparently, because she was enjoying the heat of his body a little too much.

What man would follow a woman into a stable just because she looked upset? No. He'd followed her for one reason and one reason only. A reason she certainly didn't think she was ready for.

"I'm fine," she lied.

Ian nuzzled her hair. Oh…when he did that she forgot all arguments about why being attracted to someone so full of himself was wrong. Her mind completely voided out any pep talks she'd given in regard to steering clear of lustful feelings and attractive charmers.

"You're a very beautiful woman, Cassie." His soft voice slid over her body, reinforcing those tremors that were becoming the norm where he was concerned. "I tried to ignore this pull I have toward you, but it was damn hard when I saw you during the shoot. How do you do that to a guy?"

Um…she had no clue. Power over men had certainly never been something she'd mastered. If it had, she'd still be married.

"Ian, we just met and…"

He used one hand and slid the hammer from her grasp, letting it fall to the concrete floor with a loud thud.

"And I'm older than you," she continued. "I'm thirty-four. You can't even be thirty."

With an arm around her waist, he hauled her off the ladder and spun her around until she faced him—their mouths inches apart.

"I'm twenty-nine, and I assure you I'm old enough to not only know what I want, but to act on it."

His mouth came down on hers, hard, fast, hungry. Cassie didn't have time to think or refuse because her body was already melting into his.

The passion pouring from him stirred her desire even more as she gripped his thick biceps. Giving in to just a few seconds of bliss wouldn't hurt.

And when Ian's mouth traveled from her mouth down the column of her throat, Cassie tipped her head back as her breath caught. What was he doing to her? A full-on body attack. His mouth may be in one spot, but Cassie could feel every inch of her body tingling and wanting more.

Wait...this wasn't right. She couldn't do this.

Pushing him away, Cassie slid her hand up over the exposed skin peeking out of her shirt...the skin his mouth had just explored.

"Ian, I can't... We can't..." Words were useless because her mind was telling her one thing and her body was telling her another. "I just met you."

"You're attracted to me."

She couldn't deny the statement. "That doesn't mean I should act on it. I don't just go around kissing strangers."

"After you learned my name this morning, I was no longer a stranger."

Those dark eyes held her gaze. Even without a word the man exuded power, control. Derek had been so laid-back, so uncaring about everything that this was quite a change.

And Cassie would be lying if she didn't admit the fact that Ian was the polar opposite of her ex turned her on even more.

"You're only here for a short time," she went on, crossing her arms over her chest. "We can't just...you know."

"Have sex?" he asked, quirking a brow.

Oh, mercy. The words were now out, hovering in the air, and from the smirk on his face, she was the only one feeling awkward at this moment.

"Yes, that." *Dear Lord.* It wasn't as if she hadn't had

sex before; she'd had a baby, for crying out loud. But she couldn't discuss something like that with him. Now she felt foolish and juvenile. "Acting on sexual attraction isn't something I normally do."

That was an understatement, considering she'd had sex with one man and that had been her husband. What if she did throw caution to the wind? What if she had some sordid affair?

Seriously? Was she contemplating that? She was a mother—a mother to a little girl. What kind of example was she?

"You're thinking too hard." Ian started to step forward, but he stopped when Cassie held up a hand.

"Don't. I can't think when you're touching me."

"I'll take that as a compliment."

Cassie rolled her eyes. "You would."

"See? You know me already."

One of them had to think rationally. Apparently it would be her. She maneuvered around him toward the opening of the stable.

"You're going to have to keep your hands and your mouth to yourself."

Those tempting lips curved into a smile. "You're no fun."

"I don't have time for fun, Ian."

And more than likely he was the proverbial good time back in L.A. She could easily see him hopping from one party to the next, beautiful women draped over his arm, falling into his bed.

Cassie flicked the main switch to light up the pathways between the stalls. The brightness from the antique horseshoe-style chandeliers put a screeching halt to any romantic ambience that had been lurking in the darkening stable.

When she turned back around, Ian had his hands on his narrow hips, his focus still locked on her. There was a hunger in his eyes she'd never seen from any man before.

Without a word, he closed the gap between them. Cassie's heart had just started to settle, but now it picked back up again. She should've known better than to think the intense moment would pass.

Ian framed her face with his hands and brought his mouth to within a fraction of an inch of hers. "A woman who kisses, who responds to my touch without hesitation, has pent-up passion that needs to be released."

His lips barely brushed hers. "Come find me when you're ready."

Ian walked around her, leaving her still surrounded by that masculine scent, his arousing words and the tingling from his touch still on her lips.

She'd known the man twelve hours. There was no way she could handle him being on the grounds for two more months. She was a woman—a woman with needs.

And a part of her wondered just what would happen if she allowed herself to put those needs first for once.

Three

Two days had passed since she'd been up close and personal with Ian, but Cassie was more than aware of his quiet, yet dominating, presence on the estate. She'd seen him from a distance as he talked with Max. She'd found out she'd just missed him on the set of one scene she'd gone to watch, but she refused to admit she was wondering about his schedule, about when she'd see him again. Feel his body against hers.

She refused to fall for another man who set her hormones into overdrive, so where did that leave her? Considering a fling?

Groaning, she made her way from the stables to the main house. The sun was making its descent behind the mountains and Emily was at her weekly sleepover with Tessa and Grant. After witnessing the shooting of the engagement scene over the past couple of days, Cassie was feeling more and more nostalgic.

She missed her mother with each passing day; seeing Rose's life depicted in the film had Cassie wanting to feel closer to her. And with Emily away for the night, this was the perfect opportunity to reminisce and head up to the attic, where all her mother's things were stored.

Rose's unexpected death had shaken up the family in ways they'd never even imagined. As teen girls, Tessa and Cassie had really taken it hard, but they'd all been there for each other, forming an even stronger bond. But Cassie still ached for her mother's sweet smile, her encouraging words and her patient guidance.

Because right now she truly wanted a mother's advice. Ian had her completely tied in knots. When he'd left her in the stables two days ago, Cassie had never felt so torn, so conflicted in her life. And he hadn't approached her since. What was up with that? Had he changed his mind? Had he decided she wasn't worth the trouble?

Why was she even worried about this anyway? No doubt Ian was used to those flawless women who had been surgically perfected. More than likely Cassie's extra pounds and shapelier curves were not what Ian was looking for in a...fling? What was he doing exactly with his flirting? Where had he expected this to go?

Never mind. He'd thrown out the word *sex* like nothing. Cassie knew exactly where he was headed with his flirting.

Leaving the attic door propped open, Cassie headed up the narrow wooden staircase. At the top she flicked on the small light that was so soft, it really only set off a glow on one wall. But that was the wall where her mother's boxes were stacked.

In the silence of the evening, Cassie was all alone with her thoughts, her memories. She pulled the lid off the first bin and choked back tears.

How could anyone's life, especially that of her beautiful,

loving, vivacious mother, be condensed to a few boxes? All the memories, all the smiles, all the comfort Rose Barrington had offered to the world...all gone. Only tangible items remained stored neatly in plastic bins.

Cassie couldn't help but smile. Her very organized mother wouldn't have had it any other way.

After going through pictures from her parents' simple, elegant wedding day, Cassie knew the wedding dress was around. Tessa actually planned on wearing it for her upcoming vows, and Cassie couldn't wait to see her baby sister in their mother's gown. Just that image was enough to have her tearing up again.

This film was certainly wreaking havoc on her emotions, that was for sure.

Cassie kept searching through storage bins, looking for a box or a folded garment bag. Would the crew need to duplicate that dress for the wedding scene? More than likely they'd already researched pictures to find inspiration for the costumes, just as they had for the settings.

Cassie had been itching for a chance to look through the old photos again herself.

Moving from the bins, Cassie went and looked inside the narrow antique wardrobe, where she discovered a white garment bag. Slowly unzipping, so as not to tear the precious material inside, Cassie peeled back the bag and pulled out the classy gown she'd been hunting for.

The dress had been preserved so that the cream-colored material was still perfect. Tessa would be just as beautiful a bride as their mother had been.

Cassie had thought about wearing it for her own wedding, but her ex had insisted on getting married at the courthouse. She should've known then that he wasn't the one. Not that there was anything wrong with a small civil ceremony, but Derek had known she'd always wanted a wedding in the small church where her parents had married. She'd wanted the lacy gown, the rice in her hair as they ran to their awaiting car…the special wedding night.

None of those young-girl dreams had come true.

Unable to resist, Cassie stripped from her jeans, boots, button-up and bra and pulled on the strapless floor-length dress. A straight cut with lace overlay may be simple to some, but the design was perfect to Cassie.

Smoothing a hand down the snug bodice, Cassie went to the antique mirror in the corner. If she fell in love one day—real love this time—maybe she could wear it. Wouldn't that be a beautiful tradition? Rose, Tessa and Cassie all wearing the same gown. Perhaps if the material held up and the gown was well preserved again, little Emily would one day walk down the aisle wearing the dress her grandmother had.

If it weren't for baby weight, the frock would fit perfectly. Unfortunately, right now her boobs threatened to spill out the top and lace was definitely not a forgiving material, so her curves were very…prominent.

Behind her, the attic door clicked. Cassie turned, her hand to her beating heart as footsteps sounded up the stairs. No time to cover up all her goods, so she kept her hand in place over her generous cleavage.

"Hello?" she called.

Ian rounded the landing and froze. He took in her state of dress—or undress, really—of course zeroing in on where her hand had settled.

So much for her evening of reminiscing. Could fate be any more mocking? Dangling this sexy stranger in her face when she knew full well that nothing could or should happen?

"What are you doing?" she asked, keeping her hand in place and trying to remain calm. Kind of hard when she was on display and just the sight of the man had her heart accelerating.

"I wanted to apologize for the other day," he told her, coming up the last couple of steps. "I never force myself on a woman, and I didn't want you to have that impression of me. But if I'm going to be here any length of time, and I am, we need to clear the air."

Clear the air? Cassie sighed and prayed because she had a sinking feeling they may be there for a while.

"Well, now's the perfect time because if that door latched all the way, we're locked in here."

Ian drew his brows together. "Locked in?"

"The door locks from the outside. That's why I had left it standing open."

Pulling up the hem of the dress with one hand and trying to keep the bodice up with the other, she moved around him down the steps and tugged on the handle. She leaned her forehead against the door and groaned.

"I didn't know," he murmured behind her.

Cassie turned and looked up the steps to see Ian looking menacing and dangerous—in that sexy way only he could—standing at the top. His muscles filled out his long-sleeved T, those wide shoulders stretching the material, and his dark jeans fit his narrow hips beautifully.

She knew firsthand exactly how that body felt against hers. Knew just how well he could kiss a woman into forgetting her morals.

In a house this size, with only her father living here and his bedroom on the first floor, no one would hear them yell until morning, when they could open the small window and catch someone's attention.

Risking another full-body glance at Ian, Cassie knew she was in big, big trouble. Her attraction to him was the strongest she'd ever felt toward a man. But it wasn't so much the level of heat between them that scared her; it was the quick onset of it. It felt as if she had no control over her own reaction. She'd been helplessly drawn to this intriguing man. How could she trust her emotions right now? He was honestly the first man to find her desirable since her ex. Was he just a sexy diversion or were her feelings more in-depth than that?

Earlier tonight she'd flirted with the idea of a fling, but now the reality of being trapped with Ian made her heart flutter and nerves dance in her belly.

Her gaze met his. Crackling tension vibrated between them in the soft glow and the silence.

And Cassie had all night to decide what to do with all her attraction and the hungry look in Ian's eyes...

Ian stared down at Cassie, struck by those creamy exposed shoulders, that poured-on, vintage-style wedding gown molded to her sweet curves. From his vantage point, he could see even more of her very exposed breasts and most impressive cleavage—even though she was trying her hardest to keep gravity from taking over the top of that dress.

Mercy. Being straight in front of her had been torture, but this angle offered a much more interesting, gut-clenching view. Not that he was complaining.

Being stuck in an attic with Cassie would be no hardship because he'd caught a glimpse of the passion she held beneath her vulnerability. And there wasn't a doubt in his mind that her war with herself stemmed from some past hurt.

Cassie attempted to cross her arms over her breasts, which only tortured him further, because she failed to cover the goods and actually ended up offering him an even more enticing view. Was she doing this as punishment?

"Text Max and have him come to the main house and ring the doorbell. Dad won't be in bed yet."

Ian shook his head. "Sorry. I only came over to apologize to you, so I left my phone in my trailer to charge."

Groaning, Cassie tipped her head back against the door and closed her eyes. "This isn't happening to me," she muttered. "This cannot be happening."

Ian had to smile. Of all the scenarios he'd envisioned on his short walk from his trailer to the main house, he hadn't once thought of being stuck for hours with someone so sexy, so unexpected, and wearing a wedding dress to boot.

This couldn't have been scripted any worse...or better, depending on the point of view.

Cassie lifted the dress and stomped back up the steps, her shoulder slamming into him as she stormed by.

"Wipe that smirk off your face, Ian. Nothing about this is comical."

"Can't you call someone with your phone?" he asked, turning to face her.

Cassie propped her hands on her hips. "No. I came up here to be alone, to think."

Damn, she was even sexier when she was angry. But getting too wrapped up with Cassie Barrington was a dangerous move. She wasn't a fling type of girl and he'd pushed too hard in the stables. Had she given in to his blatant advances, he knew she would've regretted it later.

He needed to do the right thing and keep his hands off her. He was here for two main purposes: keep Max happy and sign Lily so she didn't go to his rival. Period.

But his hormones didn't get the memo, because the more he was around Cassie, the more alluring and sexy she became. Of course, now that he'd seen a sample, he had to admit, he wanted to see more. That dress... Yeah, she looked like a 1950s pinup. Sexy as hell, with all the right curves and none of that stick-thin, anorexic nonsense, and she was even hotter with a slight flush from anger.

For the past two days he'd seen her working with her sister, training the horses and driving him unbelievably mad with the way her lush body filled out a pair of jeans. He'd seriously had to get his damn hormones in check and then approach her with a much-needed apology for his Neanderthal tendencies.

But now that he was here, those hormones were front and center once again, overriding all common sense and rational thoughts.

"How did you know I was up here?" she asked. "I figured all the crew was either in their trailers or back at the hotel."

"I ran into Grant on my way to your cottage. He told me you were here. As I was coming in the back door, your cook, Linda, was going out for the night and she said you mentioned coming to the attic."

"You came all this way just to apologize? I'm sure you would've seen me tomorrow."

Ian shrugged, shoving his hands into his pockets. "True, but I knew too many people would be around tomorrow. I assumed you wouldn't want to discuss this in front of an audience. Besides, I think we need to address this spark between us and figure out what to do with it since I'll be here several weeks."

Cassie threw her hands in the air. "Could you at least turn around so I can put my clothes back on?"

His eyes traveled down her body, darting to the pile of clothes behind her, zeroing in on the leopard-print bra lying on top.

"Sure," he said, trying to get the visual of her in that leopard bra out of his mind before he went insane.

Fate may have landed him up here with the sassy, sexy

Ms. Barrington, and fate also provided a window directly in front of him, where he was afforded a glorious view of Cassie's reflection as she changed. Of course, that made him a bit of a jerk, but no man with air in his lungs would look away from that enticing view. This evening just kept getting better and better.

Cassie would probably die before she asked for help with the zipper, so he didn't offer. And she didn't have any trouble. As the dress slid down her body, Ian's knees nearly buckled.

Lush didn't even begin to describe her. Her full breasts, rounded belly and the slight flare of her hips were a lethal combination.

"As I was saying," he went on, cursing his voice when it cracked like that of an adolescent. "I realize that neither of us was prepared for the instant physical attraction—"

"You're delusional," she muttered as she tugged her jeans up over her hips and matching bikini panties.

"But just because I find you sexy as hell doesn't mean I can't control myself."

Her hands froze on her back as she fastened her bra. Apparently his words had struck a chord. She glanced up and caught his gaze in the reflection. Busted.

"Seriously?" she asked with a half laugh. "Why did you even turn around?"

"I didn't know the window was there." That was the truth.

"And you weren't going to say anything?"

Ian spun around—no point in being subtle now. "I'm a guy. What do you think?"

Rolling her eyes, Cassie shrugged into her shirt and buttoned it up with jerky, hurried motions.

Fighting the urge to cross the room and undress her again, Ian slid his hands into his pockets and met her gaze.

"You are stunning," he told her, suddenly feeling the need to drive that point home. "I'm not sure why that statement caught you off guard."

Most women in Hollywood would pause at such a comment, try to deny it in order to hear more pretty words in a vain attempt to boost their own egos, but Ian knew Cassie was different. She truly didn't believe she was beautiful, and he had a feeling all that insecurity circled back to whatever the basis was for her vulnerability.

Damn, he didn't have time to delve into distressed damsels. But there was a desire in him, something primal, almost possessive that made him want to dig deeper, to uncover more of Cassie Barrington. And not just physically.

That revelation alone scared the hell out of him.

"I don't need to be charmed, Ian." She propped her hands on her hips. "We're stuck up here and lying or trying to make me want you isn't going to work."

"I don't lie, Cassie." When she quirked a brow, he merely shrugged. "I find you sexy. Any man would be insane or blind not to."

Cassie shook her head. After zipping the dress into a white garment bag, she headed over to a storage box and popped off the lid. She flopped down on the floor, crossing her legs and offering him the view of her back.

He waited for her to say something, but she seemed to have dismissed him or was so wrapped up in the memories of the photos she was pulling out, she just didn't care that he was there.

"You ever look at a picture and remember that moment so well, you can actually feel it?" she asked, her soft voice carrying across the room.

Ian took that as his invitation to join her. He closed the distance between them, taking a seat directly beside her. Cassie held a picture. A young girl, he presumed it was her, sat atop a horse, and a dark-haired beauty, who he assumed was her mother, held the lead line.

"That was my first horse," she told him, her eyes still on the picture. "I'd always ridden with Dad and helped him around the stables, but this one was all mine. I'd picked him out at auction and Mom and Dad told me I had to care for him all by myself."

Ian looked at the image of a young Cassie. "How old were you?"

"Eight. But I knew as soon as I saw him that I'd want him. He was skittish and shied away from the men, but when I approached him, against my father's advice, he came right to me and actually nuzzled my neck."

Ian listened to her, refusing to let himself fall into her sea of emotions. He'd noticed her and Tessa holding hands at the shoot, tears swimming in both of their eyes.

"I've never ridden a horse," he admitted.

Cassie dropped the picture back into the bin and turned to stare at him. "Seriously? We'll have to rectify that while you're here."

Ian laughed. "I wasn't asking for an invitation. Just stating a fact."

She turned a bit more to face him, her thigh rubbing against his. Did she have a clue that she was playing with fire? She may be older than him, but something told him she wasn't necessarily more experienced.

Arrogance had him believing they weren't on a level playing field. He had plenty he wanted to show her.

"I love teaching people how to ride," she went on, oblivious to his thoughts. "It's such an exhilarating experience."

Cassie's wide smile lit up her entire face. The room had a soft glow from the single-bulb sconce on the wall and Ian could resist those full lips for only so long…especially now that he knew exactly how they tasted.

Without warning, he slid his hands through her hair and captured her lips. She opened freely, just like when they'd been in the stables.

Ian tipped her head, taking the kiss deeper. He wanted more, so much more. He wanted to feel her hands on him as he explored her mouth, relishing her taste, but she didn't touch him. Maybe she did know how to play this age-old game of catch and release.

Easing back, Ian took in her swollen lips, her heavy lids and flushed cheeks and smiled. "Actually, *that's* an exhilarating experience."

And God help them both because between the interlude in the stables and that kiss, he had the whole night to think about how this sexual chemistry would play out.

The real question was: Could he make it all night without finding out?

Four

Cassie jumped to her feet, instantly feeling the chill without Ian's powerful touch. The man was beyond potent and he damn well knew it.

"You seriously think because we're locked in here and we kissed a few times that I'll just have sex with you?" Cassie ran a shaky hand through her hair, cursing her nerves for overtaking her as fast as those heated kisses had. "I don't know what lifestyle you lead in L.A., but that's not how I work."

Ian stared up at her, desire still lurking in those dark-as-sin eyes. "Are you denying you were just as involved in those kisses as I was?"

"You had your hands all over me," she threw back. "Just because I like kissing doesn't mean I always use it as a stepping-stone for sex. I technically just met you, for crying out loud. I don't know anything about you."

Moving as slowly as a panther hunting its prey, Ian came

to his feet and crossed to her. "You know how quick you respond to my touch, you know how your heartbeat quickens when you wonder what my next move will be and you know you're fighting this pull between us."

Cassie raised a brow, trying for her best bored look. "That has nothing to do with Ian Shaffer. That's all chemistry."

"So you don't deny you want me?" he asked with a smirk.

Crossing her arms and taking a step back, Cassie narrowed her eyes. "Drop the ego down a notch. You just proved how very little we know about each other. You may sleep with virtual strangers, but I don't."

Ian laughed, throwing his arms in the air. "Okay. What do you want to know?"

"Are you married?"

Shock slid over his face. "Hell no. Never plan to be."

Commitment issues? Lovely. Hadn't she just gotten out of a relationship with a man of the same nature?

On the other hand, Ian wasn't cheating on a wife back in California. That was at least one mark in his favor. Okay, the toe-curling kisses were major positive points in his favor, but she'd never confess that out loud. And she wasn't actually looking to jump back into another relationship anyway.

"No girlfriend?" she asked.

"Would I be all over you if I did?"

Cassie shrugged. "Some guys wouldn't care."

That heated gaze glided over her and was just as effective as a lover's touch. Her body trembled.

"I'm not like a lot of other guys."

He was powerful, sexy and wanted in her pants. Yeah, he was just like some guys.

With a sigh, Cassie laughed. "I can't believe this," she

muttered more to herself than to Ian. "I'm actually playing twenty questions because I want to have sex."

"Sweetheart, I don't care a bit to answer a hundred questions if you're considering sex."

Lord have mercy, it was hot up there. Not just because of the ridiculous way her body responded to this charmer, but literally. The heat in the attic was stifling.

Cassie unbuttoned the top two buttons of her shirt, exposing her cleavage area, but she needed air. She rolled her sleeves up and caught Ian's eyes taking in her actions.

"Don't get excited there, hotshot. I'm just trying to cool off."

Sweat trickled between her shoulder blades and she so wished she'd at least pulled her hair up earlier. There had to be something up here. As she started to look around in boxes for a rubber band of any type, she tried not to think of Ian and if he had sweat on the taut muscles beneath his shirt.

Okay, that mental blocker was broken because all she could see was glistening bronzed skin. And while she hadn't seen him without a shirt, she had a very good imagination.

"Can I help you find something?" he asked.

Throwing a glance over her shoulder, she caught his smirk as he crossed his arms over his chest. "I just need something to pull my hair up. I'm sweating."

There, that should douse his oversexed status a little. What man found a sweaty woman attractive? And she was pretty sure her wavy red hair was starting to look like Bozo the Clown's after a motorcycle ride...sans helmet. She lifted the flap off a box in the far corner and shuffled things around in her hunt.

"So, why is an agent needed on a film set?" she asked,

truly wondering but also wanting to keep his mind on work—which was what he should be doing anyway.

"Max is one of my top clients." Ian unbuttoned his shirt halfway. "I often visit my clients on set to make sure they're taken care of. And with this being a very impressive script and plot, I knew I had to be here. I've actually blocked off a good bit of time to spend at Stony Ridge."

And wasn't that just the news she needed to hear? Mr. Tall, Dark and Tempting would be spending "a good bit of time" here. Just what her very inactive sexual life needed... temptation.

"Yes," she shouted as she grabbed a rubber band off a stack of school papers from her primary days.

"Max is a great guy, from what I've seen." After pulling her hair into a knot on top of her head, she turned to Ian. "He and Lily are doing an amazing job, too. Lily seems like a sweetheart."

Nodding his agreement, Ian rested a hip against an old dresser. "She's rare in the industry. L.A. hasn't jaded her or sucked the goodness out of her. She had a rough patch with a scandal at the start of her career, but she's overcome it. She's a rare gem."

"And I'm sure you've tried to get her into bed."

Rich laughter filled the space. The fact he was mocking her only ticked Cassie off more. But, if she were honest, she was ticked at herself for wanting him.

"I've never slept with Lily," he told her, a grin still spread across his handsome face. "I've never even tried to. I'm actually hoping to sign her to my agency. I respect my clients and they respect me. This business is too risky and too exposed for anything like that to remain a secret. There are no secrets in Hollywood."

"Is that all that's stopped you? The fact that people could find out?"

Ian straightened to his full height and took a step toward her. *Great.* She'd awoken the sex beast again.

"What stopped me," he said as he took slow steps toward her, "was the fact that, yes, she's beautiful, but I'm not attracted to her. Added to that, I want a professional relationship with her, not a sexual one. If I want a woman in my bed, she won't be on my client list. Plain and simple."

He'd come close enough that Cassie had to tip her head back. Thankfully, he hadn't touched her. Too much more touching—or, heaven forbid, kissing—and she feared her self-control would be totally shot.

Cassie swiped a hand over her damp neck. "Is everything a business strategy with you?"

"Not at all. Right now, I'm not thinking anything about business."

The way his eyes held hers, as if she was the only person that mattered right now, made her wonder...

She may be naive and she was certainly still recovering from Derek walking out on her, but what would a fling hurt? Tessa had even verbally expressed Cassie's thoughts on the matter. She'd married for "love," or so she'd thought. Hell, she'd even saved herself for marriage and look how that had turned out.

"I promise I won't ravage you if you'd like to take something off," he told her with a naughty grin. "I'm sure your shirt will be long enough to cover things if you need to get out of those jeans. If not, I've seen naked women before."

Yeah? Well, not *this* naked woman, and with that last bit of baby weight still hanging on for dear life, she most definitely wasn't comfortable enough with her body to flaunt it. Even if she did indulge in a fling with the sexy agent—and she couldn't believe she was seriously considering such a thing—she wasn't going to make the catch so easy for him. What fun would that be?

Deciding to teach him a lesson, Cassie reached up and patted the side of his face. "You're so sweet to sacrifice yourself that way."

Cassie knew her mother had a box of old clothes up here. Perhaps something could be used to cool her off and make Ian squirm just a bit more.

As she went toward the area with the clothing boxes, she opted to keep Ian talking.

"So, tell me more about Lily." Cassie pulled the lid off an oblong box and nearly wept with relief at the colorful summer dresses inside. "She's very striking and has a strong resemblance to my mother."

"When this film came across my desk, I knew I wanted Max to try for it and I was sincerely hoping they paired him with Lily. This role was made for her. She's already got that Southern-belle charm your mother had, according to everyone on set. Lily has the sweet little twang in her voice like all of you Barringtons do."

Cassie turned, clutching a simple strapless cotton dress to her chest. "I do not have a twang."

Ian quirked a brow. "It's actually even more prominent when you get ticked. Very cute and sexy."

Rolling her eyes, Cassie turned back to the box and placed the lid back on. "I'm going to change. Could you try not to stare at me through the reflection again?"

Ian shrugged one broad shoulder. "I promise."

Cassie waited for him to turn around or move, but he just sat there smiling. Damn that man. Now that she'd reminded him he'd seen her pretty much naked, Cassie had no doubt she'd just thrown gasoline on the fire.

"Aren't you going to turn around?" she finally asked.

"Oh, when you just said not to look at you through the reflection, I assumed you wanted to let me in on the full viewing."

"I didn't want to let you into this room...let alone treat you to a viewing."

Cassie resisted the urge to kiss that smirk off his face. He knew he was getting to her, and she wondered just how much longer she'd deny it to herself.

"I'll move, then," she told him, stomping to the other end of the attic behind a tall stack of boxes. "And don't you follow me."

"Wouldn't dream of it." He chuckled. "But you're just putting off the inevitable, you know."

She quickly wrestled out of her clothes and yanked the strapless dress up over her heated body. Her bare arms and legs cooled instantly.

"I'm not putting anything off," she informed him as she came back around the boxes. "I know your type, Ian. Sex shouldn't just be a way to pass the time. It should mean something, and the couple should have feelings for each other."

"Oh, I feel something for you. And I plan on making you feel something, too."

Why did her body have to respond to him? And why did she always have to be so goody-goody all the time?

She didn't even have the ability to make him squirm. No wonder her husband had left her for another woman.

"I'm not sure what put that look on your face, but I hope it wasn't me."

Cassie drew her attention back to Ian, who had now moved in closer and was very much in her personal space. His dark eyes stared at her mouth and Cassie really tried to remember why she was putting up such a fight.

Had her husband ever looked at her like this? As though he was so turned on that all that mattered was the two of them? Had he ever made her tingle like this or feel so feminine and sexy?

No to all the above.

Cassie swallowed. If she was really going to do this, she needed to be in control. She'd been dominated enough in her marriage and right now she wanted something totally different. She wanted sex and she wanted Ian.

Mustering up all her courage, Cassie looked up at him with a wide smile and said, "Strip."

Five

It wasn't often Ian was shocked—he did live in Hollywood, after all. But that one word that had just slid from Cassie's lips truly took his breath and left him utterly speechless.

"Excuse me?"

Raising a brow, she crossed her arms as if she dared him to refuse. "I said strip. You want this, fine. But on my terms."

"I don't do sex with rules."

Cassie shrugged. "I don't do flings, but here we both are, stepping outside of our comfort zones."

Damn, she was hot. He never would've guessed the shy, quiet sister had this vixen streak. Of course, she admitted she was stepping outside her comfort zone, so perhaps this was all new territory. He had to hand it to her—she was doing a spectacular job. But he couldn't let her have all the control.

Reaching behind his neck, Ian fisted his shirt and tugged it off, flinging it to the side. Hands on his hips, he offered a grin.

"Now you."

Cassie laughed. "You're not done yet."

"No, but I'm ahead of you." He met her gaze, the silent challenge thrown down between them. "I'm waiting."

Even though her eyes never left his, he didn't miss the way her hands shook as she reached beneath the dress and pulled her panties down her bare legs.

Just that simple piece of silk lying discarded at her feet had his pulse racing, his body responding.

She quirked a brow again, as if waiting for him to proceed.

Without hesitation he toed off his shoes and ripped off his socks. "Looks like you're down to only one garment now," he told her, taking in the strapless dress she'd donned.

And it was about to get a whole hell of a lot hotter in here.

She eyed the lamp across the room and started for it.

"No," he told her. "Leave it on."

Glancing over her shoulder, she met his stare. "Trust me when I say you'll want that off."

"And why is that?"

Turning fully to face him, she pointed to her body. "In case you haven't noticed, I'm not one of those Hollywood types who starve themselves for the sake of being ultra-thin."

Crossing the narrow space between them, Ian ran both his hands up her bare arms and tucked his fingers in the elastic of the top of the dress, causing her arms to fall to her side.

"Oh, I've noticed." He yanked the dress down until it

puddled at her feet, leaving her bare to him. "And that's precisely why I want that light on."

Her body trembled beneath his. No way did he want her questioning her gorgeous curves or the fact that he wanted the hell out of her.

Without a word he shucked off his pants and boxer briefs and tossed them aside.

Her eyes drank him in, causing the same effect as if she'd touched his entire body with her bare hands. Dying to touch her, to run his fingers along her curves, Ian snaked his arms around her waist and tugged her against him.

"As much as I want to explore that sexy body of yours, I'm hanging on by a thread here," he admitted as his mouth slammed down onto hers.

Cassie wrapped her arms around his neck. Their damp bodies molded together from torso to thigh, and she felt so perfect against him.

Perfect? No, she couldn't be perfect for him. Perfect for right now, which was all either of them was after.

They were simply taking advantage of the moment...of the sexual attraction that had enveloped them since she'd literally fallen into his arms only a few days ago.

Ian gripped her waist and lifted her.

"Ian, don't—"

"Shh," he whispered against her mouth. "I've got you."

Her lips curved into a smile. "What about a condom? Do you have that, too?"

Condom, yes. They needed a condom. His mind had been on the subtle moans escaping from her lips and getting those curves beneath his hands.

He eased her down his body and went to his jeans, where he pulled a condom from his wallet and in record time had it on.

When he turned back to her, he fully expected her to

have her arms wrapped around her waist, maybe even be biting her lip out of nerves. But what he saw was a secure woman, hands on her hips, head tilted and a naughty grin on her face.

"Your confidence is sexy," he told her as he came back to her.

"You make me feel sexy."

Yeah, she wasn't a Hollywood size zero. Cassie Barrington was more old-school Hollywood starlet. She was a natural, stunning, vibrant woman, and now that she'd agreed to leave the light on, he could fully appreciate the beauty she was.

And when she reached for him and nearly wrapped herself around him as she claimed his mouth, her sexy status soared even higher.

Damn, he wasn't going to make it through this night.

Ian backed her against the wall and lifted her once again. This time her legs went around his waist and he had no control. None. The second he'd shucked that dress off her he'd been holding on by that proverbial thin thread.

Ian took her, causing her body to bow back, and her head tilted, eyes closed as she groaned once again.

As their hips moved together, Ian took the opportunity to kiss his way across her shoulders and the column of her throat before taking her face between his palms and claiming her mouth.

Sweat slick between them, the air around them grew even hotter as Cassie gripped his bare shoulders. Her nails bit into his skin; her heels dug into his back.

He wouldn't have it any other way.

She tore her mouth from his. "Ian, I—"

Yeah, he knew. He was right there with her as her body stilled, trembled. Following her over the edge, watching her face as she succumbed to the passion was one of the most erotic moments of his life.

Her body slid down his and he was pretty sure she would've collapsed to the floor had he not been leaning against her. He needed to lean into her or he'd be a puddle, too.

And the night had just begun.

Cassie slid back into her dress, ignoring the panties. Why bother with modesty at this point?

She may not live in Hollywood, but she'd put on one hell of an acting display. Ian thought her confident? She'd played along simply because she secretly wanted to be that wanton, take-charge woman, that woman who claimed what she wanted. And if he thought she was so comfortable with her body in this situation, then who was she to tell him different?

She'd been meek in her marriage, not a sex goddess in any way. But the way Ian had looked at her, touched her, was nothing like she'd ever experienced.

How could a man she'd known only a handful of days provide so much self-assurance? He'd awakened something within her she hadn't even known existed.

Cassie was certainly not used to one-night stands or flings, but she couldn't regret what had just happened. A virtual stranger had just given her one of the greatest gifts…self-esteem. Not too long ago she'd thought she'd never have that back, but right now, with her body still tingling from his talented hands and lips, Cassie knew without a doubt that she was better than the husband who had left her for another woman.

She'd just scooped up her discarded panties from the floor when Ian placed his hands around her waist and tugged her back against his bare chest.

"How's that age thing now?" he asked, nipping her ear. "Any complaints about how young I am?"

Laughing, Cassie shook her head. "You certainly know what you're doing."

His lips trailed over her neck. "I'm not done, either."

Oh, mercy. Her entire body shivered as she let her head fall back against his shoulder, enjoying the kisses he sprinkled across her heated skin.

"I'm not sure why you put this dress back on," he told her between kisses. "It's so hot in here and all."

Yes, yes, it is.

Cassie turned in his arms, noticing he was still completely naked. Those ripped muscles beneath taut, tanned skin begged for her touch.

"I didn't get to appreciate all of this a moment ago, before you attacked me," she told him, trailing her fingertips along his biceps and across his pecs.

"Appreciate me all you want," he told her with a crooked grin. "But let it be known, I didn't attack. You ordered me to strip, so I believe you started this."

Cassie playfully smacked his chest. "Who started what? You were the one who propositioned me in the stables."

"How's a man supposed to react when a sexy woman falls into his arms?"

"Yes, naturally that's what most people would do," she said, rolling her eyes.

Ian reached down, cupped her backside and widened his sexy smile. "I'm glad this little incident happened with the lock."

Cassie had to admit she was, too. There was no way she would've been able to focus on work with all her emotions fluttering around inside her. Now hopefully she wouldn't have to worry about this overwhelming physical attraction to Ian. They'd had sex, gotten it out of their systems and could move on.

His body stirred against hers. Okay, maybe they hadn't gotten it out of their systems.

"We still have hours before anyone will find us." He started backing her up again. "I have so many ideas to fill the time."

The backs of Cassie's thighs hit the edge of an old table. Ian wasted no time hoisting her up onto the smooth wooden surface.

"Do you have more condoms?" she asked.

His heavy-lidded gaze combined with that Cheshire-cat smile had her quivering before he even spoke.

"I may be out of condoms, but not out of ways to pleasure you."

And when he proceeded to show her, Cassie was suddenly in no hurry for daylight to come.

Six

Unable to sleep for appreciating the feel of this sexy woman tangled all around him on the old chaise, Ian smoothed a hand down Cassie's bare back. Trailing down the dip in her waist, up over the curve of her hip had his body stirring again.

What on earth was he doing? Sex was one thing, but to lie awake most of the night rehashing it over and over in his head like some lovesick fool was, well…for fools. Not that he was any expert on relationships.

His mother was gearing up to divorce husband number four, no doubt with number five waiting in the wings, and his father… Ian sighed. His father probably wasn't even capable of love. Ian hadn't spoken to his father in years and rarely talked with his mother. He had nothing to say to either and it was obvious both of his parents were battling their own issues that didn't include him.

It shouldn't come as a surprise that Ian didn't do relationships.

He was great at his job, however, and what he wanted was to take his client roster to the next level. Lily Beaumont was the key.

Yet here he was, getting involved with Cassie Barrington. And, yes, they'd just had sex, but during the moments in between their intimacy, he'd gotten a brief glimpse of a playful, confident woman and he couldn't deny he liked what he saw.

The sound of a car door jarred him from his thoughts. He eased out from beneath Cassie's warm, lush body and moved over to the small window that faced the side of the house.

Tessa and Grant had arrived. He didn't know if he wanted to call for their attention or crawl back over to Cassie and give her a proper good-morning wake-up.

But their night was over, and he had responsibilities. He honestly had no clue how she'd react once she woke up. Would she regret what they'd done? Would she want more and expect some sort of relationship?

Ian gave the window a tug and it rose slowly with a groan.

"Hey," he yelled down. "Up here."

Tessa and Grant both looked around and Ian eased his arm out to wave. "We're locked in the attic," he called.

"Ian?" Grant shouted. "What on earth? We'll be right up."

Of course, now it dawned on him that both he and Cassie were as naked as the day they were born, and he turned around to see her already getting up. Shame that he hadn't ignored the rescue party and gone with his original idea of waking her, especially now that she was covering that made-for-sex body.

"Was that Tessa and Grant?" she asked, tugging on her jeans from the previous day.

"Uh-huh." He pulled on his own clothes, trying to keep his eyes off her as she wrestled into her bra.

Several moments later, the door below creaked open and Ian rushed over to the top of the stairs to see Tessa.

"We'll be right down," he told her, hoping to save Cassie some time to finish dressing.

He didn't know if she wanted it public knowledge that they'd slept together. This was all her call. He was much more comfortable with a fling than he figured she was. Plus this was her home, her family, and the last thing he wanted to do was put her in an awkward position.

"Who's up there with you?" Tessa asked, her brows drawn together.

"Your sister."

Tessa smiled. "Really? Well, we'll meet you all down in the kitchen. Take your time."

Once she walked away, Ian glanced up to Cassie, who was wearing a lovely shade of red over her neck and face.

"I tried," he defended, holding out his hands. "But I'd say your sister knows."

Cassie nodded. "That's okay. Tessa won't say anything."

Okay, maybe he hadn't wanted a relationship, but her statement hit a nerve. Seconds ago he'd thought he was fine with a fling and she wasn't, but perhaps he'd had that scenario backward.

"Is that what we're going to do? Keep this quiet?"

Smoothing her tousled hair away from her face, Cassie eyed him from across the room and sighed. "I don't know. This is all new to me. Can we just go downstairs and talk later?"

The voice of reason had him nodding. He didn't want to

analyze what had happened too much. They both needed to concentrate on their jobs. After all, he had a mission and she was in the middle of the biggest racing season of her life.

Cassie started to ease by him when he stepped in front of her, blocking her exit. Her eyes went wide, then dropped to his mouth. Why was he doing this?

Quit stalling and let her go.

But he needed one more taste before their night officially came to an end.

He shoved his hands into her hair, tilting her head as he closed the distance between them. "Before you go," he whispered as his mouth slid across hers.

She melted into him as she returned the kiss. Her hands gripped his wrists as he held on to her. As much as Ian wanted her naked once again, he knew that was not an option.

Easing back, he smiled when her eyes took a moment to open. He released her, and, without a word, she walked by him and down the stairs.

And like some nostalgic sap, he glanced around the attic and smiled. This was definitely his favorite place on the estate.

Ian met up with Cassie in the kitchen. As soon as he entered the open room, he took in several things at once.

Tessa and Grant were seated at the bar, where Linda was serving cinnamon rolls. Both Tessa and Grant were eyeing Ian with knowing grins on their faces.

But it was Cassie, yet again, who captured his attention.

The woman he'd spent the night with was currently squatting down in front of a little girl with soft blond curls. The little girl looked nothing like Cassie, but the interaction didn't lie. The way she clung to Cassie, Cassie's sweet smile and laughter as she kissed her—it all had a sickening feeling settling deep in his gut.

"And who's this?" he asked, hoping it was Linda's grandchild or something because he knew Tessa and Grant had no children.

Coming to her feet with the little girl wrapped in her arms, Cassie still wore that vibrant smile as she turned to face him. "This is my daughter, Emily."

All eyes were on Ian. Granted, they were watching him because of the unspoken fact that he and Cassie had spent the night together, but they couldn't know the turmoil that flooded him. Cassie had a child and hadn't told him.

Not that they'd played the getting-to-know-you game before they'd shed their clothes, but wasn't that something that would come up?

Cassie's smile faded as Ian remained silent. Her protective hands held Emily close to her chest.

"Why don't you have some breakfast?" Linda asked, breaking the silence.

His eyes darted to her, then back to Cassie, who still watched him with a questioning look. Tessa and Grant had yet to move as they also took in the unfolding scene.

"I have things to do," he said as he walked by Cassie, ignoring the hurt in her eyes, and out the back door.

He couldn't stay in there another second. Rage filled him at the idea that Cassie had kept such a vital part of her life a secret. Was she the mother who pawned her kid off on other people so she could go have a good time? She'd been so confident, so eager to please him last night. Perhaps he was just the latest in a long line of men she threaded into her web.

No, he hadn't wanted anything beyond sex. And he sure as hell didn't want to discover that the woman he'd spent the night with was manipulative and selfish, looking for attention...just like his mother.

Humiliation flooded her.

The look of utter shock layered with anger had consumed Ian when she'd announced Emily was her daughter.

"Cass?"

Swallowing the hurt, Cassie turned to see her sister watching her. Because this awkward moment didn't need any more fuel added to the fire, Cassie smiled.

"Thanks for watching her last night," Cassie said as she held Emily with one arm and grabbed the overnight bag off the counter. "I need to go change and then I'll meet you at the stables."

"Cassie." Tessa slid from the stool and crossed to her. "Don't do this."

"Do what?"

Blue eyes stared back at her and Cassie wanted nothing more than to sit and cry, but feeling sorry for herself wouldn't accomplish anything. She'd tried that when Derek had left her.

"I just want to go feed Emily and change." Cassie blinked back the burn of tears. "I'll meet you in an hour."

"Leave Emily here," Linda said. "I'm keeping her today anyway. Do what you need to do. I'll make sure she's fed."

As much as Cassie wanted to keep Emily with her, she knew it was silly. She'd just have to put her in her crib with toys while she grabbed a shower.

"All right," she conceded, dropping the bag back onto the counter and easing Emily into the wooden high chair next to the wide granite island. "Thanks, guys."

Barely keeping it together, she started for the door. When Tessa called her name again, Cassie raised a hand

and waved her off. She just wanted to be alone for a minute, to compose herself.

How could she be so naive? Of course some big-city bachelor would be turned off by kids, but to act so repulsed by the fact made her flat-out angry.

She'd sworn when Derek had left she wouldn't allow herself to get hurt again. So, what did she do? Sleep with the first man who showed her any kind of affection.

Seriously, she thought she had more self-respect than that.

More angry at herself now, Cassie marched across the Barrington estate to her cottage next to the stables. Swatting at her damp cheeks, she squinted against the bright early-morning sun.

And because of the light in her eyes she didn't see Ian until she was in the shadow of her house. There he stood, resting against one of the porch posts as if he belonged there.

"Don't you have a client who needs your attention?" she asked, not stopping as she brushed past him and slid her key from her pocket to let herself in.

When she tried to close the door behind her, Ian's muscular arm shot out and his hand gripped the edge.

Those dark eyes leveled hers as she reined in her tears. No way would she let him see just how upset she truly was.

Tension crackled between them as Ian stood on the threshold, making no move to come in or leave.

"What do you want?" she asked.

"I want to know why you didn't tell me you had a daughter."

"Do you have kids?" she retorted.

He blinked. "No."

"Why didn't you tell me you didn't?"

"It never came up."

She threw her arms out. "Exactly. We didn't discuss too much personal stuff before…"

Shaking her head, Cassie looked up to the ceiling and sighed. "Just go. I made a mistake—it's over."

When her front door slammed, she jumped.

"I don't like being played." Ian fisted his hands on his narrow hips.

"This is my life, Ian." She gestured toward the Pack 'n Play in the corner and the toys in a basket next to the sofa. "I'm a mom. I'm not apologizing for it, and you won't make me feel bad."

When he continued to stare, muscle ticking in his jaw, Cassie tried her hardest not to wilt under his powerful presence. His gray T-shirt stretched over taut muscles, and she instantly recalled him taking her against the wall.

"Look, you're going to be here for a while," she said, reality sinking in. "I'm going to be here for the most part except during races. We're going to see each other."

His eyes roamed over her as if he were recalling last night, too. A shiver crept through her, but she remained still, waiting on his response.

"I wish you were different," he told her, his voice low.

Stunned, Cassie crossed her arms. "What?"

Cursing, Ian turned for the door. "Nothing. You're right," he said, gripping the handle and glancing over his shoulder. "We have to see each other, so why make this harder than necessary? Last night was a mistake, so let's just forget it happened."

He walked out the door and Cassie resisted the urge to throw something. For a second, when he'd said he wished she were different, she'd seen a sliver of vulnerability in his eyes. But he'd quickly masked it with his cruel, hurtful words. *Fine.* She didn't need anybody, especially someone who acted as if her child was a burden. Emily came first in her life. Period.

And no man, not her ex-husband and certainly not this sexy stranger, would make her feel ashamed.

Cassie turned toward her bedroom and cursed her body. She hated Ian Shaffer for his words, his actions, but her body still tingled from everything he'd done to her last night. How could someone so passionate and gentle turn into someone so hurtful?

Something about Emily had triggered such a dramatic turnaround. Unfortunately, Cassie didn't have the time or the energy to care. Whatever issues Ian had didn't concern her.

Now she just had to figure out how to see him on a daily basis and block out the fact he'd made her so alive, so confident for a brief time. Because now she didn't feel confident at all. She wished she could have a do-over of last night.

This time she'd keep her clothes on.

Seven

Ian may have had the best sexual experience of his life last night, but any desire he felt for Cassie was quickly squelched when he'd discovered her with a baby. A baby, for crying out loud.

It wasn't that he didn't like children. Kids were innocent in life, innocent in the actions of adults. How could he not love them? He just didn't see any in his future. And Cassie having a child certainly wasn't a problem in and of itself.

No, the issue had been when he'd seen her holding her child and he'd instantly flashed back to his mother, who would drag him from sitter to sitter while she went out at night.

But he wouldn't blame his past for his present problems. His body seemed to forget how angry he was and continued to betray him. Cassie was still sexy as hell and he'd forever be replaying just how hot their encounter had been.

But now that he knew she had a daughter, messing

around on a whim was definitely out. He wasn't cut out for the long term, and he refused to be the lover floating in and out of a kid's life the way his mother's lovers had floated through his.

Shaking off the unpleasant memories seeing Cassie with her baby had inspired, Ian approached Max Ford. His client had recently married his high school sweetheart and the couple had adopted a little girl. Ian couldn't be happier for the guy, but he wanted no part in the happily-ever-after myth himself.

"Hey," Max greeted him as he headed toward the makeup trailer. "Coming in with me?"

"Yeah."

Ian fell into step behind Max. The actor tugged on the narrow door and gestured for Ian to enter first. After climbing the three metal steps, Ian entered the cool trailer and nodded a greeting to the makeup artist.

Max closed the door behind him and exchanged pleasantries with the young lady. Ian took a seat on the small sofa across from the workstation and waited until the two finished their discussion of the day's events.

"You're working out in the stables and field today?" Ian asked. "I saw the script. Looked like the scene with you and Lily when the first horses were brought onto the estate after the wedding."

Max nodded as the makeup artist swiped over his face with a sponge full of foundation. "Yeah. It's a short scene. This afternoon and evening we'll be shooting some of the wedding scenes at the small church in town."

Ian settled deeper into the sofa, resting an arm across the back of the cushion. "Everything going okay so far?"

"Great," Max told him. "Raine is planning on joining me in a few days. She was excited I was shooting on the East Coast."

Ian knew Max and Raine had been through hell after years apart before finally finding their way back to each other in Max's hometown of Lenox, Massachusetts. Ian couldn't imagine trying to juggle a family while working in this crazy industry, let alone from across the country. Speaking of crazy, Ian never thought Hollywood heartthrob Max Ford would settle down, much less on some goat and chicken farm in New England, but to each his own and all that. Love apparently made you do some strange things.

"You talking to Lily soon?" Max asked.

Max had been one of Ian's first clients. They'd both taken a chance on each other, the risk had paid off and here they were, at the top of their games. They had no secrets and oftentimes their relationship was more like friends than business associates.

"Yeah. Hoping to get a few more minutes with her today."

The makeup artist reached for a brush and started stroking a shadow across Max's lids. Yeah, Ian would much rather stay on this side of the industry...the side where his face stayed makeup-free.

"I'll keep you posted," Ian said, not wanting to get too detailed since there were other ears in the room. "I plan on being on set for the next several weeks, so hopefully something will come from that."

Something positive. There was no way Ian wanted his ex-partner to get his clutches on Lily. Not to mention Ian was selfish and now that Lily was between agents, he wanted her because she was one of the top Hollywood leading ladies.

Added to that, she was the rare celebrity who hadn't been jaded or swayed by the limelight. Lily was the real deal who made a point to keep her nose out of trouble.

Any agent's dream client.

"I've discussed some things with her," Max stated. "She's

interested in hearing your terms and ideas, so hopefully she makes the right decision."

Ian was counting on it. Lily was smart enough to know the industry. After all, she'd just left her agent, who'd been a bit shady with her career. She'd put a stop to that immediately.

Ian could only hope she saw the hands-on way he worked and how invested he was as an agent. Visiting movie sets was his favorite job perk. Getting out of a stuffy office and being on location was always the highlight. Plus he wanted to make sure his clients were comfortable and there were no glitches.

"I'll be around if you need me." Ian came to his feet and moved toward the trailer door, pulling his phone from his pocket to check his emails. "I plan on being at both scenes today."

"Sounds good. I assume you've met all the Barringtons?" Max asked as the makeup artist ran the powder brush over his neck.

Ian swallowed. "Yeah. I've met them."

Met them, slept with one and still felt the stirrings from the continuous play of memories.

"They're one impressive family," Max went on, oblivious to the turmoil within Ian. "Damon is an amazing man with all of his accomplishments, but I swear, Cassie and Tessa are a force to be reckoned with."

Ian bit the inside of his cheek to avoid commenting on one of those "forces." The image of her in that body-hugging dress still made his knees weak, his heart quicken.

"That's why this movie is going to kick ass," Ian said, circling back to work, where his mind needed to stay. "Everyone loves a story like this, and having it on the big screen with two of Hollywood's top stars will only make it pull in that much more at the box office."

"I hope you're right."

Ian was confident this movie would be one of the biggest for both Max and Lily. Hollywood's heartthrob and sweetheart playing a married couple in a true story? It was a guaranteed slam dunk for everybody.

Which reminded him, he needed to check his emails and hopefully line up another client's role.

"I'll see you in a bit," Ian said as he exited the trailer.

He refused to glance toward Cassie's cottage. He wasn't some love-struck teen who'd slept with a woman and now wondered what she was doing every waking minute.

Okay, so he did wonder what she was doing, but love had absolutely nothing to do with it. His hormones were stuck in overdrive and they would just have to stay there because he refused to see her in any type of personal atmosphere again.

Even flings warranted a certain type of honesty, and getting involved, in any manner, with a woman who reminded him of the past he'd outrun was simply not an option.

A flash of movement from the field in the distance caught his eye. He headed toward the white fence stretching over the Barrington estate. As he neared, his gut tightened.

Cassie sat atop a chestnut-colored horse flying through the open field. Her hair danced unrestrained in the wind behind her and the breeze carried her rich laughter straight to him…and his body responded…work and emails instantly forgotten.

Ian stood frozen and admired the beauty. From behind her came Tessa on her own horse, but Ian's gaze was riveted on Cassie. He hadn't heard that deep laugh. She all but screamed sex with that throaty sound, her curves bouncing in the saddle, hair a wild mass of deep crimson curls.

Her carefree attitude would've been such a turn-on, but in the back of his mind he couldn't forget where he came from. From a father who had standards so high nobody could reach them and a mother who spent her time entertaining boyfriends and husbands, leaving a young Ian a distant second in her life.

He never wanted to go back to that emotional place again.

"You've got an audience."

Breathless and smiling, Cassie turned to her sister as Tessa came to a stop beside her. This felt good, to get out and not worry about training or anything else for a few minutes. Just getting back to their roots and racing was something she and her sister didn't do nearly often enough.

"Who's the audience?" Cassie asked, fully expecting to see some of the film crew. The cameramen and lighting people seemed to be all over the estate, moving things around, making the place their own for the sake of the film. The Hollywood scene was definitely a far cry from the usual relaxed atmosphere of Stony Ridge.

A sense of pride welled deep within her at the fact that Hollywood loved her family's story as much as she did. Horses, racing and family… That was what it meant to be a Barrington, and they excelled at it all because they worked hard and loved harder.

"Your agent," Tessa replied, nodding back toward the fence line. "I saw him stop when you raced by. He hasn't moved."

Cassie risked a glance and, sure enough, Ian stood turned in her direction. He was just far enough away that she couldn't make out his facial expression…not that she cared. But damn, why did he have to be a jumbled mess? He'd wanted her with such passion last night, had made her feel so special and wanted. How dare he pull such emotions out of her when she was still trying to piece the shards of her heart back together after her divorce?

Today when he'd seen Emily, he'd become detached, angry and not at all the same man she'd been with last night. His silence had hurt her, had made the night before instantly ugly.

And after coming home, she'd checked her phone and found a missed call from Derek. Seriously? After months of no contact whatsoever, now he decided to call? Cassie had deleted the message without listening. She didn't care what he had to say, and, after her emotional morning with Ian, she wasn't in the mood.

"He's not my anything." Cassie turned back toward Tessa, turning her back on Ian and willing him to go away.

"He was something to you last night."

Squinting against the sun, Cassie shrugged. "He was my temporary mistake. Nothing more."

Leaning across the gap between the horses, Tessa slid her hand over Cassie's. "I'm not judging at all. I just want you to know people aren't perfect. We all make rash decisions, and beating yourself up won't change what happened."

Cassie knew Tessa would be the last person to judge her, but that didn't stop the embarrassment from settling in her gut.

"I just hate that I gave in to the first man to show me any attention since being divorced," Cassie explained, gripping the reins.

Tessa's warm smile spread across her face. "Honey, Ian is a very attractive man, you're a beautiful woman and you all were locked in an attic all night. Instant attraction is hard to ignore, especially when you have nothing else to focus on."

"Self-control is a beautiful thing," Cassie murmured. "Too bad I didn't have any."

Laughing, Tessa squeezed Cassie's hand before pulling back. "Yeah, well, I didn't have any where Grant was concerned, either, and look how well it worked out for us."

Cassie's eyes darted down to the impressive diamond band surrounding Tessa's ring finger. Grant had gotten a flat band because of Tessa's riding career; he knew she wouldn't want to work with anything too bulky.

And that proved just how beautiful a relationship her sister and Grant had. The man knew Tessa inside and out, loved her and her career. He'd even overcome his own personal demons to be with her.

Cassie couldn't be happier for the two of them, but her situation was different.

"I'm pretty sure my attic rendezvous will not be leading to any proposals," Cassie joked. She had to joke with Tessa, otherwise she'd cry, and she refused to let this experience pull her down and make her feel guilty for having needs. "Besides, I think seeing Emily was like a bucket of cold water in Ian's face. I won't be with anybody who can't accept that I'm a package deal."

"I saw Ian's face when he found out Emily was yours," Tessa said, shoving her hair behind her ear. "He was definitely caught off guard, but the man wasn't unaffected by whatever happened between the two of you or he wouldn't have just stopped to watch you ride by. He may be torn, but he's still interested. You can't blame him for being shocked you're a mother."

Yeah, well, Ian's interest more than likely consisted of getting in her pants again…which she wouldn't allow.

But the memory of last night still played through her mind. His touch had been perfect. His words had seduced her until she'd forgotten about anything else but the moment they were locked in.

No matter how her body craved to be touched by his talented hands again, Cassie knew she deserved better than the way she'd been treated afterward.

So if Ian wanted her, that was his problem and he'd have to deal with it. She had enough on her plate without worrying about some big-time Hollywood agent who was only looking for only a fling.

She had a racing season to finish and a school for handicapped children to get started.

Her soon-to-be brother-in-law, Grant, had a paralyzed sister who used to ride, and her story had inspired Cassie on so many levels. Even though they hadn't met yet, just her story alone was enough to drive Cassie to want more for the next chapter of life. And what better way to teach her daughter to give back and love and care for others? Instilling love in young children made all the difference. She and Tessa were evidence of that.

Throwing a glance over her shoulder, Cassie had mixed emotions when she saw Ian was nowhere in sight. On one hand, she was glad he'd moved on. On the other, she kind of liked knowing she'd left some sort of impression on him.

No matter how things were now, for a time last night, she'd been in a sexy man's arms and that man had been attentive and giving and had made her feel more self-worth than ever.

Having regrets at this point was kind of in vain.

Besides, no matter what common sense played through her mind, she couldn't deny the physical pull she still felt toward Ian. And she was positive she hadn't seen the last of him.

Eight

After shooting wrapped for the day, Ian headed toward the stables to see if Lily was in there. He hadn't seen her for two days, and Max had mentioned he'd seen her heading that way. Ian hadn't had a chance to speak with her yet. The chaos of filming and so many people around had gotten in the way. Other than the usual small talk, he'd not been able to catch her alone.

Hopefully he could find her and perhaps they could arrange for a time to sit down and talk.

The sun was just at the edge of the horizon, casting a vibrant orange glow across the sky. The air had turned warmer as spring approached summer. Soon they'd be off to the Preakness Stakes, where Tessa would try to win the second race on her way toward the coveted Triple Crown.

The entire crew was riding the high of the shoot as well as getting sucked into the excitement of cheering the Barrington girls on toward victory. He had no doubt Tessa and Cassie were a jumble of anticipation and nerves.

Ian shoved his hands into his pockets as he approached the stables. He wasn't letting his mind wander to Cassie, because if he thought of her, he'd think of her sweet curves, her tempting smile and the fact he still wanted her.

Before he could travel too far down that path of mixed emotions, Ian rounded the corner of the open stable door and froze.

Lily was in the stable all right. But she wasn't alone. The groom, Ian believed his name was Nash, had his back to Lily, and Lily's hand rested on his shoulder, a look of concern marring her beautiful face.

She whispered something Ian couldn't make out and Nash's head dropped at the same time Lily's arms slid around his waist and she rested her forehead on his back. The intimate, private moment shocked Ian and he really had no clue what he'd walked in on.

The old-fashioned lanterns suspended from the ceiling cast a perfect glow on them and Ian quickly stepped out of the stable before he could be spotted…or interrupt whatever was happening.

He had a feeling whatever was going on between the groom and the star of the film was on the down low… especially since an affair had nearly cost Grant Carter his job when he'd been sneaking to see Tessa.

But that had all worked out and the two were headed down the aisle in the near future.

Their secret would be safe with him. For one, he wanted Lily to trust him and sign with his agency. And for another, why stir up trouble? Ian couldn't help but laugh. He and Cassie were pretty far-fetched in terms of the possibility of getting together, but look where they were now after a heated night in the attic.

Heading back toward his on-site trailer, Ian stopped when a scream cut through the evening. It was loud enough to have him trying to figure out where the sound was coming from.

He heard it again and moved toward the row of cottages settled beyond the main house. The grounds were deserted now since the entire crew had left for the hotel in town. Only a handful of people were staying on the property in trailers like the one Max had requested for him. The scream split through the air once more and Ian quickly found the culprit.

Just behind Cassie's cottage there was a small patio area and suspended from the pergola was a child's swing.

Cassie pushed her daughter, and each time the child went high, she let out a squeal. Ian's heart dropped at the sight. He didn't recall ever having that one-on-one playful time with either of his parents. Perhaps when he'd been a toddler, but he doubted it, considering they weren't affectionate when he'd been old enough to recall.

The sweet little girl with blond curls blowing in the breeze giggled and kicked her feet when Cassie grabbed the back of the plastic seat on the swing and held it back.

"Hold on," Cassie warned. "Here comes the biggest push of all."

When she let go of the swing, Cassie laughed right along with her daughter and Ian found himself rooted to his spot at the edge of her concrete patio.

The man in him watched, admiring Cassie's laid-back style, with her hair in a ponytail and wearing leggings and an oversize T-shirt that slid off one delicate, creamy shoulder. Her feet were bare and her face was void of any makeup, which was how he'd seen her since he'd arrived. Everything about her screamed country girl.

While the man in him watched, the lost little boy in him turned his attention to Emily. He took in all the delight from the sweet girl still clutching the rope holding up her swing and wondered where her father was. Did the man even know he had a child? Did Cassie have any contact with him?

All the questions forming in his head were absolutely none of his business, yet he couldn't help but want to know more.

Ian's gaze traveled from Emily back to Cassie...and he found her looking right back at him with those impressive blue eyes.

"What are you doing here?" she asked, giving the swing another light push.

Ian tried not to focus on the fact that her shirt had slipped in the front, giving him a glimpse of the swell of her breast.

"I heard screaming." He stepped onto the concrete pad, cursing himself for being drawn in even more. "I wasn't sure who it was."

Cassie's eyes held his for a second before she turned her attention back to the swing. She held on to the ropes, thus bringing Emily's fun to a screeching halt.

The little girl twisted in her seat to look back at Cassie. Cassie went to the front of the swing, unfastened the safety harness and lifted Emily out.

"We were just heading in for dinner," Cassie said, propping Emily up on her hip.

Damn if her tilted, defiant chin didn't make him want to stay longer. Why torture himself? He wanted her physically, nothing more. Yet he found himself being pulled ever so slowly toward her.

"Don't go in just because of me."

Emily stared at him with bright, expressive blue eyes like her mother's. Her hand reached toward him and he couldn't stop himself from reaching back. The moment he looked into those little baby blues something unidentifiable slid over his heart.

Emily's tiny hand encircled his finger as a smile spread across her baby face. That innocent gesture touched so many places in him: the child who'd craved attention, the teen who'd needed guidance and the adult who still secretly wished he had a parent who gave a damn without being judgmental.

Ian didn't miss the way Cassie tensed at the sight of Emily holding on to his finger, but he wasn't pulling back. How could he deny such an innocent little girl human touch? She was smiling, happy and had no clue the turmoil that surrounded her right now.

"Don't you have a client you should tend to?" Cassie asked, her meaning that he was not welcome all too clear.

"I already talked with Max after the shooting wrapped and we came back here." The crew had taken a few shots of the wedding scene in town. "I didn't see you at the church earlier."

Cassie reached up, smoothing away blond curls from Emily's forehead. "I was there. I stayed in the back with Tessa. We didn't want to get in the way."

"What did you think of the shoot?"

Why was he still here talking to her? Why didn't he just leave? He had calls to return, emails to answer, contracts to look over.

Besides the fact a little cherublike toddler had his finger in a vise grip, he could walk away. Cassie had made it clear she didn't like him, and he certainly wasn't looking for a woman with a child.

Yet here he stood, talking to her and eagerly awaiting her answer.

"It was perfect," she said, a soft smile dancing across her lips. "Lily looked exactly like the pictures I've always seen of my mother on that day. My father teared up, so I know Lily and Max hit that scene beautifully."

Ian wiggled his finger, making Emily giggle as she tugged on him. He took a step forward, now being drawn in by two intriguing ladies.

"I think the fans will fall in love with this film," he told Cassie as his eyes settled on hers. "And your family."

The pulse at the base of her throat quickened and Ian couldn't help but smile. Good to know she wasn't so unaffected. What they'd shared the other night was nothing short of amazing. No matter what transpired afterward, he couldn't deny that had been the most intense night of his life.

Damn it. Cassie and her innocent daughter were the exact picture of the commitment he could never make.

So how could he be drawn to this woman?

"I just want my father to be happy with the end result," she told him. "I want people to see what a hard worker he is and that everything didn't get handed to him."

Ian couldn't help but admire her for wanting people to see the other side of Damon Barrington. The man was a phenomenon, and Ian had no doubt whatsoever that this film would be a mega blockbuster.

Emily let go of his finger and started patting her mother's cheeks. Instantly Ian missed the innocent touch, but he stepped back and shoved his hands into his pockets.

"Was there something else you wanted?" she asked.

Clearing his throat, Ian shoved pride aside and nodded. "Actually, yeah. I'm sorry for how I handled the other morning."

Cassie's brows rose as she reached up to try to pull Emily's hands from her face. "I never expected you to apologize."

He hadn't expected it, either, but he couldn't deny the

fact he'd been a jerk. If he'd learned anything from growing up, it was to know when to apologize. He'd never seen his parents say they were sorry to each other, and he'd always wondered if such a simple gesture would have made a difference.

"I can admit when I make a mistake," he informed her.

Those bright eyes darted down as she sighed. "This is a first for me."

"What's that?"

Glancing back up, she shook her head. "Nothing. I appreciate you apologizing. Since you're going to be here awhile, I really don't want tension. Between you working and me training, I just can't handle more stress."

Ian noticed the soft lines between her brows, the dark circles beneath her eyes. This single mother was worn-out and he'd added to her worry because she hadn't wanted any awkwardness between them.

"Who helps you with Emily?"

Great, now he was asking questions before he could fully process them. He needed a filter on his mouth and he needed to mind his own business. The last thing he wanted was to worry about Cassie and her daughter. He certainly wasn't applying for the position of caregiver.

"My family." Her chin tilted as she held his gaze, unblinking. "Why?"

Yeah, why indeed? Why was this his concern? They'd slept together one night after days of intense sexual tension and now he was all up in her personal space…a space that hit too close to home and touched his heart way too deeply.

He pushed aside the unwanted emotions. He would be here only a short time. Even if his past hadn't mixed him all up, he still couldn't get too involved with Cassie Barrington.

Besides, she had her hands full and they'd definitely

done a complete one-eighty since they'd spent the night together. That night had been full of passion and surrender. Now Cassie had erected walls, thanks to him, and the only thing he saw in her eyes was exhaustion.

"I'll let you get in to dinner," he told her, not answering her question. "See you tomorrow."

When he turned away, Cassie called his name. He glanced over his shoulder and found two sets of beautiful blue eyes staring at him.

"We're not having much, but you're welcome to join us."

The olive branch had been extended and he wondered if this was her manners and upbringing talking or if she truly wanted him to stay.

"I'd be a fool to turn down dinner with two pretty ladies," he told her, turning back to face her. "Are you sure?"

With a shaky nod, Cassie smiled. "I'm sure."

Well, hell. Looked as if he was getting in deeper after all. But he followed her through the back door like the lost man that he was.

They could be friends, he thought. Friends ate dinner together; friends apologized when they were wrong. That was where they were at now because Cassie and her little girl deserved a commitment, a family life—things he couldn't offer.

As Cassie slid Emily into her high chair, Ian watched her delicate skin as her shoulder peeked from her shirt once again. Anything he was feeling right now went way beyond friendship and ventured down the path at warp speed toward carnal desire.

Nine

Cassie had no clue what had prompted her to invite Ian inside. She wasn't weak. She didn't need a man and had been just fine on her own for the better part of a year now. But something about Ian kept pulling her toward him, as if some invisible force tugged on her heart.

And when Emily had reached for him, Cassie had waited to see his reaction. Thankfully, he'd played right along. She'd barely noticed his hesitation and hard swallow, but he hadn't disappointed Emily. Maybe kids weren't the issue with him; perhaps he was just upset because she hadn't said anything. But really, when would that conversation have occurred? When she had fallen into his arms that first day or when she'd told him to strip in the attic?

The image of him doing just that flooded her mind. Cassie was thankful her back was to him as she turned on the oven.

"Hope you like grilled cheese and French fries." Cassie

reached into the narrow cabinet beside the oven and pulled out a cookie sheet.

"Considering I was going to probably have microwave popcorn back in my trailer, grilled cheese and fries sounds gourmet."

Her phone vibrated on the counter next to the stove. She saw Derek's name flash across the screen. No and no. If he was so determined to talk to her, he knew where she was.

Right where he'd left her months ago. Pompous jerk.

As she busied herself getting the meager dinner ready for the other man who was driving her out of her mind in a totally different way, she mentally cursed. Ian was probably used to fine dining, glamorous parties and beautiful women wearing slinky dresses and dripping in diamonds. Unfortunately, tonight he was getting a single mother throwing together cheese sandwiches while wearing an old, oversize T-shirt to hide her extra weight.

More than likely he'd said yes because he felt sorry for her. Regardless, he was in her house now. Surprisingly he'd pulled up a kitchen chair next to the high chair and was feeding puff snacks to Emily.

The sight had Cassie blinking back tears. Emily's father should be doing that. He should be here having dinner with them, as a family. He should've stuck it out and kept his pants zipped.

But he'd decided a wife and a baby were too much of a commitment and put a damper on his lifestyle.

In the back of her mind, Cassie knew she was better off without him. Any man that didn't put his family first was a coward. Not suitable material for a husband or father to her child.

But the reality of being rejected still hurt. Cassie could honestly say she'd gotten over her love, but the betrayal… That was something she would probably never recover from. Because he'd not just left her; he'd left a precious, innocent baby behind without even attempting to fight for what he'd created.

Being rejected by Ian was just another blow to her already battered self-esteem.

"You okay?"

Cassie jerked back to the moment and realized two things. One, Ian was staring at her, his brows drawn together, and two, she'd worn a hole in the bread from being too aggressive applying the butter.

Laughing, Cassie tossed the torn bread onto the counter and grabbed another piece from the bag. "Yeah. My mind was elsewhere for a minute."

"Were you angry with that slice of bread?" he asked with a teasing grin.

"I may have had a little aggression I needed to take out." Cassie couldn't help but laugh again. "You're pretty good with her. Do you have nieces or nephews?"

Ian shook his head. "I'm an only child. But there was a set I visited not too long ago that had a baby about Emily's age. He was the cutest little guy and instantly wanted me over anyone else. I guess kids just like me."

Great. Now he had a soft spot for kids. Wasn't that the exact opposite of the image he'd portrayed the other morning when seeing Emily for the first time?

Ian Shaffer had many facets and she hated that she wanted to figure out who the real Ian was deep down inside.

Dinner was ready in no time, and thankfully, the silence wasn't too awkward. Eating and caring for a baby helped fill the void of conversation. When they were done, Ian went to clear the table and Cassie stopped him.

"I'll get it," she told him, picking up her own plate. "It's not that much."

"You cooked. The least I could do is help clean." He picked up his plate and took it to the sink. "Besides, if you cook more often, I'll gladly clean up after."

Cassie froze in the midst of lifting Emily from her high chair. "You want to come back for dinner?" she asked.

"I wouldn't say no if you asked."

Cassie settled Emily on her hip and turned to Ian, who was putting the pitcher of tea into the refrigerator. Okay, now she knew this wasn't pity. He obviously wanted to spend time with her. But why? Did he think she'd be that easy to get into bed again? Of course he did. She'd barely known his name when she'd shed her clothes for him. What man wouldn't get the impression she was easy?

Cassie turned and went into the living room, placed Emily in her Pack 'n Play and handed her her favorite stuffed horse. Footsteps shuffled over the carpet behind her and Cassie swallowed, knowing she'd have to be up front with Ian.

"Listen," she said as she straightened and faced the man who stood only a few feet away. "I have a feeling you think I'm somebody that I'm not."

Crossing his arms over his wide chest, Ian tilted his head and leveled those dark eyes right on her. "And what do you believe I think of you?"

Well, now she felt stupid. Why did he make this sound like a challenge? And why was she getting all heated over the fact he was standing in her living room? No man had been there other than her father and her soon-to-be brother-in-law. She'd moved into the guest cottage on the estate after Derek had left her so she could be closer to the family for support with Emily.

So seeing such a big, powerful man in her house was a little…arousing. Which just negated the whole point she was trying to make. Yeah, she was a juxtaposition of nerves and emotions.

"I think because we slept together you think I'm eager to do it again." She rested her hands on her hips, willing them to stop shaking. She had to be strong, no matter her physical attraction to Ian. "I'm really not the aggressive, confident woman who was locked in that attic."

Ian's gaze roamed down her body, traveled back up and landed on her mouth as he stepped forward. "You look like the same woman to me," he said, closing the gap between them. "What makes you think you're so different from the woman I spent the night with?"

She couldn't think with him this close, the way his eyes studied her, the woodsy scent of his cologne, the way she felt his body when he wasn't even touching her.

"Well, I…" She smoothed her hair back behind her ears and tipped her head to look him in the eye. "I'm afraid you think that I look for a good time and that I'm easy."

A ghost of a smile flirted around those full lips of his. "I rushed to judgment. I don't think you're easy, Cassie. Sexy, intriguing and confident, but not easy."

Sighing, she shook her head. "I'm anything but confident."

Now his hands came up, framed her face and sent an insane amount of electrical charges coursing through her. As much as she wanted his touch, she couldn't allow herself to crave such things. Hadn't she learned her lesson? Physical attraction and sexual chemistry did not make for a solid base for family, and, right now, all she could focus on was her family. Between Emily and the race with her sister, Cassie had no time for anything else.

But, oh, how she loved the feel of those strong, warm palms covering her face, fingertips slipping into her hair.

"You were amazing and strong in the attic," he told her.

He placed a finger over her lips when she tried to speak. "You may not be like that all the time, but you were then. And that tells me that the real you came out that night. You had no reason to put on a front with me and you were comfortable being yourself. Your passion and ability to control the situation was the biggest turn-on I've ever experienced."

Cassie wanted to tell him he was wrong, that she wasn't the powerful, confident woman he thought she was.

But she couldn't say a word when he leaned in just a bit more, tickling his lips across hers so slowly that Cassie feared she'd have to clutch on to his thick biceps to stay upright.

She didn't reach up, though. Didn't encourage Ian in tormenting her any further.

But when his mouth opened over hers so gently, coaxing hers open, as well, Cassie didn't stop him. Still not reaching for him, she allowed him to claim her. His hands still gripped her face, his body pressed perfectly against hers and she flashed back instantly to when they'd had nothing between them. He'd felt so strong, so powerful.

More than anything to do with his looks or his charming words, he made her feel more alive than she'd ever felt.

Ian's lips nipped at hers once, twice, before he lifted his head and looked her straight in the eyes.

The muscle ticked in his jaw as he slowly lowered his hands from her face and stepped back. "No, Cassie. Nothing about you or this situation is easy."

Without another word, he turned and walked through her house and out the back door. Cassie gripped the edge of the sofa and let out a sigh. She had no clue what had just happened, but something beyond desire lurked in Ian's dark eyes. The way he'd looked at her, as if he was wrestling his own personal demon...

Cassie shook her head. This was not her problem. Sleeping with the man had brought up so many complications—the main reason she never did flings.

Was that why she kept feeling this pull? Because sex just wasn't sex to her? For her to sleep with someone meant she had some sort of deeper bond than just lust. How could she not feel attached to the man who made her feel this alive?

Glancing down to sweet Emily, who was chewing on her stuffed horse, Cassie rested her hip against the couch. This baby was her world and no way would she be that mother who needed to cling to men or have a revolving door of them.

Better to get her head on straight and forget just how much Mr. Hollywood Agent affected her mind.

Trouble was, she was seriously afraid he'd already affected her heart.

Ten

"My girls ready for next week?"

Cassie slid the saddle off Don Pedro and threw a glance over her shoulder to her father. Damon Barrington stalked through the stables that he not only owned, but at one time had spent nearly every waking hour in.

Even though the Barringtons' planned to retire from the scene after this racing season, Damon still wasn't ready to sell the prizewinning horses. He'd had generous offers, including one from his biggest rival in the industry, Jake Mason, but so far no deal had been made. Cassie highly doubted her father would ever sell to Jake. The two had been competitors for years and had never gotten along on the track…or off it.

"We're as ready as we'll ever be," Tessa said as she started brushing down the Thoroughbred. "My time is even better than before. I'm pretty confident about the Preakness."

Damon smiled, slipping his hands into the pockets of his worn jeans. The man may be a millionaire and near royalty in the horse industry because of his Triple Crown win nearly two decades ago, but he still was down-to-earth and very much involved in his daughters' careers.

"I know you'll do the Barrington name proud, Tess." He reached up and stroked the horse's mane as Cassie slid in beside her father.

"What are you doing down here?" Cassie asked. "Thought you'd be keeping your eye on the film crew."

Damon patted the horse and reached over to wrap an arm around Cassie's shoulders. A wide grin spread across his tanned, aged face. His bright blue eyes landed on hers.

"The lighting guys are reworking the living room right now," he explained. "The scene they shot the other day wasn't quite what they wanted. They're shooting a small portion again this afternoon."

This whole new world of filming was so foreign to her, but the process was rather fascinating. "I plan on heading into town and picking up some feed later," she told him. "I guess I'll miss watching that."

And more than likely miss seeing Ian again—which was probably for the best. She needed space after that simple dinner and arousing kiss last night. He hadn't been by the stables and she hadn't seen him around the grounds, so he was probably working...which was what she needed to concentrate on.

"I thought I'd take Emily with me and maybe run her by that new toy store in town," Cassie went on. "She's learning to walk now and maybe I can find her something she can hold on to and push around to strengthen her little legs."

Damon laughed. "Once she starts walking, she'll be all over this place."

Cassie smiled. "I can't wait to see how she looks in a saddle."

Tessa came around Don Pedro and started brushing his other side. "Why don't you take her for a ride now? I'm sure she'd love it and it's such a nice day out. We're done for a while anyway."

The idea was tempting. "I still need to get feed, though."

"I'll send Nash to get it," Damon spoke up. "He won't mind."

Cassie leaned her head against her father's strong shoulder. "Thanks, Dad."

Patting her arm, Damon placed a kiss on top of her head. "Anytime. Now go get my granddaughter and start training her right."

Excited for Emily's first ride, Cassie nearly sprinted to the main house and through the back door to the kitchen, where Linda was washing dishes.

"Hey, Linda." Cassie glanced over the island to see Emily in her Pack 'n Play clapping her hands and gibbering to her animals. "I'm going to take Emily off your hands for a bit."

"Oh, she's no trouble at all." Linda rinsed a pan and set it in the drainer before drying her hands and turning. "I actually just sat her in there. We've been watching the action in the living room. She likes all the lights."

Cassie scooped up her girl and kissed her cheek. "I'm sure she does. She'd probably like to crawl all over and knock them down."

Laughing, Linda crossed to the double ovens in the wall and peeked inside the top one. "I'm sure she would, but I held on tight. The cranberry muffins are almost done if you'd like one."

Yeah, she'd love about six warm, gooey muffins dripping with butter, but she'd resist for the sake of her backside.

"Maybe later. I'm taking Emily for her first ride."

A wide smile blossomed across Linda's face. "Oh, how fun. She's going to love it."

"I hope so," Cassie said. "I'll be back in a bit."

When Cassie stepped back into the barn, Tessa had already saddled up Oliver, the oldest, most gentle horse in the stables. Cassie absolutely couldn't wait to see Emily's excitement as she took her first horseback ride.

"He's all ready for you," Tessa exclaimed, reaching for Emily.

Cassie mounted the horse and lifted Emily from Tessa's arms. Settling her daughter in front of her and wrapping an arm around her waist, Cassie reached for the rein and smiled down to Tessa.

"Get a few pics of us when we're in the field, would you?"

Tessa slid her hand into her pocket and held up her phone. "I'm set. You guys look so cute up there," she said, still grinning. "My niece already looks like a pro."

Cassie tugged on the line and steered Oliver out of the barn and into the field. The warm late-spring sunshine beat down on them and Cassie couldn't help but smile when Emily clapped her hands and squealed as the horse started a light trot.

"This is fun, isn't it, sweetie?" Cassie asked. "When you get big, Mommy will buy you your own horse and he will be your best friend."

Cassie didn't know how long they were riding, and she didn't really care. Memories were being made, and even though Emily wouldn't recall this day at all, Cassie would cherish it forever. She thought of her own mother and held Emily a little tighter. Her mom lived in her heart and there was an attic full of pictures and mementos to remember her by.

Turning Oliver to head back toward the front fields, Cassie swallowed as new memories overtook her. That attic wasn't just a room to store boxes and old furniture. Now the attic was a place where she'd given herself to a man…a dangerous man. He made her feel too much, want too much.

And what was with him wanting to eat dinner with her and Emily? Not that she minded, but having him in her house just once was enough to have her envisioning so much more than just a friendly encounter.

She had to admit, at least to herself, that Ian intrigued her. And if she was going that far, she also had to admit that every part of her wished he weren't just passing through. She missed the company of a man…and not just sex. She missed the conversation, the spark of excitement in harmless flirting… Okay, fine, she missed the sex, too.

But it really was so much more than that. There was a special connection, a certain bond that strengthened after being intimate. At least there was for her. Perhaps that was why she couldn't dismiss what had happened between her and Ian so easily.

As she neared the stables, she caught sight of Ian walking toward the main house with the beautiful Lily Beaumont at his side. The gorgeous actress was laughing and Cassie had to ignore the sliver of jealousy that shot through her. Ian wasn't hers by any means, no matter what she may wish for.

And Lily was a very sweet woman, from what Cassie had experienced on the set. As Cassie watched the two head toward the front door, she couldn't help but get a swift kick back into reality. Ian and Lily were from the same world. They were near the same age, for crying out loud.

In comparison, Cassie was just a worn-out single mom. Squeezing Emily tight and placing a kiss on her little mop of curls, Cassie knew she wouldn't wish to be anything else. Being the solid foundation for Emily was the most important job of her life, and for now, all her daughter's needs had to come first. One day, Cassie vowed, she'd take time for herself and perhaps find love.

"I'm actually considering your offer and one other," Lily stated.

Ian rested his hand on the knob of the front door. "You don't have to tell me the other agency. I already know."

And damn if he'd lose this starlet to his rival. They'd ruin her and not give a damn about reputation, only the bottom line, which was money to them.

"It's not a decision I'm going to make overnight." Lily lifted her hand to shield her eyes from the afternoon sun. "I am glad you're on set, though, because that will give us more of a chance to discuss terms and what I'm looking for in an agency."

Good. That sounded as though she was interested in him. "I'm ready to talk anytime you are."

A bright smile spread across her face. "Well, right now I'm needed for a scene, but perhaps we could have lunch or dinner one day while we're both here?"

Returning her smile, Ian nodded and opened the door for her, gesturing her in. "Let me know when you're not filming and we'll make that happen."

Nodding her thanks, Lily headed into the house. Ian wasn't sticking around for the short scene retake. He had other pressing matters to attend to. Like the beauty he'd seen out in the field moments ago. With red hair blazing past her shoulders and a heart-clenching smile on her face, Cassie had captured his attention instantly. So what else was new? The woman managed to turn him inside out without even being near. More times than not she consumed his thoughts, but when he'd seen her taking her daughter on a horseback ride, Ian had to admit that the sight had damn near stopped him in his tracks.

Emily's sweet squeals of delight, the loving expression on Cassie's face... The combination had shifted something in Ian's heart, something he wasn't quite ready to identify.

But he did know one thing. He'd been wrong. He was wrong about Cassie in thinking she was just like his mother. His mother never would've taken the time to have precious moments with him like the ones he'd seen with Cassie and Emily. His mother had been too busy on her quest for love and Mr. Right.

Ian ran a hand over his hair and sighed. He'd turned out just fine, no thanks to Mom and Dad, but getting involved with a woman and an innocent child was a hazardous mistake that would leave all parties vulnerable and in a risky position. What did he know about children or how to care for them?

And why was he even thinking this way? He was leaving in a few weeks. No matter his attraction and growing interest in Cassie Barrington, he couldn't afford to get personally involved.

Hours later, after he'd drafted a contract he hoped would entice Lily Beaumont into signing with his agency, Ian found himself leaving his trailer and heading toward Cassie's cottage.

Night had settled over the grounds and all was quiet. No bustling crew or noisy conversation. Max's wife and baby had shown up earlier in the evening, so they were probably holed up in his trailer for family time. And the producer's and director's families had arrived the day before. Bronson Dane and Anthony Price were at the top 1 percent of the film industry and still made time for their growing families.

Everyone had a family, a connection and the promise of love.

Ignoring the pang of envy he didn't want to feel, Ian stepped up onto Cassie's porch, which was illuminated with a lantern-style light on either side of the door. As soon as he knocked, he glanced down to his watch. Damn, maybe it was too late to be making a social call.

The door swung open and Ian took in the sight of Cassie wearing a long T-shirt and her hair down, curling around her shoulders. Long legs left uncovered tempted him to linger, but he brought his eyes back up to her surprised face.

"I'm sorry," he said, shoving his hands into his pockets. "I just realized how late it was."

"Oh, um…it's fine." She rested her hand on the edge of the oak door and tilted her head. "Is everything okay?"

Nodding, Ian suddenly felt like an idiot. "Yeah, I was working and lost track of time. Then I started walking and ended up here."

A sweet smile lit up her features. "Come on in," she told him, opening the door and stepping aside. "I just put Emily to bed, so this is fine."

He stepped inside and inhaled a scent of something sweet. "Is that cookies I smell?"

Cassie shut the door and turned to face him. "I thought I'd make some goodies for the wives who arrived. This way they can stock their trailers with snacks. I already made a batch of caramel corn."

His heart flipped in his chest. He hated the fact he kept going back to his mother, but he honestly couldn't recall a time when his mother had baked anything or even reached out to others by doing a kind act.

A shrink would have a field day in his head with all his Mommy and Daddy issues. *Jeez.* And here he'd thought once he'd left for L.A. he'd left all of those years behind.

"They will really appreciate that," he told her.

Shrugging, Cassie maneuvered around him and grabbed a small blanket from the couch and started folding it. "I'm no Linda, but I do enjoy baking when I have the time."

She laid the folded blanket across the back of the couch and looked back at him. He couldn't stop his eyes from traveling over her again. How could he help the fact he found her sexier than any woman he'd ever met? She probably wouldn't believe him if he told her that her curves were enticing, her low maintenance a refreshing change.

Cassie tugged on the hem of her shirt. "I should probably go change."

"No." He held up his hand to stop her. "This is your house—you should be comfortable. Besides, I've seen it all."

Her eyes flared with remembrance and passion as Ian closed the space between them and looked down at her mouth. "I've tasted it all, too, if you recall."

With a shaky nod, she said, "I remember."

The pulse at the base of her throat increased and Ian ran a hand over his face as he took a step back. "I swear, I didn't come here for this."

Cassie's bright blue eyes darted away. "I understand."

"No, you don't." Great, now she thought he was rejecting her. "It's not that I don't want you, Cassie. That's the furthest from the truth."

Shoving her hair back from her shoulders, Cassie shook her head. "Ian, it's okay. You don't have to make excuses. I'm a big girl. I can handle the truth. Besides, we're past this awkward stage, right?"

"Yeah," he agreed because right now he was feeling anything but awkward. Excited and aroused, but not awkward. "I don't know what possessed me to show up at your door this late, but…"

Cassie produced that punch-to-the-gut smile. "You can stop by anytime."

How did she do that? Instantly make him feel welcome, wanted…needed. There was so much more to Cassie Barrington than he'd first perceived. There were sides to the confident vixen, the single mother and the overworked trainer he had yet to discover.

Cassie was giving, loving and patient. He'd known instantly that she was special, but maybe he just hadn't realized how special. This woman embodied everything he hadn't known he'd been looking for.

"Why are you looking at me like that?" she asked, brows drawn together, smile all but gone.

Ian took a step toward her. He'd been mentally dancing around her for days and now he was physically doing it as he made up his mind on how to approach her.

"Because I just realized that all of your layers are starting to reveal themselves, one at a time." He slid his fingertips up her arms and back down, relishing the goose bumps he produced with such a simple touch. "I didn't want to see all of that before. I wanted you to be unattainable. I wanted you to be all wrong and someone I could easily forget."

Those vibrant eyes remained locked on his as her breath caught.

"But there's no way I could ever forget you, Cassie. Or us."

He didn't give her time to object. He claimed her lips and instantly she responded—opening her mouth to him, wrapping her arms around his neck and plunging her fingers into his hair.

Ian knew he wasn't leaving anytime soon. He also knew her T-shirt had to go.

Eleven

Cassie had no idea what she was doing. Okay, she knew what she was doing and who she was doing it with, but hadn't she just had a mental talk with herself about the hazards of getting wrapped up in Ian's seductive ways? Hadn't she told herself she'd already been burned once and was still recovering?

But the way his mouth captured hers, the way he held her as if she were the rarest of gems, Cassie couldn't help but take pleasure in the fact that Ian pulled out a passion in her that she'd never known existed.

When Ian's hands gripped the hem of her T-shirt and tugged up, she eased back and in an instant the unwanted garment was up and over her head, flung to the side without a care.

Dark-as-sin eyes raked over her body, which was now bare of everything except a pair of red lacy panties. The old Cassie wanted to shield herself with her hands, but the way Ian visually sampled her gave her the confidence of a goddess.

"I could look at you forever," he said, his voice husky.

Forever. The word hovered in the air, but Cassie knew he was speaking only from lust, not in the happily-ever-after term.

Ian pulled his own shirt off and Cassie reached out, quickly unfastening his pants. In no time he was reaching for her, wearing only a smile.

"Tell me you know this is more than sex," he muttered against her lips. "I want you to know that to me, this is so much more."

Tears pricked the backs of her eyes as she nodded. The lump in her throat left her speechless. She really didn't know what label he wanted to put on this relationship, but right now, she couldn't think beyond the fact that Ian's hands were sliding into her panties and gliding them down her shaky legs.

Cassie wrapped her arms around his broad shoulders and kicked aside the flimsy material. Ian's hands cupped her bottom as he guided her backward.

"Tell me where your room is," he muttered against her lips.

"Last door on the right."

He kissed her on the throat, across the swells of her breasts, all the while keeping his hands firmly gripped on her backside as he maneuvered her down the hallway and into her room.

A small bedside lamp gave the room a soft glow. Ian gently shut the door behind him and looked her right in the eyes. There was an underlying vulnerability looking back at her, and Cassie knew what he was thinking.

"I've never had a man in this room," she told him. "And there's no other man I want here."

As if the dam had broken, Ian reached for her, capturing her lips once again and lifting her by the waist.

When she locked her legs around his hips and they tumbled onto the bed, Ian broke free of her lips and kissed a path down to her breasts. Leaning back, Cassie gripped his hair as he tasted her.

"Ian," she panted. "I don't have any protection."

His dark gaze lifted to hers. "I didn't bring any. I hadn't planned on ending up here."

Biting her lip, Cassie said, "I'm on birth control and I'm clean. I've only been with my ex-husband and you."

Ian's hands slid up to cup her face as he kissed her lips. "I've never been without protection and I know I'm clean, too."

She smiled. "Then why are we still talking?"

Cassie moved her hands to his waist. Before she could say another word, Ian slid into her. Closing her eyes, Cassie let out a soft groan as he began to move above her.

"Look at me," he demanded in that low tone. "I want you to see me and only me."

As if any other man could take his place? But as she stared into his eyes, she saw so much more than lust, than sex and passion. This man was falling for her. He may not even recognize the emotion himself, but it was there, plain as day, looking back at her.

When his pace increased, Cassie gripped his shoulders and arched her back. "Ian...I..."

Eyes still locked on to her, he clenched the muscle in his jaw. "Go ahead, baby."

Her body trembled with her release, but she refused to close her eyes. She wanted him to see just how affected she was by his touch...his love.

When his arms stiffened and his body quivered against

hers, Cassie held on, swallowing back the tears that clogged her throat.

One thing was very certain. The night in the attic may have been all about lust, but this moment right here in her bed, Cassie had gone and fallen in love with Ian Shaffer.

"I have to be on set early," Ian whispered into her ear.

Pulling himself away from the warm bed they'd spent the night in, Ian quickly gathered his clothes and dressed. Cassie eased up onto one elbow, and the sheet slipped down to stop just at the slope of her breasts. All that creamy exposed skin had him clenching his jaw and reliving what had just transpired hours before between those sheets.

"How early?" she asked, her voice thick with sleep.

"I'd like to see Max before he starts."

Okay, so the lie rolled easily off his tongue, but he couldn't stay. He couldn't remain in her bed, smelling her sweet scent, playing house in her little cottage, with her innocent baby sleeping in the next room.

What did he know about family or children…or whatever emotion was stirring within him? His career had always taken precedence over any social life or any feelings. With his parents' example of the epitome of failed marriages and love, he knew he wanted something completely different for his own life, so perfecting his career was the path he'd chosen.

How could he put his career, his agency and the impending addition of Lily to his client roster in jeopardy simply because he'd become entangled with Cassie Barrington? She was the poster child for commitment, and an instant family was something he couldn't get wrapped up in.

Cassie was a beautiful, intriguing complication. His eyes darted to the bed, where she studied him with a hint of desire layered with curiosity.

"Everything okay?" she asked.

Nodding, he shoved his feet into his shoes. "Of course. I'll lock the door behind me."

Unable to avoid temptation completely, Ian crossed the room, leaned down and kissed her lips. Just as her hand came up to his stubbled jaw, he pulled away and left her alone.

He stepped onto the front porch, closed the door behind him and leaned against it to catch his breath. The easy way Cassie welcomed him into her bed—and into her life with Emily—terrified him. Last night she'd accepted him without question and she'd given him everything she had... including love. He'd seen it in her eyes, but even more worrisome was what she may have seen reflected in his.

Because in those moments, when they were one and her bright blue eyes sought his, Ian had found himself completely and utterly lost. He wanted so much, but fear of everything he'd ever known regarding love and family made him question his emotions and his intentions.

Damn it. His intentions? What the hell was this? He wasn't the kind of man who had dreams of driving a minivan or heading up a household. He was a top Hollywood agent and if he didn't get his head on straight, he could lose one of the most important clients he'd ever had the chance of snagging.

Shaking his head, Ian pushed off the door and forced himself to walk toward his trailer. Twenty-nine years old and doing the walk of shame? *Classy, Shaffer. Real classy.*

Darkness and early-morning fog settled low over the estate. He shoved his hands into his pockets and decided he needed to shower and change before seeing Max...especially considering he was wearing the same clothes as yesterday.

He hadn't totally lied when he'd left Cassie's bed. He would talk to Max, but it wasn't dire and they could always talk later. Yet he worried if he stayed, he'd give Cassie false hope.

Okay, he worried he'd give himself false hope, too, because being with her was like nothing he'd ever experienced before and he wanted to hold on to those moments.

But the reality was, he was passing through.

Ian took his time getting ready for the day, answered a few emails and jotted down notes for calls he needed to make later in the week. He hated to admit he was shaken up by this newfound flood of emotions, but he had to come to grips with the fact that whatever he was feeling for Cassie Barrington was most definitely not going away.... It was only getting stronger.

By the time he exited his trailer, he had a plan of action, and today would be all about work and focusing on the big picture and his agency.

Crew members were gathered around the entrance of the stables, and off to the side were Max and Lily, holding their scripts and chatting. Ian headed in their direction, eager to get the day started.

"Morning," he greeted them as he approached.

Max nodded. "Came by your trailer last night to discuss something. Have a late night?"

The smile on Max's face was devilish—and all-knowing.

"What did you need?" Ian asked, dodging the question.

With a shrug, Max shook his head. "It can wait. I'm going to talk to Bronson before we start filming. Excuse me."

Ian figured Max left so Ian could chat with Lily. *Good boy.*

"I glanced over today's filming schedule." Ian stepped in front of Lily to shade her face from the sun. "Looks like after three today you guys are free."

Lily smiled. "We are indeed. Are you available to talk then?"

He'd be available anytime she wanted if it meant persuading her to sign with him. "I am. Would you like to stay here or go out to grab something for dinner?"

"I say go out," she replied. "Hopefully we can talk privately without everyone around."

Before he could respond, Lily's gaze darted from his to a spot over his left shoulder. A smile like he'd never seen before lit up her face and Ian couldn't help but glance around to see who she was connecting with.

Nash.

More confirmation that this Hollywood starlet and the groom on the Barrington estate had something going on.

Ian only hoped whatever was happening with the two of them was kept quiet and didn't interfere with filming or hinder her judgment in signing with him.

"Going out is fine," he told her.

Blinking, she focused back on him. "I'm sorry. What?"

Yeah, definitely something going on there.

"I said we could go out for a bite to eat. I can come by your trailer about five. Does that work?"

"Of course," she replied with a nod. "I'll see you then."

As she walked away, Ian turned and caught Nash still staring as Lily entered the stable. Nash had the look of a man totally and utterly smitten and Ian couldn't help but feel a twinge of remorse for the guy. Nash and Lily were worlds apart.

Exactly like Ian and Cassie.

What a mess. A complicated, passion-induced mess.

Ian stood to the side as lighting and people were set in place to prepare for filming. Bronson was talking with Max, and Lily's hair was being smoothed one last time.

Grant and Anthony were adjusting the bales of hay at the end of the aisle.

Ian wasn't sure what Cassie's plans were for the day, but he intended to keep his distance for now. He needed to figure out exactly how to handle this situation because the last thing she needed was more heartache. And he, who knew nothing about real intimacy, would most certainly break her heart if he wasn't careful.

Damon Barrington settled in beside him and whispered, "Their chemistry on set is amazing."

Ian watched Max and Lily embrace in the middle of the aisle, horses' heads popping out over their stalls. The set was utterly quiet except for Lily's staged tears as she clung to Max. The couple was the perfect image of a younger Damon and Rose Barrington, according to the pictures Ian had seen.

As soon as Anthony yelled, "Cut!" the couple broke apart and Lily dabbed at her damp cheeks.

Damon glanced around. "I can't believe my girls aren't down here. You haven't seen Cassie or Tessa, have you?"

Ian shook his head. "I haven't."

No need to tell Cassie's father that just a few hours ago Ian had slipped from her bed. Best not bring that up.

"I'm sure they'll be along shortly." Damon looked over at Ian and grinned. "My girls haven't let too many scenes slip by. They've enjoyed this process."

"And you?" Ian asked. "Have you enjoyed the Hollywood invasion?"

Nodding, Damon crossed his arms over his chest. "It's not what I thought it would be. The scenes vary in length and everything is shot out of order. But I'm very interested in seeing how they piece this all together."

Ian liked Damon, appreciated the way the man had taken charge of his life, made something of it and encouraged his children to do the same. And when his wife had passed, the man had taken over the roles of both parents and loved his children to the point where both women were now two of the most amazing people he'd met.

Ian had never received encouragement from his father and couldn't help but wonder what his life would've been like had his father been more hands-on.

Shrugging off years that couldn't be changed, Ian excused himself from Damon. If Cassie was going to come watch the filming, he needed to be elsewhere.

Because he had no doubt that if he hung around and had to look Cassie in the eye in front of all these people, there would be no hiding the fact that he'd developed some serious feelings for her.

Twelve

Who was he kidding? There was no way he could stay away from Cassie. All during the business dinner with Lily, his mind had been on Cassie and what she was doing.

By the end of the night he'd nearly driven himself crazy with curiosity about what Cassie and Emily had done all day. Added to that, Lily hadn't signed with him. Not yet. She'd looked over his proposed contract and agreed with most of it, but she'd also said she needed to look over one other contract before deciding.

He was still in the running, but he'd rather have this deal signed and completed so he could move on to other deals waiting in the wings...not so he could focus on the woman who had his head spinning and his gut tied in knots.

After walking Lily to her trailer, Ian crossed the estate toward the two cottages. Only one of Cassie's outdoor lights was on and she was on her porch switching out the bulb in the other.

"Hey," he greeted her as he stepped onto the top step. "Need help?"

"I can manage just fine."

As she stood on her tiptoes and reached, her red tank top slid up over her torso, exposing a tantalizing band of flesh.

"I can get that so you don't have to stretch so far," he told her.

She quickly changed out the bulb and turned to face him, tapping the dead bulb against her palm. "I've been doing things on my own for a while now. Besides, I won't be anybody's second choice. I figured you were smart enough to know that."

"I'm sorry?"

Somehow he was not on the same page as her and she was mad at someone. From the daggers she was throwing him, he'd done something to upset her. Considering he hadn't sneaked out of her bed that morning without saying goodbye, he really had no clue what was going on.

"Forget it." She shook her head and opened her front door, then turned before he could enter. "I'm pretty tired, but thanks for stopping by."

Oh, hell no. He wasn't going to just let her be mad and not tell him what was going on. More than that, did she really believe he'd just leave her when she was this upset?

His hand smacked against the door as she tried to close it. "I'm coming in."

Cassie stepped back and let him pass. Emily sat in her Pack 'n Play and chattered with a stuffed horse, oblivious to the world around her.

"I need to get Emily ready for bed." Cassie maneuvered around him and picked up Emily. "I may be a while."

Code for "I'm going to take my time and let you worry." That was fine; he had no intention of going anywhere.

If Cassie was gearing up for a fight, he was ready. Seeing her pain, masked by anger, had a vise gripping his heart, and he cared too much about her to just brush her feelings aside.

Ian glanced around the somewhat tidy living area and started picking up toys before he thought better of it. He tossed them into the Pack 'n Play; then he folded the throw and laid it on the back of the sofa, neatened the pillows and took a plate and cup into the kitchen and placed them in the dishwasher.

By the time he'd taken a seat on the couch, he found himself smiling. Where had this little domestic streak come from? He hadn't even thought twice about helping Cassie, and not just because she was angry. He found himself wanting to do things to make her life easier.

Ian had no clue what had happened with her life before he'd come along, but he knew she was divorced and assumed the ex had done a number on her.

Well, Ian intended to stick this out, at least for as long as he was here. He would make her smile again, because she deserved nothing less.

Cassie wasn't jealous. Just because she'd heard Ian and Lily had had dinner didn't mean a thing. Really.

But that green-eyed monster reared its ugly head and reminded Cassie that she'd fallen for a cheating man once before.

On the other hand, what hold did she have over Ian? He wasn't staying and he'd never confessed his undying love to her. But she'd seen his eyes last night, she'd seen how he looked at her, and she'd experienced lovemaking like she never had before. How could he deny that they'd formed an unspoken bond?

Cassie quickly dried off Emily and got her dressed in

her footed bunny pajamas. After giving her a bottle and rocking her gently, Cassie began to sing.

This was the time of night she enjoyed most. Just her and her precious baby girl. Cassie might sing off-key, she might even get an occasional word wrong, but Emily didn't care. She just reached her little hands up and patted Cassie's hand or touched her lips.

They had a nightly ritual and just because Ian was out in her living room didn't mean she would change her routine. Before Emily fell asleep in her arms, Cassie laid her in her crib, giving her a soft kiss on her forehead, then left the room.

Cassie took a moment to straighten her tank and smooth her hair over her shoulders before she started down the hallway. As she entered the living room, she noticed that Ian was reclined on her sofa, head tilted back, eyes closed, with his hands laced across his abdomen. He'd picked up the toys and neatly piled them in the Pack 'n Play in the corner.

No. She didn't want that unwelcome tumble of her heart where this man was concerned. She couldn't risk everything again on the chance that he could love her the way she loved him.

Tears pricked her eyes as she fully confessed just how much she did love this man. But he could never know.

Her feet shuffled over the hardwood floors, and Ian lifted his lids, his gaze seeking hers.

"Thank you for picking up," she told him, still standing because she intended to show him out the door.

Shifting to fully sit up, Ian patted the cushion beside him. "Come here, Cassie."

She didn't like being told what to do, but she wasn't going to act like a teenager who pouted over a boy, either.

She was a big girl, but that didn't exempt her from a broken heart.

Taking a seat on the opposite end of the couch, she gripped her hands in her lap. "What do you want, Ian? I don't have time for games."

His eyes locked on to hers. "I don't play games, Cassie, and I have no idea what you're so upset about."

Of course he didn't. Neither had her ex when he'd cheated.

She eased back against the arm of the sofa and returned his stare. "Do you know why I'm divorced?"

Ian shook his head and slid his arm along the back of the couch as if to reach for her.

"My husband got tired of me," she told him, tamping down the sliver of hurt and betrayal that threatened to make her vulnerable. Never again. "The whole marriage-baby thing was cramping his style. Apparently he'd been cheating on me for most of our marriage and I was too naive and dumb to realize it. You see, I assumed that when we took our vows they meant something to him."

"Cassie—"

"No," she said, holding up her hand. "I'm not finished. After Emily was born, Derek left. She was barely two months old. He left me a note and was just…gone. It seems the sexy wife he once knew was no longer there for him, so, in turn, his cheating and the divorce were my fault. I know now that he was a coward and I'm glad he's gone because I never want Emily to see me settle for someone who treats me like I'm not worth everything.

"I want my daughter to see a worthy example of how love should be," she went on, cursing her eyes for misting up. "I want her to see that love does exist. My parents had it, and I will find it. But I won't be played for a fool while I wait for love to come into my life."

Ian swallowed, his eyes never leaving hers as he scooted

closer. He wasn't stupid; he could put the pieces together and know she'd assumed the worst about his dinner meeting with Lily.

"I didn't play you for a fool, Cassie." His tone was light as he settled his hand over both of hers, which were still clasped together in her lap. "I have never lied to a woman and I've never pretended to be something I wasn't."

With a deep sigh, Cassie shook her head. "Forget I said anything. I mean, it's not like we're committed to each other," she said as she got to her feet.

But Ian jumped right up with her and gripped her shoulders before she could turn from him.

"Do you seriously think for one second that I believe you're so laid-back about the idea of me seeing you and another woman?" he demanded. "I had a business meeting with Lily. I told you I've wanted to sign her to my agency for months. She's the main reason I came to the set and why I'm staying so long."

Cassie's eyes widened, but he didn't give her a chance to speak. He needed her to know she didn't come in second... and she should never have to.

"I spent the entire evening trying to win her over, outlining every detail of the contract and all the perks of having me as her agent." Ian loosened his grip as he stepped closer to Cassie and slid his hands up to frame her face. "But the entire evening, I was thinking of you. Wondering what you were doing, how long it would be until I could see you again."

Her shoulders relaxed and her face softened as she kept those stunning baby blues locked on his. The hope he saw in her eyes nearly melted him on the spot. He knew she wanted to trust. He knew she'd been burned once and he completely understood that need, the yearning for that solid foundation.

"I'm sorry," she whispered. Cassie's lids lowered as she shook her head before she raised her gaze to his once more. "I don't want to be that woman. I seriously have no hold on you, Ian. You've promised me nothing and I don't expect you to check in."

Ian kissed her gently, then rested his forehead against hers. A soft shudder rippled through her and Ian wanted nothing more than to reassure her everything would be all right.

But how could he, when he knew he wasn't staying? How could they move forward with emotions overtaking them both?

"I hate what he did to me," she whispered, reaching up to clasp his wrists as he continued to cup her face. "I hate that I've turned bitter. That's not who I want to be."

Ian eased back and tipped her face up to his. "That's not who you are. You're not bitter. You're cautious and nobody blames you. You not only have yourself to think of—you have Emily, too."

Cassie's sweet smile never failed to squeeze his heart, and Ian had no clue how a man could leave behind a wife and child. Ian wouldn't mind getting ahold of Cassie's ex. He obviously was no man, but a coward. Selfishly, Ian was glad Derek was out of the picture. If the man could throw away his family so easily, he wasn't worthy.

"What's that look for?" she asked. "You're very intense all of a sudden."

He had to be honest because she was worth everything he had inside him.

"Where is this going?" he asked. "I care about you, Cassie. More than I thought I would, and I think we need to discuss what's happening between us."

A soft laugh escaped her. "You sound like a woman."

Ian smiled with a shrug. "I assure you I've never said this to anyone else, but I don't want you getting hurt."

Cassie nodded and a shield came over her eyes as if she was already steeling herself. "Honestly, I don't know. I care for you, too. I question myself because I'm still so scarred from the divorce and I told myself I wouldn't get involved again. Yet, here we are and I can't stop myself."

Her inner battle shouldn't make him happy, but he couldn't help but admit he liked the fact she had no control over her feelings for him.... At least he wasn't in this boat of emotions alone.

"I don't want you to be the rebound guy," she murmured. "But I'm so afraid of how you make me feel."

Stroking her silky skin, wanting to kiss her trembling lips, Ian asked, "How do I make you feel?"

He shouldn't have asked. Cassie pursed her lips together as if contemplating her response, and Ian worried he'd put her on the spot. But he had to know. This mattered too much. *She* mattered too much.

"Like I'm special."

She couldn't have zeroed in on a better word that would hit him straight in the heart. *Special.* She was special to him on so many levels. She was special because he'd never felt more alive than he did with her. He'd never let his career come second to anything before her, and he sure as hell had never thought, with his family issues, that he'd be falling for a woman with a child.

Cassie inspired him to be a better person, to want to care for others and put his needs last.

But most of all he understood that need to feel special. He'd craved it his entire life, and until this very moment, he hadn't realized that was what he'd been missing.

"You make me feel special, too." Before now he never would've felt comfortable opening up, showing how vulnerable he was on the inside. "I don't want to be the rebound guy, either."

Her eyes widened as she tried to blink back the moisture. "So what does that mean?"

Hell if he knew. Suddenly he wanted it all—his career, the Hollywood lifestyle, Cassie and Emily. Cassie had him rethinking what family could be.

There was that other part of him that was absolutely terrified and wanted to hightail it back to Hollywood. But for now, he would relish their time together until he could come to grips with this mess of emotions.

"It means for now, you're mine." He kissed the corners of her mouth. "It means you are more to me than any other woman has ever been." He kissed her directly on the mouth, coaxing her lips apart before murmuring, "It means I'm taking you to bed to show you just how much you mean to me."

Only wanting to keep her smiling, keep her happy for as long as he was here, Ian slid his arms around her waist and pulled her body flush against his own.

When Cassie's fingers slid up around his neck and threaded into his hair, Ian claimed her mouth and lifted her off the ground. She wrapped her legs around his waist and he carried her toward the bedroom, where he fully intended to make good on his promise.

Thirteen

The day couldn't be more perfect. God had painted a beautiful setting with the sun high in the sky and the temperature an ideal sixty degrees. The stage was set for Tessa to win the Preakness and take the second step toward the Triple Crown.

But no matter the weather, the thrill that always slid through Cassie at each race had to do with the stomp of the hooves in the stalls as the horses eagerly awaited their shining moment, the thick aroma of straw, the colorful silks adorning each horse, the tangible excitement of the jockeys as they shared last-minute talks with their trainers.

Which was exactly what Cassie and Tessa had just finished doing. Cassie had the utmost confidence that this race would go in their favor, but strange things always happened and they both knew better than to get cocky—especially at this point.

The first third of the Triple Crown was theirs, but this

was a new day, a new race and a whole other level of adrenaline rushes.

Cassie followed behind as Tessa rode Don Pedro from the stables through the paddock and entered the track. No matter the outcome, Cassie was proud of her sister, of what they'd accomplished in their years together.

Soon their racing season would come to an end and Cassie would move on with her goal of opening a riding camp for handicapped children. Training a Triple Crown winner would put her in high demand in the horse-breeding world, but she hoped to use that reputation as a launching point for her school.

And beyond the school worries, her father was getting offers from his most heated rival, Jake Mason, to buy the prizewinning horses. Their season wasn't even over yet, for heaven's sake.

But those thoughts would have to wait until after the competition.

As would her thoughts of a certain Hollywood agent who had stayed behind on the estate to get some work done without distractions. The majority of the film crew had accompanied the Barringtons to Baltimore, Maryland, but today they were spectators, enjoying the race. They'd gotten many great shots from Louisville a couple of weeks ago, so now they were able to relax…somewhat. Cassie knew they were still taking still shots for the ad campaign, but not as many as at the derby.

As Tessa rode onto the track, Cassie couldn't help but smile. There was so much to be thankful for right now in her life. One chapter of her career was coming to an end. Another was going to begin in a few months. Her daughter was happy and healthy and nearing her first birthday.

And, delicious icing on the cake, Ian Shaffer had entered her life. For how long she didn't know. But she did know that, for now, they were together and he had admitted his feelings were strong. But did that mean he'd want to try something long distance? Or would he stay around a little longer after the film was finished?

So many questions and none of them would be answered today. She needed to concentrate and be there for Tessa. All else could wait until this race was over.

In no time the horses were in their places and Cassie felt her father's presence beside her. His arm snaked around her waist, the silent support a welcome comfort. Each race had nerves balling up in her stomach, but nothing could be done now. The training for the Preakness was complete and now they waited for the fastest, most exciting moment in sports.

Cassie glanced toward the grandstands, and the colorful array of hats and suits had her smile widening. Excitement settled heavily over the track as everyone's gaze was drawn to the starting gate.

"You're trembling," her father whispered into her ear.

Cassie let out a shaky laugh. "I think that's you."

His arm tightened around her waist as a robust chuckle escaped. "I believe you're right, my dear."

The gun sounded and Cassie had no time for nerves. She couldn't keep her eyes off the places switching, the colored numbers on the board swapping out as horses passed each other and inched toward the lead.

Don Pedro was in forth. Cassie fisted her hands so tight, her short nails bit into her palms.

"Come on. Come on," she muttered.

Tessa eased past third and into second on the last turn.

The announcer's tone raised in excitement as Tessa inched even farther toward the head of the race. Cassie wanted to close her eyes to pray, but she couldn't take her gaze off the board.

Just as the first two horses headed to the finish line, Cassie started jumping up and down. Excitement, fear, nerves... They all had her unable to stand still.

And when the announcer blared that the winner was Don Pedro by a nose, Cassie jumped even higher, wrapped her arms around her father's neck and squealed like a little girl.

"We did it," he yelled, embracing her. "My girls did it!"

Damon jerked back, gripped her hand and tugged her toward the winner's circle, where Tessa met them. Her radiant smile, the mass of people surrounding her and the flash of cameras all announced there was a new winner.

Grant was right there in the throng of people, his grin so wide there was no way to hide the pride beaming off him.

Cassie's heart lurched. She loved that Tessa had found the man of her dreams, couldn't be happier for the couple. But, for the first time, Cassie was not the first one Tessa turned to after a race.

And that was not jealousy talking.... Cassie loved seeing Tessa and Grant so happy, and sharing Tessa's affection was fine. It was the fact that Cassie still felt empty when monumental things happened. Whom did she turn to to celebrate or for a shoulder to cry on?

Tessa turned her head, caught Cassie's eye and winked down at her. Returning the wink, Cassie smiled to hide her sad thoughts.

Soon reporters were thrusting microphones in her face, as well. Very few ever won the Triple Crown, and a team of females was practically unheard of. History was definitely in the making.

The Barrington sisters had done it again, and with only one more race to go to round out the season and secure the coveted Triple Crown, Cassie knew she needed to focus now more than ever on training for the Belmont.

Which meant keeping her heart shielded from Ian, because if he penetrated too much more, she feared she'd never be able to recover if it all fell apart.

They were gone for days, weeks.

Okay, maybe it wasn't weeks, but Ian felt as if he hadn't seen Cassie forever. Which told him he was going to be in trouble when it came time for him to head back to L.A.

She'd arrived home late last night and he'd known she'd be tired, so he had stayed away to let her rest and spend time with Emily. But knowing she was so close was hard.

As he headed toward the stables just as the sun peeked overtop the hilltops, Ian wanted to spend some time with her. He'd actually ached for her while she'd been away. Like most of the nation, he'd watched with eyes glued to the television during the Preakness and he'd jumped out of his seat and cheered when Don Pedro crossed the finish line for the win.

The familiar smell of hay greeted him before he even hit the entrance. As soon as he crossed the threshold, Ian spotted Nash cleaning out a stall.

"Morning," Ian greeted him.

Nash nodded a good-morning and continued raking old hay. "Cassie isn't here yet," he said without looking up.

Ian grinned. Apparently he and Cassie weren't very discreet...not that they'd tried to be, but they also hadn't been blatant about their relationship, either.

"Hey, Ian."

He turned to see Tessa striding into the stables, all smiles with her hair pulled back.

"Congrats on the win." Ian couldn't help but offer a quick hug with a pat on her back. "That was one intense race."

Tessa laughed. "You should've seen it from my point of view."

Her eyes darted to Nash, then back to Ian. "What brings you out this early?"

Ian shrugged, sliding his hands into his pockets. "Just looking for Cassie."

Tessa's grin went into that all-knowing mode as she quirked a brow. "She actually was up most of the night with Emily. Poor baby is teething and nobody is getting any sleep."

"But Cassie has to be exhausted. You just got back late last night," he argued, realizing he was stating nothing new to Tessa.

Shrugging, Tessa sighed. "I know. I offered to take Emily for the night, but Cassie wouldn't hear of it."

Probably because the last time Cassie had been without her child, she had been locked in the attic with him.

"She's spreading herself too thin," Ian muttered.

Nash walked around them and pulled a bale of hay from the stack against the wall, then moved back into the stall. Ian shifted closer to the doorway to get out of the quiet groom's way.

"Follow me," Tessa said with a nod.

Intrigued, Ian fell into step behind the famous jockey. She stopped just outside the stables, but away from where Nash could overhear.

"This isn't where you tell me if I hurt your sister you'll kill me, is it?" he asked with a smile.

Tessa laughed and shook her head, eyes sparkling with amusement. "You're smart enough to know that goes without saying. I wanted to discuss something else, actually."

"And what's that?"

"Did Cassie ever tell you about the little getaway she and Grant came up with for me? Grant felt I was pushing myself too hard, never taking time for myself to regroup and recharge."

Ian grinned. "Must run in the family."

"Yeah, we Barringtons are all made of the same stubborn stuff."

Ian had no doubt the almighty Damon Barrington had instilled all his work ethic into his girls and that hard work and determination were paying off in spades.

"I'd like to return the favor," Tessa went on. "Are you up for taking a few days away from here?"

Was he? Did he want to leave Lily when they were still negotiating a contract? He didn't mind leaving Max. The actor could handle anything and Ian was very confident with their working relationship.

It was Lily that worried him. But he couldn't be in her face all the time. He'd spoken with her a few times since their dinner meeting. She'd promised a decision once she realized which agency would offer her the most and which one she'd feel most at home with.

He had to believe she'd see that his company was hands down the front-runner.

And a few days away with Cassie? He had deals and meetings to get back to, but after days without her, how could he not want to jump at that chance?

"Should I take that smile to mean you're going to take me up on this offer?"

Ian nodded. "I think I will. What did you have in mind?"

Fourteen

How long could a baby be angry and how many teeth would be popping through?

Cassie had just collapsed onto the couch for the first time all day when someone knocked on her door. She threw a glance to Emily, who was playing on the floor and crawling from toy to toy…content for now.

Stepping over plush toys and blankets, Cassie opened the door and froze. Ian stood on her porch looking as handsome as ever, sporting aviator sunglasses and a navy T-shirt pulled taut across his wide shoulders and tucked into dark jeans.

She didn't need to look down at her own outfit to know she was just a step above homeless chic with her mismatched lounge pants with margarita glasses on them and her oversize T-shirt with a giant smiley face in the middle.

And her hair? She'd pulled it up into a ponytail for bed and hadn't touched it since. Half was falling around her face; the other half was in a nest on the side of her head.

Yeah, she exuded sex appeal.

"Um...are you going to invite me in?"

Cassie shoved a clump of hair behind her ear. "Are you sure you want to come in? Emily is teething. She's cranky more often than not since last night, and I'm...well..."

Ian closed the gap between them, laying a gentle kiss on her lips. "Beautiful."

Okay, there was no way she couldn't melt at that sweet declaration even if he was just trying to score points. He'd succeeded.

When he stepped into the house, Cassie stepped back and closed the door behind him. Emily grabbed hold of the couch cushion and pulled herself to her feet, throwing an innocent smile over her shoulder to Ian.

Cassie laughed. "Seriously? She smiles for you and I've had screaming for over twelve hours?"

"What can I say? I'm irresistible."

No denying that. Cassie still wasn't used to his powerful presence in her home, but she was growing to love it more and more each time he came for a visit.

"Hey, sweetheart," he said, squatting down beside Emily. "Did you have your mommy up last night?"

Emily let go of the couch to clap her hands and immediately fell down onto her diaper-covered butt. She giggled and looked up at Ian to see his reaction.

Cassie waited, too. She couldn't help but want to know how Ian would be around Emily. He hadn't spent too much time with her, considering he stopped by at night and he'd gone straight to Cassie's bed.

Reaching forward, Ian slid his big hands beneath Emily's delicate arms and lifted her as he came to his full height.

Cassie couldn't deny the lurch of her heart at the sight of this powerful man holding her precious baby. Was there a sexier sight than this? Not in Cassie's opinion.

"I know we talked on the phone, but congratulations." A smile lit up his already handsome face. "I'm so happy for you and Tessa."

Cassie still couldn't believe it herself. Of course they'd trained to win, but what trainer and jockey didn't? The fact they were that much closer to winning that coveted Triple Crown still seemed surreal.

"I'm still recovering from all the celebrating we did in Baltimore," she told him. "I've never been so happy in all my life. Well, except for when Emily was born."

"I have a surprise for you," Ian told her as Emily reached up and grabbed his nose.

Cassie went to reach for Emily, but Ian stepped back. "She's fine," he told her. "I love having my nose held so my voice can sound a little more like a chipmunk when I ask a sexy woman to go away with me for a few days."

Shocked at his invitation, Cassie shook her head, trying to make sense of it. "Go away with you?"

Ian nodded as Emily reached up on his head and tugged his glasses off. Immediately they went to her mouth.

"She's still fine," Ian told Cassie as he dodged her again. "They're sunglasses. She can chew on them all she wants."

"They'll have drool on them."

Ian's eyes darted to the lenses, but he just sighed. "Oh, well. So, what do you say? You up for getting away for a few days?"

Oh, how Cassie would love to get away. To not worry or train or do anything but be with Ian because their time together was coming to an end and she was certainly not ready to let go.

"Ian, going away with you sounds amazing, but I can't."

Ian glanced at Emily. "She's going to use you as an excuse, isn't she?"

Cassie laughed. "Actually, yes. But she's not an excuse.

I mean, I can't ask anyone to keep her for days, especially with her teething and upset."

Bringing his gaze back to Cassie, Ian crossed the space between them until he stood so close she could see the flecks of amber in his dark eyes.

"I'm not asking you to hand her off to anybody. I want to take you both away."

Cassie stared back at him, sure she'd heard him wrong. He wanted to take her and a baby? A cranky baby?

"But...but...are you sure?"

Ian dipped his head and gently kissed her before easing back and giving her that heart-melting grin. "I wouldn't have asked if I wasn't sure."

A million things ran through her mind. Could she actually take off and be with Ian for a few days? Did he honestly know what he was asking? Because she really didn't think he knew how difficult playing house could be.

"Stop thinking so hard." He shifted Emily to his other side and reached out to cup the side of Cassie's face. "Do you want to go?"

Cassie nodded. "Of course I do. It's just—"

"Yes, you want to go. That's what I need to hear. Everything else is taken care of."

Intrigued, Cassie raised her brows. "Oh, is it?"

A corner of Ian's mouth quirked into a devilish half smile. "Absolutely. How about I come back and get you in an hour. Just pack simple clothing and whatever Emily can't live without. I'll be back to help you finish up and then we'll go."

"Where are we going?" she asked.

Handing Emily back to Cassie, Ian shrugged. "I guess you'll find out when we get there."

She tried to get the sunglasses away from Emily and

noticed slobber bubbles along the lenses. Ian waved a hand and laughed.

"No, really, keep them," he said as he headed toward the door. "She apparently gets more use out of them than I did."

Cassie was still laughing after he'd closed the door behind him. A getaway with Ian and Emily? How could she not want to jump at this chance?

And how could she not read more into it? Was Ian silently telling her he wanted more? Or was he getting in all the time he could before he said his final goodbye?

Ian didn't know if he was making a mistake or if he was finally taking a leap of faith by bringing Cassie and Emily to his beachfront home. They'd flown from the East Coast to the West and he'd questioned himself the entire way.

Tessa had suggested he take Cassie to Grant's mountain home for a getaway, but Ian wanted Cassie on his turf. Deep down inside he wanted her to see how he lived, see part of his world.

And he wanted to find out how well she fit into his home. Would she feel out of place or would she enjoy the breathtaking views from his bedroom, which overlooked the Pacific Ocean?

Surprisingly, Emily was wonderful on the plane ride, thanks to the pain reliever aiding in her teething process. As Ian maneuvered his car—it had been waiting for him at the airport—into his drive, he risked a glance over to Cassie. He wanted to see her initial reaction.

And he wasn't disappointed. Her eyes widened at the two-story white beach house with the porch stretching across the first floor and the balcony wrapping around the house on the second. He'd had that same reaction when his Realtor had shown him the property a few years ago. Love at first sight.

"Ian, this is gorgeous," she exclaimed. "I can't believe you managed to get a beach house on such short notice."

He hadn't told her he was bringing her to his home. He'd wanted to surprise her, and he was afraid if he told her, then she'd back out.

As he pulled into the garage and killed the engine, Ian turned to face her. "Actually, this is my house."

Cassie gasped, jerking her head toward him. "Your house? Why didn't you tell me we were coming to your house?"

He honestly didn't have an excuse unless he wanted to delve way down and dig up the commitment issues he still faced. His fear of having her reject his plan, his fear of how fast they'd progressed and his fear of where the hell all of this would lead had kept him silent.

"I can't believe you live on the beach," she said, still smiling. "You must love it here."

Yeah, he did, but for the first time in his life, he suddenly found himself loving another location, as well. Who knew he'd fall in love with a horse farm on the other side of the country?

While Cassie got Emily out of the car, Ian took all the luggage into the house. He put his and Cassie's in the master bedroom and took Emily's bag into the room across the hall.

Thankfully, he'd called ahead and had his housekeeper pick up a few items and set them up in the makeshift nursery. Since she was a new grandmother, she knew exactly what a baby would need. And judging from the looks of the room, she'd gone all out.

Ian chuckled. The woman was a saint and deserved a raise...as always.

"Ian, this house is—"

He turned around to see Cassie in the doorway, Emily on her hip, eyes wide, mouth open.

"I had a little help getting the place ready," he informed her, moving aside so she could enter. "I hope you don't mind that I had my housekeeper get Emily some things to make her comfortable while you guys are here."

Cassie's gaze roamed around the room, pausing on the crib in the corner. "I don't know what to say," she whispered as her eyes sought his. "This is... Thank you."

Warmth spread through him. Cassie was absolutely speechless over a package of diapers, a bed and some toys. Cost hadn't even factored into his plan; Emily's comfort and easing Cassie's mind even a little had been his top priorities.

Before he could respond, Emily started fussing. Cassie kissed her forehead and patted her back. "It's okay, baby. You're all right."

The low cries turned into a full-fledged wail and a sense of helplessness overtook him. Yes, he could buy anything for her, but what did he know about consoling a child or what to do when they were hurting or sick?

With a soft smile, Cassie looked back to him. "Sorry. I'm sure this isn't the getaway you'd hoped for."

Ian returned her smile and reached out to slide his hand over Emily's back. "The only expectation I had was spending time with both of you. She can't help that she's teething."

Her eyes studied him for a moment before she said, "I don't know what I did to deserve you, Ian."

"You deserve everything you've ever wanted."

He wanted to say more, he wanted to do more and give more to her, but they were both in uncharted territory, and taking things slow was the best approach. God knew they hadn't started out slow. Working backward might not have been the most conventional approach, but it was all they had to work with.

"Can you get in the side of her diaper bag and get out the Tylenol?" she asked.

While Cassie got Emily settled with pain medication and started to sing to her, Ian watched from the doorway. Had his father ever felt this way about him? Had the man wanted to be hands-on? Because Ian desperately found himself wanting to be more in not just Cassie's life, but Emily's, as well. He didn't have the first clue about caring for children, but he wanted to learn.

How could he ever be what they needed?

But how could he ever let either of them go?

Fifteen

Thankfully, after a round of medicine and a short nap, Emily was back to her happy self. Cassie put on her bathing suit, wrapping a sheer sarong around her waist, then put Emily into her suit, as well.

Why waste time indoors when there was a beach and rolling waves just steps away?

"You ready to play in the ocean?" Cassie asked Emily as she carried her toward the back door. "You're going to love it, baby girl."

The open-concept living room and kitchen spread across the entire back of the house, and two sets of French doors led out onto the patio. Cassie stepped out into the warm sunshine and stopped.

At the edge of the water, Ian stood with his back to her wearing black trunks and flaunting his excellent muscle tone. The fabric clinging to the back of his well-toned thighs, his slicked-back hair and the water droplets glistening on his tanned shoulders and back indicated he'd already tested the waters.

The man was sinful. He tempted her in ways she never thought possible, made her want things that could never be. They couldn't be more opposite, yet they'd somehow found each other. And they'd grown so close since their encounter in the attic.

The night of the lock-in had been filled with nothing but lust and desire. Now, though, Cassie was wrestling with so many more emotions. At the top of her list was one she'd futilely guarded her heart against...love.

She completely loved this man who had brought her to his home, shown her his piece of the world. But the clincher was when he'd assumed Emily would accompany them. He knew Cassie and Emily were a package deal, and he'd embraced the fact and still welcomed them.

How could she not fall hard for this intriguing man? He was nothing like her ex, nothing like any man she'd ever known, really. And that was what made him so special.

Emily started clapping and pointing toward Ian. Cassie laughed. "Yeah, we're going, baby."

Sand shifted beneath her toes as she made her way toward the man who'd taught her heart to trust again. Just the sight of him had her anticipating their night alone after Emily went to bed.

It wasn't as if she hadn't seen or touched him all over, but still, his sexiness never got old.

Emily squealed and Ian turned to face her. His gaze traveled over her modest suit and Cassie tamped down that inner demon that tried to tell her that her extra baby weight was hideous. Ian never, ever made her feel less than beautiful, so that inner voice could just shut the hell up.

"You look good in a suit, Cass."

His low voice, combined with that heavy-lidded gaze, had her insides doing an amazing little dance number.

"I was thinking the same thing about you," she told him with a grin.

"Mom, Mom, Mom," Emily squealed again, clapping her little hands and staring out at the water.

"Can I?" Ian asked, reaching for Emily.

Handing Emily over, Cassie watched as Ian stepped into the water. Slowly, he waded in deeper, all the while taking his hand and cupping water to splash up onto her little pudgy legs. Emily's laughter, her arms around Ian's neck and seeing Ian bounce around in the water like a complete goofball had Cassie laughing herself.

This getaway was exactly what she needed. Coming off the win at the Preakness and rolling right into a special weekend had Cassie realizing that her life was pretty near perfect right now. For this moment, she would relish the fact that Ian had to care for her on some deep level… possibly even love her. If he only had feelings of lust, he wouldn't have brought her to his home, wouldn't have invited a teething, sometimes cranky kid, and he certainly wouldn't be playing in the water with Emily like a proud daddy.

Cassie hated to place all her hope, all her heart, on one man…but how could she not, when he'd captured her heart the instant they'd been intimate in that attic?

Not wanting to miss out on a single moment, Cassie jumped into the ocean, reached beneath the water and pinched Ian on the butt.

The grin he threw over his shoulder at her told her she was in for a fun night.

Rocking a now peaceful baby had Ian truly wishing for so much. He'd convinced Cassie that he could put Emily to bed. He figured the little one was so tired from the day of playing in the ocean and taking a stroller ride around his neighborhood that she'd fall fast asleep.

She'd been fussy at first and Cassie had shown Ian how to rub some numbing ointment onto Emily's gums. He'd given Emily a bottle, even burped her, and rocked her until her sweet breath evened out.

He glanced down to the puckered lips, the pink cheeks from the sun—even though they'd slathered her with sunscreen—and smiled. Was it any wonder Cassie worked herself to death? How could a parent not want to sacrifice herself to make such an innocent child happy?

Cassie worked so hard with her sister, worked harder in the stables caring for horses, and she busted her butt to make a secure life and happy home for Emily…all without a husband.

Oh, she'd be ticked if she knew he worried about her not having someone in her life to help her. Granted, she had her father, Tessa and Linda, but whom did she have at night? Who helped her at home?

God help him, but Ian wanted to be that man. The weight of a sleeping baby in his arms, the sweet smell of her skin after her bath and the thought that this innocent child had complete and total trust in him were truly humbling.

Once he knew she was asleep, Ian eased from the rocking chair and laid Emily into the new crib, complete with pink-and-white-striped sheets. When he stood up, she stirred a little, but she settled right in.

A sigh of relief escaped Ian. He'd mastered numerous multimillion-dollar movie deals, he rubbed elbows with A-list actors and he'd managed to start his own agency at the age of twenty-four. But putting a child to sleep all by himself felt like quite an accomplishment.

He glanced at the monitor beside the crib and made sure it was on before he stepped out into the hall and quietly shut the door behind him.

He barely managed not to jump when he noticed Cassie across the hall, leaning against the doorway to his bedroom.

"You did it," she said with a wide smile. "I'm impressed."

All thoughts fled his mind as he took in the muted glow that surrounded her from the small lamp in his room. Her long red curls slid around her shoulders, lying against the stark white silk robe she wore—and what she wasn't wearing beneath. The V in the front plunged so deep, the swells of her breasts begged for his touch.

"I like your pajamas," he told her, crossing the hallway and immediately going to the belt on her robe. "Reminds me of something…"

Cassie lifted her arms to wrap around his neck. "What's that?"

"The fact I haven't seen you naked in several days."

She shifted, allowing the material to slide from her shoulders and puddle at her feet. Ian's hands roamed over the soft, lush curves he'd come to love and crave.

"You feel so good," he groaned as he trailed his lips from her jawline down the smooth column of her neck. "So perfect."

When she trembled beneath his touch, Ian cupped her behind and pulled her flush against his body. Nothing had ever felt so right. Every time Cassie was in his arms, contentment settled deeper and deeper into his heart.

She undressed him rapidly, matching his own frenzy. Ian had brought other women to his home. Not many, but a few. Yet he knew the second he laid Cassie beneath him and looked down into her blue eyes…he never wanted another woman in this bed.

***

He knew she wasn't asleep. The full moon shone through the wide expanse of windows across the room from the king-size bed and directly across their tangled bodies.

Cassie's breathing wasn't even and he'd felt the soft flutter of her lashes against his arm. Whatever thoughts consumed her mind, they were keeping her awake.

More than likely they were the same things that had him awake hours after they'd made love…twice.

Ian trailed his fingertips over her hip, down into the dip of her waist and back again. Goose bumps prickled beneath his touch.

"Talk to me," she whispered in the darkened room.

Words that had frightened him on more than one occasion after sex. But this was so different from any other time. First, Cassie was like no other woman. Second, what had just happened between them was so far beyond sex. And third, he actually didn't cringe as the words hovered in the air between them.

Moreover, he *wanted* to talk to her. He wanted her to know about his past, his life and what had brought him to this point…and why the thought of commitment scared the hell out of him.

Part of him truly wanted to try for her. Never before had he even considered permanent anything in his life, let alone a woman and a child. Cassie changed everything for him, because she was starting to *be* everything for him.

Of course, there was that devil on his shoulder that kept telling him he couldn't just try out playing house with this woman. She was genuine, with real feelings and a heart of gold that she had to protect. If he attempted to try for a long-term spot in her life and things didn't work out, he would never be able to forgive himself.

"My childhood wasn't quite as rosy and enjoyable as

yours." The words tumbled out before he thought better of opening up about the past he hated to even think about. "My father was a military man. Things had to be perfect, and not just perfect, but done five minutes ago. When he was home on leave, if I had a chore, I had better get to it the second he told me or I would face punishment."

Cassie gasped next to him. "He hit you?"

Ian stared up at the darkened ceiling as he continued to trail his fingertips over her lush, naked curves. "On occasion. But it wasn't a beating. He was old-school and a hand to my backside wasn't unheard of. But then he came home less and less because he and my mother divorced. That's when she started bringing her male friends into the house."

Ian recalled how weird it felt having a strange man at the breakfast table when he woke up, but eventually he didn't question his mother...and he didn't ask the names of the men. Would it matter? They'd be gone when she finished with them anyway.

"My mom is currently in the middle of her fourth divorce and I've no doubt number five is waiting in the wings absolutely convinced he's the one."

Cassie's arm tightened around his abdomen. "I'm sorry. I can't imagine."

Her warm breath tickled his chest, but Ian wouldn't have it any other way. He loved the feel of her tucked perfectly against him, her hair falling over his shoulder, the flutter of her lashes against his side.

"Don't be sorry," he told her. "There are kids way worse off than I was. But I always wished I had parents who loved each other, who loved me. A family was everything to me when I was younger, but I wanted the impossible."

A drop of moisture slid down his side. Ian shifted his body, folding Cassie closer as he half loomed over her.

"Don't cry for me." In the pale moonlight, her eyes glistened. Had anyone ever cried for him before? "I'm fine, Cassie. I guess I just wanted you to know what I came from."

Soft fingertips came up to trail down his cheek. Her thumb caressed his bottom lip, and his body responded instantly.

"I'm crying for the little boy who needed love and attention," she whispered. "And I'm crying for the man who fits so perfectly into my family, I'm terrified of how we'll get along without him."

Her declaration was a punch to his gut. The fact that they'd never mentioned his leaving after the film wrapped hung heavy in the air between them. And knowing she not only worried about his absence, but she'd cried over it had him hating himself on so many levels.

"I don't want to hurt you," he murmured as he slid his lips across hers. "That's the last thing I'd ever want."

Adjusting her body so she could frame his face with her hands, Cassie looked up at him with those damn misty eyes and smiled. "I know. I went into this with my eyes wide-open. For right now, though, you're mine and I don't want to think about tomorrow, Ian. I don't want to worry about that void that will inevitably come when you're gone."

Her hips tilted against his. "I just want you. Here. Now."

As he kissed her lips he had a hard time reining in his own emotions, because Cassie was dead-on about one thing.... There would most definitely be a void—the one he would feel without her by his side.

Sixteen

Cassie reached across the bed, only to encounter cool sheets. Quickly she sat up, clutching the material to her chest and glancing to the nightstand clock.

How on earth had she slept until nine? Between having a career set around a working horse farm and being a single mother, sleeping in was a foreign concept and a luxury she simply couldn't afford.

Another reality hit her hard as she jerked to look at the baby monitor on the dresser across the room. The red light wasn't on, which meant at some point the device had been turned off. Throwing the covers aside, Cassie grabbed the first available article of clothing—which happened to be Ian's T-shirt—and pulled the soft cotton over her head. She inhaled the embedded masculine scent of Ian as she darted across the hall.

The nursery was empty. Giggling erupted from downstairs, so Cassie turned and headed toward the sweet sound. At the base of the steps, Cassie froze as she stared into the living room. Ian stood behind Emily, her little hands held high, clutching on to his as he helped her walk across the open space. He'd pushed the coffee table against one wall, leaving the dark hardwood floor completely open.

Emily squealed as she waddled through the area, and Cassie, who still stood unnoticed, had to bite her lip to control the trembling and wash of emotions that instantly consumed her.

Ian Shaffer had officially stolen her heart, and there was no way she could go back to her life before she'd ever met him. The man had opened his home to her and her daughter. He wasn't just interested in having her in his bed. Granted, that was how they'd started out, but over a brief period of time they'd grown together and meshed in such a way that had Cassie hopeful and wishing. Dare she set her sights so high and dream for things that once seemed unattainable?

"Mamamama," Emily cried when she saw Cassie in the doorway.

Cassie stepped toward her daughter and squatted down. "Hey, sweet pea. Are you making Ian work this morning?"

Emily's precious two-toothed grin melted her heart. When she glanced up to meet Ian's gaze, her breath literally caught. He still clung to Emily's fingers and he'd been hunched over so he could accommodate her height, but he just looked so at peace and happy.

"What time did she get up?"

Ian shrugged. "Maybe around seven."

Cassie straightened. "Why didn't you get me up?"

Scooping Emily into his arms, Ian smiled. "Because you needed to sleep, so I turned the monitor off and got her out of the crib. She's been changed and fed—probably not how you'd do it, but it's done nonetheless."

Cassie was utterly speechless. The man had taken such care of her daughter all so Cassie could sleep in. He'd been watching and loving over Emily...over another man's baby, and all without a care or second thought. And now he stood holding her as if the act were the most natural thing in the world.

"Don't look at me like that," he told her. Emily turned her head into Ian's shoulder and his wide, tanned hand patted her tiny back. "I wanted to help and I knew you'd refuse if you even thought she was awake. Besides, I kind of wanted to see how Emily and I would get along. I'm pretty sure she loves me."

Cassie couldn't help but laugh. "I'm sure she does love you. She knows a good thing when she sees it."

Ian's eyes widened, and the muscle in his jaw moved as if he were hiding his words deep within. Had she said too much? At this point, with time against them, Cassie truly believed she couldn't hold back. She needed to be up front and honest.

"I'm not saying that to make you uncomfortable," she informed him, crossing her arms over her chest. "But you have to know this is so much more than physical for me, Ian."

Those dark eyes studied her a second before he nodded. "I'd be lying if I said this was all sexual for me. You and Emily..."

He shook his head as his words died on his lips. Cassie wanted him to go on, but she knew the internal battle he waged with himself and she didn't want to push him. He'd opened up to her last night, bared his soul, and she knew what he'd shared hadn't come easy for him.

Placing a hand on his arm, Cassie smiled. "We don't need to define anything right now," she assured him. "I just wanted you to know this thing between us—it matters so much to me."

With Emily lying against one shoulder, Ian pulled Cassie to his other side and wrapped an arm around her. "Everything in my arms right now matters more to me than I ever thought possible," he told her with a kiss to the top of her head.

Before she could completely melt into a puddle at his feet over his raw, heartfelt words, Ian's hand slid down her side and cupped her bottom beneath his T-shirt.

"This shirt never looked this sexy on me," he growled into her ear. "So unless you want to end up back in bed, you better go get some clothes on."

Shivers of arousal swept through her. Would she ever get enough of him? More so, would he get enough of her?

Tipping her head back, she stared up into his eyes. Desire and, dare she say, love stared back at her. No, she didn't think they'd get enough of each other, which meant whatever they were building wouldn't come crumbling down when he left Virginia after the film was done shooting. But how they would manage was a whole other hurdle to jump.

Extracting herself from his side, Cassie pulled Emily from his arms. "How about we spend the day on the beach?" she suggested.

Emily's little hand went into Cassie's hair, and she started winding the strands around her baby fingers.

"You in a suit?" Ian's gaze raked over her once more. "I'd never say no to that."

With this being their last day of complete relaxation, Cassie wanted to live for the moment, this day, and not worry about what obstacles they faced tomorrow or even next week. She was completely in love with Ian. He wasn't a rebound; he wasn't a filler or a stepping-stone until the next chapter of her life.

Ian Shaffer *was* the next chapter of her life.

Seventeen

"I just need someone who's good with advertising," Cassie muttered as she stared down at the new plans for her riding school for handicapped children.

"How about that hunky agent you're shacking up with?"

Cassie threw a glare across the room at her sister. Tessa silently volleyed back a wicked grin.

"We're not shacking up." Not technically, anyway. "And that's not his job."

"Maybe not," Tessa replied, coming to her feet. "But he'd know more about it than we would, and I guarantee he'd do anything to help you."

More than likely, but Cassie wasn't going to ask. Venturing into personal favors would imply something…something they'd yet to identify in their relationship.

Yes, they'd admitted they had strong feelings for each other, but after the giant leap into intimacy, they'd pulled back the emotional roller coaster and examined where they were going.

And they still didn't know.

Cassie spoon-fed another bite of squash and rice to Emily. Right now she needed to focus on the final race of the season, getting her school properly advertised and caring for her daughter. Ian, unfortunately, would have to fall in line behind all of that and she highly doubted he would want to. What man would? He deserved more than waiting on her leftover time.

"You're scowling." Tessa came to stand beside the high chair and leaned against the wall. "What's really bothering you?"

Sisters. They always knew when to dig deeper and pull the truth from the depths of hell just to make you say the words aloud.

"Ian is out to dinner with Lily."

A quirk of a smile danced around Tessa's mouth. "You're jealous? Honey, the man is absolutely crazy about you. All you'd have to do is see how he looks at you when you aren't paying attention."

The idea that he studied her enough to show emotion on his face for others to see made her way more thrilled than she should be. She wanted to tell him she'd fallen for him—she wanted to tell everybody. But there was that annoying little voice that kept telling her this was too good to be true and that she needed to come back to reality before she ended up hurt.

"He's not like Derek," Tessa informed her as if she were reading her mind. "Ian may be younger, but he's all man and he's only got eyes for you."

Cassie smiled with a nod and scooped up the last bite, shoving it into Emily's waiting mouth. "I know. There's just that thread of doubt that gets to me, and I know it's not Ian's fault. He can't help the mess that is my life."

Laying a hand over Cassie's arm, Tessa squeezed. "Your

life is beautiful. You have a precious baby, an awesome career and the best sister anyone could ever ask for. What more could a girl want?"

To be loved. The words remained in her head, in her heart.

"So where's your guy tonight?" Cassie asked, wiping off the orange, messy mouth, hoping to unearth her daughter. "You two aren't normally separated for more than an hour at a time."

With a smile that could only be equated to love, Tessa positively beamed. "He's going over some things with Bronson and Anthony. I'm pretty sure Dad weaseled his way into that meeting, as well."

Cassie scooped Emily from the high chair and settled her on her hip. "I've no doubt Dad is weighing in with his opinion. I need to give her a bath. You sticking around?"

Shaking her head, Tessa sighed and started across the living room. "I think I'll head home and make some dinner. It's not often I get to cook for Grant, and he's worked so hard lately. He needs to relax."

Cassie squeezed her eyes shut. "I don't want to hear about you two relaxing. Just a simple no would've answered my question."

With a naughty laugh, Tessa grabbed her keys from the entry table and waved. "See you tomorrow."

Once Cassie was alone, she couldn't help that her thoughts drifted to Ian, to the days they'd spent at his home in L.A. and to the fact he'd taken such good care of her sweet Emily.

Yes, the man may be five years her junior, but so what? Her ex-husband had been two years older and look how well that had turned out. Cassie couldn't hang a single argument on age, not when Ian went above and beyond to show her just what type of man he was.

After Emily was bathed and dressed in her lightweight

sleeper, Cassie set some toys on a blanket and let her daughter have some playtime before bed. Settling on the couch, curling her legs to the side, Cassie rested her elbow on the arm of the sofa and watched Emily smack soft yellow and red cubes together, making them jingle.

Exhaustion consumed her, but how could she not be tired? Her plate was not only full—it was overflowing. Physically, mentally, she was drained. Her head was actually pounding so fiercely her eyes ached. Maybe she could just lay her head on the arm of the couch while Emily played for a bit longer.

Adjusting her arm beneath her head, Cassie closed her eyes, hoping to chase away the dull throb.

After the flash of panic in seeing Cassie slumped over the arm of the couch and Emily holding herself up against the edge of the couch by her mama, Ian realized Cassie had merely fallen asleep.

"Hey, sweetie," he said softly when Emily smiled up at him, flashing her two little baby teeth. "Your mama is pretty tired. Why don't we let her sleep?"

Ian scooped Emily up, set her in her Pack 'n Play across the room and made sure she had her favorite stuffed horse. He had to ignore her slight protesting as he crossed back and gently lifted Cassie into his arms. Murmuring something, she tilted her head against his chest and let out a deep sigh. She was exhausted and apparently couldn't even keep her eyes open. It was so unlike her to fall asleep with Emily still up and not confined to one area.

A small bedside lamp sent a soft glow through her bedroom. After gently laying her down, he pulled the folded blanket from the foot of the bed and draped it over her curled form. Smoothing her hair from her face, Ian frowned and leaned in closer to rest his palm across her forehead.

She wasn't burning up, but she wasn't far from it. Careful not to wake her, he peeled the throw back off her to hopefully get her fever down. Her cheeks were pink and the dark circles beneath her eyes were telltale signs of an illness settling in. He had a feeling Cassie would only be angry to know she was getting sick.

He went into her adjoining bath, got a cool cloth and brought it back out, carefully laying it across her forehead. She stirred and her lids fluttered open as she tried to focus.

"Ian?"

"Shh." He curled a hand over her shoulder to get her to remain down. "It's all right. You need to rest."

"Emily..." Cassie's eyes closed for a moment before she looked back up at him. "I don't feel very well."

"I know, baby. I'm not going anywhere and Emily is fine. Just rest."

He had no clue if she heard him; her eyes were closed and her soft, even breathing had resumed.

The woman worked herself too hard. Not that he could judge. After all, he hadn't grown to be one of Hollywood's most sought-out agents at such a young age by playing assistant and errand boy. No, he'd done grunt work, made his career his since he'd left home determined to prove to his free-spirited mother and domineering father that he could manage on his own and succeed way above anything they'd ever dreamed.

And he'd done just that.

But now that he looked down at Cassie resting peacefully, he couldn't help but wonder if there wasn't more in store for him. Work was satisfying on so many levels, but it didn't keep his bed warm, didn't look to him for support and compassion and sure as hell didn't make his heart swell to the point of bursting.

Cassie and Emily, on the other hand...

After clicking off the bedside lamp, he went straight to the hall bath to wash his hands. If Cassie was contagious, he didn't want to get her daughter sick. Granted, the child had been with her mother all evening, but still. Weren't people supposed to wash their hands before dealing with kids?

Yeah, he had a lot to learn. As he lathered up and rinsed, he glanced across the open floor plan to Emily, who had long since forgotten she was angry with being confined. Ian dried his hands on a plaid towel and smiled. Definitely had a lot to learn about little people.

And suddenly it hit him that he actually wanted to do just that. Who knew that when he came out here to sway Lily into signing with his agency that he'd completely get sidetracked by a beauty who literally fell into his arms?

After getting a bottle ready—thank God he'd had those alone days with Cassie and Emily in California so he knew a bit more about Emily's care—Ian set it on the end table and went to retrieve one happy baby.

"Are you always in a good mood?" he asked as he lifted her from the baby prison. "Your mama isn't feeling good, so it's just you and me."

Emily patted his face and smiled. "Dadadada."

Ian froze. *Oh, no. No, no, no.* As if a vise was being tightened around his chest, Ian's breath left him.

"No, baby. Ian."

Emily patted his cheek again. "Dadada."

Okay, he had to put his own issues aside at the thought of someone calling him Daddy because this poor girl honestly didn't know her daddy. She didn't remember the man who was supposed to be here for her and her mother.

Ian held her closer, silently wanting to reassure her that she was not alone. But was he also silently telling himself that he'd be here beyond the rough night right now? Would he be here after the film wrapped up?

Since he was alone with his thoughts he might as well admit to himself that being with Cassie and Emily for the long term was something he wanted and, dare he say… ached for?

As he settled into the corner of the couch with Emily, he slid the bottle between her little puckered lips and smiled as those expressive blue eyes looked back up at him. Eyes like her mother's. Both ladies had him wrapped around their fingers.

Emily drifted off to sleep about the time the bottle was empty. He set it back on the table and shifted her gently up onto his shoulder. If she spit up on his dress shirt, so be it. He hadn't taken the time to change after his dinner meeting with Lily. She was pretty confident she'd be signing with his agency.

And the fact this was the first time he'd thought of that monumental career development since he'd come in and discovered Cassie ill should tell him exactly how quickly his priorities had changed where the Barrington females were concerned.

Once Emily had fallen asleep, he figured it was okay for him to rest on the couch with her. He carefully got up and turned off the lights in the living room, leaving on only the small light over the stove in the kitchen. Pulling the throw off the back of the sofa with one hand and holding Emily firmly with the other, Ian toed off his shoes and laid the little girl against the back of the sofa before he eased down onto his side beside her. Not the most comfortable of positions, but he was so tired he could've slept standing up, and there was no way he'd leave Cassie alone with the baby tonight.

Resting with the baby on a couch was probably some

sort of Parenting 101 no-no, but since he'd taken no crash courses in this gig, he was totally winging it.

The next thing he knew someone was ringing the doorbell. Ian jerked up, taking in the sunlight streaming in through the windows. It was Sunday and the crew was taking the day off. Was someone looking for him? The doorbell chimed again and Emily's eyes popped open, too.

Ian picked her up and raked a hand over his hair as he padded to the door. The last thing he needed was for someone to ring that bell again and wake Cassie. Apparently they'd all slept uneventfully through the night.

As he flicked the lock, Ian glanced out the sidelight, frowning when he didn't recognize the stranger on the porch.

Easing the door open slightly, Ian met the other man's gaze. "Can I help you?"

The stranger's eyes went from Emily back to Ian before the muscle in his jaw jumped. "Who the hell are you, and where is Cassie?"

Shocked at the immediate anger, Ian instantly felt defensive. "I should be asking you who you are, considering you're on the outside."

Narrowed eyes pierced Ian. "I'm Cassie's husband. I'll ask again. Who the hell are you?"

Husband. Ian didn't miss the fact the prick left out the "ex" part.

"I'm her lover," Ian said, mentally high-fiving himself for wiping that smug look off the man's face.

Eighteen

Cassie held on to the side of her head, which was still pounding, but now she had a new problem.

Frozen at the end of her hallway, she had full view of Ian holding Emily and the front door wide-open with Derek standing on the other side looking beyond pissed. This was the dead-last thing she wanted to deal with in her life, particularly at this moment.

"Derek, what are you doing here?" she asked, slowly crossing the room, praying she didn't collapse.

"Go back to bed, honey." Ian turned to her, his face softening as he took in what she knew was impressive bed head. "Emily is fine and he can come back later."

"Don't tell my wife what to do," Derek practically shouted as he shouldered his way past Ian and into the living room.

"She's not your wife." Ian's eyes narrowed. When Emily started to fidget, Ian patted her back and murmured something to her. "I need to feed her and change her diaper."

Derek's gaze darted from Ian to Cassie and back to Ian.

"What the hell is this? You move in your lover to shack up? Never took you for a whore."

Cassie didn't think she could feel worse. She was wrong. But before she could defend herself, Ian had turned back, clenching the muscle in his jaw.

"Apologize," Ian said in a low, threatening tone.

Cassie had no doubt if Ian hadn't been holding the baby, he would've been across the room in an instant.

"This has nothing to do with you," Derek shot back. "Why don't you give me my daughter and get out."

No matter how awful Cassie felt, she raised her hand to silence Ian and moved closer to Derek. Too bad whatever bug she'd picked up couldn't be fast-acting or she'd so exhale all over him.

"You relinquished any right you had when you walked out on us." Cassie laid a hand on the back of the couch for support. She'd be a little more intimidating if she wasn't freezing and ready to fall onto her face. "You can't just barge into my house and try to take control. I don't know why you're here, but I don't really care."

Cassie felt Ian's hard body behind her, his strong hand settled around her waist. The man offered support both physically and emotionally with one simple, selfless touch. And the sea of differences between the two men in this room was evident without so much as a spoken word.

Ian had watched her with care, concern and, yes, even love. Derek stood glaring, judging and hating. When he'd first walked out she would've done anything to get her family back, but now that he was here, she loathed the sight of him.

"I'm here to see my wife and daughter," Derek told her.

"I'm not your wife," Cassie fired back. "And if you want to see Emily, you can contact your attorney and he can call mine. You can't just charge in here after being gone for nearly a year and expect me to just let you see her. Did you think she'd be comfortable with you?"

"She seems fine with him." Derek nodded his chin in Ian's direction.

"That's because she knows who I am," Ian stated from behind her. "Now, Cassie has asked you to leave. She's not feeling good and my patience has just about run out. Leave now or I'll escort you out personally, then notify the crew's security to take you off the estate property."

Derek looked as if he wanted to say more, but Ian stepped around Cassie, keeping his arm wrapped around her waist. He said nothing and kept his gaze on Derek until Derek stepped back toward the front door.

"I plan on seeing my daughter," Derek threatened. "And my wife. I'll go through my lawyer, but I will be getting my family back."

He slammed the door, leaving the echoing sound to fill the silence. Cassie hadn't seen Derek in so long, she had no idea how to feel, how to react. She didn't feel like battling him.

And had he threatened to take Emily? Was that what he'd implied?

Cassie sank onto the back of the couch and wrapped her arms around her waist. Maybe she should have listened to those voice mails.

"Go back to bed, Cass. Don't think about him—just go rest for now."

Cassie looked up at Ian, still holding Emily. The image just seemed so...right. The three of them *felt* right. They'd all been random puzzle pieces and when they'd come together they'd instantly clicked into place without question.

Shoving her wayward hair behind her ears, Cassie shook her head. "I can't rest, Ian. He just made a veiled threat to take Emily. He can't do that, right? I mean, what judge would let him have my baby after he walked out on us?"

Tears pricked her eyes. She couldn't fathom sharing custody of her baby. Emily belonged here.

"She doesn't even know him," Cassie murmured, thinking aloud. "There's no way he could take her. Emily would be terrified."

Ian rested a hand on her shoulder and held on to Emily with his other strong arm. "You're jumping the gun here. He didn't say he was going to ask for custody. I honestly think those were just hollow words. He wants to scare you because he's angry I was here. I guarantee had you been alone, his attitude would've been completely different. One look at me, especially holding his daughter, and he was instantly on the defensive."

Emily started to reach for Cassie, but Ian shifted his arm away. "Go on back to rest. I'll feed her breakfast and then I'll check on you to see if you feel like eating. You're exhausted and working too hard."

Cassie raised a brow. "Working too hard? Are you the pot or the kettle?"

Laughing, Ian shrugged. "Does it matter?"

Cassie pushed away from the couch and sighed. "Thanks, Ian. Really. I don't know what I would've done without you here last night."

After a light kiss across her forehead, Ian looked into her eyes. "There's nowhere else I would've rather been."

As Cassie got back into bed, she knew Ian wasn't just saying pretty words to try to win her over. The man was full of surprises, and she found herself falling harder with each passing revelation.

And now here she was, 100 percent in love with a man who lived on the other side of the country, who would be leaving in a couple of weeks to go back to his life. And, of all the rotten timing, her ex had decided to show up now.

Cassie curled into her pillow and fisted her hands beside her face as the tears threatened to fall. Somehow this would all work out. She had faith, she had hope and, for the first time in her life, she had love. All of that had to count for something...didn't it?

Once Cassie had gotten a little food in her, she seemed even more tired, so Ian insisted on taking Emily for a few hours and then checking back. There was no way he could leave her alone with a baby, but he still had work to do.

Single parents worked while caring for their babies all the time, right? Shouldn't be too hard to send some emails and make a few phone calls.

After fighting with the straps on the stroller and narrowly missing pinching Emily's soft skin in the buckle, he finally had her secured and ready to go. Diaper bag over his shoulder, Ian set out across the estate, pushing Emily toward his trailer.

Bright purple flats covered her feet as she kicked her little legs the entire way. Ian knew he was smiling like an idiot, but how could he not? Emily was an absolute doll and she was such a sweet kid. He was actually looking forward to spending time with her.

Max Ford and his wife, Raine, were just stepping out of their trailer as he passed by. Max held their little girl, Abby, who was almost two now.

"Look at this," Max said with a wide grin. "You seeing how the family life fits you?"

Ian didn't mind the question. Actually, he kind of warmed at the idea of it. "Cassie isn't feeling too great, so I told her I'd take Emily for the day."

Max's daughter pointed down to Emily. "Baby."

Laughing, Raine took the little girl and squatted down to the stroller to see Emily. "Her name is Emily," Raine explained.

"You're pretty serious about Cassie," Max said in a softer tone. "Happened pretty quick."

Ian shook his head and raked a hand over his hair, which was probably still sporting a messy look after sleeping on the sofa all night. "Yeah, it did. But I can't help it, man. I didn't see this coming."

"You plan on staying after the film is done?" Max asked.

Ian watched the interaction between the two little girls and Raine and his heart swelled. "I honestly don't know," Ian said, looking back to Max. "How hard was it for you with the transition?"

Max's gaze drifted to his family, and a genuine smile, not what he used for the cameras or his on-screen love interests, but the one that Ian had seen directed only at Raine, transformed his face. "When you want something so bad you'd die without it, there's no transition. It's the easiest and best decision I've ever made."

Yeah, that was kind of where Ian's mind was going. Having Cassie and Emily in his life made him feel things on a level he hadn't even known existed inside him.

Ian said his goodbyes to Max and his family and stepped inside his trailer. After settling Emily on a pink fuzzy blanket from her house, Ian placed her favorite toys all around her. Standing back to admire his feat of babysitting, he went to boot up his laptop, grabbed his phone and sat at the small kitchenette. Thankfully, the trailer was all open and small, so Emily couldn't leave his sight.

After answering a few emails, Ian glanced at the little girl, who was chewing on one toy and pounding the other one against the side of her rainbow-striped leggings. So far so good.

As he dialed one of his clients, rising star Brandon Crowe, who was on his way to Texas for filming, Ian scrolled back through his emails, deleting the junk so he could wade through and find things that actually needed his attention.

"Hello."

"Brandon, glad I caught you." Ian closed out his email and opened the document with his client's name on it to make notes. "You arrive in Houston yet?"

"About an hour ago. I'm ready for a beer, my hotel room and about five days of sleep. In that order."

Ian chuckled. His client had been filming all over with a tight schedule; the crew had literally been running from one location to another.

"What's up?" Brandon asked.

"I know your mind is on overload right now, but I need to discuss the next script. I have a film that will be set in Alaska and the producer has specifically asked for you. I'd like to send this script to you and see what you think."

Brandon sighed. "Sure. Did you look it over?"

"Yeah. I think this character would be a perfect fit for you. I can see why they want you for the role."

"Who's the producer?" Brandon asked.

Ian told him more specifics and turned to see Emily... only she wasn't there. Panic rushed through him as he jerked to his feet, sending his chair toppling to the floor behind him.

"Emily," he called, glancing around the very tiny area.

"Excuse me?"

Ian glanced at the phone. For a second he'd forgotten about the call. "I need to call you back. The baby is gone."

"Baby?"

Ian disconnected the call and tossed his phone on the

table. Stepping over the toys and blanket, Ian crossed to the other end of the trailer. He peeked into the tiny bathroom: no Emily.

"Emily," he called. "Sweetheart?"

In the small bedroom, Ian saw bright rainbow material sticking out from the side of the bed. He rounded the bed. Emily sat on her bottom, still chewing her favorite stuffed horse. Of course, when she saw him she looked up and gave that heart-melting smile.

"You're rotten," he told her. "Your mom is not going to let you come play with me anymore if you give me a heart attack."

He scooped her up and was rewarded with a wet, sloppy horse to the side of the face. *Nice.*

The next hour went about as stellar as the first, and by the end of hour two, Ian knew he was an amateur and needed reinforcements. There was just no way he could do this on his own.

How the hell did Cassie manage? Not only manage, but still put up the front of keeping it together and succeeding at each job: mother, sister, daughter, trainer. She did it all.

Of course, now she was home, in bed, flat-out exhausted and literally making herself sick.

As Ian gathered up all Emily's things, she started crying. The crying turned into a wail in about 2.5 seconds, so Ian figured she was hungry. Wrong. He changed her diaper. Still not happy.

He picked up the bag and Emily, stepped outside and strapped her into the stroller. Perhaps a walk around the estate would help.

Keeping toward the back of the main house, Ian quickly realized this also wasn't making her very happy. That was it. Reinforcements were past due.

He made his way to the back door, unfastened the very

angry Emily and carried her into the house, where—*thank you, God*—Linda greeted him with a smile and some heavenly aroma that could only be her cinnamon rolls.

"I've done something wrong," Ian yelled over Emily's tantrum. "We were fine." A slight lie. "But then she started screaming. She's not hungry. She has a clean diaper. We took a walk. I don't know what to do."

Linda wiped her hand on a plaid towel and tossed it onto the granite counter before circling the island and holding her hands out for Emily. The baby eagerly went to the middle-aged woman and Ian nearly wept with gratitude that someone else surely knew what they were doing.

"She probably needs a nap," Linda told him as she jostled and tried to calm Emily.

Ian laughed and pushed a hand through his hair. "After all of that, I need one, too."

Smiling, Linda patted Emily's back. "You say you fed her?"

Ian nodded. "She took a bottle. I have some jar food, but Cassie said to save that for a bit later."

"If she's had her bottle, then her little belly is full and she's ready to rest. I'll just take her into the master bedroom. Damon has a crib set up in there for when Cassie is over here."

Ian sank to the bar stool, rested his elbow on the island and held his head in his hands. Good grief, being in charge of one tiny little being was the hardest job he'd ever had… and he'd had the job only a few hours.

Hands down, parenting was not for wimps.

A slither of guilt crept through him. Had he been too hard on his parents all those years? His free-spirited mother who was always seeking attention and his by-the-book father who could never be pleased…were they just struggling at this whole parenting thing, too?

Ian didn't have the answers and he couldn't go back in time and analyze each and every moment. The most pressing matter right now was the fact that he was in love with Cassie and her sweet baby, and the ex had just stepped back into the picture.

Great freakin' timing.

But Ian needed to wait, to let Cassie deal with this matter in her own way. He wasn't stepping aside, not by any means. He'd offer support any way she wanted it, but this was her past to handle, and with a baby involved, Ian had a bad feeling things were about to get worse before they could get better.

Nineteen

Cassie jerked when the loud knock on her door pulled her out of her sleep. Glancing to the clock on the bedside table, she realized she'd slept most of the day. Damn, she'd never slept that much.

Throwing off the covers and coming to her feet, Cassie was thrilled when she didn't sway and within moments knew she was feeling better. Perhaps her body was just telling her she needed to slow it down every now and then. The pounding on her door continued and Cassie rolled her eyes. There wasn't a doubt in her mind who stood on the other side of the door. Ian wouldn't pound on her door. He'd knock or just come on in, and so would her father and Tessa.

And that left only one rude, unwanted guest.

Shuffling down the hall, probably looking even more stellar than earlier today when Derek had stopped by, Cassie actually laughed. Was he really here to plead for his family back when she looked like death and after he'd left her for some young, hot bimbo? Oh, the irony was not lost on her.

Cassie took her time flipping the lock on the knob and opening the door. Sure enough, Derek stood there, clutching a newspaper. Disapproval settled in his eyes.

"Funny," she told him, leaning against the edge of the door. "That's the same look you wore when you left me. What do you want now?"

He slapped the paper to her chest and pushed past her to enter.

"Come on in," she muttered, holding on to the paper and closing the door. "I thought I told you to have your lawyer contact mine."

Derek scanned the living area, then stretched his neck to see down the hall. "Where's Emily?"

"With Ian." Crossing her arms, crinkling the paper, Cassie sighed. "What do you want, Derek?"

"First of all, I don't want my daughter with a stranger."

Hysterical laughter bubbled out before she could even try to control it. "Seriously? If anyone is a stranger to her, it's you. We've already established what you think of Ian, so state your reason for this unwanted visit or that threat of calling security will become a fast reality."

He pointed toward the paper. "Apparently you haven't seen today's local paper. Maybe your pretty boy is a stranger to you, as well."

Cassie unfolded the paper. She'd play his game if it meant he'd leave sooner.

Her eyes settled on the picture of Lily and Ian. Cassie had known they were having a business meeting the evening before, she'd known they were discussing a major career move for both of them, but she hadn't known the media would spin the story into something…romantic.

Her eyes landed on the headline: Hollywood Starlet on Location Still Finds Time for Romance.

The way their two heads were angled together in the grainy picture did imply something more than a business meeting. The intimate table for two complete with bouquet and candles also added to the ambience of love.

Cassie glanced back up to Derek. "What about it?"

She would not give her ex the satisfaction of letting it get to her, of coming between something she and Ian had built and worked hard at.

"Looks like your boy toy has someone else on the side." Derek smirked. "Is this really what you've moved on to?"

"Why are you here?" she demanded. "What do you want from me?"

"If you'd answered my calls or texts you'd know I want my family back. I had no idea you opted to replace me with such a younger man."

Cassie smacked the paper down on the table beside the door. "Don't you dare judge me. You left me, remember? And if we're casting stones, I'll remind you that when you left, you moved on with a much younger woman with boobs as her only major asset."

Fired up and more than geared for a fight, Cassie advanced on him. "You're just upset because Ian is a real man. He cares about me, about Emily. My looks don't matter, my size doesn't matter and he's taken to Emily like she is his own, which is a hell of a lot more than you ever did for either of us."

Derek clenched his jaw as he loomed over her and held her gaze. "I just want you to know that this man, this kid, really, will get bored with the family life. He'll move on, and then where will you be? I'm man enough to admit I was wrong and that I'm willing to try again."

She hated that she felt a small tug, hated that for months

she'd prayed for this moment. But she loved Ian. How could she deny herself the man she felt she'd been waiting for her whole life?

But on the other hand, how could she deny her daughter the bond of her parents raising her in the same house?

Cassie shook her head, refusing to listen to the conflicting voices in her head. She needed to think, needed to be alone.

"I waited for months for you to come back," she told him, hoping her words would make him squirm, make him feel the heavy dose of guilt he was due. "I cried myself to sleep when I thought of Emily not knowing her father. But you know what? After the tears were spent, I realized that Emily was better off. Both of us were, actually. Neither of us needed a man in our life who didn't put us first. We needed a man who would love us, put our needs above his own selfish ones and be there for us no matter what."

When he opened his mouth, Cassie raised a hand to silence him. "I would've given you the same in return. I married you thinking we were both in love, but I was wrong. You didn't love me, because if you did, you wouldn't have found it so easy to leave me."

"I'm back, though." He reached out, touched her face. "I want my family back, my wife back. I know I made a mistake, but you can't tell me you're ready to throw everything away."

When the door opened behind her, Cassie didn't have to turn to know Ian stood just at the threshold. She closed her eyes and sighed.

"Actually," she whispered. "You already threw it all away."

Derek's eyes darted from hers to just over her shoulder before he dropped his hands. "You can keep the paper. Maybe it will give you something to think about."

She didn't move as he skirted around her. When the door shut once again, Cassie turned slowly to see Ian, hands on his hips. Even with the space between them, Cassie saw so many emotions dancing in his eyes: confusion, hurt, love.

"Where's Emily?" she asked, hoping to keep the conversation on safer ground.

"I actually just left her with Linda. She's taking a nap."

Cassie nodded, worry lacing through her. "What you just saw was—"

"I know what I saw," he murmured. "I know he wants you back. He'd be a fool not to. It's just—"

Ian glanced down, smoothing a hand over the back of his neck, then froze when his gaze landed on the paper. Slowly he picked it up, skimming the front page.

Cassie waited, wondering how he would react.

When he muttered a curse and slammed the paper down, Cassie jumped.

"Tell me this wasn't Derek's defense," Ian begged. "He surely wasn't using me as his battle to win you back."

Shrugging, Cassie crossed her arms around her waist. "It's a pretty damning photograph."

Closing the spacious gap between them, Ian stood within a breath of her and tipped her chin up so she looked him in the eyes. "The media is known for spinning stories to create the best reaction from viewers. It's how they stay in business."

Cassie nodded. "I'm aware of that."

Ian studied her for a moment before he plunged his fingers through her disheveled hair and claimed her lips. The passion, desire and fury all poured from him, and Cassie had to grip his biceps to hold on for the ride.

He attacked her mouth, a man on a mission of proving something, of taking what was his and damning the consequences.

When he pulled away, Ian rested his forehead against hers. "Tell me you believe that I could kiss you like that and have feelings for another woman. Tell me that you don't trust me and all we have here is built on lies. Because if that's the case, I'll leave right now and never come back."

Cassie's throat tightened as she continued to clutch his arms. "I don't believe that, Ian. I know you wouldn't lie to me. You've shown me what a real man is, how a real man treats a lady."

Taking a deep breath, she finally stepped back, away from his hold. "But I also know that this is something I'm going to have to deal with if we're together. The media spinning stories, always being in the limelight."

"I'm an agent, Cassie. Nobody cares about me. If I had been out alone, nobody would've known who I was."

Cassie smiled. "But you were out with the breathtaking Lily Beaumont. All of your clients are famous, Ian. There will be other times, other photos."

Shaking her head, she walked around and finally sank onto the sofa. Ian joined her but didn't touch her. She hated this wedge that had settled between them…a wedge that had formed only once Derek had entered the picture.

"I want to be with you, Cassie," he told her. "As in beyond the movie, beyond next month or even next year. I want to see where this can go, but if the idea of my work will hold you back, maybe we both need to reevaluate what we're doing."

Tears pricked her eyes as she turned to face him fully. "You want to be with me?"

Reaching out to swipe the pad of his thumb across her cheek to clear the rogue tear, Ian smiled. "Yes. I know it's crazy and we've only known each other a short time, but I do want to be with you."

"Is this because my ex is back? Are you feeling threatened?"

Shaking his head, Ian took her shoulders and squeezed. "This has nothing to do with Derek. His appearance is just bad timing, that's all. I can't deny myself the fact that being with you has made me a better person. Finding myself wrapped around yours and Emily's lives makes me want more for myself. I never thought about a family before, but I want to see where this will lead and how we can make it work."

Hope filled Cassie as she threw her arms around Ian's neck and sniffed. "I know I'm a hot mess right now," she told him. "I have no idea how I was lucky enough to get you, but I want to see where we go, too. I'm just sorry you'll have to deal with Derek." Cassie eased back and wiped her cheeks. "He's Emily's father, and even though he abandoned us, I can't deny him if he wants to see her."

"What if he wants custody? Did he mention that again?"

"No. I hope he was just trying to scare me, like you said."

Smoothing her hair behind her ear, Ian smiled and settled his palm against her cheek. "No matter what, I'm here for you. Okay?"

For the first time in a long time, Cassie knew there was something to be hopeful about, something more than her career and Emily to fight for. And that was the love of a good man.

Ian was right. Damn if Derek's visit hadn't come at the worst possible time. Not only was the estate covered in film crew and actors, but Ian had settled so perfectly into her life and now the Belmont Stakes was upon them.

The final of the three most prestigious races in the horse world. There was no way Cassie could possibly think of

Derek and his threats right now…and yet he had left her with a doozy last night.

He'd called her and issued an ultimatum—either she take him back and give their marriage another go or he would go to his lawyer with a plea to get full custody. Of course, she doubted he could, but the threat was there, and even if he didn't get full, there was always a chance he could get shared. And then where would she be?

Cassie sank down onto the bed in her hotel room and rested her head in her hands. Crying would be of no use, but she so wished she could cut loose and absolutely throw a fit. Being an adult flat-out sucked sometimes.

The adjoining door to the bedroom next to hers creaked open and Cassie glanced up to see Tessa standing in the doorway wearing a gray tank top and black yoga pants.

"I know you're not in a good spot, and as much as I think you could use a drink, that won't help us any in tomorrow's race." Tessa held up a shiny gold bag. "But I do have chocolates and I'm willing to share."

Cassie attempted a smile. "Are they at least rum balls?"

Laughing, Tessa crossed the room and sank onto the bed, bumping Cassie's hip. "Sorry. Just decadent white-chocolate truffles. You ready to talk about Derek being back and wreaking havoc? Because it's been all I could do not to say something to you, but I figured you'd tell me on your own."

Cassie took the bag and dug out a chocolate. No, the sweetness wouldn't cure all, but it would certainly take the edge off her rage.

"I was hoping if I ignored the fact he was in town he'd just go away," Cassie said as she bit into the chocolate.

"How's that working?"

"Not well. How did you find out anyway? He's only been in town two days."

Tessa reached into the bag and pulled out a piece for herself. "Ian and Max were discussing the problem, and I may have eavesdropped on their conversation."

Swallowing the bite and reaching for another truffle, Cassie shifted on the bed to face her sister, settling the bag between them. "I planned on telling you. I was just trying to focus on Ian, make sure Emily was all settled with Linda before we left and praying Derek didn't try to get back onto Stony Ridge while we were gone. I've got security keeping an eye out for him."

"Can you legally do that?" Tessa asked.

Shrugging, Cassie smoothed her hair back and tugged the rubber band from her wrist to secure the knotty mess. "I have no clue. But if he's trespassing on the property, that's all the guards need to know to have him escorted off. If he wants to play the poor-father card, I doubt he'll have a leg to stand on."

"After the race tomorrow, go on home." Tessa reached in the bag and offered Cassie another chocolate, but Cassie wasn't in the mood anymore. "Nash and I will make sure everything is handled and taken care of. Take the truck Nash brought, and he and I can take the trailer and other truck."

Cassie bit her lip when tears threatened. "I don't want him to ruin this, Tessa. We've worked too hard, come too far, and we're both retiring after this season. I can't let him destroy our dreams of going out on top."

Reaching between them to take Cassie's hand, Tessa smiled. "Derek won't destroy anything. You won't give him that power. He's a jerk and he'll probably be gone when we get back because you weren't falling all over yourself to take him back when he appeared on your doorstep."

"He's threatening to file for custody," Cassie whispered.

Tessa let out a string of words that would've made their mother's face turn red. "He's an ass, Cassie. No judge will let him take Emily."

"What about joint custody?"

With a shrug, Tessa shook her head. "Honestly, I don't know, but the man has been gone almost a year, so I would certainly hope no judge would allow someone so restless to help raise a child."

Cassie had the same thoughts, but life and the legal system weren't always fair.

Flinging herself onto the bed, Cassie crossed her arms over her head. "I just never thought I'd be in this situation, you know? I mean, I married Derek thinking we'd be together forever. Then when we had Emily I really thought my family was complete and we were happy. Derek leaving was a bomb I hadn't expected, but now that he's back, I don't want him. I feel nothing but anger and resentment."

Tessa lay on her back next to Cassie and sighed. "You know, between me, Dad, Grant, Linda and Ian, Derek doesn't stand a chance. There's no way we'd let him just take Emily without a fight. If the man wants to play daddy, he'll have to actually stick around and prove he can man up."

"I agree," Cassie told her, lacing her fingers behind her head and staring up at the ceiling. "I won't deny my daughter the chance of knowing her father if I truly believe he won't desert her in a year just when she's getting used to him. I will do everything in my power to protect her heart from him."

And wasn't that just the saddest statement? Protecting a little girl's heart from her own father. But Derek had given her little choice.

"So, you want to tell me what you and Ian are doing?"

Tessa asked. "Because I'm pretty sure the two of you are much more than a fling."

Cassie laughed. "Yeah, we're definitely much more than a fling."

"Who knew when you got locked in that attic the man of your dreams would come to your rescue?"

"Technically he didn't rescue me," Cassie clarified.

Tessa glanced over, patted Cassie's leg and smiled. "Oh, honey. He's rescued you—you just might not see it yet."

She was right. Ian had come along at a time in her life when the last thing she'd wanted was a man. But he'd shown her love, shown her daughter love. He'd shown her what true intimacy was all about. When she'd been sick he hadn't thought twice about taking Emily, even though he knew next to nothing about babies.

He made Cassie's life better.

There was no way that she could not fight for what they had. Maybe she should look into a riding school in California. With her income and her knowledge, she technically could start it anywhere.

She had to deal with Derek first; then she would figure out how being far away from her family would work.

Tessa's brows lifted. "I know that look," she said. "You're plotting something. Share or I'll take my chocolates back to my room."

"Just thinking of the future," Cassie replied with a smile. "Thinking of my school. I've already started putting the wheels in motion for Stony Ridge, but who's to say that's where it has to be?"

Tessa hugged her. "I was so afraid this is what you'd do. Damn, I'm going to miss you if you move."

"Don't go tearing up on me," Cassie ordered. "Ian hasn't asked me, but if he did, I can't say that I would tell him no. On the other hand, Grant has a home out in L.A., too, so I'm sure you'd spend time out there."

"It wouldn't be the same." Tessa sniffed, blinked back tears. "But I want you happy and this is truly the happiest I've seen you in your entire life. I'll support any decision you make."

Cassie reached out, grabbed Tessa's hand and settled in with the fact she'd move heaven and earth to be with Ian. And now she couldn't wait to get home to tell him just that.

Twenty

Ian had a wonderful surprise planned for Cassie. He couldn't wait for her to get home.

Not only had Tessa and Cassie taken the Belmont Stakes and the coveted Triple Crown, but Cassie was on her way back and Ian had to get the stage set. They had so much to celebrate.

Very few had ever taken home the Triple Crown title, and Tessa was the first female jockey to own the honor. The Barrington sisters had officially made history and Ian was so proud he'd been able to witness a small portion of their success. He hated he wasn't there in person, though.

Ian had opted to stay behind for two reasons. So they could both concentrate on their own work without distractions and to see if he could handle being without her.

He couldn't.

After a perfect morning in which Lily officially signed with his agency, he was now in town hitting up the quaint little florist, about to buy an exorbitant amount of flowers in a variety of colors and styles. He wanted her cottage to be drowning in bouquets for the evening he had planned. Not only because he had high hopes about their future, but because she deserved to be placed on a pedestal after such a milestone win.

He may have also had Linda's help in the matter of planning.

The days they'd been apart had been a smack of reality to the face. He didn't want to be without her, without Emily. He was ready to make a family with them.

He also realized that love and marriage—and fatherhood—weren't scary at all once you found the person who totally completed you.

This family had instantly been so welcoming, so loving, and Ian couldn't be happier. From Linda to sweet Emily, he was so overwhelmed by how easily they accepted him. And now Cassie was about to get the surprise of her life.

As Ian rounded the building that housed the flower shop, he smacked into someone…Derek. *Great.*

"You're still in town?" Ian asked, eyeing the man clutching a massive bouquet of roses.

Derek shielded his eyes from the warm afternoon sun. "I'm not leaving until I get what I want."

Becoming more irritated by the moment, and a tad amused, Ian crossed his arms over his chest. "That will be a while, considering what you want is mine."

"Yours? My family is not your property," Derek clarified.

"They're also not your family. Not anymore. Cassie made her choice."

"Did she? Because the Cassie I know loves family." Derek adjusted the flowers to his other hand and shifted beneath the awning of the flower shop to shield himself from the sun. "It means more to her than anything. Do you think she'd honestly choose some young guy who she just met over the father of her child? Because I can assure you, she'll put Emily's needs ahead of her own."

There was a ring of truth to Derek's words, but there was also no way Ian would show any emotion or allow this guy to step into the life he was trying to build.

"Don't blame me or Cassie because you realized too late that you made a mistake," Ian said, propping his hands on his hips and resisting the urge to take those flowers, throw them on the ground and crush them. "Cassie and I have something, and there's no way you're going to come charging in like you belong. You missed your chance."

Derek smiled. "I didn't miss anything. You see, no matter how much you hate me, I am Emily's father. She will want to know me and I will make damn sure my lawyer does everything he can to get my baby girl in my life. Now, if Cassie wants to come, too, that's her decision, but I'll fight dirty to get what I want. Considering the fact that you are a Hollywood playboy, combined with the perfectly timed image in the paper, I don't see how I can't use that against Cassie. Obviously she's eager to get any man's attention—"

All control snapped as Ian fisted Derek's shirt and slammed him against the old brick building. Petals flew everywhere as the bouquet also smacked against the wall.

"Listen here, you little prick." It was all Ian could do not to pummel the jerk. "I will not be bullied into giving up what I want, and Cassie will not be blackmailed, either. If you want to see your daughter, then go through your attorney the proper way, but don't you dare use your own child as a pawn. Only a sick ass would do that."

Stepping back, Ian jerked the bouquet from Derek's hand and threw it down on the sidewalk. He'd held back long enough and Ian knew full well whom that arrangement was meant for.

Ian issued one final warning through gritted teeth. "Stay away from me and mine."

As he walked away, he didn't go into the flower store as originally intended. He had some thinking to do.

No, he wouldn't be intimidated by some jerk who thought he could blackmail his way back into Cassie's life, but if Ian's presence was going to cause issues with custody of Emily, Ian knew he had a difficult decision to make.

As he headed back to his sporty rental car, the small box in his pocket felt heavier than ever.

Cassie had never been so eager to return from a race, especially one as important as this one.

They'd done it. The Barrington women had conquered the racing world and brought home the Triple Crown. Cassie was pretty sure she'd be smiling in her sleep for years to come. She and Tessa had worked so hard, prayed even harder, and all their endless hours and years of training had paid off.

But beyond the joy of the racing season coming to an amazing end, Cassie couldn't wait to celebrate with Emily and Ian and wanted to get Derek taken care of so he would leave her alone once and for all.

Because she'd gotten home later than intended, Linda had stayed in the cottage and put Emily to bed. Now Cassie was alone, her baby sleeping down the hall and unpacked bags still just inside the door where she'd dropped them.

She had to see Ian now. Too many days had passed since she'd seen him, touched him. Each day she was away from him she realized just how much she truly loved him.

A gentle tap on her front door had her jerking around. The glow of the porch light illuminated Ian's frame through the frosted glass. She'd know that build anywhere and a shiver of excitement crept over her at the thought of seeing him again. She hadn't realized she could miss someone so much.

But the second she flung the door open, ready to launch into his strong hold, she froze. Something was wrong. He wasn't smiling, wasn't even reaching for her. Actually, his hands were shoved in his pockets.

"What's wrong?" she asked, clutching the door frame.

Ian said nothing as his gaze moved over her. Something flashed through his eyes as he settled back on her face...regret?

"Ian?"

He stepped over the threshold, paused within a breath of her and then scooted around her. After closing the door behind her, she leaned against it, unsure of what to say or how to act.

Her eyes locked on to Ian's as silence quickly became the third party present. Moments ago she'd had nothing but hope filling her heart. Now fear had laid a heavy blanket over that hope.

"This is so much harder than I thought it would be," he whispered, his eyes glistening. "I had tonight planned so different."

"You're scaring me, Ian."

Wrapping her arms around her waist, Cassie rubbed her hands up and down her bare arms to ward off the chill.

"I love you, Cassie. I've never said that to another human being, not even my own parents." Ian stepped closer but didn't touch her. "Tonight I thought I would tell you I loved you, show you that I can't live without you and Emily, but I've thought about it all evening and came to the hardest decision of my life."

Cassie wasn't a fool. She knew exactly what he was

going to say. "How dare you," she whispered through tears clogging her throat. "You tell me you love me a breath before you're about to break things off? Because that's what this is, right?"

Ian ran a hand over his face. "Damn it, Cassie. I'm letting you go to make things easier. I can't keep you in my life, knowing I could be the one thing that stands between you and keeping custody of your daughter."

Realization quickly dawned on Cassie. "You bastard. You let Derek get to you, didn't you? I never took you for a coward, Ian."

"I'm not a coward, and if Emily weren't in the picture I would stay and fight for you…and I'd win. But Emily deserves a chance to know her father, and I can't stand the thought of you sharing custody or possibly losing because Derek is going to fight dirty. He said it himself. This way, with me gone, maybe you two can come to some sort of peaceful middle ground."

Torn between hurt, love and anger, Cassie tried to rein in her emotions. "You're leaving me because you're afraid. I understand that you didn't have a great childhood, which makes me respect you all the more for stepping up and loving Emily the way you have. But don't you dare leave now when things get tough. I thought you were more of a man than that."

He jerked as if she'd slapped him. "Trust me, Cass. In the long run, this is the best for Emily."

"What about me?" she cried. "I love my daughter and her needs will always come first, but you say you love me. So what about that? What about us?"

The glistening in his eyes intensified a second before a tear slid down his cheek. He didn't make a move to swipe it away and Cassie couldn't stop staring at the wet track.

Her heart literally ached for the man who was trying

to be strong and, in his own way, do the right thing. But damn it, she wanted more and she thought she'd found it with him.

As she stepped forward, Ian took a step back. And that lone action severed any thread of hope she had been holding on to.

"I'm barely hanging on here," he whispered. "You can't touch me. I have to be strong for both of us. Just think about what I said. You'll know that I'm right. There's no other way if you want to keep Emily. Derek won't play fair, and if I'm in your life, he'll use that against you."

He took in a deep, shuddering breath. "I want to be part of your life, Cass. I want to be part of Emily's. But it's because I want so much to be a part of your family that I must protect you both, and unfortunately, that means I need to step aside."

Cassie hated the emotions whirling about inside her. So much love for this man and so much hatred toward another. Damn Ian for being noble.

"If you're not staying to fight for me and with me, then leave." Blinking back tears and clenching her fists at her side to keep from wrapping her arms around him, Cassie held his gaze. "You've done what you came to do, so go."

Ian slid a hand from his pocket, clutched something and reached out to place it on the end table by the sofa. "What I came to do was quite the opposite," he told her as he took a step toward her. "But I want you to have that and remember that I do love you, Cassie. No matter what you think right now. I'll always love you."

Without touching her, without even a kiss goodbye, Ian stepped around her and quietly walked out of her life. Drawing in a shaky breath, she took a step toward the end table and saw a blue box. Her heart in her throat, Cassie reached for the box. Her hands shook because she knew exactly what would be beneath that velvety lid.

Lifting the lid with a slow creak, Cassie gasped. Three square-cut stones nestled perfectly in a pewter band had tears spilling down both cheeks. Cassie's hand came to her mouth to hold back the sob that threatened to escape.

Ian had put all of their birthstones in the ring…a ring he'd planned on giving her when he told her he loved her.

Unable to help herself, she pulled the band from the box and slid it on. A perfect fit—just like the man who had walked out the door moments ago.

As she studied the ring on her finger, Cassie knew there was no way she would go down without a fight. No way at all. Emily would come first, as always, but who said she couldn't have the man of her dreams *and* her family?

If Derek wanted to fight dirty, well, bring it on, because Cassie had just gotten a whole new level of motivation to fuel her fire. And there was no way in hell Derek would take her child or the dreams Cassie had for a future with Ian.

The depth of Ian's love was so far beyond what she'd dared to imagine. His strength as a man and father was exactly what she needed, wanted…deserved. She wouldn't let his sacrifice go to waste.

Twenty-One

Ian wasn't sure why he didn't book a trip somewhere exotic to just get away. He'd come back to L.A. after breaking things off with Cassie. Max had more than understood his need to leave, but his friend had also had some choice words for him regarding the stupidity of his decision.

Ian wished there'd been another way. He'd had many sleepless nights looking for another way to protect Cassie and Emily, but it was because he loved them so much—because they *were* his family—he knew he needed to remove himself from their lives.

The pain after he'd left was unlike anything he'd ever known. Sharp, piercing pain had settled into the void in his heart that Cassie and Emily had left. But he also knew, in the long run, this was the best for the ladies he'd quickly grown to love.

Now, back in his beachfront home, he saw Cassie and that precious baby. How had two females he'd known only a short time infiltrated every single corner of his life? There wasn't a spot in his house, his mind or his heart that they hadn't left their imprint on.

He'd been home almost a month, and in the phone calls and texts between Max and Lily, he knew the filming was nearing the end. He hadn't asked about Cassie.... He just couldn't. The thought of her possibly playing house with Derek to keep the peace for Emily nearly crippled him.

Ian sank down onto the sand and pulled his knees up to his chest. The orange glow from the sunset made for a beautiful backdrop and not for the first time was he elated to have all of this for his backyard.

But he'd give it up in a heartbeat for a chance at happiness with Cassie. Letting her go was hands down the hardest thing he'd ever done in his entire life.

He hadn't been lying when he'd said this decision was better for Emily in the long run. When he'd been younger he would've given anything for his parents to have stayed together. Perhaps his father would've been a little more relaxed and his mother not so much of a free spirit always seeking attention from men.

Ian couldn't alter Emily's future by coming between her parents. His broken heart was minor in comparison to their safety. All that mattered was that sweet Emily wasn't a pawn, that he gave her the best chance to know her father. A chance he'd never had.

Damn it, he loved that little girl. He missed those little fingers wrapped around his thumb as he gave her a nighttime bottle. He missed that little two-toothed grin she'd offer for no apparent reason.

He missed everything...even the diaper changes.

"Beautiful place you have here."

Ian jerked his head over his shoulder, his heart nearly

stopping at the sight of Cassie in a little green sundress, her hair whipping about her shoulders and Emily on her hip.

"I was just in the neighborhood and was curious if you had room for two more," she went on, not coming any closer.

In an instant, Ian was on his feet. "Room for two? Were you wanting to stay here?"

Cassie shrugged, her face tipped up to hold his gaze as he moved in closer. "Your house, your heart. Wherever you have room."

Ian's knees weakened. She'd come for him. When he'd thought they were finished, when he'd thought he'd done the right thing by setting her free, she'd come to him.

"I'll always have room in my heart for you and Emily." Ian reached out, slid a crimson curl behind her ear. "But my house? That depends on what's going on with you and Derek."

Cassie grabbed his hand before he could pull away from her. "Derek is being taken care of by my team of attorneys. I hired three to make sure he didn't blackmail me, you or use Emily as a bargaining chip. He's agreed to supervised visitation because Emily is young and would view him as a stranger. He's not allowed to take her from the state for any reason and I have approval over any and all visits."

Shocked, Ian merely stared. When Emily reached for him, his heart tumbled. Pulling her into his arms, he held her tight, breathing in her sweet scent.

"I've missed you," he whispered into her ear. Her little arms came around his neck and Ian had to physically fight back tears.

"We've missed *you*," Cassie told him. "But I had to make sure Derek was being handled before I could come to you."

Ian lifted his head, slid his arm around Cassie's waist

and pulled her against his side. This right here was worth everything. The heartache he'd felt, the worry, the sleepless nights.

"If you ever try to be noble again, I'll go to the press with horrid lies." Cassie smiled up at him. "I know why you left—I even admire your decision on some level—but being without you for weeks was a nightmare. I never want to be without you again."

Ian slid his lips over hers. "What about your family? What about the school?"

Reaching up to pat his cheek, Cassie smiled. "Emily and I are staying here for a while. As for the school, I'd really like to open it on the estate, but I'll move it to California if you're needed here."

Ian couldn't believe what he was hearing. She was willing to part with her life, live across the country from her family, her rock, all because of him.

"I'd never ask you to leave your family," he told her. "I actually want to be near them. What do you say we keep this home for our getaways and vacations? We can live on the estate or build nearby. The choice is totally up to you, but I want you to have the school at Stony Ridge."

Cassie's smile widened, those sparkling blue eyes glistening. "Sounds like a plan. Of course, we're missing something, you know."

Curious, Ian drew back slightly. "What's that?"

"Well, I've worn my ring since you left." She held up her left ring finger and the sight had his heart jumping. "I assumed that this ring had a question that went along with it. I mean, I'm assuming the man I've fallen in love with plans on carrying out his intentions."

Ian looked to Emily. "What do you think, sweetheart? Should I ask your mommy to marry me?"

Emily clapped her hands and grinned. "Mom-mom-mom."

Laughing, Ian glanced back to Cassie. So many emotions swam in her eyes. So much hope and love, and it was all for him.

"How did I get to be so lucky?" he murmured.

Shrugging, Cassie said, "I'd say fate has been pushing us together since the moment I fell into your arms."

Pulling her tighter against him, he held the two most precious ladies. "This right here, in my arms, is my world. Nothing will come between us again. Not an ex, not my tendency to be noble, nothing. You're mine, Cassie."

Easing back to look down into her eyes, Ian saw his entire future looking back at him. "Tell me you'll marry me. Tell me you'll let me be Em's dad. That you'll even teach me all about horses. I want to be part of everything in your life."

"I wouldn't have it any other way," she told him, wiping a lone tear that had slid down her cheek. "Besides, I still owe you that horseback ride you've never been on."

Ian laughed. "How about we lay Emily down for a nap and we'll discuss other plans for our family?"

The gleam in her eye told him she hadn't missed his hidden meaning. "*Our family.* Those are two of the most beautiful words I've ever heard."

He kissed her once again. "Then let's get started on building it."

* * * * *

THAT NIGHT WITH THE RICH RANCHER

SARA ORWIG

With many thanks to Stacy Boyd, Senior Editor

One

Tony Milan felt ridiculous. Standing in the wings of the wide stage of the elegant Dallas country club ballroom, he promised himself that next time, he would be more careful making bets with his oldest brother. Losing at saddle bronc riding in a rodeo last April had put him backstage tonight at this gala charity event, which included a dinner dance as well as an auction. One that would auction *him* off. At least it was all for a good cause, he reminded himself. The funds raised would go to Parkinson's disease research.

As he'd made his way to the stage earlier, he had seen some of the attendees: beautiful women dressed in designer gowns accompanied by men in tailored tuxedos. The highest bidders would win a night with "Texas's most desirable bachelors," according to the brochure that had been mailed to a select group wealthy enough to afford the event. He couldn't imagine any woman bidding much for an evening out with a guy she won in an auction, but after the opening bid, he realized he was wrong. The Texas ranchers who'd gone before him had stirred up high prices.

Looking out at the latest bachelor who now pranced offstage, Tony could not recall ever feeling more out of place. And then he heard his name called.

Taking a deep breath and forcing himself to smile broadly, he stepped forward, striding out of the darkened shadows into the blinding spotlights in front of a glittering audience. Applause was loud as he waved at the audience, most of which he could no longer clearly see because of the spotlights shining in his eyes.

After a spiel about his bachelor status, the master of ceremonies opened up the bidding. Tony was startled by the number of women who jumped into the bidding, but as the amount climbed, first one and then another dropped out until only three women were left.

Shocked yet pleased by the amount he was going to draw, he grinned and walked around the stage as the bidding climbed.

When a woman in a front table bid, he glanced down and saw it was an ex-girlfriend. He hoped she didn't win. As far as he was concerned, he'd said a final goodbye to her when she'd started getting serious. No long-term relationships for Tony Milan. He liked to flirt, play the field, just have a good time with no strings attached. Thankfully, after a flurry of bidding, his ex-girlfriend dropped out and only two women were left.

Tony couldn't see either one of the women, hidden by the blinding lights, but he heard their competitive bids. They were calling outrageous sums of money—all for an evening with him. When one graciously dropped out, the MC brought down the gavel.

"We have a winner," he said, not able to hide his outright glee at the final amount for the charity. "Would our lucky woman please come up onto the stage?"

Tony couldn't contain his curiosity. He scanned the audience for a glimpse at her, and then a spotlight found her at a table off to the right. His pulse jumped when a stunning blonde stood up. Her hair was piled atop her head with a few spiral curls falling about her face, and she wore a fiery red dress as she threaded her way to the stage. Even from a distance he could see the dress clung to a breathtaking figure. Jeweled straps glittered on her slender shoulders and her full breasts pillowed above the low-cut neckline.

One of the auction's ushers took her hand as she climbed the steps to the stage and Tony's gaze finally swept over her from head to toe, taking in her long, shapely legs revealed by a high slit in the skirt. Instantly Tony began to feel immensely better about the entire auction and the upcoming evening.

As the blonde crossed the stage, his gaze swept over her features. She wasn't a local resident, he thought, because he didn't recognize her. But then as she neared center stage to give the MC her name, he had a niggling feeling that he did indeed know her. He looked at her again. Something about her features seemed familiar. Perhaps… There was a faint resemblance to a local—his neighbor and lifetime enemy, Lindsay Calhoun.

He shrugged away that notion. The woman talking to the MC could not be Lindsay Calhoun. For one brief moment, a memory flashed through his mind of Lindsay dressed in skintight jeans and driving her muddy pickup, her long sandy braid bouncing beneath her floppy old hat. That was followed by another memory—Lindsay wagging her finger at him and accusing him of taking her ranch's water—something unethical he would never do to any neighbor, even Lindsay. She was mule stubborn, never took his advice and wouldn't agree with him if he said the sun set in the west.

Most of all, she was serious in every way, all business all the time. With their many confrontations, he had wondered if she'd ever had any fun in her life. So there was no way on earth that the vision who had won an evening with him was Lindsay.

Curiosity ran rampant as the MC took the mystery woman's hand and she turned to the audience, shooting a quick glance at Tony and then smiling at the audience while the MC held her hand high like a boxer at a heavyweight fight.

"Our winner—a beautiful Texan, Miss Lindsay Calhoun!"

Tony was stunned. His gaze raked over her again. Why had she done this? Their families had maintained a perpetual feud since the first generation of Milans and Calhouns had settled in Texas, and he and Lindsay kept that feud alive. Besides, she didn't even date. Nor would she spend a dime for an evening with him. She never even spoke to him unless she was accusing him of something.

He squeezed his eyes shut as if to clear them, and then looked at her again. Actually, he stared, transfixed. Not one inch of her looked like his neighbor.

She turned as another man in a black tux came forward to escort her toward Tony while the MC began to talk about the next bachelor.

"Lindsay?" Tony's voice came out a croak. The woman he faced was breathtaking. He wouldn't have guessed all the makeup in Texas could have made such a transformation.

Her huge blue eyes twinkled and she leaned close, giving him a whiff of an exotic perfume—another shock.

"Close your mouth, Tony," she whispered so only he could hear. "And stop staring."

The tuxedo-clad man stepped forward. "Lindsay, it seems you've already met your bachelor, Tony Milan. Tony, this is Lindsay Calhoun."

"We know each other." Tony hoped he said it out loud. His brain felt all jumbled and he couldn't force his gaze from Lindsay. He still couldn't believe what he was seeing. He had known her all his life. Not once had she even caused him to take a second glance. Nor had he ever seen her as anything except a colossal pest. Saying she wasn't his type was an understatement.

But was there another side to her? Why was Lindsay here? Why had she bid a small fortune to get the evening with him? No doubt she wanted something from him—and wanted it badly.

Would she go to this length to get water? He ruled that out instantly, remembering her fury and harsh words when she had accused him of buying bigger pumps for his wells to take more groundwater from the aquifer they shared. He had told her what she should do—dig her wells deeper. She had charged right back, saying she wouldn't have to go to the added expense if he wasn't depleting her water with bigger pumps. And there it went. Once again her usual stubborn self refused to take his advice or believe him.

Then she had started calling him devious, a snake and much worse. She pushed him to the edge and he knew he had to just walk away, which he did while she hurled more names at him.

That was the Lindsay Calhoun he knew. This Lindsay tonight had to be up to something, too. Surprisingly, though, he couldn't bring himself to care much. Thoughts of ranching and feuding fled from his mind. He was too busy enjoying looking at one of the most beautiful women he had ever seen.

How could she possibly look so good? They were being given the details of their evening, beginning with a limousine waiting at the country club entrance to take them to the airport where a private jet would fly them to Houston for dinner. He barely registered a word said to him; he couldn't focus on anything but the sight of her.

"Excuse me a moment. I'll be right back," their host said, leaving them alone momentarily.

"You've got to give me a moment to come out of my shock," Tony said with a shake of his head.

"You take all the time you want. I've been waiting for this," she drawled. "If necessary, I would have paid a lot more to get this night with you."

"If you'd come over to the ranch dressed the way you are now and just knocked on the door, you could have had my full attention for an evening without paying a nickel, but this is for a good cause."

"It's for two good causes," she said in a sultry voice, and his heartbeat quickened. He still couldn't quite believe what was happening. Before tonight, he would have bet the ranch he could never be dazzled or even take a second look, let alone willingly go out with his stubborn neighbor.

"Lindsay, I've never fainted in my life, but I might in the next thirty seconds, except I don't want to stop looking at you for anything."

"When you saw I had won, I was afraid you'd turn down this evening."

"I wouldn't turn down tonight if I had to pay twice

what you did," he said without thinking, and her smile widened, a dazzling smile he had never seen in his life.

"If you two will follow me, I can show you to the front entrance," their host said, returning to join them. "First, Miss Calhoun, you need to step to the desk to make arrangements about payment."

"Certainly," she answered. "See you in a few minutes, Tony," she added in a soft, breathless voice.

Where had that sexy tone come from? He recalled times when he had heard her shout instructions to hands on her ranch. She had a voice that could be heard a long stretch away and an authoritative note that got what she wanted done. As he watched her, she turned to look at him. She smiled at him, another dazzling, knee-weakening smile, and he couldn't breathe again.

Holy saints, where had Lindsay gotten that enticing smile? It muddled his thoughts, sent his temperature soaring and made him want to please her enough to get another big smile.

He had seen her stomping around horses, yelling instructions and swearing like one of the men, the sandy braid flopping with her steps. He had faced her when she had yelled furious accusations at him about dumping fertilizer. How could that be the breathtaking woman walking away from him? His gaze ran down her bare back to her tiny waist, down over her flared hips that shifted slightly in a provocative walk.

With the tight dress clinging to her every curve, he caught a flash of long legs when she turned and the slit in her skirt parted. That's when he noticed the stiletto heels. He would have sworn she had never worn heels in her life, yet she moved as gracefully as a dancer. He wiped his heated brow. This was rapidly turning into the most impossible night of his life.

Befuddled, totally dazzled by her, he tried to remind himself she was Lindsay, and he should pull his wits together. That might not be so easy. He would never again view her in the same manner.

Why hadn't he ever really looked at her before? He knew full well the answer to his question. He had been blinded by their fights over every little thing, from her tree falling on his truck to his fence on her property line. Not to mention her usual raggedy appearance when she worked.

If she had gone to such lengths tonight to wring something she wanted out of him, he had better get a grip, because it was going to be all but impossible to say no to the fantastic woman in red standing only yards away and writing a check for thousands of dollars for an evening with him. Not even a night— just a dinner date and maybe some dancing.

But Lindsay Calhoun wasn't interested in dinner dates and ballroom dancing, boot scooting or even barn dances. He eyed her skeptically. To what lengths was she prepared to go tonight to get what she wanted?

He gave up trying to figure her out.

Still, he couldn't take his eyes off her. The skintight red dress left little to the imagination. Why had she hidden her gorgeous figure all these years? Why had she always pulled her hair back in a braid or ponytail? He looked at the beautiful silky blond hair arranged on her head, some strands falling loosely in back. He had never seen her hair falling freely around her face—would he before this night was over?

She looked seductive, like pure temptation, and he knew he should be on his guard, but there was no way he could be defensive with the woman standing only yards away. He wanted her in his arms. He wanted to kiss her.

And, if he was truthful with himself, he wanted to make love to her.

When she finished writing and handing over her check, their host led them to a garden, where they had pictures taken together. As he slipped his arm around her tiny waist while they posed for the camera, the physical contact sizzled. He was so heated he thought he would go up in flames.

He made a mental note to get a picture. His brother-in-law and sister were in the audience, so they had seen her tonight. So was his oldest brother, Wyatt. He was certain Jake Calhoun had seen his sister look this way before, but Wyatt was probably as shocked as he had been.

Talking constantly, their host escorted Lindsay and Tony through the wide front doors of the country club, where a long white limousine waited.

As soon as the door closed on the limo, they were alone, except for the driver on the other side of a partition.

"Maybe you've been using the wrong approach," Tony remarked.

She smiled another full smile that revealed even, white teeth that made him inclined to agree with whatever she said.

"That's what I decided. So we'll see how it helps letting my hair down, getting out of my jeans and into a dress, smiling and being friendly. So far, it seems to be working rather well, don't you think?"

"Absolutely. I don't know why you waited this long. I keep reminding myself not to give you the deed to my ranch tonight."

She laughed with a dazzling, irresistible smile on her lips. "The other way is a more direct approach. You know where you stand."

"And this is a sugarcoated enticement to get what you want?"

"Oh, my, yes. I'm just getting started. When I walked up on stage, I'm sure you wanted to refuse keeping your part of the bargain."

"You're wrong. Not the way you look tonight," he said in a husky voice. "With you in that red dress, there's nothing that would cause me to turn down an evening with you."

When had he reacted like this to a woman? He escorted beautiful women, was friends with them, had them continually around in his life and yet never had he been dazzled senseless as he was tonight. He wouldn't ever have guessed Lindsay could generate such attraction and make him overlook all their battles.

It had to be the shock of who she was that was setting him ablaze. He'd better get a grip on reality and see her as the person he knew her to be. But that wasn't going to happen tonight. His thought processes worked clearly enough to know that.

She smiled sweetly. "Penny for your thoughts."

"I'm wondering why I haven't ever heard from anyone about how gorgeous you can be."

"I suppose because I rarely go out on dates and never with anyone in these parts."

"Why not?"

She shrugged. "I've just never met anyone around here I wanted to go out with very much. And there's nowhere close by here to go dressed up."

"There's Dallas."

With a twinkle in her blue eyes, she answered, "In Dallas, our paths probably wouldn't cross."

"I've known you all my life and I know your family

well. Tonight I feel as if I'm spending the evening with a complete stranger I've just met."

She looked amused. "In some ways, Tony, we are strangers. There's a lot you don't know about me," she said in the breathless, sultry voice that made the temperature in the limo climb again.

"I should have asked you out long ago," he said.

"You know how likely that was to have happened, and what my response would have been."

He nodded. "Our past is better left alone and forgotten tonight."

"We fully agree on that one," she answered as the limo slowed. "Tonight is filled with illusions."

"The way you look is no illusion. You're gorgeous," he said, and was rewarded with another coaxing smile.

The limo turned into the airport and in minutes they slowed to a stop. While the chauffeur held the door, Tony took her arm to escort her to the waiting private jet. The moment he touched her, awareness burned in a fiery current. Her arm was warm, her skin silky smooth. He caught another whiff of her exotic perfume, and he couldn't wait to get her to their destination so he could ask her to dance and have an excuse to hold her in his arms.

In the plane he was aware of how close she sat. It was difficult to keep from staring because her red dress had fallen open, revealing those beautiful, long shapely legs. He took a deep breath.

"I need to keep pinching myself to make sure this is actually happening," he said. "And I keep reminding myself you're the same neighbor I see across the fence with your horses."

"I love my horses. You should come visit and really look at them sometime. I have some fine horses."

"I've seen them across the fence. Everyone in the county knows you have some of the finest horses."

"They're working horses or horses for my riding. I like to ride."

"We have that in common, Lindsay."

"I've never seen you riding just for pleasure."

"If it's for pleasure, I don't ride in the direction of your ranch." He smiled sheepishly. "I figure we're both better off that way."

"We're in agreement there, too," she remarked in a tone that was light and held no rancor.

"Have you attended one of these charity bachelor auctions before?"

"Sure, because it's a good cause." She held up a hand but stopped before it touched his arm. "I don't need to ask, I know you haven't. What prompted you to agree to participate in the auction tonight? You seem to be more the type to just donate the money."

"I lost a bet with Wyatt over bronc riding in an Abilene rodeo."

She laughed. "So because of your brother you're trapped into a night with me now."

"I was filled with thoughts of revenge until you stood up to walk to the stage. Since then, this night has taken the best possible turn."

She smiled. "I must admit I'm pleasantly surprised by your reaction. I never, ever thought I'd hear you say that. But you know, underneath this red dress, I'm still me."

He inhaled deeply, his temperature spiking at her mention of what was beneath the red dress, even though she had intended a different meaning.

He cleared his throat. "I have a feeling I better not say anything about what's underneath your red dress."

She looked as if she held back a laugh. "I knew there

had to be another side to you besides the one I always see. I've wondered how the evening would go and so far, so good. I think, Tony, we've set a record already for the length of time we've been civil to each other."

"I intend to be more than 'civil to each other.' We're just getting started," he said. "Frankly, Lindsay, it's damn difficult to remember that you're the same woman whose ranch adjoins mine. I feel as if I'm with a beautiful woman I've just met," he said softly, taking her hand in his and rubbing her knuckles lightly with his thumb. His brows arched and he turned her hand over to open her palm, looking up at her.

"You have soft hands. I know how you work with the cowboys. You should have hands like mine—with scars, calluses and crooked bones from breaks. How did you get these?" he asked, running his thumb lightly over her palm.

"I wear gloves most of the time," she said. "And I haven't been out working quite as much for the past two weeks because I was shopping for a dress and getting ready for tonight."

Her voice had changed, becoming throaty, losing the humor, and he wondered if she had a reaction to his touch. That idea made the temperature in the limo climb again. He gazed into her big blue eyes. "I hope tonight will be far better than you dreamed possible and worth all the effort you put into it," he said softly, and raised her hand to brush her palm with his lips.

His thumb brushed across her wrist and he felt her racing pulse, making his own pulse jump again in response. As he looked into Lindsay's eyes, he wanted to pull her close and kiss her. He couldn't help the thought that came to mind. How much was this night going to complicate his life?

He couldn't answer his question, but he was glad for the auction and thankful she hoped to win him over with sweet talk. It was a dazzling prospect.

He tried to pour on the charm and avoid any topics about the ranch, their relationship or their families. The feud between their families had been far stronger when they had been children and their grandparents had influenced the families. As a small child, Tony was taught to avoid speaking to any Calhoun, and she'd been taught the same about the Milans. In fact, they hadn't spoken to each other until they became neighboring ranchers and had their first dispute over her tree falling on his fence and hitting his truck.

The plane ride seemed to take mere minutes. Before he knew it, they touched down in Houston and were ushered to another waiting limo. A short while later, they pulled into a circular drive lined by manicured shrubs strung with tiny white lights and stopped in front of a sprawling stone building he recognized as an exclusive club.

When they stepped out of the limo, Tony took her arm to walk through the canopied entrance. Inside, when he told the maître d' they were from the Dallas auction, they were welcomed and led to a linen-covered table by a window overlooking the wide patio that held hundreds more twinkling lights and a splashing water fountain.

A piano player sang as he played a familiar old ballad and several couples danced on a small dance floor.

In minutes they were presented a bottle of Dom Pérignon champagne. As soon as they were alone with drinks poured, Tony raised his glass in a toast. "Here's to the most beautiful woman in Texas."

She smiled. "A very nice exaggeration, Tony," she said, touching his glass lightly with hers and taking a sip. "Actually, you look rather handsome yourself."

He smiled and wondered if she felt any real attraction. "Lindsay, I can't imagine why you've been hiding that beauty all these years."

She laughed. "Not so many years, Tony. And thank you. I'm far from the most beautiful woman in Texas, but it's nice to hear."

"You could have had most of the single guys in the county asking you out if you'd wanted," he said.

"Actually, that's not my aim in life," she remarked. "And I do get asked out."

"To talk about someone's horses. If they could see you tonight, though, horses wouldn't come up in the conversation." He waited a second and then asked the question that flitted into his mind. "Speaking of which, Lindsay, will you go to dinner with me next Friday night?"

She grinned at him. "Aren't you jumping the gun? You don't know if we can make it through tonight and get along the entire time."

He leaned across the table to take her hand again. "I promise you, we're going to get along tonight," he said, his tone lowering as it did when he was aroused. "A lot of people saw you at the auction tonight. I think you'll be inundated with invitations from guys when you get home. I want you to myself," he added softly, and something flickered in the depths of her eyes as her smile vanished and she gazed at him solemnly. Electricity flashed between them, and he wanted to be alone with her and kiss her more than ever.

As their waiter appeared, Tony released her hand and leaned back in his chair, listening to a menu recited by the waiter. When they were alone again, Tony raised his flute of champagne. "Here's to a fabulous evening that we'll both remember and want to repeat."

With a seductive smile, she touched his glass with hers

lightly, causing a faint clink, and sipped again, watching him the whole time with a look that made him want to forget dinner and find somewhere to be alone with her.

"I'm beginning to see that you have a sensual side you've kept well hidden."

"Well, yes, Tony. I've kept it hidden from *you*," she said with good humor, and he laughed.

"I suppose I brought that on," he said, wondering whom she had allowed to see this aspect of herself. He sat back to study her. "As well as I know your family, I really don't know much about you. You went to Texas Tech, didn't you? And you were an agriculture major?"

"Yes, with a minor in business. I knew I'd come home to run a ranch."

"Good background. Do you ever feel overwhelmed with the ranch?"

"Sometimes the problems seem a little overwhelming, but I love the ranch too much to feel at odds with it. It's my life."

"I agree, but it's different for you. Don't you want a family someday?"

"Owning the ranch doesn't mean I can't have a family," she retorted.

"I suppose." He nodded as he considered her remark. "Everyone in the county knows you work as hard as the guys who work for you. It's difficult to look at you now and remember how tough and resilient you are."

"Did you know my big brother came out to the ranch, sat me down and lectured me to try to get me to be nicer to you?"

"The hell you say. Is that why you're here tonight?" he asked. Still, he couldn't believe that the gorgeous creature flirting with him now was only here to make nice.

She leaned over the table, reaching out to take his

hand in hers, and his heart jumped again. Every touch, her flirting, the looks she was giving him, all stirred responses that shocked him. No other woman had ever had the same instant effect on him from the slightest contact.

"No," she replied, her voice lowering. "Before the night is over, you'll know this was all my idea and not one of my brothers had anything to do with my plans for tonight."

Her plans? His mind began to race with the possibilities and they were all X-rated. His blood pulsed hot through his veins. "I'm beginning to wish we were alone right now."

With a satisfied expression, she sat back. "Mike and Josh weren't at the auction and I haven't talked to them lately. They have no idea what I'm doing tonight. Jake was in the audience, with Madison, but across the room from me. Otherwise, I'm sure he would have tried to stop my bidding because he would have suspected my motives. But he more than any of my brothers should know you can take care of yourself."

Tony nodded. "I'll bet it was Jake who tried to talk you into being nicer. Mike has had his own problems with losing his first wife, caring for four-year-old Scotty and getting married to Savannah. And Josh is too busy making money with his hotels."

"You're right about all three." She glanced down to their joined hands. "Although I don't think this was exactly what Jake had in mind when he told me to be civil to you."

Tony couldn't help but smile. "I'm sure it wasn't." He turned his hand so that his was holding hers and rubbed his thumb across her smooth skin. "You know, I've heard little Scotty adores his aunt Lindsay. I'm beginning to see how that's possible."

"I don't think Scotty sees me the way you do."

He laughed. "No, I'm sure he doesn't. But you have a whole different side to you that I'm seeing tonight." And he was still having quite a time wrapping his mind around this Lindsay. If this auction night had happened when she first moved to her ranch, would they have avoided their big clashes? Or would that same stubborn Lindsay still have been lurking beneath this beauty?

"I've gotten the same lecture from my brother Wyatt about cooling our fights," he told her. "As county sheriff, he just wants peace and quiet in his life and he doesn't want to have to continually deal with our battles—which will be less in the future, I promise you."

"I hope we can end the clashes altogether."

"If you're like this, you'll have my complete cooperation. You know, I have to tell you. Over the years, some things you've wanted or accused me of destroying, I had nothing to do with. Hopefully, after this, you'll listen to my side a little more. But enough about our past. It doesn't exist tonight, Lindsay."

"That suits me fine," she said softly as she licked her lower lip.

"That does it." He pushed back his chair and went around to her. "If you do one more sexy thing, I may go up in spontaneous combustion." He held out his hand to her. "Let's dance. I don't want the table between us anymore." He also needed to move around and cool down.

Her blue eyes sparkled. "Ah, so I have your attention."

"You've had my full attention since that spotlight revealed you."

He led her to the dance floor, where he turned to take her into his arms. He was intensely aware of her enticing perfume, of her soft hand in his, of her other hand skimming the back of his neck. She was soft, lithe and a good dancer, one more surprise for the evening.

"You have really hidden yourself away from a lot of fun and a lot of attention."

"I have a life. Around the ranch and in Verity, I don't think I've missed a thing. You don't know what I do when I go to Dallas, Houston or New York."

"No, I don't, but I'm curious now."

"I have a lovely time. I have friends in other places besides Verity and the ranch, you know."

"I'll bet you do," he said, smiling at her.

He had seen Lindsay in one of the bars in Verity, playing poker and downing whiskey like one of the men. Now he had a hard time reconciling that image with the woman in his arms. He stared at her, amazed it was her and wondering how long this facade would last.

Even when she returned to her normal self—and she eventually would—he knew he'd never look at her in the same way again. Discovering there was an enticing side to her changed his entire view of the woman who took life too seriously.

For once, she wasn't so serious and earnest. He knew that was her nature, though, and he warned himself not to have high expectations of partying or lovemaking. She was not the type of woman he wanted to get entangled with, but for tonight he was going to break one of his basic rules of life.

Tonight he was going to stop thinking about the past and their problems. Tonight he was simply going to enjoy being with a stunning woman whose intention was to please him. And he wanted to return the favor.

When the dance ended, he took her hand. "I think our salads have been served. Shall we go back?"

As they ate, he listened attentively while she talked about growing up a Calhoun. She avoided mentioning the family feud or any touchy subject. Instead, she related childhood memories, college incidents and ranch success stories. The whole time she spoke, he couldn't stop picturing her blond hair long and soft over her shoulders. He wondered if she would let him take it down later. He wanted to run his fingers through the long strands, hold her close and kiss her. He wanted seduction.

Again, he wondered about her plans for the night. She had surprised him constantly since the bidding began back at the auction. In a way she was being her most devious self, but he hoped she never stopped. So far, he had loved every minute of this night since the spotlight first picked her out of the crowd.

Over their dinners, which were a thick, juicy steak cooked to perfection for him and a lobster for her, she asked about his life, and he shared some stories.

Finally, their desserts were brought out, fancy, beautifully crafted dishes that they both ignored because they were more interested in each other.

"Would you like to dance again?" he asked when she sat back.

"Of course."

The piano player had been joined by four more musicians, and the group played a ballad that allowed him to hold Lindsay close in his arms.

"Remember," he whispered in her ear, "for tonight, we'll forget our battles."

"I already have," she said, squeezing his hand lightly and making his breath catch.

The band changed to a fast number and he released Lindsay reluctantly. Instead of returning to her seat, she began to dance in front of him, and he followed suit. As he watched her, he could feel his body heat rising. She was like a flame, her hips gyrating sensuously, her blue eyes languid and heated as if thoughts of making love were inspiring her every movement. She was sexy—another shocking discovery. She had to know the effect she was having on him. While her eyes glittered, a faint, satisfied smile hovered on her face. He wanted to yank her into his arms, lean over her until she held him tightly and plunder her soft mouth.

He danced near the wide glass doors overlooking the veranda. He opened the doors and whirled her through them onto the patio, where warm night air enveloped them.

"We can dance out here?"

"The night has cooled enough and we have this to ourselves," he said, moving to the music that was only slightly muted. He danced out of the light spilling through the glass doors, into the shadows and stopped, looking down at her as she tilted her face up.

She was taller than most women he had gone out with, but still shorter than he was. His eyes adjusted to the August night and he could see her looking up at him as he tightened his arm around her, feeling her softness press against him.

"Ever since you walked across the stage at the country club, I've been wanting to do this." Slowly, inch by inch, he leaned in closer, taking his time to steal the kiss he craved.

He wondered if it would be worth the wait.

Two

As Lindsay gazed into Tony's eyes, her heart thudded—and not just from desire. Wanting his kiss disturbed her because it was not part of her plans for enticing him. Still, there was no denying it. Some crazy chemistry burned between them. Actually being attracted to Tony Milan had not even occurred to her as a remote possibility when she'd initially come up with her plan to get him to be friendly and to influence him to stop overpumping his groundwater, which was taking water from her wells. Somewhere in the back of her mind, a question formed in the sultry haze. Could he have been truthful when he said he wasn't using bigger water pumps?

From the first encounter they were at odds. The initial confrontation was over the boundary between their neighboring ranches. Each had come armed with over a century's worth of documents to prove their property lines. Tony had been the condescending Mr. Know-It-

All, telling her she was wrong and how to run her ranch. He'd changed little since that first meeting. He was still a classic alpha male who had to control everything and when it came to ranching, that attitude was annoying. Tonight, though, was a whole different matter.

She was in control.

Or so she planned.

Right now she had to admit she was nearly speechless, because she had never planned or considered an attraction to Tony. She thought she could have a fun, pleasant evening and get on better footing with him. He had lots of friends, so she figured he had to have a nice side and that's what she hoped to get to know tonight with her bachelor-auction ploy.

She had hoped to entice him, make him see her as a desirable woman, have fun and maybe even share some kisses with him so their battles would not be so bitter and he would stop doing annoying things. Instead, she was breathless around him. An attraction between them that she had not expected had flared to life.

How could he be so attractive to her? She knew already that it was because of his charm, his seductive ways, his same alpha male that annoyed her with his know-it-all, take-charge attitude, but now it thrilled her. It was aimed at her, like a missile locked on its target, and, incredibly, she found it appealing…and sexy. She was definitely seeing him in a whole new way tonight.

Still, she couldn't help feeling her carefully laid-out plan was going off the rails a bit. Now wasn't the time to analyze her feelings, though. Not while she was in his arms. She knew this could never continue past tonight. Feelings for Tony Milan could complicate her life bigtime. But for one night only, she would go where her heart and body led her. She could only tilt her head back and go with them. And right now they were taking her closer and closer to Tony. She wanted his kiss.

Her heartbeat raced as her gaze lowered to Tony's mouth, and she closed her eyes when his lips finally touched hers.

All thoughts fled and her heart slammed against her ribs as Tony's warm mouth moved on hers. His lips brushed hers lightly, a tantalizing touch that heightened her need for his kiss. Every inch of her tingled as desire electrified her nerves, hot and intense.

Another warm brush of his lips and she tightened her arm around his waist, sliding her hand behind his neck to wind her fingers in his thick, short hair. Every contact was unique, special, something she'd never expected and would never forget.

His mouth settled on hers, parting her lips as his tongue thrust deep and stroked hers, slowly. It was a kiss to make her moan and cling to him, to make her want him more than was sensible and beyond what she had set as limits for tonight's "date." His kiss set her ablaze with desire, making her quiver for his touch and dare to touch him in kind. How could Tony's kisses do this to her? How could he cause responses that no other man ever had?

Her knees felt weak while desire was too strong. Her heart pounded and she moaned softly against his lips. She felt as if she could kiss him for hours and still want so much more from him. As her hand slipped down over his arm, she felt the hard bulge of solid muscle even through the sleeves of his tux and shirt. The feel of that strength, that powerful maleness, rocked her. She felt as if she was hanging on to her senses by a thread.

What she was doing? Somewhere in her mind the question formed, but her thoughts were too scrambled and hungry with need to articulate an answer.

Nearby voices dimly reached her ears, barely registering in her thought processes. Tony released her slightly and for a few seconds they stared at each other. He looked as dazed as she felt, his half-lidded eyes smoky and dark, his lips wet and smeared with her lip gloss.

His voice was thick and deep when he finally spoke. "Damn, Lindsay, there's another side to you I never knew. You're a stranger that I've never met before tonight."

"I think I can say the same thing about you," she whispered. "All I hoped was to get you to talk to me."

He dragged his eyes away from hers and cast a glance to the side of the veranda. He frowned slightly as voices grew louder.

"We're not alone out here anymore," he whispered, still studying her solemnly as if she were the first woman he had ever kissed. But she knew better than that.

"Logic says we should go inside," she replied without moving. For seconds they continued to stare at each other until Tony took her arm and led her silently back inside. The small band was playing another fast number and they moved to the dance floor, stepping out in time to the throbbing beat. Still stunned by his kiss, she watched him dance, his black tux jacket swinging open as he moved with a masculine grace that was sensual, sexy, his hips gyrating and making her think of being in bed with him.

She felt her cheeks flame and looked up to meet his gaze. It was as if he read her mind. Desire was blatant in his eyes.

The band slipped into a slow ballad and Tony took her hand, drawing her into his arms to dance close. Their bodies were pressed together, his hardness against her curves, and she didn't know how long she'd be able to stay in his arms like this before she would combust. He pulled back ever so slightly to look down at her, and she was caught in his solemn gaze. For the first time, she realized his eyes were blue, with green flecks in their depths. He had thick dark brown eyelashes, straight brown hair that was neatly cut and short.

Tony Milan was *handsome*.

Down deep she had always thought that, in spite of how annoyed she had usually been with him. But up close like this now, she could no longer view him in any such detached manner. Not after that kiss. Tony Milan wasn't dime a dozen "handsome." No. He was drop-dead gorgeous.

And she wanted him to kiss her again.

The realization surprised her on top of the other jolting shocks of this night. Was she going to regret her decision to see if she could win him over with enticement and sweetness? It wasn't sweetness Tony was bringing out in her tonight. It was desire. She wanted to be alone with him and she wanted him to kiss her again. She wanted to kiss and hold him, to run her hands over him. There was no way she was going to bed with him—she'd established that boundary from the start—but she wanted more than she'd originally planned.

The night had lost its sense of reality and become a moment out of time. Everything had changed. Desire was hot, constant. Tony was sexy, virile, charming, appealing, and tonight he was the most desirable man she had ever known.

She had never expected or planned on a night like this one. Since she had decided to own a ranch, she had never wanted to date other ranchers or cowboys. She knew them too well and she didn't want them telling her how to conduct her business on the Rocking L Ranch. She loved her ranch—it was her whole life. No one had the right to come along and tell her how to run it. How many times had Tony done exactly that?

Tonight was different, though. Tony was different. How much would tonight change their relationship as neighboring ranchers? Or would they go back home with the same attitudes they had always had?

She knew she wouldn't and she didn't think he would, either.

And then she couldn't think anymore. Tony moved her hand against his chest and covered it with his own, pulling her even closer, as if wrapping their joined hands in the heat from their bodies. She inhaled the scent of his woodsy aftershave, a musky scent that was all male. She gave herself over to him and let him lead her with his sure steps. They were totally in sync as they moved, their long legs pressed against each other's. The contact was electrifying. She wanted to keep dancing with him for hours, almost as much as she wanted to be alone with him, in his arms and kissing him. Was that where the evening would lead, or would he follow the auction itinerary and go back to the Dallas country club, kiss her goodnight and each of them drive away? To her surprise, that wasn't the way she wanted to end the evening.

For the next hour they danced and she realized Tony was fun to be with when he wanted to be. He had her laughing over things he had done with her brothers over the years. She knew he was friends with them even though they were older. She was the only Calhoun who actively fought with him, but she had always blamed Tony for being such a know-it-all and so uncooperative as a neighbor. For tonight, though, she saw none of that. Far from it. He looked as if he was having a wonderful time and he helped her to have a wonderful time.

There was one rational part of her that cried out a

warning: she needed to remember why she bid on him. She couldn't let her plan backfire on her. When this night was over, she'd still need what she came here for—and that wasn't a relationship with Tony Milan. A relationship was the one thing she needed to avoid at all costs, because it would vastly complicate her life. She was here only to win his friendship so he would discuss their problems with her. If possible, even talk about their water situation.

From her earliest memories she had been taught by her grandparents not to trust Milans. Now her brother had married one and he was blissfully happy. She had to admit that she liked and trusted her sister-in-law Madison. And a distant Calhoun cousin—Destiny—had married a Milan—Wyatt, who was sheriff of Verity. Wyatt had been a shock because he proved untrue everything Lindsay had been taught by her grandparents and mother about Milans. In all her dealings with Wyatt, she had found him to be honest, friendly, fair and definitely trustworthy.

She gazed at Tony's handsome features and wondered if he could be trusted, as well. As they danced, he constantly touched her, looked intently at her. He paid her compliments, got her whatever refreshment she wanted. All his attention, his casual touches, increased her awareness of him, as well as her desire for him. She fought the temptation to tell him that she wanted to go someplace where they could be alone. She had a hotel room in Dallas for the night provided by the auction board. She could invite him back for a drink.

As much as she told herself she wanted to kiss him again, she knew where the kissing might lead. And she couldn't make love with Tony. Difficult as it was to curb her desire, she had no other choice.

Finally, as the band took a break, Tony turned to her.

"It's time for us to meet our chauffeur so we can take the plane back to Dallas. It's all arranged to get us back by midnight, so we should go now."

"Let me pick up my purse," she said.

On their flight home, Tony embodied the perfect gentleman, continuing to surprise her. She'd known he had to have a good side to him, but she'd never expected to be charmed by him or even find him such enjoyable company. Certainly not once had she thought she would be attracted to him or see him as a sexy, exciting man whose kiss set her heart pounding.

As they flew back to Dallas, Tony reached for her hand, holding it in his. "The evening will still be young when we get home. We can go dancing or just go have a drink and talk. Better yet, I have a condo in Dallas. Come back with me. I'll take you to your hotel whenever you want. We can have the place to ourselves."

Eagerness to draw out the evening made it easy to answer. "Let's go to your place," she said. "I don't want tonight to end yet. It's been fun, Tony. I know things will go back somewhat to the way they were because that's reality, but this has been a special night."

"You have no idea how special it has been. Things may go back to sort of like they were, but they won't ever again be the same as before. You'll no longer have an antagonistic neighbor. I promise."

"Dare I hope," she gasped, clutching her heart, making him laugh. Shaking her head, she smiled. "There's no way this truce is going to last."

"I'll try if you will," he said, his eyes twinkling with mischief, and she had to laugh in return.

"I promise I'll try, too," she said, looking into his eyes and again feeling an electrifying current spark between them.

"I keep waiting for a pitch from you to get me to agree to something. You all but admitted that's the purpose of your bidding for me tonight."

"Maybe I've delayed that original agenda," she said in a sultry voice. "I'm having fun, Tony. Fun that I don't want to spoil. The night is magical, a trip into a world that doesn't really exist. But for a few hours, we can pretend it does and enjoy it."

He raised her hand and brushed a light kiss on her knuckles, his breath warm on her hand.

"I'm glad," he said. "I'm not ready to tell you goodnight and watch you walk away." He placed his hands on the arms of her seat, facing her and leaning close, his voice dropping to a whisper as he said, "I want to hold you and kiss you again."

Her heart thudded and for the first time she realized she might be in trouble. Was Tony the one who would get what he wanted out of tonight instead of her? She'd planned to wring concessions from him, but now it seemed he was once again in control and she was under his spell. Not once had it crossed her mind that she could be so beguiled by him.

And she was powerless to stop it.

His gaze lowered to her mouth and suddenly she couldn't get her breath. She tingled, feeling as if she strained to lean closer to him while she actually didn't move at all. He moved closer, until his mouth settled on hers. He kissed her, another kiss that set her heart racing and made her want to move into his lap, wrap her arms around him and kiss for the rest of the flight.

Instead, in seconds—or was it minutes?—she shifted away. "This plane isn't the place," she whispered reluctantly. She had to keep her wits about her. Had to mind her goal of working out her water problem, at least partially. Still, her breath came quick and shallow, matching his own.

Looking at her mouth, he didn't move for a moment and her heart continued to drum a frantic rhythm. He leaned closer to whisper in her ear, "I want to kiss you for hours." His words caused a tremor to rock her. Another shock added to the continual shocks of the night. She had no choice but to admit the truth—she wanted him to kiss her for hours.

As his gaze met hers, he scooted back into his seat and buckled his seat belt again.

When her breathing returned to normal, she tried for conversation.

"Why do you have a condo in Dallas? I thought you were as much into ranching as my brother Mike, that both of you had devoted your lives solely to ranching."

"I'm on two boards that meet in Dallas—for my brothers. Wyatt has recently acquired a bank and I'm on that board. Nick recently became owner of a trucking company with two close friends and I'm on that board, too. In Dallas, I have a small condo and I like having a place of my own I can go relax when I'm in the city. It's convenient even though I don't spend a lot of time there. I don't have a regular staff in Dallas unless I plan to stay a long time, which rarely happens. Then I hire from a local agency to cook and clean."

"That makes sense."

"I spend most of my time on my ranch. When we're back in our regular routines, I'd like for you to come over to the MH Ranch sometime. I have a new horse and I'm boarding a new quarter horse that Josh bought. You're welcome to come see them, ride them and tell me what you think."

"Sure," she said. "I suspect you better let all the guys

who work for you know that you invited me or they'll tell me I'm trespassing and toss me off your ranch."

He laughed. "I'll tell them. Now if you'll come wearing a dress with your hair down, they'll be so dazzled, there's no way they'll mention trespassing. Far from it. We'll all welcome you with open arms."

Smiling, she shook her head. "Nice try, but I don't wear a dress to ride a horse." She shrugged. "In fact, I don't wear a dress anywhere around home. But you can tell them I'm coming."

"Sure. Better yet, let me know beforehand and I'll pick you up. I probably should do that anyway, so they all know we have a truce of sorts." He turned more so that he faced her in his seat. "And it is a truce, Lindsay. Definite and permanent. I'll never again be able to fight with you."

"Don't say things you don't mean, Tony. Your intentions might be good, but there is no way this side of hell that you'll be able to stick by that statement."

Once again he leaned in closer and her heartbeat quickened as it had before. "Yes, there is definitely a way that I can be influenced to stick by that statement. You can wind me around your little finger if you really want to."

"I don't believe that one."

"You should," he said, settling back in his seat again. "Before tonight, did you ever think we would get along as well as we have?"

"Of course not." She tilted her head to study him. "In some ways, we're strangers. There's a lot I don't know about you."

"That's true and a lot I don't know about you. But strangers? No way, Lindsay. There is much I want to explore and discover about you and I intend to do that tonight," he said in a husky voice that made her heartbeat jump again.

Cutting into their conversation, their pilot announced descent into Dallas, and in a short time Lindsay looked out at the twinkling city lights spread far into the distance.

"Do you have your car at the club?" Tony asked.

"No. I left it at the hotel and took a cab."

"Good thinking," he said.

Once they arrived back at the country club, a valet brought Tony's car around and in minutes they drove through the iron gates to his condo complex.

As soon as Lindsay entered his unit, she walked through his entry hall to cross the spacious living room and look out over the sparkling lights of downtown Dallas.

"You have a gorgeous view."

"Do I ever," he said, and she smiled when she turned to see him looking at her.

"I meant the city lights," she explained, knowing he understood exactly what she had referred to.

"Want a drink?" he asked.

"Yes. White wine, please."

He removed his jacket and tie, dropping them on a chair, and walked to a bar in a corner of the room.

"This is a large living area. It's very nice," she said, looking at comfortable brown leather chairs and a long leather sofa.

"It's convenient when I'm here, which is not too often. A few days here and I'm ready for the ranch."

"That I understand," she said, crossing to the bar to perch on a stool and watch him pour her wine.

"I have a full bar if you prefer something else."

"The wine is good."

He handed her the glass and picked up a cold beer. "I figured you for a cold brew," he said, smiling at her.

He set his bottle on the counter, his gaze skimming over her legs when her skirt fell open just above her knees. "Lindsay, it's a crime to hide legs like yours all the time."

"You have no idea what I do all the time. We see each other about once every four or five months at best."

"That I intend to change."

She shook her head. "You know as well as I do that we'll go right back to our usual way of life when the sun rises in the morning."

"I hope to hell not," he said, holding up his bottle of beer in a toast. "Here's to the most beautiful neighbor I'll ever have and to a night I'll never forget."

Laughing softly, she touched his bottle with her wineglass and sipped her wine.

"Here's to the day we can both be civil to each other," she said.

"I'll drink to that." He touched her glass, took a sip of beer and set his bottle on the bar. "But we're going to be much more than civil to each other," he said, the amusement no longer visible in his expression. With his deep blue eyes gazing intently at her, he took her drink from her hand and placed it on the bar. Her heartbeat quickened in anticipation while desire burned in the depths of his eyes.

"I've waited all evening for this moment—to be alone with you," he said, stepping closer. His arm circled her waist and he lifted her off the bar stool easily, standing her on her feet and drawing her into his embrace as his gaze lowered to her mouth.

Desire made her draw a deep breath as he leaned closer, and then she closed her eyes, winding her arms around his neck, surrendering to his kiss.

The moment his mouth settled on hers, her heart slammed against her ribs as passion ignited and desire overwhelmed her. Tony was hard, his chest sculpted with muscles, his biceps like rocks from constant ranch work. She breathed in his scent and knew she would remember it forever. She wound her fingers through his short hair and returned his kiss, wanting to stir him as much as he did her. She tightened her arms around him without having to stand on tiptoe to kiss him because her heels added inches to her height.

As Tony drew her more tightly against him, his warm hand played over her bare back and then up to her shoulders. Dimly she felt him push away her straps as they slipped down on her arms. In seconds she was aware of slight tugs to her scalp when he removed the pins and her hair fell over her shoulders and down on her back.

Slowly, while he kissed her senseless, he drew away each pin until finally her hair framed her face.

He raised his head to look at her, running his fingers slowly through the long locks. "You're so beautiful. You take my breath away, Lindsay," he whispered, sounding as if he meant every word. How could she find this pleasure with Tony? Or want him so desperately?

She had meant this night to be lighthearted, friendly, seductive, so afterward he would be civil to her and try to cooperate with her. She hadn't considered there could be this unbelievable, fiery attraction that he seemed to feel as much as she did.

No matter what he said, they'd go back to their old ways after tonight, though maybe not as contentious. This blazing attraction was for one night only. Tonight she wanted this time with him because she had never before desired or reacted to a man the way she did Tony.

His gaze shifted to her mouth and he leaned down to kiss her again. How long they stood kissing, she didn't know, but at some point, Tony picked her up to carry her to the sofa, switching off the overhead lighting, leaving only the bar light glowing softly.

She planned on some kisses and caresses and then she'd stop. Truthfully, she had never even planned on this much. Dancing, some laughs, a good time, maybe some flirting as she tried to soften him up so he would be more receptive to what she wanted.

She had never dreamed it was possible for Tony's kisses to turn her world upside down, to make her heartbeat race and cause her to desire him more than any other man. She was on fire. As if of their own accord, her hips shifted slightly against him, pressing tightly and feeling his hardness. He was ready for her.

Astounded by the need she felt for him and the response his kisses evoked in her, she kissed him wildly, her fingers unfastening the studs on his shirt, finally pushing away the fabric. Wanting to touch him, she ran her hands over his warm, rock-hard chest, growing bolder when she heard him take a deep, trembling breath. He set her on her feet while he continued to kiss her.

She felt his fingers at her waist at the back of her dress and then felt him tug down the zipper. He ran his hand lightly over her bottom and she moaned softly as her desire intensified.

While he kissed her, his hands slipped lightly up her back and across her shoulders and then came down to push her red dress over her hips so it fell softly around her ankles.

Tony stepped back to look at her. She wore only lacy bikini panties.

His eyes had darkened to a stormy blue-green and he let out a ragged breath. "I'll never forget this moment," he whispered, and stepped to her to crush her against him, kissing her deeply, a kiss that made her feel wanted and loved. She knew she wasn't loved by him, but he made her feel that way, as if he needed her more than he had ever needed any other woman.

He showered kisses on her throat while his hands cupped her full breasts and his thumbs circled their tips. His kisses moved lower until his lips met one breast while his hands caressed the other.

Running her fingers in his hair, she gasped with pleasure when his tongue circled her nipple. She was awash in desire, wanting him more than she had ever dreamed possible. She wanted his loving; she wanted all of him.

She had made a decision much earlier to end this night before it led to lovemaking, and she'd stuck with it even as they flew back to Dallas. But now desire forced her to rethink her decision, instinctively feeling that this moment would not come again.

Common sense told her that, come morning, they would go back, at least partially, to the arguments they had had all their adult lives. Tonight was special, a once-in-a-lifetime magical night that would never come again, and what they did tonight, all their loving, would carry no ties after dawn.

Tony was incredible. No man had ever excited her the way he had, and no man would ever make love to her the way she knew he would. Beyond that, she was unable to think when his hands and mouth were on her. But she was able to make a decision. She pulled back and looked into his eyes.

"Tony, I'm not protected."

He raised his head, kissing her lightly. "I'll take care of it," he whispered, and leaned down to kiss and fondle her other breast.

She wanted him with all her being, wanted to make love with him for the rest of the night. With deliberation her fingers unfastened his trousers. He grasped her wrist and she paused as he released her to yank off his boots and then his socks. He dropped them carelessly to the floor and returned to kissing her while she pushed down his trousers and then peeled away his briefs.

Her heartbeat raced as her gaze swept over his muscled body. His manhood was thick and hard, ready to love. Stepping closer, she caressed him while he stroked and showered her with kisses.

He picked her up again, kissing her when he carried her through his condo. She clung to him with her eyes closed as they kissed. He touched a light and she glanced quickly to see they were in a bedroom. She returned to kissing him until he stood her on her feet. He reached down to yank away the comforter covering his high, king-size bed.

Watching him, she felt her heart drum in anticipation of the pleasure he would give her. As her gaze swept over his muscled body, she trembled. He stepped back, looking at her in a slow, thorough study that made her tingle as much as if his fingers had moved over her in feathery caresses.

"So beautiful, so perfect," he whispered, drawing her into his embrace as he leaned over her to kiss her hungrily. His hard erection pressed against her, his hard body hot and solid against her.

Why did she want him so desperately and respond to him so intensely? His slightest touch set her quivering and his kisses rocked her, building in her a need unlike she had ever felt before. How could she have found this with Tony?

She couldn't answer her question. Nor did she care. She just wanted Tony and his loving for the rest of the night.

He lifted her into his arms again and placed her on the white sheets, kneeling beside her, his knees lightly pressing against her thighs. Then, as if in a dream—or a fantasy—he rained kisses from her ankles to her mouth.

She writhed, her hips moving slightly as blinding need built inside her until she wanted him more than she ever thought possible.

"Tony, make love to me," she whispered.

"Not so fast, darlin'. We're going to take our time and love for hours," he whispered, still showering her with kisses.

His endearment, spoken in a tender voice that she had never heard before from him, was as effective as his caresses.

"Tony," she gasped, sitting up to grasp his shoulders. "Make love to me. Let me love you."

"Shh, darlin'," he said softly while he kissed her breasts between his words. "Lie down and turn over, let me kiss you," he said, pushing gently.

She rolled onto her stomach and he picked up her foot to kiss her ankle lightly and then brush kisses higher up the back of her leg. He traced circles with his tongue on the back of her knee.

Digging her fingers into the bed, she raised her head slightly to look over her shoulder. "Tony, I can't touch or kiss you this way."

"You will soon," he whispered, and returned to his tender ministrations, trailing his tongue slowly up the back and then along the inside of her thigh.

Aflame with longing, she twisted and rolled over, sitting up to wrap her arms around his neck and kiss him, pouring all her hunger for him into her kiss, wanting to drive him as wild as he had her.

They fell back on the bed with Tony over her, his weight welcome against her. While she moved her hips against him, he kissed her as he rolled beside her. "Do you like me to touch you here?" he whispered, fondling her breast. "Do you want me to kiss you here?" he whispered, moving to brush kisses on her inner thigh, watching her as he did. "You're beautiful."

His words heightened the moment, making her more aware of him and what he was doing while she was lost in sensation and desire.

While he kissed her, his hand trailed up her leg to the inside of her thighs. When he stroked her she gasped with pleasure.

His hand moved against her, driving her to new heights. She didn't think she could take more and she reveled in the feelings he evoked in her. Needing him, she reached out and took him in one hand as her other played over his chest.

She wanted him to feel the same heady sensations he was strumming in her, so she caressed him, eliciting a growl deep in his throat. He stopped her, but he continued to love her, driving her to the brink, lifting her to the precipice of release. And then, when she was about to fall over, he pulled his touch away, shifting his hands to caress her breasts as he also showered them with kisses.

Her fingers wound in his hair. "Tony, I want you. I'm ready," she gasped, moaning with pleasure as he continued to kiss each breast, his tongue drawing lazy circles over each nipple. His fingers dallied on her stomach, but when they slipped lower, she arched against him, thrusting her hips and spreading her legs to give him access.

That was all the urging he needed. Or so she thought. He moved between her legs and she clutched his buttocks, pulling him toward her. "Tony, I want you now," she whispered. But he didn't enter her.

The warm, solid weight of him pressed against her as he stretched over her and kissed her with a hunger that made her heart pound even harder. She wrapped her long legs around him, wanting him more with each second that ticked past. Never before had she wanted to make love as much as she did now.

"Tony," she whispered again, the rest of her words smothered by his mouth covering hers and his tongue entwining with hers.

How could she want him so much? She couldn't answer her own question, she just knew she did. She ached for him, her pulse pounding. "Tony, I can't keep waiting..."

"Yes, you can and it'll be better than ever," he said. He laved her breasts, teasing her nipples between his teeth, and she felt a tug between her legs. All the while, his hands caressed her, binding them in one night of lovemaking that she would always remember. Though this night could not be repeated, she knew this was the time to make memories she'd carry with her forever.

"I want you now," she finally gasped, tugging him closer.

He stepped off the bed to open a night table drawer and then he watched her, his eyes burning her, as he stood beside the bed to slowly put on the condom.

As she caressed his thigh, her hips shifted slightly in anticipation. She wished he would hurry. Then, he knelt between her legs, his eyes still on hers, as he finally entered her. She wrapped her legs around him again, caressing his smooth, muscled back and hard buttocks, as he slowly thrust into her. She cried out, arching to meet him, wanting him to move with her to give her release for all the tension that coiled tightly in her.

Hot and hard, his manhood filled her, moving slowly, driving her to greater need as she clung to him and moved beneath him in perfect sync.

"Now," she cried, running her hands over his muscled thighs. He obeyed her, and her hips moved faster, her head thrashing as she was lost in the throes of passion, until finally he gave one last thrust, deep and hard, and she cried out. Arching under him, her fingers raking his back, her hips thrusting against him, she found that elusive release and he followed her, bursting within her.

"Tony," she cried.

"Ah, darlin'..." He ground out the words through clenched teeth as his body continued to move over hers.

Finally, satiated, they stilled.

"You're fantastic in every way," he whispered, kissing her temple lightly, trailing light kisses down her cheek and sighing as he lowered his weight carefully onto her.

Gasping for breath, she clung to him while her heartbeat and breathing returned to normal. Tony rolled to his side. He kept her with him, his legs entwined with hers.

"I don't want to let you go."

"You don't have to right now. I want to stay here in your arms, against you. Tony, this has been a wonderful, once-in-a-lifetime night."

"I agree," he said, hugging her lightly and kissing her forehead. "Our lives have changed."

"Not really. It may not ever again be as bad or as hateful, but tonight doesn't really change what we'll face tomorrow. My water problems, you telling me what I should or should not do, not to mention the next thing that'll come up between us."

There was silence while he toyed with locks of her hair. It seemed to her that many minutes went by until he finally spoke. "There's one question I'd like you to answer. Is water what was behind your high bid tonight? You wanted something from me, Lindsay, and I haven't heard one word about what it is."

Three

At his question, she felt her very core stiffen. She didn't want to get into that with him lying beside her and her wrapped in his arms. She didn't want to say anything that would upset him and break the spell that had been woven around them.

"We'll talk about that tomorrow. Tonight is special, Tony. I want to keep it magical until the sun rises and brings the reality of our regular lives back to us. Is that okay with you?"

"Sure, because I have plans for the rest of this magical night. Big plans."

"I do hope they involve me and your sexy body and your wild kisses."

"My sexy body and wild kisses? Wow. Definitely back to my plans for tonight," he said, leaning down to kiss her again. In minutes he propped his head on his hand to look at her again.

She couldn't tell from his eyes what he was thinking. "What?" she asked him.

He toyed with a strand of her hair as he answered. "At this moment I can't imagine ever returning to the way we were. All I'll have to do is remember tonight. All of it, darlin'."

"You better stop calling me darlin' when we go back to real life."

"I can call you that if I want."

"I suspect you won't really want to, but it's very nice tonight under the circumstances."

He smiled at her. "As you said, this is a magical night. One giant surprise after another. And deep down, I know you're right. We'll go back to our ordinary lives and our usual fights, except maybe they won't be quite so bad. After tonight I'll listen, I'll try to cooperate with you and maybe even do what you want."

She couldn't hold back a laugh. "Like hell you will!"

He chuckled, a deep throaty sound that she could feel in her hand as it lay on his muscled chest. Her fingers traced the solid muscles in his shoulders, chest and arms. Occasionally, she would feel the rough line of a scar. His daily outdoor work not only showed in the strength of his fit body but in his scars, as well.

He pulled her close against his side. "Do you have to go home tomorrow? I hope not. I want to stay right here."

"I suppose I don't, until late afternoon. I'll need to be home early Monday morning," she answered, thinking more about his flat stomach, hard with muscles and dusted with hair, over which she ran her fingers.

"Good. I have plans and they involve staying right here and not talking to anyone except each other."

"I have to check out of the hotel tomorrow by noon,

though. That room was paid for by the auction board." She drew another circle slowly on his stomach.

"I'll call and have tomorrow night put on my card, so you can get your things whenever you're ready," he said, rolling over and stretching out his long arm to retrieve his phone. "What hotel?"

"I can do that."

"Don't argue. We're not going to disagree with each other this weekend."

She smiled as she told him the name of her hotel and watched him get the number on his phone. Once again she thought his take-charge attitude was delightful when he focused on her. When he finished and she had the room for another night, he turned to take her into his arms again.

"Thanks, Tony. That was nice of you," she said, running her fingers over the dark stubble on his jaw. "I have to say, I didn't know I could ever be quite so fascinated by a cowboy's body."

"I guarantee you, I'm totally fascinated by a cowgirl's body," he said, trailing his fingers lightly over her breasts. Even though she had a sheet pulled up over her, she felt his feathery caresses, and her rapidly heating body responded to them.

"A beautiful blonde cowgirl," he continued, as his eyes seemed to feast on her. "I want you here with me as long as possible."

She felt the same way and had no desire to get up and leave him. Though her heart wished the night could go on forever, she couldn't get her head around the fact that she was in Tony Milan's bed. "My family would never believe we're together tonight. No one would."

"All those people who heard what you paid for a night with me will believe it."

She laughed. "I suppose you're right." She rolled over

and sat up slightly to look down at him. "You're really amazing, you know that? Tonight is astonishing. I never dreamed it would be like this."

"I promise you that I didn't, either." His face took on a sheepish look. "When I stepped out on that auction stage earlier, I didn't really think anyone would bid for me."

"Now that is ridiculous."

"I'm just a cowboy."

"A cowboy named Milan—a name that's well known in these parts. And a very wealthy rancher," she remarked. "With all the ranches and businesses owned by your family, I think you could count on someone bidding for an evening with you."

"Who bid against you? I couldn't see either one of you because of the lights in my eyes, not until you stood to come to the stage and a spotlight picked you out. As soon as I laid eyes on you, my attitude about the evening did an immediate reversal."

She smiled at him. "I don't know who bid against me. There were people from Dallas and Lubbock there, and from other places, as well. Probably one of your old girlfriends who wasn't ready to say goodbye," she said.

"Let's not discuss my old girlfriends," he said through a grin. "I'd much rather talk about you anyway. I still say if you'd wear a dress to town, you'd have a slew of guys asking you out."

"I don't want a 'slew' of locals asking me out, thank you very much."

"Why not? There are nice guys out there."

"Sure there are, but they're ranchers and cowboys. I don't want to go out with ranchers or cowboys."

"You could've fooled me. You paid a small fortune to go out with a rancher tonight, in case you've forgotten."

"I won't ever forget you," she said, hoping she kept

her voice light, but a shiver slithered down her spine because she suspected she had spoken the absolute truth. This had turned into the best night of her life because of Tony. He'd charmed her, seduced her and become the most appealing man she had ever known—as long as she didn't think about him as a rancher.

He didn't let the subject drop. Instead, he questioned her. "Why don't you want to go out with ranchers or cowboys? We're nice guys."

"I know you guys are nice. It's just that—" She stopped, hesitating to tell him the truth. But Tony deserved an answer to his question. "I'm a ranch owner, remember? I'm not a party girl out for fun. I'm also not a sweetie who'll go dancing and come home and cook and have a family and kiss a cowboy goodbye every morning while he goes out to work and listen politely to him at night while he tells me bits and pieces about what he had to do at work. Even worse, I don't want to fall for another rancher and have him tell me how to run my ranch."

"I should have guessed. Two bosses can't run a ranch."

"Not my ranch," she said.

"If you don't marry a rancher or a cowboy, the guy is going to want to move you to the city."

"Now you're beginning to get the picture—the complete picture—of why I never wear dresses. I can't imagine marrying a city guy, either, so there you are." She gave a nod of her head, then shrugged. "I have a nice life. I have my nephew, Scotty, who stays with me a lot, and soon there will be another baby in Mike's family."

"But, Lindsay, you were meant for marriage in so many ways. I hope some guy comes along and sweeps you off your feet and you can't say no. Rancher or city guy."

She giggled. "My, oh, my. Is this a sideways proposal?"

He grinned. "You know better than that. We're doing

well together tonight, but for a lifetime…? Would you want that?"

She studied him, knowing she had to make light of his question, but another shiver ran down her spine and she couldn't explain why. She squeezed his biceps. "Mmm, you do make good husband material. You have all your teeth and they look in good shape and you're healthy and strong and light on your feet. And you're incredibly sexy." She gave an exaggerated sigh. "Given our past and probably our future, I think I have to answer…no."

"Incredibly sexy? Oh, darlin', come here." He drew her closer, but she resisted and placed her hand against his chest.

"Whoa, cowboy. Don't let that compliment go to your head…or other parts," she said, and he grinned.

"I told you our future will not be like our past."

She had to agree. "I don't think it will, either."

"Right now I want to relish the present. How about a soak in the tub?"

"A splendid idea," she said, already eager to be naked in the water with him.

He stood and picked her up. She yelped in surprise as she slid her arm around his neck. "I never dreamed you could be so much fun or so charming."

"I promise you, I have to say the same about you. And, to boot, you're breathtakingly beautiful and hot and sexy. I guarantee that sentiment will not end when morning comes," he added with an intent look that made her heart skip a beat.

He carried her to a huge two-room bathroom. One room held plants, mirrors, two chaise longues with a glass-topped iron table between them, plus dressing tables, a shower and an oversize sunken Jacuzzi tub.

Soon they were soaking in a tub of swirling hot water while she sat between his legs, leaning back against him.

"Tony, this is decadent. It feels wonderful."

"I suspect you're referring to the hot water and not my naked body pressed against yours. Right?"

"I won't answer that question."

"An even better choice than I expected from you. Also, I seem to remember a short time ago hearing you say something about my sexy body and wild kisses," he whispered, fondling her breasts as he kissed her nape.

"That I did and I meant it," she concurred, running her hands over his strong legs.

In no time, desire overwhelmed her, and their playful moment transformed. She turned to sit astride him. Placing her hands on both sides of his face, she leaned forward to kiss him, long and thoroughly, her hair falling over his shoulders. He was ready to love her again, too—she felt it. His hands caressed her breasts, then slid down over her torso to her inner thigh. His fingers glided higher, stroking her intimately until she closed her eyes and clung to him, her hips moving as he loved her.

"Tony, you need protection," she said, her eyes flying open.

"So I do," he said, reaching behind him for his terry robe on the footstool. He took a condom out of the pocket and, in seconds, he was sheathed and ready. He pulled her close again, lifting her so he could enter her in one smooth stroke. She locked her legs around him and lowered herself onto his hard shaft.

Her climax came fast, as if they hadn't made love earlier, and she achieved another before Tony reached his. When he was sated, he watched her with hooded eyes and she wondered what he thought.

She picked up a towel to dry herself, her gaze running

over broad shoulders that glistened with drops of water. "I'll see you in bed," she said, leaning close to kiss him. His arm snaked out to wrap around her neck.

"I want to keep you right here in my arms," he said between kisses. Damp locks of his hair clung to his forehead and he felt warm and wet.

"I'll see you in bed," she repeated with amusement. "You're insatiable. When do you run out of energy?"

"With you, I hope never."

She laughed, snatching up another towel to wrap around herself as she got out of the tub and headed to bed.

She felt as if she was having an out-of-body experience. The night continued to shock her—Tony continued to shock her. She couldn't believe he'd given her the best sex of her life, three bone-shattering orgasms—and the night wasn't over yet.

She walked into a big closet and looked at his clothes so neatly hanging. Boots were lined in rows. She found what she wanted—a navy terry robe—and she pulled it on, belting it around her waist.

She climbed into bed, detecting a faint scent of Tony's aftershave, wondering how long it would be before he joined her.

In minutes he walked through the door and her heart skipped a beat. With a navy towel knotted around his waist, he oozed sex appeal as he crossed the room.

"I couldn't wait to be with you. You look more gorgeous than ever," he said, discarding his towel and scooting beneath the sheet. "Want a drink? Something to eat? Music and dancing?"

She laughed out loud. "You've got to be kidding. Relax, Tony. Sit back and enjoy the moment." She sobered and ran her fingers over his smooth jaw. "You shaved."

"Just for you." Turning on his side, he pulled her close against him. "This is better. I like your hair down best."

"I rarely wear it that way, but I'll keep that in mind."

"No, you won't. You'll forget." He ran his fingers through the damp locks. "You know you never gave me an answer to my invitation to go to dinner next Friday night."

She was silent, mulling over his question. She had wanted to accept instantly when he had asked her the first time, but reluctance had filled her. It still did. "I think when we go back to our real lives, you'll wish you hadn't asked me."

"Not so."

"Call me next week and ask me again if you still want to go out. I don't think you will."

"Darlin', if I didn't want you to go, I wouldn't ask you."

"Just call me next week."

He gave her a long look and she wondered what was running through his mind. Had their mild clash reminded him of the big fights they'd had? From the shuttered look that had come to his eyes, she suspected it had. She didn't want any such intrusion on this night. She scooted close against him. "In the meantime, I intend to keep you happy with me," she said, hoping for a sultry voice.

The shuttered look was replaced by blatant desire, and she guessed she had succeeded in making things right between them again. When he turned to kiss her, she was certain she had.

It was midafternoon the next day when she walked out of the shower. Wearing the navy robe again, she roamed through his sprawling condo into a big kitchen that had an adjoining sitting room with a fireplace.

Exploring the refrigerator and his freezer, she saw

some drinks, a few covered dishes and an assortment of berries. She had leaned down to look at the lower shelves when Tony's arms circled her waist to draw her back against him. He nuzzled her neck.

"I know what I want," he said.

She turned to wrap her arms around his neck. He wore another thick navy robe that fell open over his broad chest.

Aware their idyll was about to end, she kissed him passionately. She dreaded stepping back into reality, where she would have to wrangle with him again.

He released her. "Hold that thought and let me put something in the oven so I can feed us."

"At last…food," she said, clutching her heart and batting her eyelashes dramatically at him. When she licked her lips slowly as she watched him remove the covered casserole dish from the fridge and nudge the door closed, he placed the dish on the counter and turned to draw her into his arms.

"You were going to get fed until you did that," he said in a husky voice, pulling her close.

"Did what?"

"You know what," he said, leaning closer to kiss her, a hungry kiss that ignited fires more swiftly than ever.

In minutes she wriggled out of his grasp. "I think we should eat. Whatever I did, I won't do again. How can I help?"

He was breathing hard, looking down, and she realized the top of her robe was pulled apart enough to reveal her breasts. She closed the robe more tightly. "As I was saying, what can I do to help?"

He seemed to not even hear her, but in seconds he looked up. "If you want to eat, I suggest you go sit over there on the sofa and talk to me while I get something heated up. If you stay within arm's reach, I'm reaching."

She smiled and left him alone, watching him put the dish into the oven and get plates, pour juice, wash berries. Her gaze raked over him. He was a gorgeous man. Sexy, strong, successful. Why hadn't some woman snatched him up already? As far as she knew from local gossip, there had never been a long-term girlfriend. Just a trail of girlfriends who'd come and gone. Apparently, he didn't go in for serious affairs.

"Tony, you really should let me help you. I feel silly sitting here doing nothing except watching you work."

"This isn't hard work. You stay where you are so I'm not too distracted to get breakfast on the table."

"I do that to you? Distract you?"

"Lindsay," he said in a threatening tone, "do you want breakfast or do you want to go back to bed?"

She laughed. "Breakfast. I'm famished. And I'll help any way I can."

"You know what you can do, so do it," he said.

"Yes, sir," she answered demurely, teasing him. When his gaze raked over her, she became aware of the top of her robe gaping open enough to give a another glimpse of her breasts and the lower half of her robe falling open over her crossed legs. She closed her robe and belted it tightly, glancing up to find him still watching her.

"Show's over," she said.

He nodded and turned to finish preparing the meal.

After a breakfast of egg-and-bacon casserole and fruit, he turned on music as they cleared the table, and took her wrist. "Stop working and come dance with me," he said, moving to a familiar lively rock number.

Unable to resist him, she danced with him, aware as

she did that her robe gaped below her waist, revealing her legs all the way to her thighs.

Next a ballad came on and he drew her into his arms to slow dance. He was aroused, ready to make love again. His arms tightened around her and he shifted closer to kiss her. Dimly she was aware they had stopped dancing.

His hand trailed down between them to untie her robe while he continued kissing her. When she reached out to do the same, his belt was tightly knotted and she needed his help, but soon both robes were open. He shoved them aside, pulling her naked body against his.

Her soft moan was a mixture of pleasure and desire as he kissed her and picked her up to carry her back to bed.

It was almost two hours later when he held her close beside him in bed and rolled over to look at her. He wound his fingers in the long strands of her hair, toying with her locks.

"I know you have to go home soon," he said. "I think it's time we get to the reason behind this weekend and your incredible bid for me at the auction. You paid a mind-boggling sum to get my attention, so now you have it. What's behind this? What did you want me to agree to do?"

Tony looked into her big eyes that were the color of blue crystal. His gaze went to her mouth and he wanted to kiss her again. He stifled the urge, difficult as it was. Their time together had been fabulous, a dream, but it would end shortly and they would go back to their regular lives. How much would it change because of the auction? For a moment a memory flashed in his mind of the second and most direct encounter they had, when a big tree on her property fell during a storm in the night. It had fallen on his fence, taking it down and also smashing one of his trucks, which had stalled in the rainstorm.

One of the men had called to tell him. When he drove out to view the damage, she was already there with a crew working to cut up the fallen tree and haul it away. She held a chain saw and had a battered straw hat on her head with a long braid hanging over her shoulder. He'd known her all his life but rarely paid any attention to her. He knew she was two years younger than he was, but right then he thought she looked five years younger. The noise of chain saws was loud, the ground spongy from the rain when he stepped out of his truck.

Even though she had to pay for the damage because it was her tree, he'd tried to curb his anger that she hadn't called him first. She saw him and walked over.

"My tree fell in the storm. Sorry about the damage. But I'm insured."

"Did you call your agent?"

"No, I will. I want to get the fence up as soon as possible so I don't lose any livestock."

"Lindsay, that's my fence and I'll fix it. You should have called me. Your insurance should cover the damages when a tree falls on something, but only if you have notified your company. They would have sent someone out to see what happened, take pictures and write a report. Now the tree is back on your property, cut up as we speak, and I doubt if you can collect anything."

She had looked surprised. "I haven't had a tree fall on anything before. I'll check with my insurance company, and I'll pay you for the damage."

"Stop cutting up the tree. I'm going to call and see if my adjustor wants to come out anyway."

She'd frowned but agreed.

"And leave the fence alone. It's my fence and I'll get it replaced today."

She had scowled at him. "Today?"

"This morning," he said. "As soon as we can. If you have livestock grazing here, move them. Don't let them in this pasture. That's simple enough," he said, wondering if she knew how to run that ranch of hers.

"I know that," she snapped.

"Leave the fence to me. Stop cutting up and hauling away the tree. I'll get someone out here to look this over," he repeated, suspecting she was stubborn enough to keep cutting up the tree.

She had clamped her mouth closed as her blue eyes flashed. "Anything else you want to tell me to do?" she snapped, and his temper rose a notch.

"Probably a lot, but I'm not going to," he answered evenly.

"Why was your truck parked right by my property?"

He had been annoyed by her question, though he tried to hang on to his temper. "It was on my property and we can park the truck wherever we want on this side of that fence. If you want to know, one of the men was headed back in the storm and checking to see if the fences were okay. He'd been driving through high water in several low places and the truck quit running here. Unfortunately, near your tree."

She'd been silent a moment as if thinking about what he had said. "I know it was my tree on your truck. My word should be good enough for the insurance."

Impatiently, he shook his head. "No, it's not good enough. Next time, remember to call your adjustor before you do anything else. You may have a hard time collecting."

He remembered her raising her chin defiantly and he'd

wondered if she would argue, but then she looked around and seemed lost in thought until she turned back to him. "That isn't a new truck. Get three estimates in Verity for the repairs and I'll cover the lowest bidder's charges."

"Look, I can't get that kind of damage fixed in Verity. At least not at three different places and you know it. The truck will be totaled."

"I'm not buying you a brand-new truck."

"Tell your guys to stop working and then go home, Lindsay, and call your insurance company. They'll tell you what to do next."

Her cheeks had grown red and fire had flashed in her eyes, but he hadn't cared if his instructions made her angry. She had already annoyed the hell out of him.

Yes, Lindsay Calhoun had that unique ability to boil his blood.

Right now, though, as he reined his thoughts back to the present and looked down at her naked body, she had the ability to heat his blood in a different way.

Tony pushed aside the past to gaze into her big blue eyes. He didn't expect what they'd had this weekend to last much longer because the real world was settling back into their lives.

Last night he hadn't cared what she wanted from him. He'd been totally focused on her as he adjusted to his new discoveries about her. Now, though, curiosity reared its ugly head and he wanted to learn her purpose behind the evening.

"You should know what I want to talk about," she said, scooting to sit up in bed and lean back against pillows, pulling the sheet demurely high and tucking it beneath her arms. Her pale yellow hair spilled over her shoulders. She looked tousled, warm and soft, and he wanted to wrap his arms around her and kiss her again, but he refrained. It was time he heard her out and learned what was so important to her that she would pay several thousand dollars just to get his attention.

"Two things, Tony," she said, and he sighed, trying to be quiet and listen, to be patient and talk to her calmly. He had already given her the solution to her water problem, but she didn't believe him. He could deal with this in a civilized manner, but underneath all her sex appeal, breathtaking beauty and their dream weekend, there still was the real woman who was mule-stubborn and did not take advice well.

Lindsay was all he avoided in women—stubborn, far too serious and constantly stirring conflict.

The irony of the fact that she was now sharing his bed was not lost on him. But he ignored it as he focused on her.

She continued her explanation. "First and foremost I hope that we have some sort of truce where we can be civil to each other, with no tempers flaring."

"I'd say we can be mighty civil to each other. You should have some of your money's worth there," he said, caressing her throat, letting his fingers drift down lightly over her breast.

"I hope so," she said solemnly.

"I'm willing," he said. "So continue."

She squared her shoulders and fussed with the sheet. Then she cleared her throat and spoke. "My wells are running dry and I figured you've replaced your old pumps with bigger ones that are drawing on the aquifer and depleting my groundwater. I can get bigger pumps, too, but that might take water from other neighbors and I don't want to do that."

He held up his hand. "I told you, Lindsay, I do not have bigger pumps."

"Well, for some reason, my water is dwindling away to almost nothing."

"It's a record drought," he said, as if having to explain the obvious to a child.

"I've asked Cal Thompson and he doesn't have bigger pumps. Neither does Wendell Holmes. I figured it was you."

"It is not. According to the weather experts, this is the worst drought in these parts in the past almost sixty years—before you and I were born, much less before we became owners of neighboring ranches. I told you the solution to my problem. You can do the same. Just dig deeper wells and you'll have much more water. Then when it rains, the aquifer will fill back up again. If you don't want to dig deeper, buy water and have it piped in. That's what Wendell is doing."

She stared at him thoughtfully in silence for several minutes. It was difficult to keep his attention on her water worries while she sat beside him in bed, naked, with only a sheet pulled up beneath her arms. He couldn't resist reaching out to caress her throat again, letting his hand slide down and slip beneath the sheet to caress her bare breasts. It took an effort to sit quietly and wait when all he wanted to do was take her in his arms and kiss her thoroughly. Well, that wasn't all he wanted to do.

The instant his fingers brushed her nipple, he saw a flicker in her eyes.

"You really had them dug deeper?"

Thinking more about her soft skin and where his fingers wanted to go, he hung on to his patience. "Yes, I did. When we get home, come over anytime and I'll show you my old pumps."

When she merely nodded, he felt a streak of impatience with her for being so stubborn. She didn't seem convinced he was telling the truth, and he suspected she wasn't going to take his advice. With every passing minute he could see her sliding back into her serious, stubborn self, stirring up conflict unnecessarily. Lindsay seemed to thrive on conflict. Except for last night. For that brief time she had been sexy, appealing, cooperative and wonderful. Now they were drifting back to reality and he had to hang on to his patience once again.

"I might do that."

As his gaze ran over her, it was difficult to think about anything else except how sexy she was and how the minutes were running out on this brief truce. She looked incredibly enticing with her bare shoulders and just the beginning of luscious curves revealed above the top of the sheet. How could she be this appealing and he had never noticed? He knew his answer, but it still amazed him that he hadn't had a clue about her beauty. In the past, once she started arguing he couldn't see beyond his anger. He saw now.

He was unable to resist trailing his fingers lightly over her alluring bare shoulder, looking so soft and smooth. If his life depended on it, he couldn't stop touching her or looking at her. He wanted to pull away the sheet, place her in his lap and kiss her senseless. They were wasting their last few moments together talking about the drought, when he had other things he wanted to do.

He leaned forward to brush a kiss on that perfect shoulder.

"Tony, you're not even listening," she snapped, her voice taking on the stubborn note he had heard her use too many times. Right now, he didn't care, because he knew how to end her annoyance.

He trailed kisses to her throat and up to her ear while his hands traveled over her, pulling the sheet down as they set out in exploration. Suddenly, she pushed him down and moved over him to sit astride him. She had tossed aside the sheet completely and was naked. It still startled him to realize what a sexy body she had.

"This weekend has opened possibilities I never thought of when I was bidding," she said in a throaty voice while her hands played over his chest.

He cupped her full breasts, their softness sending his temperature soaring. He was fully aroused, hard and ready and wanting her as if they hadn't made love ever.

"I'll leave you with memories that will torment you," she whispered, leaning down to shower kisses over his chest.

He sighed as she moved down his body, her hand stroking his thick rod as she trailed kisses over his abdomen and lower. When she reached his erection, he groaned.

He relished her ministrations, but he didn't want their last time to be like this. He wanted to be inside her. In one smooth motion he rolled her over so he was on top. His mouth covered hers in a demanding, possessive kiss at the same time that he grabbed a condom from the bedside table.

In seconds he entered her, taking her hard and fast while she locked her legs around him and rocked wildly against him in return.

He wanted to bring her to more than one climax, as he'd done before, but this time was too unbridled, too untamed. The second he sent her flying over the edge of an orgasm, he joined her, reaching the stars together on a hell of a ride.

When they slowed and their breathing became regular, he stayed inside her, too exhausted to move. Finally he kissed her lips and said softly, "You can't imagine how beautiful and sexy I think you are."

A smile lit up her eyes, though it did not grace her mouth. "I hope so. I don't want you to forget this weekend," she whispered.

He gazed into her eyes and doubted if he ever would.

This time with her had been special, but now they would be going back to their real lives. While they should be more neighborly in the future, they were still the same people, with the same personalities. Lindsay was not his type—she was way too serious for him and far too stubborn. He suspected today would be goodbye.

He pulled out of her and rolled over.

"I should get ready to go home," she said.

He turned to her. "I'll fly you home if you want to have someone pick up your car. Or I can take you home when I go."

She shook her head. "Thank you, but I'll drive home. I'd better get in the shower now. It's time," she said.

He caught her arm and she pulled up a sheet to cover herself while she paused getting out of bed.

"Lindsay, more water is a poor return on your money. For your bid and for this weekend, you should get a whole lake of water in return."

To his surprise she smiled, standing to wrap the sheet around herself in toga fashion. She walked to the other side of the bed to put her arms around his neck. When she did, he placed his hands on her tiny waist, wanting to kiss her instead of listening to whatever she had to say.

"Maybe not such a poor return," she said in the throaty voice that conjured up images of them in bed together. "We've made some inroads on our fighting that will make a huge change in our relationship. At least the fights in the future might not be so bitter."

He grinned. "We'll see how long we can both hold on to our tempers. All I have to do is remember you like this," he said, leaning down to kiss her lightly as he ran his hands over her back.

"I need to shower," she said, stepping away from him.

"Shucks. I hoped I was irresistible," he drawled, and she smiled.

"You are, Tony. Far too much," she said as she walked away from him, picking up the navy bathrobe on her way to the shower.

After her last statement he was tempted to catch up with her and kiss her again. He wanted to hold her, to see how truly irresistible he could be. But they were getting ready to go home and return to their regular lives and there would be no lovemaking in their future. With a sigh he pulled out some fresh clothes and went down the hall to another bathroom.

All the time she showered, Lindsay wondered how much this weekend would change how they treated each other at home. Tony was still Tony, telling her what to do. She hadn't said anything to him, but she wanted to check his pumps by herself. She wouldn't put it past him to be bluffing with his invitation to come look. After all, he was a Milan.

One of her earliest memories had been her grandmother telling her to never trust a Milan. Could she trust Tony now?

The Tony she had just been with for the past twenty hours was a man she would trust with her life. That thought startled her; it was completely at odds with how she'd been raised. Then again… Had her grandmother just been passing down family opinions that could have gone back generations?

Thirty minutes later, dressed and ready to go, Lindsay joined Tony in the living room. He came to his feet when she entered, his gaze sweeping over her, making her tingle. To her surprise, reluctance to see the weekend end filled her. After all, she and Tony had always known it wouldn't—couldn't—last.

Even in jeans, boots and a navy Western shirt, Tony looked sexy and handsome. A short while ago, as they'd talked about ranching, she'd felt the old annoyance with him for telling her what she should do. Now, simply looking at him made her heart beat faster.

She looked down at the red dress she'd worn last night and wore again now. "I have to go back to my hotel in this. It's four in the afternoon, so I may turn heads," she said, forcing a grin that never made it fully to her lips.

He crossed the room to place his hands on her shoulders. "Lindsay, in that dress, you'll turn heads any hour of the day or night. You're gorgeous." He reached out to play with her hair, which fell about her shoulders. "I like your hair down."

For some reason she hadn't put it up when she got ready. She couldn't say why.

"Thank you. I'm ready to go. You know what the drive is like back to the ranch. Are you going home today?" She knew he was driving her to her hotel, but wasn't sure where he was headed after that.

"No, I have an appointment in Dallas in the morning. Otherwise, I would have pushed harder to go home together."

"I see." She gave one nod. "Well, now we go back to our real lives and the real world. But it was a wonderful, magical weekend that I never, ever expected."

"My sentiments exactly," he said. "I don't want you

to go. I don't want this to end, but I know it has to and it won't be the same."

"Afraid not," she agreed with him. "I'm ready. Shall we go?"

"Yes. But how about one last kiss?" He took her in his arms and he kissed her, hard, as if his kiss was sealing a bond that had been established between them this weekend. His lips were making sure that she would never forget his lovemaking, even though she knew it wouldn't happen again.

She kissed him in kind, wanting just as much to make certain he couldn't forget her, either.

He raised his head. "How about a picture of the two of us to commemorate the occasion?" he asked, pulling out his phone. "Do you know how few selfies I've taken? I think one—with a friend and my horse at a rodeo."

She laughed. "I rank right up there with your horse. Wow."

He grinned as he held out the phone and took the shot, then he showed it to her. "You're gorgeous, Lindsay."

"Look at that picture the next time you think about dumping trash on the entrance to my ranch."

He shook his head. "I'm still telling you that I did not do any such thing. You might have annoyed someone else, you know."

Startled, she studied him. "You really mean that?"

"I really mean it."

"If you didn't do it, then I owe you an apology," she said, still staring at him. But, even if she had accused him of something he didn't do, there was bound to have been things he did do. And he still had those take-charge ways that drove her nuts. Besides, he liked to play the field and never get serious. No, Tony was not for her.

"One picture, Lindsay, just of you, so I can look and

remember. Okay?" he asked, stepping away and taking her picture as she placed her hand on her hip and smiled.

"We have to go. I need to get home," she said, shouldering a delicate, jeweled purse that matched the straps on her dress.

"Sure thing," he said, taking her arm to walk her out to the car. As she slid onto the passenger seat, her skirt fell open and she glanced up to see him looking at her legs. She tucked her skirt around her while he closed the door and walked around to his side of the car.

He was quiet on the ride to the hotel, and so was she. As he drew up to the front entrance a short while later, he stepped out and talked to a valet, then came around to escort her into the lobby. "I'm glad you were the high bidder. But I don't want to say goodbye."

"We both know the weekend is over. Really over. Reality sets in now, Tony. As we've already agreed, it might be a little better than it was."

He nodded. "You take care."

"You, too. Thanks for a weekend that was worth my bid."

"That'll go to my head. I didn't dream I could bring such a price." He smiled as he stepped away. "Goodbye," he said, turning and walking out of the hotel.

She stood watching him, unable to understand the feelings of sadness and loss as he walked away.

Four

When he vanished from sight, she turned to go to her room to change to jeans and get her things to drive back to her real life at her ranch. She wished she had gotten a selfie for herself and then she laughed at herself. If she had, at the first ornery thing he did, she would have erased it. And she didn't expect one weekend to change Tony's alpha-male ways or his flitting from woman to woman.

Even if he changed, which couldn't happen, she didn't care to break her rule about avoiding entanglements with cowboys and ranchers. Tony would be the last man on earth she would want to fall in love with because it would be disaster for each of them from the first minute. They were both ranchers, with clear ideas of how they wanted to run things and opposing ideas on most everything. Life with Tony would be a continual battle. Unless he retired and just stayed in the bedroom. That thought made her laugh out loud as she drove all alone in her car, heading west out of Dallas and back to her ranch.

Midmorning on Tuesday as Tony sat at his ranch desk and worked at his computer, trying to find Texas water sources, his phone rang and he answered to hear his brother Wyatt.

"I thought I better call and see if you survived Saturday night. I heard you didn't come home until Monday evening."

"Keane, my foreman, always knows how to get hold of me. You didn't know I was worth so much money, did you?" Tony asked.

Wyatt laughed. "You brought in a fortune at the auction. And it was all for a good cause, so thanks. You really contributed, but don't let it go to your head. Even though this is bound to bring another slew of admiring females into your life."

Tony hadn't thought of that. "Maybe, but there's one thing I do know. I will never bet with you on saddle bronc riding events again."

Wyatt gave a belly laugh. "How'd the date with Lindsay go, bro? I was worried what she might want to do with you. I gotta tell you, I had no idea she could look like she did."

Tony recalled the blonde beauty who was such a surprise. "Lindsay's looks sent me into shock, and once I caught sight of that red dress, the evening instantly improved. But you shouldn't worry. We did fine together."

"I figured her looks would smooth things over. Don't know if you know yet, but the two of you are all the gossip in Verity and in the sheriff's office. I've been asked more than a few questions. I think around my office, they're waiting for a report from me about how the evening went."

"Civilized. That's what you tell them. We just set aside our differences—for charity."

"I'll bet you did," Wyatt said, and Tony could hear the amusement in his brother's voice. "No way in hell would you fight with someone who looked like she did Saturday night. And she must have wanted something from you badly to pay that kind of money."

"Yeah, she wants more water."

"Don't we all. She should know you can't help her out there. No rain in the forecast, either. Hang on a sec, Tony." Wyatt put him on hold while he consulted with one of his deputies. When he returned, he was back on what appeared to be his favorite subject. "Like I was saying, some people will never look at Lindsay the same way. Those who didn't see her at the auction are curious as hell. I don't know why she keeps those looks hidden."

"She's not interested in dating cowboys or ranchers. She doesn't want anyone telling her how to run her ranch. You can figure that one out."

"Definitely. I was shocked to see who had won the bid," Wyatt remarked drily.

Tony would agree with that. "We had a good time Saturday night, but she's still Lindsay, all stubborn and serious. But we did agree to ease off the fights from now on."

"Thank heaven for that one. My life will get a hell of a lot more peaceful. Call when you come to town."

"Sure, Wyatt."

After he hung up, he stared at the phone, thinking about Lindsay, and he was tempted to pick up the phone and call her. Then reason reared its head. Beneath all that beauty, he reminded himself, she was still the stubborn, obstreperous woman she had always been. She was as wise to avoid ranchers as they were to avoid her. She was not his type. Still...that weekend with her had been the sexiest in his life, and she had been the sexiest woman he'd ever been with.

He had to shake his head to get rid of the images that flooded his mind. The two of them in bed, in the Jacuzzi... No, he had to leave things alone. The weekend was over and it wouldn't happen again.

Breathing a sigh, he turned to the ledger he needed to work on and tried to forget her and the steamy memories of their weekend.

The next few days slipped by without a cloud in the bight blue sky, the drought growing more severe as water dwindled in the creeks and riverbeds and strong, hot winds warmed the parched earth. Lindsay threw herself into work, trying to forget the weekend with Tony, but she was unable to do so. It surprised her how much she thought about him. Even worse, she finally admitted to herself that she missed seeing him. She gritted her teeth at the thought. She didn't want to miss Tony. She didn't want him or the weekend they'd had to be important. Her reactions to him continually shocked her.

All her adult life she had avoided going out with men who would want to tell her how to run her ranch. She had managed, until Tony. That was the road straight to disaster. She didn't want to marry a take-charge male— and a Milan, to boot!—and then fight over running everything. There was no way she would be in agreement on everything or turn her ranch over to someone else to run. She shook her head, knowing she needn't worry. Tony wouldn't ever get close to proposing to her. He wasn't going to propose to any woman. He was not even the type of person she wanted to go out with again, and she was certain he felt the same way about her.

It was done. They were done. It was that simple.

Turning back to work, she forced him out of her mind. Soon she wouldn't even think about him.

But that resolve didn't stop her from mulling over his property. That afternoon when she drove her pickup along the boundary between her ranch and Tony's, she stopped, switched off the engine, got binoculars and climbed up on her pickup to find out if she was close enough to see his pump on the water well nearest her land.

It was visible in the distance, but she couldn't tell whether it was old or new. Damn. Time was running out for her.

How much longer could she go without rain?

Her other neighbors were buying water and having it piped or shipped in.

Tony had told her to come look at his pumps. If he still had the old pumps and he had dug deeper—if he was telling the truth—then that would be the best thing for her to do. She frowned. Why did it rankle so much to do what he told her to do?

As she looked at his land, she couldn't keep from moving her binoculars in a wide swing, curious whether Tony worked in the area. She didn't see him and she hated to admit to herself that she was disappointed. She missed his company. Now she was sorry she hadn't accepted his dinner invitation for Friday night, instead telling him to call her this week if he still wanted to take her out again. She hadn't expected to hear from him and so far, she had been right. It was Thursday and he hadn't called, so he must have had second thoughts when he got home.

She hated to admit that she was disappointed, but she told herself it was for the best. Still, she couldn't stop the memories... She remembered being in his arms, his kisses, his blue-green eyes that darkened to the color of a stormy sea when he was in the throes of passion. How could he be so handsome and so sexy? Maybe it had been the tux. Or his naked body that was male perfection. Or his—

Her ringing phone cut off that steamy train of thought. Shaking her head as she wiped her brow, she yanked her cell out of her pocket expecting Abe, her foreman, but the caller ID read T. Milan. Her heart missed a beat as she stared at the phone until the next ring jolted her out of her surprise. She said hello and heard Tony's deep voice.

"How are you?" he asked politely, and suddenly she was suspicious of why he was calling, but at the same time, she was happy to hear his voice.

"I'm fine. Actually, I'm at our boundary line and looking at your closest well trying to see your pump."

"Hey, are you really? I'm not far. Stay where you are and I'll join you and give you a closer look."

She laughed. "You don't need to."

"Of course I don't need to, but I'm already headed that way, so don't drive off."

"I wouldn't think of it."

"Oh, I almost forgot. I called to ask about dinner tomorrow night."

So he hadn't had second thoughts after all. She couldn't stop the smile from spreading across her lips.

"How about something simpler than last weekend?" he continued before he had her answer. "Like Marty's Roadhouse? I know it's two counties away, but if we go anywhere around here, you'll be besieged by cowboys wanting to take you out. Also, we'll be the top of the list for local gossip."

"I don't want either to happen."

"We'll do a little two-steppin' and eat some barbecue and discuss what you can do to get water."

She should say no. They could talk about water on the phone or when he arrived in a few minutes. Common sense told her to decline. But then she thought about dancing with him. If she just had some self-discipline and had him bring her home after dinner, an evening with him couldn't hurt. "That would be good," she said.

"Great. I'll pick you up at six. We'll have a good time dancing."

She heard a motor. "I think I hear you approaching."

"You do. Stay where you are."

"See you in seconds," she said, and broke the connection. Amused, she pulled on leather gloves and parted strands of barbed wire that formed the fence that divided their property. She had been climbing through or over barbed wire since she was little. She straightened to watch him approach.

He drove up in a red pickup, stopped and jumped down. As he came into view, she saw that he wore a light blue long-sleeved shirt with the sleeves rolled up, tight jeans, boots and a black broad-brimmed hat.

She knew she was going against good sense getting involved any more deeply with Tony. So why did her entire body tingle at the sight of him?

"You look great," Tony said as he approached her and reached out to tug her braid. "I never realized how good you look in jeans."

She laughed. "Until last weekend, I never realized you could look at me without getting annoyed."

Grinning, his gaze roamed down her legs again and every inch of her felt his eyes on her. "Oh, darlin', those jeans do fit you. I just should have taken a second look." He looked into her eyes and her breath caught. How could he cause such a reaction in her now? She had known him all her life and until last weekend she'd never once had this kind of response to him just saying hello.

"I'm glad you said yes to tomorrow night," he said, the amusement fading from his expression.

Her smile vanished when his did. "Tony, we're probably doing something we shouldn't. You and I have no future with each other in a social way."

He didn't argue with her and, instead, continued to stare at her. He shrugged and stepped closer to run his finger along her cheek. The feathery touch sizzled and she had to draw a deep breath and resist walking into his arms.

"It's just a fun Friday night, Lindsay. Surely we can do that just one more time."

She knew the more time she spent with him, the more she could get hurt. Tony would not change, and neither would she. At the next problem to come up between them, he would be telling her what to do and she would be angry with him all over again. She needed to stay rooted in reality for the good of her ranch, because she couldn't afford to be sidetracked by him. "Come on," he urged. "We'll have a good time dancing. Marty's on Friday night is fun."

"Until the fights break out."

"That doesn't happen often and if it does, we'll get out of there. I have no intention of spending any part of my night in a brawl."

"So it's two-stepping and eating."

He caught her braid in his hand again as he gazed into her eyes. "Plus some kissing."

She drew a deep breath, wanting him to lean closer and kiss her now yet knowing at the same time that she shouldn't want any such thing.

His phone rang and he looked at it. "I have to go, so let's look at the pumps another time. I have an appointment, but I thought as long as I was close, I'd come say hello. Tomorrow night can't come soon enough." He looked at her as if he still had something he wanted to say. Silence settled between them and she wondered what it was and what was keeping him from saying it.

"I've missed being with you," he finally said. He placed his hands on her shoulders, and an odd expression came over his face. "You seem shorter."

She laughed. "I am. I'm not in my high heels like last weekend."

"Oh, yeah," he said, still staring at her. "But you weren't always wearing heels last weekend," he added in a low voice. "Oh, dang," he said, on a ragged exhale. "I shouldn't, but I'm going to anyway." Pulling her closer, he kissed her.

Her heart thudded and she couldn't catch her breath. His kiss was thorough and sexy, making her heart race. And she responded to it instantly.

When he released her, he was breathing hard. "I have to go. I'll see you tomorrow night at six. Leave your hair down so I can see if it looks as good as I think it did last weekend." As she laughed, he grinned while he placed his hands on her waist to pick her up and set her on the other side of the fence. She remembered how easily he'd carried her in his arms Saturday night. He went back to his pickup in long strides, climbed in, waved and drove away.

Her lips still tingled as she stood there staring after him in a daze. "I should have said no," she whispered to herself. "I should not be going out with him. He's still Tony, all alpha male, a man I've always fought with."

Each hour she spent with him only meant more trouble. She knew that as well as she knew her own name. But she'd already accepted, and besides, it was just dinner and dancing, in a place with lots of people. And talking about water. Far from romantic. She wasn't going back to his ranch afterward. Their evening together would be meaningless.

So why couldn't she wait for tomorrow night?

Lindsay studied herself in the mirror while her two Australian shepherd dogs lay nearby on the floor. It was ten to six; Tony would be here any minute. Time for a last check in the mirror. She'd brushed her hair, curled it slightly in long, spiral curls and finally tied it behind her head with a blue silk scarf. She wore a black Resistol, a denim blouse with bling, washed jeans with bling on the hip pockets and her fancy black hand-tooled boots.

She turned to her dogs and each raised his head.

"I promise you, Tony Milan will not be invited inside tonight. When he comes to the door, don't bark at him and don't bite him."

Both animals thumped their tails as she patted their heads and left the room. The dogs followed her to the front room, where she could watch the drive.

In minutes she heard Tony's pickup approach the house. Hurrying to the door, she turned to tell the dogs to sit. As soon as they did, she opened the door. The sight of Tony took her breath away, just as it had when she had seen him yesterday. His black hat, long-sleeved black Western shirt, tight jeans and black boots made him look 100 percent gorgeous cowboy.

She kept a smile on her face as he approached, even as she silently reassured herself there was no way an attraction between them could possibly develop into anything meaningful. With Tony that was impossible and she was certain he felt the same way. As the dogs barked, she gave them commands that caused them to stop, and they came forward quietly to meet Tony, who patted their heads.

"Hi, cowboy," she said.

"Oh, yeah, you don't go out with cowboys. Well, consider this a business dinner," he said, his eyes twinkling.

"Of course. And business kisses."

"Who said one word about kisses?" he asked, his voice lowering a notch as he placed his hand on the jamb over her head. While she looked up at him, her pulse raced.

"I thought there might be a few kisses as well as dinner."

"We could just skip dinner and go inside and you can show me your bedroom."

She smiled and tapped his chest. "What finesse. I think not. You promised dancing and barbecue."

"Whatever the beautiful lady wants," he said, sounding serious, as if he had stopped joking and flirting. She wanted to step into his arms and kiss him. Then she remembered Tony had broken more than a couple of hearts with his "love 'em and leave 'em" ways.

"Let me turn on the alarm, lock up and we can go," she said in a breathless voice that she hoped he wouldn't notice.

"Sure thing." As she moved back, his eyes raked her body. "Each time I see you, you look fantastic."

"Thank you." She said goodbye to the dogs, who now sat near his feet. "You must have a way with dogs. They don't usually take to strangers."

"Women, children and dogs," Tony said.

"I suppose I have to agree on the women and dogs because that's definitely proven. I don't know about children."

"They love me, too," he said with humor in his voice. "Ask your nephew, Scotty."

Smiling, she switched on the alarm and stepped out with him, hearing the lock click.

He linked her arm in his and they walked to his red pickup.

"Allow me," he said as he held the door for her. She climbed in, aware of his constant scrutiny.

"I do love tight jeans," he said, closing the door behind her.

Laughing, she watched him walk around the pickup, feeling excitement mount as she looked forward to being with him again.

"Some of my family has called me to ask about our evening. My guess is that yours has called you," she said, turning toward him as much as her seat belt allowed. She could hardly believe she was sitting here next to him. Her anticipation of this night with him had built all day.

There still was no danger of it becoming a habit for either of them, just one more night—only a few hours of dancing and talking and, maybe, kisses at her door. As they turned on the road toward the county highway, she gripped his arm. "Tony, look over there in the trees. That's a wolf."

Tony followed the direction of her hand and looked toward a stand of scrub oaks. He didn't see any animal. "I don't see anything and there are no wolves in Texas."

"There's one on my ranch. Look."

She was insistent, so he slowed and backed up, stretching his arm over the back of the seat as he reversed the car around the curve. He saw a furry gray animal at the edge of the trees.

"That has to be a coyote," he said. "It looks like a wolf, but it's not. There aren't any in Texas."

"It's too big and furry to be a coyote," she said. As they

watched, the animal turned and disappeared into the darkness of the trees.

"That animal didn't really look like a dog," Tony said, putting the car in gear and continuing to drive. "Well, we've always got wild animals around here. My money's on a coyote."

"It's a gray wolf. They have them now in New Mexico, and a wolf doesn't know state boundaries. They could easily roam into Texas and probably already have. That was only a matter of time. Remember, there's an old legend around these parts about a gray wolf roaming West Texas and anyone who tames him will have one wish granted."

Tony glanced at her with an exaggerated leer. "I know what my wish would be," he said, his gaze sweeping over her.

She laughed. "You lusty man. You've got no chance of taming it. You'd have to catch the wolf first." She returned to her earlier topic. "About our families…"

"Yeah," Tony said. "Wyatt called me Tuesday morning and said we're the hot topic in Verity."

"Imagine that. Me—the hot topic in Verity. Well, let them talk. It'll die down soon because there won't be enough to talk about."

He cast a glance at her. "I'll bet some new guys have asked you out since last Saturday night."

"They have," she said, "but I turned each one down. A couple were at the auction and a couple heard about the auction," she said, having no intention of telling him six guys who saw her Saturday night had asked her out and three who had simply heard about the auction had called and one more had dropped by the ranch.

"All ranchers, I suppose."

"Ranchers, cowboys and an auctioneer from Fort Worth. No way will I get involved with any of them."

"I can understand that, except you're with me tonight."

She smiled. "Maybe you've moved into the classification of an old friend. Besides, there's no danger of involvement for either one of us. I figure this for our last time together."

"You're probably right," he said.

"You can dance, you're fun, and after last weekend, we're civil to each other. I'm sure we'll have a good time."

"I agree about the good time. I can't wait to get you on the dance floor."

"Also, I want something from you."

He shot her a quick glance and then his attention went back to the road. "What can I do for you?" he asked evenly, but his voice had changed, taken on the all-business tone that she was more familiar with.

"I'm trying to see if I can finagle an invitation to your ranch."

He smiled. "Darlin', I thought you'd never ask! I'll take you home with me tonight."

"Cool it, cowboy. I just want to take you up on your earlier offers to look at one of your water pumps."

His smile disappeared and she wondered if he wanted to turn around now and take her home. "Sure, Lindsay. Tell me when you want to come."

His voice had turned solemn and a muscle now worked in his jaw. She knew she was annoying him, but she wanted to see for herself if he still had his old water pumps.

"Thanks, Tony. I appreciate your offer. You told me to come look."

"So I did," he answered, and then he became silent as they drove on the empty road.

After they reached the county road, he glanced at her

once again. "Lindsay, if that's what you wanted tonight, and why you accepted, do you still want to go?"

"But, Tony," she said in a sultry voice, "that wasn't the sole purpose of accepting your offer to go dancing tonight." She ran her fingers lightly along his thigh. "I also remember how much fun and sexy you can be."

She received another one of his glances and saw him inhale deeply. "Then I'm glad you're here, darlin'. That makes the evening much better. 'Fun and sexy,' huh? I'll try to live up to that description."

She laughed. "I'm sure you will," she said.

Flirting with him made the drive seem shorter, and he flirted in return, causing her to forget about water pumps.

When they reached the roadside honky-tonk, loud music greeted them outside the log building. Inside, they found a booth in the dark, crowded room that held a few local people she knew but more that she didn't.

As soon as they had two beers on the table, Tony asked her to dance. The band, made up of a fiddler, drummer and piano player, had couples doing a lively two-step. As they stepped into the group, Tony held her hands, staying close beside her as they circled the room, and then he turned her, so she danced backward as he led. His gaze locked with hers. Desire was evident in the depths of his eyes as he watched her while they danced. She had his full attention and she tingled beneath his gaze and forgot about her problems.

They danced past midnight and after they returned to their table, he leaned closer. "Ready to leave? We can't talk in here anyway."

When she nodded, he stood, waiting as she slid out of the booth to walk out with him. The air was warm outside, the music fading as they climbed into his pickup.

Light from the dash highlighted his prominent cheekbones, but his eyes were in shadow. The ambience reminded her of their night together, when the dim light of his condo bedroom had shielded his eyes from her view. The memories stirred her as she recalled making love with him. She had tried to avoid thinking about him all week, yet here she was with him. This was crazy. She had to get over Tony, forget him and go on with her life. No way did she want to think about their lovemaking or give him a hint that she would ever want to make love to him again.

As they approached her ranch house, lights blazed from it. "Looks like you have a house filled with people."

"I leave it that way. I don't like to come home to a dark, empty house. And I leave some lights for the dogs," she explained. "Drive around to the back door. It'll be easier for me."

He drove through her wrought iron gates, which closed automatically, and did as she instructed. "I can tell you a better way to avoid a dark, empty house. Come home with me." He unbuckled his seat belt and turned to her. "My house will be neither dark nor empty, and I promise you some fun."

She smiled at him, able to see his eyes now; their blue depths seemed to sparkle even in the darkness. "Thanks, but I belong here. Besides, we agreed on the parameters for tonight."

"It's temptation. You're temptation, Lindsay. Beyond my wildest imaginings," he said, leaning forward to unlock her seat belt. As he did, his lips nuzzled her throat while his fingers caressed her nape. Then he turned to get out of the truck and strode around to open her door for her.

He draped his arm across her shoulders as they walked to her door. "Tonight was fun. I could dance with you for hours. There are a lot of things I could do with you for hours."

Her insides tightened and heated, but she forced a grin. "Is playing chess one of them?" she asked, trying to lighten the moment and get his mind off making love.

"No, chess is not what I had in mind at all," he said as he stopped and turned her to face him in the yard under the darkness of a big oak. As he slipped his arm around her waist, her heart thudded. He leaned close to trail kisses on her neck, her ear. "No, what I want to do is hold you close, kiss you until you melt," he said in a deep, husky voice.

His words worked the same magic on her as his lips and hands. Her knees felt weak and she wanted his mouth on hers. Forgetting all her intentions to keep the evening light, she slipped her arm around his neck and raised her mouth for his kiss.

"Why do I find you so damn irresistible?" she asked.

The moment his mouth touched hers, her heart thudded out of control. More than anything she wanted a night with him, wanted to ask him in, but she intended to stick with her promise to herself to say goodbye to him at her door. He deepened the kiss, his tongue stroking hers, slowly and sensually, and she could barely remember what promise she was thinking about. He was aroused, ready to make love, and she, too, ached to take him to her bedroom and have another night like before.

She didn't know how long they had kissed when she finally looked up at him. She had no idea where her next words came from. "I better go in now."

He stared at her, his hot gaze filled with desire that wrapped itself around her and held her in its spell. Stepping out of its heat, she turned to walk onto her porch. Reluctantly he followed.

When they entered the house, the dogs greeted them. She turned them into the fenced yard, closed the door and faced him.

Though he didn't ask for one, she wanted to give him an explanation.

"Tony, we both agreed last weekend was an anomaly. As special as it was, it's over and we need to leave it over. I don't want an affair and I don't think you do, either. With our families intermarried, we would complicate our lives. We're not really all that compatible anyway. I'm too serious for you and you're too much a playboy for me. If I have an affair, I want it long-term, with commitment. You're not the type for that."

"Don't second-guess me, Lindsay. You're incredibly desirable."

"Do you really want us to get deeply involved?"

He inhaled and gazed at her while seconds ticked past.

"I think that's an answer," she said, "and I agree with it."

"There will never be a time when I can look at you and honestly say I don't want you. I—" He stopped when she placed her fingers against his lips.

"Shh. Don't say things that you don't really know."

Kissing her fingers before she took them away, he nodded as he released a breath. "Okay, so we say good-night now. But I'm not going without a goodbye kiss."

He reached out to take off her hat and toss it onto a nearby chair along with his. "Hats get in the way sometimes," he said as he pulled loose the silk scarf that held her hair behind her head and dropped it into her hat. She shook her head and her hair swung across her shoulders to frame her face.

"You're beautiful, Lindsay," he whispered before his mouth covered hers. He kissed her hard, a passionate kiss that tempted her to throw away common sense and invite him upstairs for one more fabulous night.

She felt his arousal, knew he was as ready to make love as she.

But suddenly, before she could speak, he released her. "Good night, Lindsay. If I don't go right now, I won't go at all. I know what you really want is for me to leave." Before she could move, he turned and hurried out the door.

She fled to her bedroom before she called him to come back. Her heart pounded and she ached with longing for him. How could she feel this way about Tony? A Milan, and her nemesis for so many years?

She had to get beyond this heart-pounding reaction she had to him. She couldn't afford to see him again because each time bound her more closely to him.

He had walked out of her life tonight and there wasn't any reason for him to come back into it. At least not in the immediate future. Things would always happen that would cause them to see each other, but her usual encounters with Tony had been only three or four times a year.

When she had asked him if she could come to his ranch and look at one of his pumps, the question had made him angry. Would he be even angrier if she actually went to his ranch? He probably would, but she was going anyway to see for herself whether he had been truthful. It had been ingrained in her by her family not to trust a Milan and she found it difficult to trust Tony on ranch matters.

And personal matters? After last weekend, she might have to answer that question differently.

She lay across the bed, the lights out, and as thoughts of Tony swirled in her mind, she knew she'd never sleep tonight. Not when she was wishing she were with him, in his arms, naked beside him. Would he sleep? Knowing him, she figured he'd sleep like a bear in winter.

She closed her eyes against the tears that stung them. Tony was out of her life—where he should be. There was no way they had any future as a couple. She'd accomplished all she'd set out to do that night at the bachelor auction. She'd bid on him to butter him up, to make him more amenable. At least that seemed to have worked. With any luck, the fights had stopped or at least changed to simple quarrels. If that had happened, it all would have been worthwhile.

There'd be no more calls from Tony after tonight. The thought swept her with a sense of loss. She shook her head as if she could shake away the feeling. How long would it take her life to get back to normal?

Five

He hadn't been ready to tell her goodbye tonight. The whole time he'd cruised down the driveway he'd watched her house in the rearview mirror, fighting the urge to turn around.

If he let himself, Tony could envision the scene clearly. He'd stop sharply, his tires spewing dirt and gravel as he spun around and gunned his engine. When he pulled up at her back porch, she'd be there throwing open the door, and she'd run to him just as he stepped out of the truck. He'd pick her up in his arms and carry her back into her house, right up to her bedroom. They wouldn't say a word to each other; they wouldn't need to. They'd simply make love. And it would be amazing.

A nice image, he had to admit. But one that wouldn't happen.

Instead, he drove the pickup onto the county road toward his own ranch.

He couldn't help but feel tense, and not just sexually.

He'd been looking forward to this night with Lindsay, and to say it hadn't ended the way he'd hoped would be an understatement. But she was right. They had no future. And Lindsay wasn't the type of woman to have an affair without a future.

And she was too serious, just as she said.

Not to mention the whole business with her wanting to see his water pumps. Damn, she still didn't believe that he hadn't installed bigger pumps to steal her water. She wanted to see it with her own two eyes. Because he was a Milan, no doubt, and Milans never told the truth!

He banged the palm of his hand on the steering wheel. He needed to forget her.

As he drove along the darkened road, he turned on the radio, but the guy who sang—some guy who'd won one of those ubiquitous TV reality shows—strummed a soulful guitar and sang about the cute filly he was pining for. Tony didn't want to hear it. He shut it off. He had enough of his own problems with his own cute filly. A spirited one, at that.

He had to let out a laugh at the thought of Lindsay knowing he had referred to her as a filly. She'd probably take out her shotgun and fill him with buckshot.

The drive home seemed endless, but by the time he pulled onto the long driveway up to his ranch house, he knew what he had to do. He had to forget everything about Lindsay Calhoun, starting with last Saturday night. From the moment he'd seen her in that red dress all the way to tonight. As sexy, as enticing, as appealing as Lindsay was, she wasn't the woman for him. They could never be together. She was commitment with a capital *C*, and that was one thing he couldn't—wouldn't—ever be willing to give.

He entered the house and went up to bed, not even bothering to turn on a light.

* * *

She hadn't bothered to turn on the light.

For some reason, that thought struck her as she woke up. She remembered running up to her room, in the dark, after Tony left, and throwing herself on the bed, sad and uncharacteristically near tears. She thought she'd never sleep tonight, but apparently she had.

She felt beside her and at her feet, but the dogs weren't in their usual position. Then she remembered. She'd let them out when she got home and then forgotten about them. They'd probably gone over to the bunkhouse for the night.

She sat up, glancing at the clock on her bedside table to see it was after three in the morning. A long, sad howl sent chills down her spine and she ran to the window to look out. Another sad howl filled the night.

Moonlight splashed over open spaces and something moved. Chills ran down her spine again as she saw the wolf standing at the edge of a grove of trees. As she watched, it threw back its head and howled again.

She shivered. For the first time since being on the ranch, she felt alone and didn't like it. She wished she had kept the dogs with her and hoped no one at the bunkhouse turned them out, because she didn't want them tangling with a wolf. She also hoped no one at the bunkhouse got his gun. The men were good shots. If they wanted to kill the wolf, they would surely succeed. She grabbed her phone to call her foreman, thought about it and decided it would be ridiculous to wake him. When morning came, she would talk to Abe about the four-legged intruder.

Another lonely howl caused a fresh batch of shivers to crawl up her spine. Impulsively, telling herself she shouldn't, she called the one person she thought of.

She felt silly when Tony answered, and she suddenly

wished she hadn't called him. But she'd awakened him and she had to explain why.

"Sorry, Tony. I know I woke you."

"Lindsay? Are you okay?" he asked, in a surprisingly clear, alert voice.

"I'm fine, Tony." Now that she had him on the phone she couldn't seem to tell him about the wolf. What did she expect him to do about it?

"Okay then, darlin', what's on your mind at…3:17 a.m.?"

"I feel really silly now."

"Lindsay, you didn't call me in the middle of the night to tell me you feel silly."

"The wolf/coyote/dog—except it looks like a wolf—is howling near my bedroom. I can see it and the animal sounds hurt."

"All animals sound hurt when they howl. So? I know you're a crack shot even with that big .45 you own. Take him out and go back to sleep."

"A gunshot would wake everyone on the ranch and create an uproar. Anyway, I can't kill him. Or her. He or she sounds pitiful and eerie, and for the first time since I've owned the ranch I don't like being here alone."

"I'm coming over."

"No, Tony. I just wanted to hear your voice. Don't get up and come over."

"I can be there in a few minutes."

"Stay in bed," she said, hearing another long howl and looking at the animal standing half in the moonlight and half in shadow. "I feel sorry for it. It sounds hurt and lonesome."

"I'll be over in a flash. I can really take your mind off the wolf, howls or no howls."

She smiled and sat back in the chair by the window.

"You're succeeding right now and you just stay home. We'll both be better off."

She didn't want a repeat of the scene they'd endured only hours ago at her back door. Watching him walk away was hard enough then; she couldn't go through seeing him—and losing him—again.

"That may be true for you, but if I come over, I would definitely be better off."

Despite herself, she laughed softly. "You make me feel so much better. But I still think you should stay home."

"Lindsay, I'm already pulling on my jeans."

"Don't. I really mean it. I feel better now and I can go back to sleep, and I know you can roll over and go to sleep the minute your head is on the pillow." She refused to picture him taking off his jeans and getting back into bed, shirtless and sexy.

"Fine," he said. "The guys will take care of the animal for you and, hereafter, you won't have to listen to it howl again."

"I don't know why, but I feel sorry for it. Unless it kills some of the livestock, I'd hate for them to shoot it."

"Well, this is a change. You're usually pretty damn tough and I know you've shot plenty of wildlife."

"Now how would you know that?"

"The guys talk. And I remember a few marksmanship competitions over the years. Come to think of it, you haven't participated in any in a long time."

"Nope. It doesn't seem to matter any longer. When I first got the ranch, I felt I had to prove that I could handle running the place and a few other things. I don't feel that way any longer."

"I would think not. Half the ranchers around here call you about their animals."

"Not really half, but a few have," she said. She settled

back in the chair to talk, forgetting about everything but the sound of his voice, soothing and smooth as it settled around her in the darkness. It was an hour later when they finally said goodbye and she went to bed. That's when she realized the howls had stopped long ago, but she hadn't actually noticed when, thanks to Tony.

As the next week passed, Lindsay tried to keep busy and struggled to stop thinking about Tony, but that was impossible. She heard nothing from him for eight more days, but, instead of forgetting about him—something she once could easily do—she thought about him constantly, to the point where she had been distracted at work.

It was Thursday, in the middle of a hot, dry afternoon, after she'd helped move steers to another pasture, when her phone rang and she saw it was Tony. She pulled her truck off the road into the shade of an oak and opened the windows.

"It's Tony. I thought it was time to see if you want to come look at the pumps on my water wells."

She was surprised, to say the least. Even though he'd offered, she'd never really expected him to have her over to his ranch—because she still figured he had installed new and bigger pumps. She glanced at her watch. "Give me about two hours and I'll be there. Tell everyone I'm coming so they don't send me away if they see me."

"Nobody's going to send you away and my foreman knows I was going to call you. Come on over. See you in two hours," he said, and ended the connection.

She looked at her phone for seconds, as if she could see Tony. Was he up to some trickery to convince her that he still had his old pumps and had just dug deeper?

She would never tell Tony, but she had already started checking into having her wells dug deeper, and Tony had been right. If she went deeper, there was still water in the aquifer, and when the rains finally came, that depleted water would be replenished and everything would be like it was.

She had already told the men she was headed home, so she started her truck and drove back to her house to shower. She changed into washed jeans, boots and a short-sleeved blue cotton shirt. She knew Tony liked her hair down and not fastened, but she was back at home and she didn't care to change her appearance, so she braided her hair and got her wide-brimmed black hat.

She hadn't been to Tony's ranch house even though she had seen pictures of it on the web, along with a map of his ranch land. As she approached, she looked at the sprawling two-story ranch house that appeared even larger than hers. A porch ran across the front and a wide circle drive joined a walk leading to the front porch.

Flower beds surrounded the house with rock and cactus gardens, plants well adapted to the drought that usually hit West Texas. As she approached, Tony crossed his porch, coming to meet her, his long legs covering the distance. His hair was combed and he had on a clean short-sleeved blue-and-red-plaid shirt, tucked into his jeans. She smiled, happy to see him again.

Tony opened the door of her truck and watched her step out.

"Oh, lady, you do look great," he said, his gaze sweeping over her and making her tingle and momentarily forget why she was here.

"And hello to you. Thank you."

"You've never been to my home, have you?"

"Nope, I haven't. And you haven't been in mine, yet. Not really," she amended, as she thought about last week and how he'd barely made it through her back door before he left.

"Well, I hope to remedy that soon," he said.

"We'll see."

They stepped into an entry foyer that held a full-length mahogany mirror, two hat racks, hooks for coats, shelves that housed several pairs of boots. Stepping through the hallway, they came to a huge kitchen with state-of-the-art-equipment and luxurious dark wood cabinetry. The adjoining family room held a stone fireplace, a big-screen television, a game table, as well as a desk with two computers and other electronic devices.

"All the comforts of home, huh?" she asked. "It's a marvelous home."

"I suspect you have one to match," he remarked.

"Odd that we've never been in each other's houses in all the years we've known each other," she said.

"There's a lot we didn't do in all the years we've known each other," he said, setting her nerves on edge. "C'mon, I'll show you more."

They walked down a wide hall with Western paintings and beautiful tapestries that surprised her. The hall held finely crafted furniture, double front doors where floor-to-ceiling windows let in light and offered a grand view of the front of his property.

"Very beautiful, Tony. And a little surprising."

"You probably pictured me in a log cabin with brass spittoons and bawdy paintings," he said grinning.

She smiled. "Not that extreme, just maybe a little more rustic than this. After all, you're a rancher at heart. This fancy home could belong to a Chicago stockbroker."

He shrugged. "It's comfortable, what I like and a haven when I come home."

"That I understand." She followed him as he directed her down another hallway.

"I don't really know much about you as a person," she

said when he stopped outside a closed door. "Just as an annoyance in my life—until this month," she said.

"I'm glad you added that last part. Here, Lindsay," he said, ushering her into a suite with a sitting room that held floor-to-ceiling windows affording a panoramic view of a terrace and fields beyond it where horses grazed. "Here's my living room. Want to see my bedroom next?"

Smiling at him, she shook her head. "I think we're skirting the edge of temptation too much as it is. Thanks, I'll pass."

"Okay, then, on to the study."

They went down the hall to another room, as elegant as the last, with leather furniture, oils on the walls, heavy shelves and polished cherrywood floors.

As she looked around, he said, "We can finish the tour later." He glanced out the window. "Because I want you to see one of the pumps before the sun goes down."

"Good idea," she said. She wanted to see it in daylight, too, because if it really was his old pump, it would have rust.

"I'm ready."

He placed a hand on the small of her back. "So am I," he said in the husky tone he'd had when making love.

She stepped back. "You're not helping the situation. We agreed that we were not pursuing…" She searched but couldn't find the word she wanted. "Not pursuing this," she said, "any further." She tried to sound forceful, but her words sounded hollow, even to herself.

Tony must have thought so, too, because he said nothing. He merely stepped close and placed his hands on her waist. Her breathing became shallow and erratic as his steady gaze met her eyes and then lowered to her mouth.

Dimly the thought nagged at her that it had been a

mistake to come here, but she wanted to see if he had been truthful with her.

She couldn't step away or protest. She saw the desire in the blue-green depths of his eyes and her mouth went dry. She wanted his kiss just one more time.

He leaned down to kiss her, a hot, possessive kiss that made her feel he wanted her with all his being. Her heart pounded as she wrapped her arms around his neck and kissed him back, once again trying to make him remember this moment and be as conflicted as she was.

Her world spun away, lost in Tony's kisses that set her ablaze. She felt his hands drifting up her back, then moving forward to lightly caress her breasts.

"Tony," she whispered, unable to tell him to stop, yet knowing they should.

She caught his wrists and leaned back. "This isn't why I came," she whispered, and then stepped away. "Water well pump, remember?" she asked, unable to get any firmness in her voice.

"When you're ready, we'll go," he said. He stood so close that her heart pounded and it took all the willpower she had to move away.

"We both have to do better than this tonight."

"I intend to do a lot better," he said, teasing and leering at her, causing her to laugh.

"You're hopeless and headed for trouble, and you're taking me with you." She smoothed down her shirt and stood tall. "I'm ready to look at that pump now."

"One thing—in case you think I might have one old pump for moments like this and the rest are new, I'll let you select which one we go see," he said. She went with him to his desk, a massive cherry table. He opened a drawer and pulled out a map, which he unfolded. "This is a map of the ranch with the water wells circled in yellow. You can select one. If you want to look at all of them, we can."

She gave him a searching look. "I'm beginning to believe you and feel really foolish."

"This is why you came. Pick the wells, Lindsay," he instructed.

She looked again and pointed to one the shortest distance from the house.

"Is that all? I want you totally satisfied when you go home." He said the last words in the tone of voice he used when he was flirting with her. He was back to sexy innuendos, which kept her thinking about his kisses and lovemaking.

"Tony, you've got to stop that," she said, unable to suppress another laugh. He grinned and took her arm.

"I don't think you really want me to. You say those words, but your body, your eyes, your voice are giving you away, darlin'."

"Time to go, Tony," she said, trying to resist him, the sensible thing to do.

They drove to the well and she could see the rust on the pump from yards away. She turned to place her hand on his arm. "Tony, I'm sorry. I've misjudged you and accused you of things you didn't do."

He turned to face her. "You don't want to see another well?"

She shook her head, "No. I apologize."

"Apology accepted."

"I've already taken your advice and called to see about digging my wells deeper."

"Good. C'mon, let's go home and have some juicy steaks."

She knew she should say no, but she couldn't. She

had been wrong about him—he had been telling her the truth all along.

She thought of all the times she had been told not to trust a Milan. Her grandmother had practically drummed it into her head. But her brother had married Tony's sister and trusted her fully. Shouldn't she have learned anything from Jake?

They rode back in silence, but when they stepped into his kitchen, she had to apologize again. She felt that bad.

"Tony, again, I'm so sorry. I—"

He turned to her and put his hands on her waist. "Don't worry about it, it doesn't matter now. This is all that matters."

He tilted her chin up, and she saw the flicker in his eyes and knew when the moment changed. He drew her into his embrace and kissed her, holding her tightly and kissing her thoroughly until she was breathless. With a moan of pleasure, she slipped her arm around his neck and another around his waist to hold him tightly, wanting his kiss in spite of all her intentions of resisting him.

When he released her, he smiled. "That's better," he said. "Let's have a drink and I'll start the steaks."

Though she knew she should go home for a quiet dinner alone, she nodded instead. She tingled from his kiss and wanted more. Each kiss was a threat to her heart and she promised herself she would stop seeing him after this evening. It was just one more night.

She drew a deep breath as her throat went dry. "We weren't going to do this."

"So we're together three times instead of two. Seeing each other will end and we both know it, so what does tonight hurt?" he asked.

"You make it sound like something silly for me to protest."

"You know I want you to stay. It won't be a big deal, Lindsay."

With her heart drumming, she watched him walk to a bar. Who would have thought it? A cowboy who could turn her world upside down, who had become the sexiest, most handsome man she had ever known. How could Tony have become important to her, able to set her heart pounding just by walking into a room where she was?

What seemed worse, the more she knew him, the better she liked him and the more she thought of him. That realization scared her. She didn't want to respect him, admire him and like him. He was still Tony, who had to run everything all the time. Physically, she was intensely attracted to him, but it was beginning to spill over into other aspects of their lives and that scared her.

Never in her life had she been attracted to someone who could put her way of life at risk—until now.

To protect her own lifestyle, she had to make tonight the last time she would socialize with him. She had to break off seeing him before her life was in shambles and her heart broken.

Could she adhere to that…or was it too late?

Six

He wasn't in the kitchen when she came back from freshening up in the powder room. Where had he gone?

She saw a column of gray smoke spiraling skyward and followed it to the glassed-in sitting room where she saw him outside at a grill. When she went out, he turned to smile at her. Tall, lean and strong, he kept her heart racing. His blue-eyed gaze drifted over her and she could see his approval.

"The steak smells wonderful," she said.

"Thanks. We have tossed salad and twice-baked potatoes, too."

"When did you fix all that? Twice-baked potatoes? You planned this?"

"No. I have Gwynne, a cook who has gone home now. She fixes dinners and leaves them for me. The potatoes were frozen and easy to thaw and heat. She lives in her own place here on the ranch and cooks five days a week."

"And what do you do the other two days?"

"Eat alone," he said.

"I can imagine," she remarked, thinking of women she knew he had taken out.

He chuckled as he turned to look at the steaks.

The terrace was broad, running across the back of the house and along the bright blue swimming pool that looked so inviting.

"What do you want to drink? Iced tea, wine, cold beer, martini—you name what you'd like."

"With a drive home tonight, I think iced tea is a good choice."

"I'll get you that, but I'd be happy to drive you home tonight."

"I'll take the tea," she answered, smiling at him, wanting to accept his offer, wanting to stay all night, but determined to do what she should.

In minutes he brought her a tall glass of tea and he held a cold beer. "Shall we sit where I can keep an eye on the steaks?"

All the time they talked, she was aware of him sitting close. His hand rested on her shoulder, rubbing it lightly, or on her nape, his warm fingers drifting in feathery caresses, all small touches that were heightening desire. Was it going to be easy to forget the times spent with him? Was she going to miss him or think about him when they parted for good? She knew the answers to both questions. What she was uncertain about was whether she could resist him.

Soon they sat down to eat in his cool, informal dining area.

"Once again, I'm surprised and impressed. You're quite a cook, Tony. The steaks are delicious."

"Thank you. Our own beef and my own cooking. Ta-da."

When she laughed, he shook his head.

"I need to make an improvement," he said, reaching out to unfasten one more button of her shirt and push it open to reveal her lush curves. His warm fingers brushed her lightly and she drew a sharp breath, longing for his touch.

She hoped what she wanted didn't show. She could barely eat. All she wanted was to be in his arms. In some part of her mind she wondered if he had an ulterior motive for inviting her to see the pumps.

He turned on the charm during dinner, smiling and telling her stories about his family and funny incidents when he started as a rancher. They sat for hours after they finished their steaks, laughing and talking over coffee, until she realized the sun had gone down a long time ago. She stood. "It's getting late, Tony. I should go home." She picked up her plate. Instantly Tony took her dish from her hands.

"None of that. Gwynne will be here in the morning and will take care of it."

"So then I should be going," she said, trying to stick to what she felt she should do.

Placing his hands on her shoulders, making her tingle in anticipation, he turned her to face him.

"Don't go home tonight, Lindsay. You have choices— you can sleep downstairs alone or upstairs with me, but stay. I don't want you to drive back tonight."

"Tony," she said, her heart drumming as she looked into his blue-green eyes, "you know I should go. We've talked about this."

He stepped closer to wrap his arms around her and kiss her. When she knew she was on the verge of agreeing to stay, she stepped out of his embrace.

"I have to go home," she said breathlessly.

He nodded and watched as she straightened her blouse and turned for the door.

Draping his arm across her shoulders, he walked her to her pickup.

"I know you're doing what's sensible. We have different lifestyles. Even so, I don't want you to go."

"I have to," she said and turned to climb into her pickup. She smiled at him. "Thanks for dinner and for showing me your water pump."

"Sure. I'll call you," he said, and closed the pickup door.

He stood on the driveway watching her as she drove away. She glanced several times at the rearview mirror and he still stood watching. Then she rounded a curve and he was gone from view.

She trembled with longing, wanting to stay, telling herself over and over that she was doing the right thing and the smart thing. She had no future with Tony. Far from it, he would be a threat to her and her ranch. Why didn't that knowledge make her feel better?

She tried to stop thinking about his kisses, the laughs they had shared. What she was doing was for the best. She missed him, but she was not brokenhearted after an affair that Tony had ended, something she wanted to avoid with all her being.

The auction had been worth the money if she got friendliness and cooperation from him. She knew he would never stop telling her what she should do, but they could have a more neighborly relationship. In a week she would probably feel differently about him if she stopped seeing him and talking to him.

Tony stood a few minutes after Lindsay drove out of sight. Longing for her tore at him and was impossible for him to ignore.

How could he have so much fun with her now, find her

so desirable when not long ago they were at each other's throats over every issue?

He knew the answer to his question. She was the sexiest, best-looking, most fun woman he had ever known. The realization still shook him.

Feeling empty, he stared at the road, wishing she would turn around and come back. Back into his arms and into his bed tonight.

He shouldn't miss her—he had never missed a woman this much or given one this much thought when he wasn't with her.

Of all the women in Texas, why did it have to be Lindsay who had turned his life topsy-turvy?

With a long sigh, he turned to go inside, knowing he wouldn't be able to stop thinking about her or sleep peacefully tonight.

As he walked back to his house, he saw a light in one of the barns. On impulse, to avoid being alone, he changed direction and strolled to the barn, where he found Keane nailing up more shelves in the tack room.

"I wondered who was working. Need help?"

"Yep. In a minute. I need a break. If you have time, four hands will be better than two trying to get these shelves in place," Keane said as he sat on a crate.

Tony sat on a bale of hay and stretched out his legs. "Lindsay just left and she's happy about my water pumps. She is going to look into doing the same, as we have to get water."

"She can be a nice lady. Good for neighbors to get along."

"It should be more peaceful. I hope it lasts, because she still can be her stubborn self."

"She's not so bad, but you know that now. The people who work for her like her."

"For a time it will probably be better between us."

"I'd bet money on that one," Keane remarked drily. "She's a strong woman who knows what she wants."

"Amen to that. Actually, I don't think we'll see any more of each other in the future."

"Maybe so. You'll work it out, I'm sure."

Tony focused on his foreman because it sounded as if Keane was trying to hold back laughter. "Ready to get back to work?" Tony asked, standing because he wanted to end the conversation about his private life.

"Sure. You can hold one of these boards in place for me."

Silently, Tony followed directions from Keane, but his thoughts drifted to Lindsay. He didn't want to go back to his empty house. He missed her and didn't want to think about her staying or having her in his arms in his bed tonight.

Once Keane stopped to look at him.

"What?"

"You're getting ready to hammer that board in and it's in the wrong place."

Startled, Tony looked at the narrow board he held in his hands. "Sorry," he said, adjusting it as he felt his face heat. He had been lost in thoughts about Lindsay. He made an effort to stop thinking about her and focus on the job at hand.

Tony managed to keep his thoughts on the task and, in minutes, Keane stepped back to look at his completed shelves.

"With your help, we're through," Keane said. "Thanks, boss. That went quickly. I'll put away the tools."

"I'll help," Tony stated, acting quickly. In minutes they parted, Keane for his house and Tony walking back to his, which was dark and empty.

He stepped inside, locked the door and went to the kitchen to get a beer. He carried it out to the patio to sit and gaze at the pool, gardens and fountain while he thought about Lindsay.

He had to get her out of his thoughts. They had no future together and neither one wanted a future together. It still amazed him how much she was in his thoughts.

"Goodbye, Lindsay," he said aloud, as if he could get her out of his thoughts that way. He didn't expect to see her again soon. He tried to ignore the pang that caused.

Lindsay stood in front of the calendar the next morning counting the days. Once and again. No matter how many times she counted it, the results were the same. She had missed her period by almost a couple of weeks now, and that had never happened before. Common sense said there could be a host of reasons and she should give it more time. But could she be pregnant? Tony had taken precautions, but there was always a chance. She knew the statistics.

Anxiety washed over her with the force of a tidal wave, and she pulled out her desk chair to sit down.

After a few minutes, she reminded herself that women were late all the time without it meaning they were pregnant and she should give it a few more days. No sense worrying needlessly. She simply put it out of her mind and got ready for work.

But when the next two days passed with no change, she had to get a home pregnancy test. She couldn't get it in Verity or any town in the surrounding counties where she knew nearly everyone.

She was having Tony's baby. She knew it. Shock buffeted her. How could she deal with it?

She was going to have to figure out how to deal with

it. She picked up her phone to send a text to her foreman. Something's come up. I'll call later.

In a minute she received a reply: Okay. She put her head in her hands. If only she could undo everything and go back to the way she and Tony had been before the auction. She didn't want to be pregnant with Tony's baby. She'd always thought someday she would marry and have a family. Now she was going to have the family without the marriage.

She didn't want Tony to know yet. She had to have plans in place so he couldn't take over.

She ran her hands through her hair. She wasn't ready for this. Tony would want to be part of his child's life, and he would take charge and tell her what to do the moment he learned she was carrying his baby.

Telling her how to run her ranch would be nothing compared to telling her how to raise a baby.

Their baby.

A Milan baby.

A Milan baby fathered by a man she could never marry.

But their families would want them to marry. Hers would pressure her, just as his would pressure him. She knew he was the family type who would think they should marry for this baby's sake. She would have a bigger fight with Tony than she had ever had before. Running two big ranches and raising a baby together. They wouldn't have a battle—they'd have a war! She put her head in her hands to cry, something she rarely did. How would she cope with this? For once in her life she felt overwhelmed.

For a few minutes as she cried, she let go, swamped by a looming disaster. She raised her head and her gaze fell on a picture of her nephew she had taken when Scotty was two. He was laughing, sitting astride a big horse and holding the reins. She loved the picture and she loved Scotty with all her heart and had always hoped she would have a little boy just like him.

She sat up, dried her eyes and stared at Scotty's picture, pulling it close. She was going to have a baby and maybe her child would be as wonderful as Scotty. And her family would stand by her. She had no doubts about that.

She had always avoided dating ranchers until Tony. When she bought a night with him at the auction, she had not expected to fall into bed with him or to even want to see him again.

She should have stuck to her rule of not dating a rancher, no matter the circumstances. But it had never once occurred to her that she could be attracted to Tony, not until she had seen him in that tux, looking so sexy, those eyes that could convey enough desire to melt her.

Logic said to make a doctor's appointment and have her pregnancy verified by a lab and a professional. She could get a home kit, but she wanted a doctor's results to be certain. That was step one. Telling Tony would be step two and the one that she could not cope with thinking about now.

Why had she ever bid for him in the damn auction? No undoing that night now, but it was coming back to haunt her. She needed to plan and to find a good doctor. She couldn't go to a doctor in Verity or anywhere around the area. Texas might not even be big enough. She didn't want word getting to Tony until she was ready to tell him herself. She should fly to a big city, like Tulsa or Albuquerque, but she didn't know any doctors there. She thought about Savannah, Mike's pregnant wife who was from Arkansas.

If Savannah gave her an Arkansas doctor's name, she

could drive to Dallas and then fly to Arkansas without anyone else in the family knowing where she had gone or why. As she thought about her older brother, Mike, she wanted to talk to him and to Savannah. Because of Scotty, she had gotten where she felt close to Mike, and now that he had married Savannah, they would be the ones to talk to about her situation. Savannah had never intended to become pregnant and when her ex-fiancé in Arkansas found out, he had been hateful and hadn't wanted his baby. Lindsay sighed. At least she would never have to worry about that with Tony. It would be just the opposite with Tony. He would want this baby in his life all the time.

Madison, Jake's wife, was expecting, too. That would help soften Jake's attitude about her situation. And Jake liked Tony. Her brothers liked him and their wives did, too. She had been the sole member of her generation to fight him. In fact, it was the older generations of Calhouns that didn't like the Milans. She had heard Destiny talk about her grandmother's intense dislike of Milans. Maybe that had eased up now that Wyatt and Destiny were married, as well as Jake and Madison.

She had always been close to all her brothers, particularly Josh when they were young, so Josh and Abby would give her support. Abby had a heart of gold and would be as kind as Josh.

Looking again at the calendar, she picked up her phone and called Savannah and in minutes made arrangements to see her.

By noon she was showered and dressed. She studied herself in the mirror, turning first one way and then another, knowing it was ridiculous to expect to see any change yet. Her cell phone rang. When she saw it was Tony, she ignored the call.

* * *

Smiling, Savannah opened the back door. "Come in. Mike is out on the ranch somewhere and you said not to call him, so I didn't. Scotty is napping."

"I'll make this short, Savannah. I wanted to talk to just you. Not Mike. And not Scotty right now."

"Sure. Come in," Savannah said, stepping back out of the way and shaking her blond hair away from her face. "Want a cool drink?" Savannah asked.

"Ice water would be fine, and you sit and let me get it and whatever you want to drink. I know this kitchen almost as well as my own."

"I'm a little clumsy, but I'm not feeble. I can get us glasses of water," Savannah said as she turned to wash her hands and get down glasses. Lindsay's gaze ran over Savannah's navy T-shirt and jeans. She knew Savannah's baby was due in October, which was only weeks away now that it was already the first day of September. Savannah's round belly didn't look big enough to deliver in another month. "You don't look very pregnant."

"I feel very, very pregnant. And believe me, there's no such thing as not very pregnant."

Lindsay laughed politely, but she still couldn't cope with the prospect of being pregnant or joke about it. Each time she thought about it, she also wondered how she would ever tell Tony. She had no answer to that one.

In minutes they had glasses of water and sat in the family room. Savannah gazed at her. "I heard you and Tony got along fine on your auction date. And you've been out with him since."

"I suppose it's impossible to keep our going out together private as long as we go out in Texas."

"I don't imagine you can. Both of you know many

people," Savannah said. She sipped her water. "Are you okay, Lindsay?" she asked finally.

"I don't know. That's why I think you're the one to talk to. I do need to keep this secret awhile and I thought about you being from Little Rock. I need to see an obstetrician without my family or anyone else around here knowing except you and Mike. Savannah, I think I'm pregnant with Tony's baby."

"Oh, my word," Savannah said, her blue eyes growing wide. "I know that's a shock."

"It is a shock that I haven't adjusted to, but I want it officially confirmed."

"Maybe you're worrying needlessly."

"I don't think so. I feel it to my bones."

"Oh, my. It'll be better than what I went through, although it led me to Mike. With Tony, it'll be good. He'll marry you, Lindsay. It's obvious you have made peace with each other. And the whole Calhoun family loves Tony. And he's so good to Scotty. Scotty is crazy about Tony even though they don't see each other often."

"I can't imagine Tony wanting to marry me and I don't want to marry Tony. I don't want to marry any rancher. Until Tony, I've never even dated one. Marriage to one would be a perpetual clash because I want to run my ranch my own way and I don't want some other rancher telling me to change the way I do things. And Tony is a take-charge person."

"Oh, dear." Savannah frowned. "You might have a problem."

"I have a big problem."

"Are you sure you're pregnant?"

"About ninety-nine percent, but that's why I want your doctor's name. I should see a doctor before I get Tony all stirred up. Other than you and Mike, I don't want anyone else to know I even suspect I'm pregnant until I verify it. Then I can tell Tony. I haven't even tried a home pregnancy test yet because I'll have to drive so far to get away from everyone I know, but I'm going today." She shook her head. "Even though I know what the outcome will be."

"Let me call my doctor's office and introduce you, then you can get on and make an appointment. Until you have a home test and the lab tests and have a doctor confirm your condition, you don't know for sure. You may not even be pregnant and may be worrying for nothing."

"Hopefully not, but if I had to bet, I'd bet the ranch that I am."

Savannah's eyes widened. "You mean that?"

Lindsay shrugged. "You get a feeling for things, you know?"

"Mike says you have a knack for knowing things and a touch that's just right. He's impressed by your abilities."

"That's nice. He hasn't mentioned that to me."

Savannah laughed. "You're his little sister. He probably doesn't realize he hasn't told you." She stood up. "Let me make that call before Scotty is up or Mike comes home. This doctor is so good about working people into his schedule."

Within the next thirty minutes Lindsay had an appointment in Little Rock on Thursday.

She sat again to face Savannah. "I really thank you for this. That was very nice."

"I'm glad to help. I only hope Mike doesn't suspect anything."

"Savannah, I don't want you to have to keep secrets from Mike. Just make it clear that you two are the only ones I'm telling at this point."

"I can wait a bit to tell Mike. He'll understand."

"You really don't need to, but thanks. I better go."

They walked to the door. "Take care of yourself," Savannah said. "Call me after you see the doctor. I'm your sister-in-law, and I'm also your friend. I can give you my doctor's name in Dallas, too." They gazed at each other and Savannah reached out to hug Lindsay.

"Thanks, Savannah. You're really good for Mike and good for our family."

"He and Scotty and the Calhouns are wonderful for me, too. Take care of yourself."

"I will," Lindsay said, and hurried to her pickup to drive home.

Thursday she drove to Dallas and flew to Little Rock to go to the doctor's office. She was thankful no one would know or question what she was doing or where she was going. The only person who came close was Abe, who had worked for her family since he was seventeen. She saw the questions in his eyes, but he didn't voice them.

The only thing that indicated his feelings was when she told him goodbye.

"Lindsay, if you want me to do anything, let me know," he said, looking intently at her, and she was certain he knew she had something she was hiding.

"Thanks. I will. I'm all right," she answered, looking into his light brown eyes. "I have my phone and if I need anything, I'll call. I'll be back tomorrow about noon."

"Sure," he said. He settled his brown hat on his head, nodded and headed back to the barn as she climbed into her pickup to drive to Dallas.

Now as she got out of the cab in front of the obstetrician's office, she felt her heart start to pound and her palms sweat.

But that anxiety was nothing to what she felt when she came out.

She felt so stressed she had to stop on the sidewalk. She stood staring and not seeing anything in front of her. Hot September sunshine blazed overhead, but chills skidded up her spine. She had known for the past two weeks that she was pregnant, but to have it confirmed by a home pregnancy test and now, to hear it officially announced by a physician after a lab test made it real.

How was she ever going to tell Tony?

Seven

Tony threw himself into work, coming home nights to an empty house that he had never felt alone in before. Constantly, he remembered Lindsay in his arms, and he wanted to talk to her or see her again. Every time he reached for the phone, he stopped, reminding himself she wanted them to break off seeing each other and he should, too, because it was inevitable.

In spite of logic, he missed seeing her. He knew from one of the men who worked for him that she had gone to Dallas and he wondered why and what she was doing there. He would get over her soon because he knew as well as she did, in spite of their truce, they were still the same people and she remained stubborn as ever. It was just a matter of time before there was another conflict between them, something she seemed to thrive on. Though common sense told him that he was better off without her, he missed her in a way he wouldn't have thought possible.

He woke up on Friday morning and she was still on his mind. He knew time would take care of this longing for her, but right now memories of her wouldn't stop coming.

He rose and got ready for a first-thing-in-the-morning meeting with Keane, who had problems with one of their trucks.

Tony stood on his porch with his foreman, who had his hat pushed far enough back on his head to reveal a pale strip on his forehead where his hat always shaded him. His tangled, curly brown hair framed his face. He was shorter than Tony, slightly stocky and the most capable ranch hand Tony had ever had.

"Keane, I heard an animal howling last night. I've seen it before on Lindsay's ranch," he said, remembering the eerie howls that had been so forlorn and sounded like an injured animal. As he had listened, he understood why the howls had unnerved Lindsay and caused her to call. They'd been jarring in the night, even to him. He'd finally got up and retrieved a rifle, switching off yard lights and stepping out on his dark porch. He'd seen it plainly in the moonlight, but he'd paused as he lifted his rifle, remembering Lindsay's request that the animal not be put down. He'd lowered his rifle and walked back inside to lock up, put away his rifle and go back to bed.

"It might be a dog," he told Keane now. "Might be a coyote. Lindsay thinks it's a wolf and she doesn't want it put down unless it starts killing livestock. Pass the word to leave it alone unless it kills something and until we know it isn't a big dog."

"Sure. Have you seen it?"

"Yes. It's big, has black and gray shaggy fur and, frankly, it does resemble a wolf, but I can't imagine it is."

Keane had a faint smile. "You know that old legend."

"If I thought that were possible, which I don't, I'd try to catch and tame the critter and I'd wish for rain."

"Amen to that one," Keane said, glancing at the sky. "Still none in the forecast. No break in the heat, either—over a hundred today. When it does rain, the ground will soak up water like a sponge. It'll just disappear. We need a month of rains."

"Right. Well, I'll see about replacing that truck," Tony said, and turned to go.

While Tony worked all day alongside the men, keeping his hands busy, he couldn't keep his mind from returning to Lindsay.

On second thought, he told himself, maybe he should tame that wolf and wish for amnesia. That might be the only way he'd forget her.

Feeling torn, miserable and caught in an uncustomary inability to make a decision, Lindsay stared at her dinner. She didn't want to eat but knew she should. Her thoughts were constantly on Tony. It seemed with each day she dreaded telling him about the baby more and more. She had to before she began to show and word got back to him. But when?

First she needed to go see Scotty, to hold him and think about having her own little baby, and then she needed to talk to Mike who would probably be a bulwark in the storm that would eventually rage around her. She didn't want to hide behind her brother from Tony, but Mike would take a levelheaded view of the situation and he and Savannah would support her in what she wanted to do.

Maybe she just needed to take Tony's call, go out with him and tell him the news. Get it over with and move on with her life and planning for her baby. Maybe Tony would back off and leave her alone.

She knew better than to expect that to happen. Mr. Take-Charge would dominate her life when she told him. Each time she thought of that happening, she was filled with dread.

She played with different scenarios in her mind: telling him soon, waiting four or five months to tell him or not saying a word until she had to. Like maybe when the baby was born.

As she headed to her house Friday afternoon, she was wrapped in worries and indecision and through it all, though she hated to admit it to herself, she missed Tony. She was so tired she paid little attention to her familiar surroundings until she steered her pickup toward the back of her house and saw a truck near the back gate. Frowning, she glanced at the house and saw Mike seated on the porch with his feet propped on the rail while he whittled.

She didn't know whether to be happy or annoyed with him and wondered whether Savannah had made him come.

As Lindsay parked behind his pickup and stepped out, Mike rose to his feet and put his knife away, along with whatever he had been whittling while he waited at the top of the steps. "What are you doing here?" she asked as she walked up the steps.

"Waiting to see if you need a big brother's hug," he said.

His kindness shook her and she walked into his arms. "I do," she whispered.

He hugged her, then stepped away to smile. "Let's go inside where we can talk and it's not a hundred degrees in the shade."

She tried to smile. "You mean where I can cry without

someone seeing me," she said, unlocking the door and leading the way. "Want a beer?"

"I'd like one, but not if it's going to make you want one."

"No. No problem there. I'll drink ice water." When they had drinks and were seated in the cool family room that overlooked the porch, patio and swimming pool, she sat facing him.

He had hung his hat on a hook in the entry hall and he raked his fingers through his hair. "Savannah said that you gave her permission to tell me." Mike leaned forward to place his elbows on his knees. "Here comes some brotherly advice and words of infinite wisdom."

She smiled. "There are moments I'm truly glad you're my big brother."

"I'm happy to hear that," he said. "There are moments I'm truly glad you're my little sis," he said, smiling at her. "Lindsay, don't forget for one minute that you have three brothers and three sisters-in-law who will support you in every way we can."

Tears threatened and she wiped her eyes. "Look at me, Mike. Do you know how few times in my life I've cried?"

"Chalk it up to hormone changes," he said. "I just want you to always remember you have our support and you can call me or Savannah anytime you want."

"Thanks. That means a lot," she said, meaning it with all her heart.

"Next thing—if being pregnant gets you down, just think of Scotty. You shower him with love and he seems to be a huge joy to you. He loves you and I know you love him. A baby in your life will be great."

"I know that and I do love Scotty beyond measure. He's adorable and I feel so close to him."

"He's a good kid. And he's going to love your baby. I

can promise you that. I'll let you tell Scotty when you're ready because he is very excited over Savannah's baby. He'll go into orbit over yours."

She smiled. "Maybe not so much if I have a girl."

"Oh, yes, he will. You wait and see. So now the next thing I want to mention, even if you don't want to hear it, is Tony. He's a good guy. I like Tony, and all the guys who work for him like him. All your brothers and sisters-in-law like him."

"I know that."

"Obviously, the two of you can get along. You were seeing each other after the auction."

"Does everyone in the state know we were going out together?"

"C'mon, Lindsay. All the Calhoun ranches and Milan ranches and the people that work on them—cleaning staff, cooks, cowboys—you think they don't get around and see who is leaving a ranch and who is entering one? Or talk about who they saw when they're out? The grapevine is alive and well in these parts. You and Tony were discreet about it, but your whole family probably knows you dated. Anyway, cut him some slack. He'll be shocked, but he's going to welcome this baby like I would, and you know it."

"Maybe that's what worries me. Tony is a take-charge guy."

Mike grinned. "I'm considering the source of that statement. Now, one last thing—would you like me to tell Mom and Dad before you talk to them?"

She thought about her parents and closed her eyes. She rubbed her hands together and looked at Mike. "Will Dad threaten Tony if he doesn't marry me? I haven't even wanted to think about dealing with our parents and, thank heavens, they're in California and have their own lives."

"Get some plans made before you tackle telling them. Tony's the one who has the difficult parents. Listen, all the rest of us will stand by you and between you and our folks. Mom will just have hysterics and faint."

Lindsay smiled and relaxed slightly. "Sounds ridiculous, but I think that might be exactly what she'll do. I've resisted her tears and hysterics plenty of times."

"The rest of us just hide from her. You're the brave one," he said, grinning. "Frankly, I don't think you'll have any pressure from our parents. They have their own lives, and I think when we grew up they let us go."

"I'm grateful for that. Tony is the person who worries me."

"You two will work it out." Mike squeezed her shoulder gently. He finished his beer and stood. "I've said what I wanted to say. I'll go home now. We're there for you—call in the middle of the night if you need us. You and Tony will work this out because you both love your families and you each will love this baby with all your hearts. You'll see."

"So when did you get to be such a counselor?" she said. Mike hadn't mentioned it, but she wondered if he or her other brothers would pressure her to marry Tony. "You know, even if we can be civil, Tony may not propose."

"There will probably be more than one pot for bets on that one," Mike remarked drily as they walked to the back door. Before they stepped outside, she closed her hand around his wrist.

"Thanks. Your advice might be a bit misguided, but your intentions are wonderful. You have cheered me up and I don't feel quite so alone."

"Lindsay, you should know your family well enough to know how very un-alone you are. Jake would be right here if you need him, or Josh. Tony's family will be the same." He stepped out on the porch, then resumed his talk. "There'll be plenty of kids on both sides of the family for your little one to bond with and to grow up with. Tony's sister, Madison, is pregnant. His brother Nick has a son, Cody, who is Scotty's age. I'll have another baby before yours is born. It'll be great." He reached out and gave her another hug.

"If only the father wasn't so take-charge and so stubborn."

"Said the kettle about the pot. You two are exactly alike in some ways and you're a strong enough woman to deal with most any man." He put his hat back on and made for the steps, then turned to her again. "Jake and Josh and I can go beat him up for you if you want."

"Mike, don't you dare!" He grinned and she saw he was teasing her. "Mike, shame on you, and I fell for it when I should know better."

"I made you smile," he said, sounding satisfied. "I gotta run, sis."

Lindsay followed him to his pickup. "Thanks for coming. I'll call Savannah and thank her. I liked her doctor—he was very nice, cheerful and kind. Now that I know for certain I'm pregnant, I'll have to find one around here. Savannah has one in Dallas she likes, so I'll probably get that name from her."

"When the time comes, you can stay at my house in Dallas if you want. If you stay on the ranch, you'll be a long way from your doctor and hospital."

"Thanks. We'll see."

"If you stay here, I guess it's a consolation that everyone on the place can probably deliver a baby."

"That's definitely not what I have in mind," she said

while she stood in the hot sun with her hands on her hips and stared at him.

"Call me and I'll do it." Grinning, he jumped into the truck and revved the engine.

"You're a wonderful brother, but you're not delivering my baby."

"For that matter, Tony can. He's good at delivering calves."

"Enough of you planning my life. How did I get tangled up with so many bossy men?"

"I think we're called alpha males," Mike corrected.

"Not in my view. I'll see you soon. Thanks for coming over."

"Sure." He smiled at her. "See you soon," he said, pulling along the driveway to head back to his ranch.

Smiling, she waved, but as the pickup drove out of sight leaving a plume of dust behind, her smile faded. None of Mike's cheerful advice or reminders of what a good guy Tony was changed the fact that Tony ran everything he could in his daily life. He was commanding, decisive, a Mr. Do-It-My-Way. Even as she enumerated those attributes, she felt a pain in her chest because she missed him. She ignored the feeling, certain it soon would stop haunting her and disappear forever.

She could tell him now, or she could tell him later. She was in for a fight and she felt it coming any which way she looked at her future.

Eight

Lost in thought, she walked into the house, mulling over how and when she would tell Tony.

By midnight she wasn't any closer to a solution. She sat in her darkened bedroom, looking out over her ranch and wondering what course of action she should follow. When the baby came, she would face more decisions. Stay home and take care of her baby all day or hire a nanny and go back to ranch work?

Eventually, she figured, that's probably what she would do, but she wanted to be home with her baby those first few months no matter what she decided to do later. Would she have to buy a house in Verity to secure a nanny or would she be able to find someone to live on the ranch? But maybe she was jumping the gun. First, she needed to find a doctor and have the baby.

She rubbed her forehead and thought about Mike's offer of his Dallas house in her ninth month. Tony might have some issue with that, being that he had a place in Dallas, too.

Tony. Mentioning his name made her remember he hadn't called her the past few days. Did he know she had been away from the ranch? She guessed he probably did, but he also knew she always had her phone. Had she heard the last from him until she contacted him?

On top of her worries and her woes, she missed Tony. He was too many wonderful things to suddenly have him disappear from her life and not feel his absence. She missed his energy, his optimism, his charm, his sexy ways. She didn't want to admit it, but a considerable amount of joy and excitement had gone out of her life. She dreamed about him at night, thought about him constantly during the day. Did Tony miss her at all?

The following Friday Tony climbed from his pickup after a long day. He'd helped some of his men clear a field. He was hot and dirty. He wanted a shower and a steak and he wanted to spend the evening with Lindsay. Since she hadn't taken his calls or answered his texts, he'd interpreted that as a sign she wanted to be left alone and he'd stopped calling. But that didn't stop him from wanting her.

He changed and went to his gym to work off the pent-up anxiety he felt from thinking about her. Exercising helped, as did swimming laps in his pool. But when he lay back in the pool, Lindsay invaded his thoughts once again. It was ridiculous, he told himself. If he didn't hear from her by next week, he promised himself he'd go out and forget all about her.

He swam laps until he couldn't stand to swim one more. Climbing out, he went in to shower and change, then work on taxes and his records. Later, he lay in the darkness, wanting sleep to come, hoping it was not another night of dreams filled with Lindsay.

During the night, he woke to hear a long, piercing howl. Stepping out of bed, he walked onto his balcony and gazed into the night. After a few minutes, another howl cut through the night. This one seemed to come from somewhere close to the barn nearest to his house.

Returning to his room, he pulled on his clothes and got a rifle. He went outside again to sit and wait, but the howls had stopped. He sat thinking about Lindsay, remembering times together, until he noticed the sky was getting lighter. It was dawn, so he went inside to shower and dress for the day.

After he had breakfast, he headed to the barn. Curious to see if he could find any signs of an animal, he knelt down and searched. But it was unlikely he'd find tracks in the hard, baked earth, so he rose and walked along slowly, studying the ground and turning a corner where thick bushes grew. He heard the faintest whine and froze for a minute. Then he moved slowly and cautiously toward the bushes, stopping instantly when he looked into a pair of brown eyes.

For a startled moment he thought it was a wolf, but then his gaze ran over the animal and he realized it was a big, furry gray-and-black male dog and it was hurt.

As the dog whimpered, Tony moved slowly, holding out his hand, wishing he had brought a piece of meat or something to offer. He spoke softly to the animal and knelt beside him. The dog tried to raise its head but lay back, watching him and giving one thump of its tail.

"Hey, boy," Tony said, speaking softly. "You're hurt." He saw the coat, tangled and matted with blood. One front leg and one hind leg each had bloody gashes. Tony pulled out his phone to call Keane.

***

Two hours later the dog was awake again, sedatives wearing off. Cleaned and bandaged, he lay in a stall in the barn on a blanket that had been tossed over hay spread on the floor. The barn was air-conditioned and comfortable.

Keane had helped Tony with the dog and, later, Doc Williams had stopped by. Now Tony was alone, sitting on the blanket by the dog and scratching its ears. He pulled out his phone and called Lindsay.

Warmth heated him at the sound of her voice. "I'm glad you answered."

"I've been in Dallas," she said, a cautious note in her voice that he'd never heard before.

He let her answer go without comment even though her phone had also been in Dallas. "Remember the howls and the coyote/wolf/dog?"

"Yes," she said, curiosity filling her voice so she sounded more like herself.

"He's in my barn. He was hurt, with lots of cuts. He may resemble a wolf, but he's actually just a big, furry gray dog that has been hurt. I thought you'd want to know."

"Oh, Tony, will he be all right?"

"Yes. Doc Williams has taken care of him. When the sedative completely wears off, he'll get a little steak. He's had some water. I held his head and sort of spoon-fed it to him. Want to come visit my patient?"

There was a pause. "Yes, I'll be there soon. Thanks for calling me. I'm headed to my pickup. By the way, how did you catch him?"

"I didn't catch him. He woke me in the night and when dawn came, I found him by the barn lying in the bushes where it was shady."

"I never thought about going to look for him. His

howling just gave me the creeps. But I'm so glad you rescued him. And it's a dog, huh?"

"Definitely. Mixed breed and looks like a wolf, but it's domesticated."

"It's wonderful that you saved him." He picked up the emotion in her voice.

"Well, well, Miss Tough Rancher is a real softie for dogs? How about men? Men named Tony?"

She laughed. "Maybe dogs."

He didn't press the point. He needed to slow down and just be happy that she'd taken his call. He brought the conversation back to the dog at his side. "Well, our patient already looks much better. Keane has a nice touch, and Doc said we did a good job. He said the dog has wounds from a fight. He's not sick, but Doc said he would stop by again and check on him."

"You're a good guy, Tony."

"I'm glad I can impress you," he said, brushing the dog's head as he talked. Despite his resolve, his eagerness to see Lindsay grew by the second. "We'll let you name him, Lindsay. Doc said no one had inquired about a lost dog that fit this one's description, and I've checked some ads and I don't see anything. I think he's homeless."

"I hope not any longer," she said breathlessly. "I hope you give him a home."

"We'll see how he fits in with the other dogs the guys keep on the ranch. I don't know what he's been fighting, but if he fights my dogs, I can't keep him."

"If you don't keep him, let me know." He heard her fumbling on the other end of the line, then she said, "I gotta go so I can drive."

"I'm in the first barn. Come on in."

"See you soon," she said and ended the call.

Putting away his phone, Tony smiled at the dog. He

was happy because Lindsay would soon be at his ranch. "Lindsay is coming to see you," he told the animal. "I hope she loves you and keeps coming to see you. Don't look too well too soon, okay, boy?"

The dog thumped its tail a few times. "I'll feed you in a while. Doc said to wait. Lindsay's going to love you and you're going to love her. Maybe you'll end up at her house and then I can come see you. Just be nice to all the ranch dogs. That's all that's required."

Big brown eyes looked up at him as the dog thumped his tail. Tony petted the dog's head gently, talking to it softly until he heard a motor. "Here she comes. Be a very nice dog now."

A pickup door slammed and Lindsay rushed in to stop in front of the stall. She had her hair in her usual braid and was in jeans and a blue T-shirt. She looked wonderful, and he fought the urge to get up, put his arms around her and kiss her.

"Hi, Tony. Oh, my, look at this beautiful dog," she said, coming into the stall to sit on the floor by Tony and reach out slowly to hold her hand in front of the dog, a treat in her palm.

He thumped his tail and raised his head slightly. His tongue licked out to take the treat.

"Oh, Tony, I'm so glad you didn't put him down. But he's all bandaged. Is he hurt badly?"

"Doc said he may limp. Other than that, he should heal just fine," Tony said, watching Lindsay instead of the dog. She smelled wonderful and she looked great. He still wanted to pull her into his arms and kiss her, but he knew that wasn't what she would want.

She placed her hand on the dog's head to pet him and he slowly thumped his tail.

"He has to get well. Thank you for calling me and

thanks for taking care of him. I think he's wonderful. Look at him. He's so sweet."

"You don't know if he's sweet yet. Remember, he still has the lingering effects of sedatives."

"He's sweet. You'll see. Look at those beautiful eyes."

"I am," Tony said, and she turned to look at him as he met her gaze.

She shook her head. "That's what I thought. You're not thinking about the dog."

"No, I'm not. It's good to see you."

She didn't respond to his statement. Instead, she teased him. "You know, if he had been a gray wolf, you could have had a wish granted, according to legend. As it is, you just became the owner of a stray dog."

"If I could have a wish, I'd wish that you'd go out with me tonight. But I guess, for the good of all, I would wish for rain this week."

"Doesn't matter. That was just a legend and he is just a dog." She petted him and Tony watched her. He couldn't help wishing those gentle hands were on his body, caressing him. But while her touch stilled the dog, it had aroused him.

"So," he prodded, "will you go out with me tonight?"

She turned to look at him solemnly, a slight frown on her brow, and he feared her answer. Then the frown disappeared and she nodded. "Tony, we need to talk," she said, suddenly sounding serious, as if she had something difficult to discuss. After her hesitation, she nodded again. "Yes. Tonight will be a big thank-you for rescuing this dog and giving him a home."

"Great. Let's go someplace fancy in Fort Worth. Someplace to dance, to talk and have a good time and super food, and then you can come back here and we'll see how our patient is doing."

Again he received a solemn look that puzzled him. "I don't know about coming back here, but we'll go out." Then, as if a thought just struck her, she asked, "But what about the dog? When you leave, he won't leave, will he?"

"I'll shut him in here where it's air-conditioned and he can be comfortable. In his condition, he can't get out. He'll have water and by that time I will have fed him something, so he should be all right."

"Do you want me to stay with him today?"

"Lindsay, I'm guessing you have a lot of things to do today."

She shrugged. "I suppose so, but I just don't want him to get up and go."

"He won't. I promise you."

She leaned down to croon to the dog and scratch behind his ears, and Tony took the opportunity to run his gaze over her. He didn't know if it was his imagination or just knowing what was beneath the clothes she wore, but she looked better than she used to with her braid, her old hat and jeans. Or was it because he hadn't seen her for a while and it was good to be with her again?

After a short time, she leaned back. "I need to get home, but I had to come see him."

They both stood and left the stall. While the dog raised its head, Tony closed the stall door and walked with Lindsay outside. "I'm glad you're going with me tonight. How about six so we have time to get to Fort Worth? I'll be glad to see you."

She smiled, but despite her acceptance of his dinner date, he sensed something off about her. Something had changed. There was a reluctance about her.

He tried to tease her out of her funk. "Still no fights between us, darlin'," he said quietly. "I'd say we've done well."

"Yes, we have, Tony. I hope it lasts," she said, and he had an even stronger feeling that something bothered her.

"Lindsay, come back into the barn for a minute."

She walked with him into the cool barn and turned to look at him with curiosity in her expression. "What's on your mind?"

"I wanted some privacy for us. Is anything wrong?"

Something flickered in her eyes and her cheeks became pink. "Not really. I just want to talk tonight."

He gazed into her eyes and wondered if he should probe more deeply. Then he figured they could talk tonight. But he couldn't let her go without doing one thing. When he stepped closer to place his hands on her shoulders, he felt her stiffen slightly. He studied her and then slipped his arm around her waist to kiss her.

"Tony, I should—" His lips on hers ended her talk.

For a moment she was resistant. Then all her stiffness vanished as she put her arms around his neck and returned his kiss passionately, a blazing kiss that meant whatever her problem was, she still couldn't cool the blazing sexual attraction between them.

When she stepped away, he let her go. She was breathing as hard as he was and they looked at each other a moment. Her blue eyes seemed clouded with worry. Turning away, she rushed out to her pickup.

"I need to get home, Tony. See you tonight," she called over her shoulder.

He hurried to watch her while she started the pickup. Gravely, she glanced at him and then drove away.

He stared after her. Something had definitely changed since the last time they were together. He didn't know what it was, unless she was trying not to tell him that she didn't care to go out with him again or receive phone calls from him. But knowing her as he did, he was certain she would have just said it.

That day was inevitable and he probably shouldn't have called her, but he knew she would want to see the dog. Oh, who was he kidding? He'd called because he wanted to see her. The dog was just an excuse. As much as he told himself to leave her alone and forget her, he couldn't stay away. His body seemed to crave her, the way a starving man craves food. Maybe tonight would be different, he told himself. Maybe tonight the reluctance and resistance he'd sensed in her would disappear. He could only hope.

He retrieved his hat and headed to his pickup to catch up with Keane and see how they were coming on clearing the land for the new pond.

But as he drove, he couldn't stop the niggling feeling that something big was going to happen tonight. Something sure as hell was wrong with Lindsay and he could only wonder what.

Lindsay spent the rest of the day at her house. Part of the time she helped her cook, Rosalee. Part of the time she was shut in her room deciding what to wear and how to tell Tony about her pregnancy.

She had wanted to wait, make her own decisions, but she couldn't go back to the carefree, happy times when she was with him after the auction. She had decided to tell him immediately and face dealing with him. It would come sooner or later and she wanted the battle over and done.

She wanted to look her best when she told him. When he was dazzled by her, Tony was much more cooperative. Take the night of the auction, for example. But then, that night she'd had surprise on her side. Oh, she had a surprise this time, all right. One that might make him faint.

Rummaging in her closet, she selected a black dress she had bought on impulse when she had been shopping in Dallas. She had never worn it, just because no occasion had arisen, but tonight should be one.

She yanked off her jeans to try on the dress. Before she pulled it on, she stopped to look at herself in the mirror. Even though it was too soon for physical changes, she couldn't keep from looking for them. It was satisfying to see she looked as slim as ever. Change was inevitable, but she hoped it didn't show really early. She wanted to keep working on the ranch, and if any of the guys noticed and realized, word would get to Abe. He would insist she stop and if she didn't, he'd probably talk to her brothers about it.

By five in the afternoon Rosalee had finished and left for the weekend. Lindsay had bathed and still worked to fix her hair, planning to leave it down in long spiral curls around her face.

As the time drew closer for Tony to arrive, her nerves became more raw. She dreaded talking to him, knowing all the peace between them would go up in flames tonight and they would each have to make a big effort to be civil and work out how they would deal with their new situation. Most of the changes would be in her life, but Tony would have adjustments and decisions, too. And their dates, their lovemaking, the fun they'd had—all that was over. It wasn't something she expected to get back in her life.

Feeling she had reached a point where her appearance was the best she could do, she went to the front window to watch for him coming up the drive. After a moment she stepped out on her porch to sit in a wooden rocker. In spite of the hot weather, she was chilled. Mounting dread about revealing her pregnancy to Tony enveloped her. She could anticipate his reactions and she suspected battles with him would fill the coming weeks. Underneath that dread was an undercurrent of anticipation, because she would finally be with him again.

When his sports car came into view, her pulse jumped. He might be bossy, but he still was the most charming, exciting, sexy man she had ever known. She went inside to take one more look at herself in the mirror, then stood waiting for the doorbell. Was she about to face her biggest struggle ever with Tony?

As Tony drove up the driveway to Lindsay's ranch house, his eagerness to see her grew. He'd been nervous all day to find out what disturbed her but, right now, knowing he'd see her in minutes, he couldn't help hoping for another hot, sexy night of lovemaking.

Never in his life had he been deeply involved in a serious relationship and he knew he wouldn't start now with Lindsay. They were just too different. Even so, at the moment he wanted to be with her; he missed talking to her and seeing her. He feared their tenuous relationship might be close to termination right now, but he intended to enjoy tonight to the fullest.

When the door swung open, his heart thudded and for seconds all he did was stare.

Lindsay wore another pair of stiletto heels with thin sexy straps crossing her slender feet, which matched her black sleeveless dress. Her plunging vee neckline revved his pulse another notch. Her straight, short skirt revealed her legs for him to view. Had she left her hair falling freely around her face to please him? Probably not, but he'd enjoy it anyway.

"You look gorgeous, Lindsay," he said. He was breathless, his voice deeper. "That black dress is killer on you."

She smiled at him, but it wasn't the wholehearted smile he had received before. "You've never been in my house. Come on in and look around."

He stepped in and the second he inhaled her perfume, he wanted to hold her and kiss her and forget about going out to dinner or eating anything for hours. He could cancel the reservations in Fort Worth and stay right here beside her.

He walked alongside her through a short hallway that opened out into a wide hall with a spiral staircase to the next floor. Above, a beamed ceiling was three stories high with skylights that let light pour into the house.

On either side of the stairs, the house opened up into spacious areas defined only by columns, furniture groupings and area rugs. The open rooms, high ceilings and lots of glass made the already large house seem twice as big.

"Like many other things about you, your house surprises me," he said. "It's beautiful, but not what I ever expected. I pictured you in a house more Western, but not the way you pictured mine would be. Just leather furniture and Western scenes in the paintings and traditional Western decor." He strolled into a living area he'd glimpsed from the hall and noticed a second-floor balcony extending over the length of one side of the room and the French period pieces upholstered in elegant silks and antique satins.

"Now I can picture you in your house," he said. "At least in part of it."

He turned to find her staring at him intently with a slight frown. Her expression jolted him. Just as he'd feared, something was very wrong and he didn't have a clue what it was.

"Lindsay, what's the problem?" he asked, unfastening the one button on his jacket and slipping out of it. He placed it on a chair. "Looks as if we need to talk."

As she wound her fingers together, her knuckles whitened. He took her hands in his.

"The weight of the world might as well be on your shoulders. Whatever is bothering you can't be that bad." He bent his knees so he could look directly into her eyes. Silently, he studied her.

"Before we talk, I think it would be wise to cancel our dinner reservation. I debated just telling you to come over for dinner, but I thought I might not have the courage to talk to you tonight—"

"Damn, Lindsay, what the hell? Is it—"

"Don't start guessing. Cancel the dinner reservation. My cook was here today and I had her leave us a casserole if either of us feels like eating later."

Watching her, he pulled out his phone, looked down and sent a short text. He put away his phone.

"I think you might like a drink. I'll get you a beer," she said.

Mystified, he stared after her. Whatever this was, the problem disturbed her a hell of a lot more than any other she'd encountered while he'd known her. From the way she was acting, it seemed even catastrophic.

Was it the ranch? Did she have to sell it? If she did, she wouldn't have any trouble telling him. Nor could it involve anyone in her family; he didn't think she would hesitate letting him know that.

He knew she had gone to Dallas recently. He also realized she had another life away from her ranch. Was it someone else? Did she have a lover in Dallas? No, she wouldn't have stayed with Tony if there'd been anyone else.

So why did she go to Dallas? Did she have some illness and need a big-city doctor?

She looked as healthy as anyone could hope to be, even though that was no indication of how she might feel or why she would have to see a doctor. The thought that Lindsay was sick was like a punch to his middle. What was wrong and how serious was it? Was it incurable? That question almost buckled his knees.

He watched her behind the bar fixing their drinks and went to join her. The more he thought about it, the more convinced he was that she had gone to Dallas because of a medical problem. She knew when she told him he'd need a drink.

What the hell could be so wrong that she knew ahead of time and it involved him enough for her to expect him to be upset?

His knees did almost cave on that one. He sat on the nearest bar stool while he stared without seeing anything and his head spun.

One possibility occurred to him and he knew in every inch of his being that he guessed correctly. Taking deep breaths, he looked up to see her coming around the bar with a glass of ice water for herself and a whiskey on the rocks for him.

"I thought you might prefer this," she said, handing him his drink. She frowned. "Tony, you look white as a sheet."

"You're pregnant, aren't you? You're carrying my baby."

Nine

"How did you find out?"

He closed his eyes. "Wow," he whispered. "I just figured it out. I tried to think of reasons for you to go to Dallas. And reasons for the big change in you since the way you were with me before you went to Dallas. And when you offered to get a drink for me, I realized it had to involve me, too. There was only one thing I could think of." He reached for the drink she held out. "I think I need that whiskey now."

He downed it in one swallow and set down an empty glass. "I'm in shock. You're going to have to give me a minute to digest this bit of news," he said. "You've had time to think about it a little."

He sat there staring at the floor but not seeing anything, just thinking about the changes coming in his life—changes that would be monumental.

He would be a father. Lindsay would have his child.

He was so dazed he knew he couldn't even fathom the changes that would downright transform his life. He couldn't even try.

There would be no financial worries for either one of them, so he could cross that concern off his list. But there was one giant problem—and only one solution.

He pulled himself together as best he could and stood up to take her hand.

"Lindsay, marry me."

His words didn't have the desired effect. Instead, he watched a transformation come over her and he had a sinking feeling a proposal wasn't what she wanted. Once again her stubbornness surfaced. He could see that in the set to her jaw and the fire in her eyes. Annoyance filled him as it always had. From the start he had known she always stirred up conflict, and this was no exception.

"Tony, that's a knee-jerk reaction. You take some time and think this through. I'm financially well-fixed, so that's not a consideration. I have a big, supportive family, so I'll have all the help I need. The biggest reason I can't marry you is that we are basically not compatible." Before he could make a point, she added, "You're bossy and arrogant and you want to take charge of every situation—which is exactly what you're doing right now. I don't want you telling me what to do."

Impatience stabbed him. Every issue was a conflict with her. Why did he think for one second this wouldn't be? She was, as always, her usual stubborn self. But then his gaze roamed over her and for an instant he forgot everything. She was stunning. Even steeped in worry, when he looked at her, she took his breath away.

"Lindsay, stop and think and consider my proposal. Don't answer now. It's the logical solution for a lot of reasons, plus we get along great in some ways."

With a slight frown, she started to answer, and he placed his finger on her soft lips. "Shh. Don't answer me now—give my proposal time and think of all the positive reasons to do this. We can be compatible, we have these big families that have drawn close and we'll be thrown together constantly. All you're thinking about right now is that I'm a rancher and how I run my ranch. Just think of all the things in our lives and give my offer consideration." He walked behind the bar to pour another drink. He stood there, not saying a word, sipping the whiskey while she was quiet. He suspected she was getting her argument lined up.

Shock still reverberated in him. Of all people—Lindsay would have his baby.

Everything fell into place—why she didn't want to see him, why she was so somber. He walked to the window with his back to Lindsay and the room and stared outside. His entire life was about to change drastically. After a few moments he turned around to find her still standing where he had left her. She looked at him but said nothing.

His mind reeled with questions. He gave one voice. "When did you find out?"

She told him. "As soon as I realized I was late, I had a feeling. I went to a doctor and had the lab work done. I wanted to confirm it before I told you."

He nodded. "This is something I thought would never happen—an unplanned pregnancy. I know you thought the same thing."

They lapsed into silence again as he contemplated the changes coming in his life. Fatherhood. Coming fast and unexpected.

"Did you get a doctor in Dallas? I assume that's why you went."

"No. I know too many people there. I called Savannah

and got an appointment with her doctor in Little Rock. I didn't want word to get back to you until I could tell you myself. I didn't think about you guessing correctly."

"Well, you'll have to find a doc closer than Little Rock," he remarked drily. "Damn."

"I will. I just couldn't take a chance going to any big Texas city where I could have run into someone I know."

Another silence fell and he was thankful again that she was giving him a chance to adjust to his new status before they talked very much.

"There are a few things I think we can decide tonight."

As he stared at her, he thought, *Here we go*. She sat at the edge of a pale antique satin sofa and crossed her legs. Long, beautiful legs—the best pair of legs he had ever seen. As he looked at her, he noted that her blond hair was like a halo around her head. In almost every respect, he knew this woman would be the best mother possible for his child. He just hadn't planned on fatherhood so soon. And he and Lindsay were not in love. She didn't like ranchers. He didn't like her stubborn streak, her knack for constantly living in conflict.

"We should keep this between us for a little longer, if possible," he said, "until we make some major decisions about the future."

She nodded. "When people hear I'm expecting a baby, I'm going to get questions."

"That's fine with me. Whatever you want. You said Savannah knows and, I'm assuming, Mike. Who else?"

"Besides you, no one else. Believe me, Mike and Savannah know how to keep quiet."

"Good. It's better for both of us to keep it quiet for now," he repeated. "You don't show at all and I doubt if you will for another month. That gives us time." He became silent, his thoughts swirling in his head. Like a mantra, one statement kept reverberating in his mind. Lindsay was pregnant with his baby.

His gaze swept over her again. She was the most beautiful woman he had ever known. And the sexiest. He remembered their lovemaking, which was never out of his thoughts long. Marriage to her would have big pluses, if her stubbornness didn't overshadow the rest.

She'd had a bit of time to think about this and adjust to the prospect of being pregnant, so she might have already made decisions about the future. He'd better come out of shock and plan what they should do.

Minutes ticked past while he tried to sort through the jumble of thoughts, possibilities and outcomes. Finally, her voice broke the silence.

"I never thought this would be a problem I'd have," she said, gazing up at him. Her blue eyes were wide and clear.

"There's a simple solution I've already given you." She directed a steady look at him and he could feel the battles looming between them. "Lindsay, we're going to have a baby," he said. "You know I'll love this baby with all my heart."

"I know you will," she replied.

"Did the doctor tell you an approximate due date?"

"Next May."

"Then we should have that wedding soon," he said, and her eyes flared.

"I'll do what I feel I have to do," she said, the old tension coming between them again. He could feel the first stir of his own anger over her answer. Trying to curb it, reminding himself of the huge upheaval this would cause in her life, he crossed the space between them to draw her to her feet and place his hands on her shoulders. She stiffened.

He could feel barriers coming up between them. Anger

plagued him over her stubborn refusal to cooperate, which showed in her body language as well as her facial expression.

But who was he kidding? In spite of the problems and differences between them, he still wanted her—in his arms, in his bed. The minute he touched her, that familiar desire flared up in every part of him, and if he wasn't mistaken, he caught the same response in her.

Unable to resist any longer, he pulled her into his arms to kiss her hard and passionately. For an instant she pushed against him, but he couldn't step away if he wanted to, and in seconds, her arm went around his neck and she surrendered to his kiss. It was all the invitation he needed.

In one motion he peeled away her black dress while he continued to kiss her. When her bra was gone, he caressed her breasts, kissing first one and then the other. Her moans and soft breaths encouraged him to take her. He paused only long enough to strip off his clothes. Then, naked and hard, he picked her up and lowered her onto the sofa. Without a second's hesitation he entered her in one smooth thrust. She was ready for him. Hard and fast, they moved together. Quickly, desperately, she clutched him to her as she climaxed with him, her cries muted by his frantic kisses. They both gasped for breath as wave after wave of ecstasy washed over them.

For Tony, though it was fast and furious, this was the best lovemaking he'd ever had. He leaned back to tell her as much till he saw the look in her eyes. He'd expected a contented haze; instead, he found a storm brewing in their blue depths.

She stared at him and he could feel her anger rising again.

Instead of lashing out, she simply pushed him off her.

"I'm going to shower, Tony. I'll be back shortly," she said, still breathless. She yanked up her clothes and left.

He watched her walk away and wondered if he could ever get her to listen and cooperate or if they were at an impasse. Gathering his clothes, he went to find a bathroom and dress. As he did, his thoughts were on Lindsay. Would she even talk to him when she came back?

He returned to wait and soon she entered the room. As always, she made his heart beat faster. "You look gorgeous."

She had changed from her dress and wore a white linen blouse and white slacks with white high-heeled sandals and she still looked good enough to model.

"Thank you," she said in a dismissive manner, as if she barely heard what he had said. "Tony, I think our evening is over. I don't feel like dinner together."

He tried to curb the flash of anger that returned. Stubborn, stubborn woman who wanted life her way and her way only.

He wouldn't leave, not without reiterating his proposal. "Lindsay, the logical thing is for us to get married. Think about it tonight."

"I will," she said, but from the way she replied, with anger in her voice, he suspected the next time he saw her, he would get only arguments about marrying.

She raised her chin. "Do you really think we can get along in day-to-day living?"

They stared at each other and he felt the palpable clash of wills.

"See. I proved my point," she said. "Frankly, Tony, I'm trying to hang on to my temper. I really would like to scream at you for getting me pregnant, except I know full well that I had as much part in that happening as you did."

"Thank you for that one." At least she was rational. "Lindsay, I just see one solution and I hope you'll come to the same conclusion."

"We irritate each other."

"Sometimes, but we can get past the problems. I know now that beneath the tough rancher is a stunning, sexy woman who can simply melt me."

"Tony," she said impatiently, "whatever we found compatible in the past few weeks since the night of the auction… it's gone. That's over."

"Not altogether," he remarked drily. "We found it again less than an hour ago."

Anger flashed in her expression. She closed her mouth tightly while she glared at him.

"I know we need to work this out," she said after a few minutes of silence. "I just can't be the same person with you that I was."

"Don't stop communicating. I won't be cut off from my child. I want this baby in my life and I feel strongly that, if possible, a baby needs both a mom and a dad. That isn't always feasible, but in this case, it damn sure is, Lindsay," he said, trying to keep his temper.

Again, he got a glacial stare. "I know it, Tony. We both caused this and I agree that we both need to be in our baby's life. But don't pressure me," she snapped.

"Dammit, Lindsay. Before you make any decisions, stop and think about our baby. I'll talk to you later." He walked out before he lost it with her.

He slammed the door and hurried to his car, then drove away. Had she already closed her mind to his proposal?

Lindsay felt as if all the frustration and anger building in her since realizing she was pregnant had finally burst and she couldn't act as if nothing had changed between them.

His controlling personality had surfaced in a big way tonight—a glimpse of what she would live with if she even considered his proposal. She couldn't imagine being married to him and taking orders from him every day.

She hadn't been able to resist his kisses, succumbing to sex, but afterward she regretted the intimacy. Sure, there was no doubt they were sexually compatible but, as she'd said many times, sex wasn't everything. Outside the bedroom, she couldn't live with him.

She had wanted him to leave. She wanted to tell him goodbye and not see him again until she worked things out for her future.

One thing her feelings were certain about was that she was not going to marry Tony. That would be disastrous for both of them.

Just as she'd expected, he had tried to take over her life tonight. In marriage he would take over her ranch, tell her what to do on a daily basis. Besides, they weren't in love.

She could imagine Tony wanting to put both ranches together with him running everything while she stayed home to raise their child. That wasn't going to happen.

In spite of her irritation with him, when she looked at the sofa, she saw Tony there, his marvelous, strong body, his vitality, his sexy lovemaking that still now made a tremor run through her. But it was over.

Though she was too upset to sleep, she got ready for bed and sat in a chair in the dark, her eyes adjusting to the moonlight that spilled into her bedroom.

Knowing she should go to bed but certain she would just stare into the darkness and sleep would still escape her, she sat where she was until she finally fell asleep in her chair.

When she crawled into bed, it was almost four in the morning. As soon as her head touched the pillow, memories of better moments with Tony bombarded her. Then she thought about tonight with him and felt her anger return.

The next day she sent a text to Abe that she couldn't work. She needed to tell him about her pregnancy, but she had to get a grip on her emotions. When she talked to Abe, she had to be able to tell him that she had decided to turn the daily running of the ranch over to him, and she had to be able to say it without tears. She loved her ranch, working on it, raising her horses, dealing with livestock and making decisions. Her land was beautiful to her, spreading endlessly to a blue horizon with gorgeous sunrises and sunsets. Tony wasn't going to marry and take that away from her.

She had been nauseated after breakfast this morning and she wondered if that was something she would have every morning. She needed to find a Dallas doctor, as well as decide where she would live in her ninth month.

Three days later she still hadn't told Abe anything except that she couldn't work. Soon he would come to see about her, but she dreaded telling him. He could keep it quiet, that she could count on. But him knowing just made it more real.

She tried to do some of her paperwork, but she couldn't keep her mind on it. There was no call from Tony, but that didn't surprise her. What did surprise her was how much she missed him.

She sat staring into space and thinking about Tony. If she wouldn't marry him, would it hurt when he married later? Would she be able to watch him go out of her life except when it was necessary to see him because of their child?

She hadn't considered that before and it hurt to think of Tony marrying someone else. If the thought of Tony marrying hurt, how much did she really care for him? Could she be in love with him?

No way she could be in love with him. He was too authoritative, too opinionated, so certain he was always right. There was a point where all her affection and his appeal came to a stop.

They would have their lives tied together for years to come, but going out with each other the way they had been had ended. She saw that clearly and felt it was for the best. Just as swiftly, she felt a pang at the thought of not going out with him, of not making love to him. Startled, she shook her head. Life with Tony was over and that was the way she wanted it. She would stop missing him soon.

And what about Tony? He might want out of seeing her just as much. He had been in shock last night. The proposal had been a knee-jerk reaction. Now that he was home to think things through alone, his conclusions about the future might have changed.

The idea made her feel even more forlorn, as if she were losing someone important. As the day passed, she tried unsuccessfully to shake the feeling of loss. How long would it be before she stopped missing him?

Ten

As each day passed, Tony tried to adjust to the situation. Without thinking, too often he reached for his phone to call Lindsay only to stop himself. He'd reminded himself how mulish she could be. But that didn't stop him from missing her.

Friday afternoon, the second of October, when he returned from work he saw Lindsay's pickup on his drive.

His heart jumped and he sped up his steps, all tiredness leaving him instantly. Lindsay stepped out of her pickup and his breath caught in his throat. She wore tight jeans, a clinging red T-shirt with a vee neckline. Her hair was in the usual braid and she had a wide-brimmed brown hat on her head. She looked great to him and his pulse raced as eagerness to talk to her made him walk even faster.

"Hi," he said as he approached, smiling.

She gave him a fleeting smile and he drew a deep

breath because she kept a wall between them. He could feel her coolness toward him and knew there was a specific reason for her visit.

"Come in, Lindsay."

"No, I just thought I'd stop in and talk in person instead of on the phone, but this won't take long. Now that my waist is getting a bit bigger—"

He looked down at her and wondered if she could even be one inch larger. "You don't look it."

"I feel it. Anyway, as I was saying, now that I'm getting bigger, I want to tell my family that I'm pregnant and I want to tell Abe and the guys."

"Lindsay, have you even thought about our baby?"

Her eyes narrowed and her cheeks flushed. He was certain she would start yelling at him any minute. He struggled to keep his temper.

"Yes, I have," she said. "I still don't want to marry you. You would want to take charge of every detail of my life and of our child's upbringing. Hell, no, I'm not marrying you."

"You're so damn stubborn, you'd mess up your own life."

"It still is my 'own life.' Are you okay with telling our families? I'll just tell them that we're working out our plans. They'll accept what I tell them."

"That's probably a good idea, because you need to get a doctor and word has a way of spreading, especially when it's about babies. I'll tell my family, too. And Keane and the guys. And I'll tell all of them I asked you to marry me and you said no—but that opens you up to some pressure."

"No more than I'll get anyway." She opened the door to her pickup. "Thanks, Tony. We got that settled."

He put his hand on her door and blocked her way from climbing in.

"It doesn't have to be this way."

"I don't see how things can be any other way," she said. He dropped his hand and held the door for her while she climbed in.

"Bye," he said as he closed the door, feeling as if this was a real and lasting farewell. That any intimacy or closeness they'd shared—the laughter and joy and steamy sex—all of it was over. Stepping away, he rested his hands on his hips as he watched her drive away, heading back to the county road to go home to her ranch. As her pickup widened the distance between them, he knew he would always remember the day she drove out of his life. He didn't think they would ever be close again. A cloud of gloom, along with his anger, settled on him as he entered the house.

The following week, Tony saw he had a text from his sister, Madison; she wanted to come see him. With a sigh he sent her a text in return.

Yes, you can come see me. Tonight's fine. Tomorrow morning is fine. Take your pick or suggest a time.

They had finally settled on early Saturday. He waited on the porch because it was a cool, sunny morning.

He watched Madison come up the walk. Her brown hair was in a ponytail. She wore jeans and a tan cotton shirt that was not tucked into her jeans. In spite of hiding her waist, it was obvious she was months along in her pregnancy. He placed his arm around her shoulders to give her a brief hug, then led her inside the house. "Haven't seen you in a while. I have breakfast ready. Or anything else you'd like."

"I've had breakfast. I'll just have a glass of ice water. It's a beautiful morning and what is even more wonderful is that rain is predicted next week—they give it a twenty-percent chance."

"If it actually happens, I'm going out to just stand in it. Might take a picture of it since it's been so long since I've seen any."

She smiled. "Is Gwynne here?"

"Not on Saturday. How are you feeling?"

"Fine. Just bigger by the day." She faced him, her green eyes sparkling. "Tony, congratulations. I've talked to you on the phone, but I wanted to tell you in person. I'm so happy for you and Lindsay. I know you have things to work out, but you will. A baby is so wonderful."

"Thanks, Madison. It's sort of a mixed blessing at this point in my life."

"It's an enormous blessing. And our babies will not be so far apart in age," she said, rubbing her stomach lightly.

"I can't think that far ahead," he remarked drily. "I'm just getting accustomed to this becoming-a-dad business."

She laughed and accepted the glass of water as he handed it to her. "I'll carry your coffee, Tony," she said as he helped himself to scrambled eggs from a pan on his stove. He added a piece of ham and picked up a slice of toast.

"I'm set. It's beautiful outside. Let's sit on the porch."

As soon as they were seated at a glass-topped iron table, he sipped his coffee and sat in silence, certain she had a mission.

"Tony, any chance you want some sisterly advice?"

"Actually, no," he said, smiling at her, "but since this drive to visit me was unprecedented and a little difficult for you under the circumstances, I'm sure I'm going to get some."

"I'm just concerned. And Jake is concerned about his sister. She's hurting, and I came to see for myself how you're faring."

"I'm faring fine," he said, startled to hear about Lindsay. He'd figured she had gotten on with her life and wasn't giving much thought to him. He knew she had stopped working with the men.

"Mike Calhoun's wife is expecting her baby this month, which is exciting. We'll have the three new babies, plus Cody and Scotty. Our families are growing and I think it's exciting and wonderful."

He smiled at her. "At the moment, you're in love with Jake, having his baby, and the whole world looks rosy to you," he said, studying her and realizing she looked happier and prettier than ever before.

"You're right," she agreed. "Are you okay?"

"I'm absolutely fine. And you're looking good yourself. I think marriage and motherhood really suit you."

"I'm happy, Tony. So happy with Jake," she said.

"Our dad should have stayed out of your lives and not deceived you about Jake, as well as driving him away," Tony said quietly. "I don't know how you can ever forgive him. Dad and I have butted heads since I was able to talk back to him. I paid for it, but I never got along with him the way Wyatt and Nick did."

"Wyatt is quiet and peaceful. Nick's the politician who's going to please the world and he started by pleasing Dad. And I always, well, until high school, did what he wanted. I never dreamed he would interfere in my life the way he did." Her frown disappeared and she smiled. "That's over. Jake and I are married, having a baby and I'm happier than I ever dreamed possible." Impulsively, she reached out to squeeze her brother's hand. "I hope you find that with Lindsay, Tony. You can't imagine how wonderful marriage can be."

He laughed. "I do believe you're in love, sis. That's good. You and Jake deserve all the happiness in the world. I'm amazed Jake hasn't punched Dad out."

"Jake isn't going to hit an elderly man, much less hit my father."

"He has a right to."

"Whatever," she said, flipping back her hair. "Anyway, I'm glad to hear you're okay. I just wanted to see for myself. I'm excited our babies will be fairly close in age. December and May aren't really far apart after the first year or two."

"Madison, you didn't drive out here to tell me how thrilled you are about our babies being close in age. You could have done that on the phone."

"Well, I more or less did. And to see if you're okay."

"I'm quite okay. But what's wrong with Lindsay?"

"I think she's just unhappy."

"Well, Jake should realize that being pregnant has put a big crimp in her lifestyle. For corn's sake, look how she's always lived—like one of the guys. Suddenly, she's a woman and her body has limitations because of her pregnancy. She's not accustomed to that, didn't expect it and evidently is having difficulty adjusting to it."

"Just be nice to her, Tony. It's a big change and for Lindsay, without a husband, without planning for a baby, changing her entire life and future is an enormous upheaval."

"She'll adjust. And she could have a husband if she wanted," he said, unable to keep the bitterness out of his voice. "She turned me down absolutely. Lindsay will handle this just like she handles everything else—in full control."

"You think a lot of her, don't you?" Madison asked.

"Sure, I do. Every rancher in the area does. She's capable and intelligent."

"You didn't take her out because she's capable and intelligent."

He laughed. "No, she can be fun and pretty."

"Lindsay has the looks of a model when she wants to. I saw her at the auction. Anyway, you be nice to her. She needs you now."

"I'll be nice to Lindsay," he said with amusement. "Though I don't think she needs me or wants to see me or talk to me."

Madison sat quietly so long that he turned to look at her. "What?" he asked.

She stood. "I've seen that you're doing fine. I don't want to pry into your life with Lindsay. I just want you to know that I'm excited about your baby. I should go home now."

"That was a short visit, but I'm glad you came. Madison, let me know when Mike's baby is born. I might not hear about it."

"Lindsay will tell you," she said.

"Lindsay isn't going to tell me one damn thing."

Madison looked startled and stared at him intently.

"We don't speak, we don't see each other. It'll have to change later, but that's the way she wants it now."

"Sorry to hear that. I'll tell you about Mike and Savannah." She gave him a hug, then leaned away to look intently at him again. "Be patient with Lindsay. This is a giant change for both of you."

"Sure," he answered, knowing his sister meant well. He stood on the porch and watched her drive away, his thoughts on Lindsay. Lindsay was unhappy? She did what she wanted to do.

And how unhappy was she? It had to be a lot to worry Jake enough to get Madison to drive out and talk to him. He wished Lindsay's unhappiness was because she missed him, but he knew better. She was probably unhappy with him and unhappy she had to change her lifestyle.

He carried his dishes into his empty house. As he passed his landline, he stared at the phone, tempted to pick it up and call Lindsay to just talk. He missed her and every time he realized that he missed her, it surprised him.

How important had she become to him?

He couldn't answer his own question.

The next week he threw himself into work, going to the corral to ride some of the unbroken horses at night with a few of the men who worked for him, just keeping busy. But none of it stopped the moments of longing for Lindsay.

Nights were long and unpleasant. He had always fallen into bed and been asleep instantly, sleeping soundly until early morning. Not anymore. His nights were filled with memories of Lindsay, dreams about her, moments of missing her.

The weekends were worse because he had no one he wanted to go out with. He missed her and the longing to see her intensified instead of diminished, until he finally sat up in bed one night, tossed back the covers and walked out on his porch.

The gray dog was still recovering, but better. The bandages were gone and his hair, where they'd had to shave it away to work on his cuts, was growing out again. He had gained weight and his coat was shiny now. Tony kept it brushed so it wasn't a tangle.

Tony let him stay at the house with him. The dog

seemed a faint tie to Lindsay, and Tony enjoyed having him around. When he went to the porch, the dog followed him, sitting with his head on Tony's knee while Tony scratched his ears. "Maybe I should invite her over to see you," he said to the dog, who wagged his bushy tail.

Tony sat quietly while he thought about Lindsay. He thought about her constantly each day. Was he in love with her and hadn't realized it when it happened?

If he was, he didn't know where it could lead. She was as stubborn as ever, refusing to give an inch, while she had accused him of being too take-charge and bossy. Plus, he was a rancher—the kind of man she said she would never marry.

He sat in the dark and mulled over his feelings for Lindsay and the problems between them.

Madison had said Lindsay was unhappy. Was their parting a cause of her unhappiness? Could he ever get past her stubborn nature? He had some of the time. His heartbeat quickened at the thought of getting past their problems. Could he think before he told her what she should do?

Could he live without her?

Was he in love with her?

Staring into the dark, he realized he was. He wanted her in his life. Lindsay would be a challenge, but if he loved her, he would cope with her. But could he get her to consider working with another rancher? That wasn't impossible. He worked with them all the time and for that matter, she did, too.

Suddenly feeling better, he wanted to call her and he wanted to be with her. One thing he knew for certain: he didn't want to lose her. Someone would come along and marry her and, at the thought, he felt as if he had been punched in his heart.

He needed to get her a ring and tell her how he felt and propose—for real this time. He had fallen in love with her and hadn't even recognized the depth of his own feelings.

He remembered her call at three in the morning when the dog was howling. It was about four o'clock now. What would happen if he called her, told her he had to see her? Could he get her to listen to him and go out with him?

Or was she out of his life no matter what he felt for her?

Lindsay sat up and shook her hair back away from her face. She stared into the dark bedroom as she clutched the phone. "Tony?" she asked, sounding more alert. "It's four in the morning. What's wrong?"

"Lindsay, I need to see you. Let me pick you up for dinner tonight."

She frowned at the phone. "You called at 4:00 a.m. to ask me to dinner?"

"You called at three to tell me a dog was howling. Will you have dinner with me? We need to talk."

She couldn't imagine what the urgency was, but her heartbeat quickened because she missed him and she wanted to be with him.

"Yes, I'll go to dinner with you. But you do know I'm pregnant and need my sleep, right?"

"I figured four is close enough to when you'll get up anyway. And can't you go back to sleep?"

"Yes," she said, but she wondered whether she would or not.

"Me, too, darling'," he said, and a warm fuzziness filled her. She hadn't heard that endearment in too long and it made it worth the wake-up call. "How about I pick you up at six?" he asked.

"That's fine," she said, curious what was on his mind.

"See you then," he said, and was gone.

She settled in bed, turning toward the windows so she could look at the bright moonlight outside. White cumulus clouds drifted rapidly across the black sky. She missed Tony more than she would have believed possible. She missed him every day and thought about him constantly and got lost in memories too often each day.

When had Tony become so important to her? At first she'd thought she would forget him as the days passed. Instead, each day she missed him and thought of him more.

She hadn't faced the question that hovered in her mind. Was she in love with him? Had she fallen in love with a man who would always want to run her life, their child rearing and her ranch? All indications said she had. She didn't know his feelings for sure, but she knew he hadn't been in love with her when she last saw him.

Tony had been so many good things—energetic, sexy, positive and upbeat, full of fun and life. She knew he was a good rancher. And she knew he was a take-charge person. Could she cope with having him back in her life? And on a larger scale? She couldn't answer her own question. The only solid answer she could give was that she had been miserable without him. She didn't want to tell him goodbye and watch him marry another woman while she raised his child.

This time without Tony had been the unhappiest stretch in her life. Excitement coursed through her at the thought of seeing him again. What was so urgent that he had to see her tonight? She hoped it was to get back together. She didn't know how they could, but she was ready to try.

She climbed out of bed, moving restlessly to a chair to think about Tony. She was guessing he wanted to see her because he missed her, too. But what if he had another reason—like a permanent parting of the ways?

That possibility filled her with concern. It couldn't happen now, she told herself, not when she finally realized she wanted him back in her life with all her being.

He still might propose to her again, even if he didn't love her. If he did, was she willing to accept that and hope she could win his love over time?

She ran her hand across her flat stomach. Their baby needed them. Could they set aside their monumental differences and give love a chance?

There was love on her part. She was ready to admit it now. She was in love with Tony, alpha male or not. She had gotten herself into this situation by bidding on him at the auction, and now she was in deep, over her head.

Would she tell him that she was in love? Or keep it from him until he declared feelings of love for her? She didn't see how she could keep from revealing her love to him. At the thought of seeing him tonight, what she most wanted was to throw herself into his arms when she opened her door. Now that she knew she would see him and had finally admitted that she was deeply in love, she ached to be with him and hoped with all her heart he might have missed her or, better yet, be as in love as she was.

She glanced at her clock and saw it was almost five. In just over twelve hours she would be with him and get an answer to the question that plagued her. What did Tony feel for her?

Only time would tell.

By six that night she had even more questions. As she left her room, she turned for one more look in the mirror. She wore a deep blue sleeveless dress with a low-cut back, a hem that ended above her knees and high heels. She had left her hair falling freely because Tony liked that best.

Downstairs, promptly at six she watched him step out of his black sports car and come up her front drive, and her breath rushed from her lungs. He looked handsome, filled with vitality. He also looked like a Texas rancher in his white Stetson, his black boots, black Western-cut trousers and a pale blue, long-sleeved cotton shirt that was open at the throat. She longed to throw herself into his embrace, but she restrained herself, opening the front door and smiling.

His blue-green eyes filled with desire that revved up her heartbeat. "Darlin', you look gorgeous," he said, his gaze moving over her slowly, a tantalizing perusal that set her pulse pounding. "You look more fantastic than ever. I'd say that pregnancy becomes you."

"Thank you. I'd say prospective fatherhood becomes you, because you're a sexy hunk, Tony Milan." As she spoke she was unable to keep from letting her gaze skim over him, wanting more than ever to be in his arms and kiss him.

"Lindsay," he said.

She looked up to meet his hungry gaze and her heart thudded at the heat and desire she saw there. He stepped inside and closed the door. She didn't have to throw herself into Tony's arms. He drew her into them and kissed her.

Her heart slammed against her ribs and she clung to him to kiss him in return. "Tony, I've missed you," she whispered breathlessly between kisses.

"I'm not doing any of this the way I planned," he said, between showering her with kisses.

Looking into his eyes, she felt a physical impact that

heated her insides. It seemed months instead of weeks since she last saw him.

He kissed her and she closed her eyes again, holding him tightly while her heart pounded.

"I might not let you go this time," he whispered. He showered kisses on her and finally picked her up, carrying her as he kissed her. "We were going to my house, but I think that's temporarily on hold. This is far too urgent," he said. "Lindsay, I've really missed you."

Clutching his shoulders, she kissed him slowly and thoroughly. "I've missed you."

He took the stairs two at a time, hurrying to the big bed in her room.

It was covered with dresses, lacy underwear, bits and pieces of clothing that she had tried on earlier.

He yanked back the cover and all of the clothing flew off. He turned to kiss her, his fingers trembling as he drew the zipper of her dress down while she twisted free the buttons of his shirt. She couldn't wait to show him how much she loved him.

Over an hour later, she lay wrapped in his arms beside him in bed while he lightly combed her hair away from her face with his fingers and showered feathery kisses on her temple and cheeks.

"I think we were going to my place for dinner," he whispered, nuzzling her neck and kissing her throat so lightly.

"We still can if you want or I can find something here to feed you."

"I had plans and I wanted to show you the dog."

She sat up so fast he rolled away slightly. "The dog? You didn't tell me. Is he okay?"

"He's more than okay," Tony said, smiling as he pulled

her back against his shoulder and held her close. "Lindsay, I've missed you, darlin', more than I thought possible and I've thought about my feelings for you."

She focused on him, her heart beginning to drum, and she could barely catch her breath upon hearing his words. He gazed into her eyes and looked at her intently. "Lindsay, I love you."

"Oh, Tony," she gasped, wrapping her arms around his neck to kiss him and hold him tightly. "I'm in love with you. I didn't want to be in love with a rancher, absolutely not the controlling type, which you are. I tried not to be. We're misfits, you and I—two ranchers. I know you think I'm too stubborn and maybe I am. Am I babbling?" she asked. Without pausing for breath or for his answer, she continued. "I've been miserable without you in my life. You're too take-charge. We'll clash and it won't be any more peaceful in the future than it was in the past—"

"Damn, Lindsay," he said, and kissed her, stopping her chatter. She clung to him, kissing him, pouring out the love that she felt along with joy and relief over his declaration.

Suddenly, she leaned away to look at him, framing his face with her hands. "You really, really love me?"

"I really, really love you. Lindsay, will you marry me?" he asked, holding her close against him with one arm wrapped around her waist.

Her heart thudded. "Yes," she gasped. "Oh, yes, Tony. We'll fight, but we'll be in love."

"We might not fight," he whispered. "We may learn to negotiate." She heard the laughter in his voice. He wrapped his fingers in her hair and tugged lightly so she had to look at him. Startled, her eyes flew wide as she looked up at him.

"Will you marry me?" he repeated.

"Yes, I will," she answered.

"Then I'm the happiest man in the world tonight," he said. "I don't care about the differences and I can cope with you and you can cope with me. You'll get used to this rancher, darlin'. You may not get used to my take-charge ways, but we'll work things out because I promise to try to keep you happy. I promise to shower you with love so you won't ever regret marrying an alpha male cowboy."

"Shh, Tony. Stop making wild promises you can't keep," she said, laughing, trailing light kisses over his face. "I love you, cowboy. I love you with all my heart."

He kissed her, a kiss of joy and promise, a kiss that melted her heart and ignited desire again, and soon she was lost in passion.

It was almost ten when she sat with him in her tub while hot water swirled around them and he held her close between his legs as she leaned back against him.

"Hungry? I was going to cook steaks."

"I hadn't thought about it," she said. "I don't know about hunger, but I'm shriveling up from being in this hot water so long."

He chuckled, cupping her full breasts in his hands to caress her. "Not too shriveled," he said. "We'll get out, dry and go eat something. I know you have something in this house and if you don't, we'll head to my place." With big splashes, he stood, pulling her up with him and helping her step out of the tub. He picked up a towel and began slow, light strokes to dry her.

She caught the towel, wrapping it around herself and picking up another folded one to hand to him. "If you keep doing that, we'll end up in bed again. I'll dry myself and you do the same, then get dressed and I'll meet you downstairs. I'm getting hungry and for some reason, I can't skip meals like I used to be able to."

Nodding, he grinned. "Not as much fun, but I'll cooperate."

When he met her downstairs in her kitchen, she already had a casserole heating and in minutes it was on the table. His fingers closed on her wrist and she looked up at him, startled.

"Darlin', I had this evening planned and it hasn't gone the way I expected from the moment you opened the door. But I came prepared for whatever happened." He reached into a pocket, pulled out a small folded bit of tissue paper tied with a tiny strip of blue ribbon. "This is for you, Lindsay."

Surprised, she looked up at him, giving him a searching look, and then she took it to tug free the bow and open the paper carefully, her heart drumming as she did. She looked at a dazzling ring. "Oh, Tony," she gasped, thrilled to look at the ring he had for her. It was a huge, emerald-cut diamond, surrounded by sapphires and diamonds with more diamonds scattered on the gold band.

He took it from her and held her hand. "One more time, the way I should have done it the first time. Lindsay Calhoun, will you marry me?"

"Oh, yes," she replied, laughing. "Yes." She threw her arms around him after he slipped the ring on her finger. Wrapping her arms around his neck, she kissed him and he held her tightly, kissing her in return.

When they finally stopped, he took her hand to walk to the table. "Lindsay, you need to eat. Let's sit and eat and talk about when we'll have a wedding. I hope we can agree on a date soon. Very, very soon."

He held her chair and then sat facing her. She could

barely think about eating because of the excitement and joy churning in her.

"Tony, I've missed you so and I realized I've been in love with you for a long time. I don't know how marriage will work with the two of us, but I can't wait to try."

"You'll be you and I'll still be me. We're in love, so we'll work it out." He grinned and picked up her hand to brush kisses over her knuckles. "I love you, darlin'. Back to the date. Lindsay, let's get married soon. Really soon.

She stared at him and then nodded. "In that, we're in agreement. The sooner the better for so many reasons, not the least of which is I love you with all my heart."

His eyes took on the greenish hue that she recognized from moments of intense emotion or passion. He held her hand and, without taking his gaze from hers, lifted it to his lips to brush more kisses lightly over it.

"Lindsay, I love you and I always will."

"Even if we fight?"

"Even if we fight. But I don't think we really will." He wagged his brows and grinned. "Well, maybe sometimes."

"Now, do you want a surprise?" she asked.

"I think my entire life will be filled with surprises. What's this one, darlin'?"

"It's early, and I'll have an ultrasound later this month, but my doctor thinks I may be having twins."

Stunned, he stared at her. "Twins?" He got up and walked around the table to reach down and draw her to her feet to kiss her hard. When he released her, he grinned. "Lindsay, why do I think my whole life will be like this night? One shock and one change after another."

"You know it won't be that way all the time."

"Get a calendar and let's have this wedding this month."

"Savannah's baby is due this month, but I'd like to

have the wedding soon, too. I've waited as long as I want to wait without you in my life. I don't ever want to go without you again," she said, holding him tightly.

He slipped his hand behind her head and leaned close to kiss her, a long kiss that made her want to be in his arms again and forget wedding plans.

"Tony," she whispered.

"Go get a calendar or I'll get my phone and we'll look at my calendar."

"I have one here." She turned to open a cabinet and came back with a calendar.

With it on the table between them, they discussed dates while they ate.

"After dinner we can call our parents and then start calling our siblings."

"Tony, I love you and I'm so happy."

"I'll show you how I feel in a little while," he said, smiling at her.

Her phone played a tune and she got up to answer it. "Sorry. Anyone calling at this hour has to have a good reason."

"Or a wrong number," he remarked, pulling the calendar close.

She picked up her phone and listened before turning to come back to the table. "That was Mike. Savannah went into labor and they didn't make it to Dallas. She delivered a little girl in the Verity hospital." She couldn't stop the smile that lit up her face. "Wyatt met him at the hospital to get Scotty. He said he texted me earlier, but he didn't hear back. He wants me to come to the hospital to see their baby. Mike sounds incredibly happy."

Tony pulled his chair close beside her. "Sit for a minute and let's pick a date so we can tell everyone and you can show them your ring."

"I don't want to detract from the baby," she said.

He gave her a look. "You're not going to. Babies are wonderful. We're probably not going to surprise anyone. We'll just announce it before we tell everyone goodbye. I didn't intend to walk in and say 'look at us,'" he said.

"You win," she said, smiling at him. "I can't keep it quiet anyway. Well, now we don't have to worry about our wedding interfering with Savannah having her baby."

Tony took her hand. "Lindsay, I want you to have a big wedding, the one you always dreamed of as a little girl. This is once in a lifetime. You won't do it again, I guarantee it."

She gazed at him and then turned to kiss him lightly. "Sometimes you're a very nice man even when you're bossy."

He smiled at her. "Don't sound so surprised." He tapped the calendar. "Pick a date so we can go see your new niece and the happy family."

Eleven

On the first Saturday in November, Lindsay stood in the foyer of the Dallas church watching Scotty walk down the aisle. Dressed in a black tux with black cowboy boots and his hair neatly combed, he was doing just as he had been told. He scattered rose petals along the aisle and took his place at the front by his dad.

Milans and Calhouns were present in abundance. Tony's best man was his older brother Wyatt. Tony had said they would kill the old feud between Calhouns and Milans, so along with his two brothers, he had asked her brothers to be groomsmen and all three accepted. Scotty stood in front of his dad and both of them looked pleased.

Lindsay had asked Savannah if she felt up to being matron of honor. After thanking her, Savannah had declined because of her new baby girl, Caitlin. Lindsay then asked Josh's new wife, Abby, and she accepted instantly, seeming grateful that Lindsay had thought of her. Madison had declined to be a bridesmaid because she was almost into the eighth month of her pregnancy.

"It's time," the wedding planner said, smoothing the train to Lindsay's white satin dress and checking her veil. She smiled at Lindsay as her dad took her arm.

"Lindsay, I wish you all the happiness possible," he said to her as they walked down the long aisle.

"Thanks, Dad," she replied. She looked at Tony in his black tux and best black boots and her heart beat faster with joy. She loved him with all her heart. It seemed like a miracle, something she once thought impossible.

When she joined him at the end of the aisle and met his gaze, she lost all awareness of their families and friends. The big Dallas church was filled, but she could see only Tony.

She repeated her vows, meaning every word, feeling as if there would be enough love between them to carry them through any kind of adversity, even the kind they stirred up themselves.

It seemed a long ceremony, but finally they were pronounced husband and wife. Above a fanfare of trumpets, an organ, and applause from the audience, thunder boomed as they rushed up the aisle.

"Wow," Tony said, glancing over his shoulder at double glass doors. "Is that really thunder?"

"Rain on our wedding day—"

"We had sunshine this morning and rain would be the best possible thing next to being alone with you within the hour."

"Rain is more likely to happen than that," she replied, laughing. "Look how dark it is outside," she said, turning to stare.

"Dare I hope?" Tony replied. "How long will this reception take?"

"Tony, you've asked me that half a dozen times. Hours. It will take hours for me to dance with all the Milan and Calhoun men who are going to ask me to dance because it's the courteous thing to do, much less all the guys who work for me that are here and will be polite and ask me to dance."

"They're not asking because they're polite. This is probably the first time they've seen you look like this and they're having the same kind of reaction I did the night of the auction," he remarked.

"I hope not." A bolt of lightning streaked in a brilliant flash, followed by thunder that rattled windows. Tony grabbed her hand. "C'mere," he said, stepping outside and drawing her beside him as he inhaled deeply.

"Smell that," he said. "And look at the trees. We have an east wind. It's going to rain. Hallelujah!" He yanked her to him to kiss her hard, and for a few minutes she forgot everything else until the first big drop hit her.

"Ki-yi-yippie-ki-ay!" Tony yelled, turning his face up to feel the rain.

"Celebrate inside." She grabbed his hand. "Let's go around where we're supposed to or everyone will be out here and we'll have a mob scene."

They rushed through an empty hall and Tony pulled her into an empty room and closed the door. "Just one more kiss," he said.

"Oh, no. You'll mess us both up for pictures. You have to wait. Come on, Tony," she said, wiggling away and stepping through the door into the hall, smiling and looking away.

"We're coming," she called. "Hurry, Tony."

He stepped out. "Yes, Miss Bossy." He looked down the hall. "Who were you talking to? I don't see a soul.

You made that up to get me out here," he accused, shaking his head but still smiling.

"Come on," she said, laughing and hurrying along the empty hall.

When they passed double glass doors, Tony pulled her to a stop. "Look at that," he said in awe, giving another whoop of joy while she clapped.

"Tony, rain! Finally."

"Just pray it lasts for a week," he said. "What a fantastic wedding gift—rain. Buckets and buckets of rain."

"Reception, remember?" she said, tugging on his hand.

Over an hour later, Tony took her into his arms for their first dance as husband and wife. "Lindsay, you're the most beautiful bride ever. You look even more stunning than the night of the auction," he said, meaning every word. He knew as long as he lived, he would never forget looking at her as she walked down the aisle to marry him.

"Tony, I'm so happy. I didn't think I could ever be this happy."

"Hang on to that as long as you can. I'll try to always make you happy, darlin'."

"Don't make wild promises."

"I'm not. I want you happy. I love you," he said, his arm tightening slightly around her waist as he held her. "Thanks again for agreeing to move into my house. My offer still stands—anytime you want me to build a new house for us, it's fine with me."

She smiled. "I think your house is wonderful," she said. "We'll see, but right now, it looks quite suitable. As long as you love me and you're in my bed at night, what more could I ask for?"

"I wish I could dance you out the door, through that pouring rain, into the limo and off to that bed right now."

"You can't do that. We have to stay and be sociable before we leave for New York."

"I hope you're still happy with going to New York for a few days."

"Very happy. After our babies are born, we can go to Paris and Italy, but I don't want that big a trip right now while I'm pregnant."

"It's your choice, darlin'." He held her close, inhaling the faint scent of her perfume. He just wanted to make her happy because she made him happier than he had ever been in his life.

"Lindsay, we still haven't told anyone we're expecting twins."

"It's just been confirmed and it's still early in my pregnancy. I want to wait a bit. We have time."

"We'll do it however you want," he said, and her blue eyes twinkled.

"I love it when you say that and I hope I hear it millions of times."

He grinned. "I'll try. That's the best I can do, just promise to try. Something I'm trying to resist doing is going out and standing in the rain. I may succumb to that one before we leave."

"Don't you dare. A soggy tux would be dreadful."

"Soggy from rainwater would be dreadful? I beg to differ."

She laughed. "Tony, life is a blast and I intend to enjoy being married to you."

"I'll keep reminding you of that. I'm going to wish I recorded it to play again."

"You still think we're going to fight. I don't think so. You're doing a great job so far of keeping me happy."

He laughed. "You can't imagine how badly I want to get you out of here and all to myself," he said.

"I'll see what I can do about that. Maybe I can hurry things up a bit."

"Darlin', you do know how to please a man."

She felt as if she'd danced with every cowboy in Texas when Mike stepped up to ask her to dance. She smiled at her brother as they danced away.

"Caitlin is a beautiful baby, Mike,"

He grinned. "Thank you. I agree. You look beautiful, too, Lindsay."

"Thank you."

"And happy. I'm glad. Tony's a good guy."

"I agree with you on that one. Savannah said Caitlin is a quiet baby."

"She is and she's a little doll. Someone's holding her constantly. When Mom and Dad arrived, they stayed with us last weekend instead of their usual hotel stay."

"Our mother?"

"Yes, she did. She thinks Caitlin is adorable."

"I'm so glad. She looks like Savannah, even as tiny as she is."

"I agree. I see Jake watching us, so I'm sure he's going to want to dance with you next. I talked to Abe. He's happy for you and he'll run the place just fine while you're gone. I told him if he needs me, call."

"That was nice, thanks," she said. "I've never been away like this."

"It's time you did, Lindsay, and time you got a life of your own. You don't have to get out there and work like one of the boys."

She laughed. "I think those days may be over. Being a mama sounds like a big responsibility."

He smiled at her and danced her toward the sideline. "I'll give you to Jake. You have so many guys who will want to dance with you that you and Tony will never get away."

"Thanks, Mike," she said, planting a kiss on his cheek as they halted and Jake stepped up to take her hand.

Mike was almost right. By the time she'd danced with all the Milans and Calhouns and talked to each of their guests, it was hours later. Finally they made it out of their reception hall.

For just a moment Tony stopped, standing in a downpour and laughing, dancing a jig until she grabbed his wrist and tugged.

They rushed to the waiting limo and fell laughing onto the seat as their chauffeur closed the door.

"The drought will lessen now and your brother told me rain is predicted for the next three days," Tony said, pulling her to him to kiss her before she could answer.

When she pushed him away she laughed as she shook her head. "You're incredibly sexy and appealing, but that wet tux is going to ruin my wedding dress."

"It's rainwater. Do you really care?"

As she shook her head, she laughed until he drew her close to kiss her again.

Tony had a private plane waiting at the airport, but it was the wee hours of the morning when he finally carried her over the threshold into the New York penthouse suite he had reserved for their honeymoon. Standing her on her feet, he pushed away her short charcoal jacket and wrapped his arms around her.

"I love you, Lindsay. I don't think I can ever tell you enough. All I can do is try to show you. I've waited all day for this moment when we would be alone together."

Wrapping her arms around his neck, she smiled at him.

"Mrs. Anthony Milan! It's a whole new life for me. Tony, once again, I am happier than I ever dreamed possible."

His smile vanished as he held her and began to unfasten the buttons down the back of her navy dress. "I hope so and I want to always make you happy, Lindsay. You've filled a huge void in my life. I want to be with you, to love you, to have a family with you. I need you, darlin'."

She tightened her arms around his neck to pull his head down and kiss him. He held her close against him, their hearts beating together.

Joy filled her. She had never known as much contentment as she had found with Tony, and so much excitement as they looked forward to their babies. She couldn't wait to start her new life, a life shared with the man she loved with all her heart—the one rancher in the whole world she could love.

* * * * *

COMING SOON!

We really hope you enjoyed reading this book. If you're looking for more romance be sure to head to the shops when new books are available on

Thursday 21st May

To see which titles are coming soon, please visit
millsandboon.co.uk/nextmonth

MILLS & BOON

TWO BRAND NEW BOOKS FROM
Love Always

Be prepared to be swept away to incredible worldwide destinations along with our strong, relatable heroines and intensely desirable heroes.

OUT NOW

Four Love Always stories published every month, find them all at:

millsandboon.co.uk

FOUR BRAND NEW BOOKS FROM
MILLS & BOON MODERN

Indulge in desire, drama, and breathtaking romance – where passion knows no bounds!

OUT NOW

Eight Modern stories published every month, find them all at:

millsandboon.co.uk

OUT NOW!

Available at
millsandboon.co.uk

MILLS & BOON

OUT NOW!

Available at
millsandboon.co.uk

MILLS & BOON

LET'S TALK
Romance

For exclusive extracts, competitions and special offers, find us online:

- **f** MillsandBoon
- **X** @MillsandBoon
- **◉** @MillsandBoonUK
- **♪** @MillsandBoonUK

Get in touch on 01413 063 232

For all the latest titles coming soon, visit
millsandboon.co.uk/nextmonth

MILLS & BOON
THE HEART OF ROMANCE

A ROMANCE FOR EVERY READER

MODERN — Prepare to be swept off your feet by sophisticated, sexy and seductive heroes, in some of the world's most glamourous and romantic locations, where power and passion collide.

HISTORICAL — Escape with historical heroes from time gone by. Whether your passion is for wicked Regency Rakes, muscled Vikings or rugged Highlanders, awaken the romance of the past.

MEDICAL — Set your pulse racing with dedicated, delectable doctors in the high-pressure world of medicine, where emotions run high and passion, comfort and love are the best medicine.

Love Always — Celebrate true love with tender stories of heartfelt romance, from the rush of falling in love to the joy a new baby can bring, and a focus on the emotional heart of a relationship.

HEROES — The excitement of a gripping thriller, with intense romance at its heart. Resourceful, true-to-life women and strong, fearless men face danger and desire - a killer combination!

 — From showing up to glowing up, these characters are on the path to leading their best lives and finding romance along the way – with plenty of sizzling spice!

To see all our latest titles, please visit
millsandboon.co.uk/NewReleases

MILLS & BOON
MODERN
Power and Passion

Prepare to be swept off your feet by sophisticated, sexy and seductive heroes, in some of the world's most glamorous and romantic locations, where power and passion collide.

Eight Modern stories published every month, find them all at:
millsandboon.co.uk

MILLS & BOON
Love Always

Celebrate true love with tender stories of heartfelt romance, from the rush of falling in love to the joy a new baby can bring, and a focus on the emotional heart of a relationship.

Four Love Always stories published every month, find them all at:
millsandboon.co.uk/LoveAlways